Kieryn Nicolas

FLAWLESS RUINS

Shakin' up
Young Readers

quakeme.com

Flawless Ruins
A Quake Book
Shakin' Up Young Readers!

First Quake paperback printing / 2011

All rights Reserved.
Copyright © 2011 by K. Ziegler

Cover © Brynna Ziegler
With Nathalie Moore

QUAKE
is a division of
Echelon Press, LLC
9055 G Thamesmeade Road
Laurel, MD 20723
www.quakeme.com

13-Digit ISBN: 978-1-59080-691-3
10-Digit ISBN: 1-59080-691-3
eBook: 978-1-59080-692-0

Published by Echelon Press LLC

For Mom

From the idea to the final edits, many people helped this book become the one you're holding. A big thank you to: Mom, Dad, Brynna, Grandma, Katie M, Katie H, Tasha, Sophie, Jacob, James, Jo, Dani, Skyanne, Pat Griffith, Kris Santillo, Beth Scott, Mandy Hubbard, Ms. Hoffman, Ms. Herrmann, Mary Welk, Karen Syed, Echelon/Quake, my family, and everyone who asked when the next book was coming out. (Here it is!)

CHAPTER 1
Morgan

Why was it hidden in the first place?

If it hadn't been hidden, I wouldn't have read it. But I couldn't exactly *say* that to the mayor of Blue City; "Well, it's not my fault I read the book. It was hidden!"

I shift in the puffy chair, nerves clawing at my intestines. Apart from me, the mayor's lobby is empty. The librarian stepped out once we'd arrived. The room, smooth blue floors and walls rippling with light, alternates between seeming too large and bordering on claustrophobic.

Victoria Amherst–or, as she insists Blue City call her, Mayor Vee–paces in her office. Despite the enormous curtains drawn over the glass walls, I can see her shadowy figure moving back and forth.

I've never really been to a discipline meeting before. There was the time Laney and I snuck into an older girl's Amora, but we were just reminded that we'd have our own Amoras soon enough, and then we were sent back to our moms.

Most disciplines, such as study packets for skipping academy classes, are decided by the mayor. That's why I wasn't originally worried to be here. It's just procedure, right?

But if it's not such a big deal, why is Mayor Vee pacing?

Finally, the mayor's door slides open. I stand up and, surprisingly, Mayor Vee smiles. Her short, platinum blonde hair contrasts sharply with the ambient lighting behind her, but the designer jeans and pale pink shirt fit right in.

"Mayor..." I begin, but she waves away my words.

"Come on in here, Morgan." She steps aside to let me pass. Her office walls pulse with a soft purple glow. Kind of like my bedroom's default setting, except mine's dark blue. And the purple totally clashes with the red shirt I'm wearing.

Mayor Vee directs me to sit. She settles in the puffy chair across from mine. On the round table between us is the book. Should I start with an apology? Laney's Amora is Saturday, and the last thing I need is to cause a problem. However, I don't even know what the problem I might have caused *is*.

I mean, I wasn't trying to get in trouble. I'd stopped by the library to look at collections of magazines and books, kept in glass cases because of their fragile paper material. I go to the library maybe once a month, so it's not unusual or anything. Last month I noticed a back room, and on my trip today I saw it was unattended. So I just slipped back and peeked in. When I did, I saw a glass storage case hanging open.

Inside there were books, real books. Stacks of them, all by the same person: Shakespeare. I've heard of Shakespeare in school, some old Writer, but we've never actually read anything written by her.

I'd pulled one off the top of the nearest stack. It felt really fragile in my hands, as if it would crumble if I turned one page. The faded print across the cover read *Romeo and Juliet*.

More curious than anything else, I'd sat with my back against the wall and started to read. I guess I lost track of time, because the next thing I knew the librarian appeared, exclaiming in shock and taking the book away before ushering me to the mayor's office.

The mayor studies me. She's a new mayor, only twenty-six, just ten years older than I am, but with her authority she might as well have been born last century. I draw in a deep breath. *Please don't say I'm in enough trouble that I have to miss any prep for Laney's Amora.*

It takes her a minute to speak. "Is there a particular reason you went into the back room of the library?"

I answer honestly. "I was curious."

"And this is what you found?" She taps the copy of *Romeo and Juliet*. Her nail leaves an impression on the delicate cover. My gaze stay locked on the crescent mark.

"Yes, Mayor."

"How much did you read?"

I don't lie, of course, but for some reason I feel hesitant about sharing the truth. "Up to the scene where Romeo is...talking to someone, a friar, after visiting Juliet."

"Hmm."

I look up. Mayor Vee lets her gaze slip past me for a moment. Her fingers lace together. She wears her Pow on one wrist and the other wrist has a ring around it too, holding a device kind of like a wall remote.

She refocuses. "What did you think?"

"Of the book?" I clarify, surprised. "I found it hard to read. The wording was...bizarre."

"Could you understand the story?"

"Yes...kind of...and no."

The mayor nods me on, so I say tentatively, "I think I figured out the storyline, but I don't understand the *story*."

Mayor Vee smiles. "I know. What in particular did you...not understand?"

I consider this. A lot of questions spun through my mind as I read, and even more have popped up since. I try to choose the most important ones. "There were so many Likes. Romeo, Benvolio, Tybalt. Whose were they? I mean, Romeo seems like he'd be Juliet's, but then what about Rosaline? If Romeo was hers, why weren't they together? How did Romeo become Juliet's?"

Mayor Vee seems to be waiting for something. So I spit out, "And there was a term Shakespeare used a lot, to describe the Likes, I think. It was...*men*." I glance at Mayor Vee's face. "What's...?"

I guess this is what she wanted me to say. She leans back now, seeming to think before she speaks. "A *man* is an old term used for a Like. At one time they were unpredictable, uncontrolled. *Men*. It was centuries ago. And this book was written centuries earlier. It's a completely archaic term."

I'm not sure that quite explains it, but she doesn't appear

mad, so I don't mention the term again. Instead I say, "Why did Shakespeare have the characters talk about love as though it's so...wild? And fickle?"

"Who knows?" Mayor Vee shrugs. "It was a long time ago, and the story's fiction, sprung out of some woman's imagination."

Her *no big deal* attitude only confuses me more. To busy myself in the silence, I bend over and adjust the tie on my boot. I'm the only one of my friends to own a pair of lace-ups. They're super cute. I found them at the Designer's annual market two years ago when I went on a trip to Red City with my mom. She attended a doctor conference I wasn't allowed to go to, so I shopped. Thank goodness my feet haven't grown too much since.

The silence stretches another minute. Does the mayor want me to say something? Should I ask the obvious question?

I can't take this suspense. "Why were the books kept in the back room? Why not in the library?" In fact, come to think of it, none of Shakespeare's books are on display. Only books and magazines less than a century old, before everything transferred to Pows, but after the Wars, are shown.

"They are irrelevant," Mayor Vee responds. "They're only in the library temporarily, for maintenance."

"Oh." I stare at the fragile book. Can I risk one more question? I'm so curious. "Mayor? How...does it end?"

I feel, rather than see, the mayor smile. "Happily, of course. The families' feuding is stopped. Romeo is Juliet's Like." She stands up again. "Even though the books being in the back room implied you weren't to open them, I don't feel any discipline is necessary. In the future, keep to the public areas of the library."

Oh, *phew*. I won't have to miss out on any Amora prep.

Somehow though, something in the back of my mind still wants to read the rest. I ignore it. "Thank you, Mayor Vee," I say and stand up. She walks me to the lobby door.

"Have a nice evening," she says. "And I'll see you

Saturday. It's a big day for your friend Laney, isn't it?"

I nod, even though she already knows. "Laney's excited," I say. "So am I." I can't help the giggle that follows. It's gonna be so much fun. Laney and I picked out an amazing color scheme and buffet and music. All I need is my dress.

"As you should be," the mayor says as I step onto the street. "And your Amora is coming up in just a few months."

"Yes, it is." The familiar excited feeling swoops through my gut when she says *Amora*. I'm so jealous of Laney. Her wait is over this weekend, but I still have to wait until June, the *end* of June, June 30th. "Bye, Mayor."

"Bye, Morgan." She disappears back into her office.

I start walking, the dry spring air filling my lungs. The tall buildings framing the street glow light blue against the darkening sky. A few women and their Likes stroll across the road, stopping at the corner diners and coffee shops. Other women exit business and arts buildings as work time ends.

I enter the nearest monorail station. The lights inside overtake the evening sky behind me. Colors ripple from the walls and burst outward under my boots, a neat floor effect. Earlier my shoeprints remained illuminated for a few seconds.

I board the monorail within minutes. It's not a long ride from the Blue City Center to the Cobalt residential station, and from there only a five-minute walk to my townhouse.

A few apartment complexes stand at the end of my block, but mostly it's lined by townhouses, all glowing the same blue color. I slow as I reach mine and open the door. The air smells like new furniture, Mom's favorite scent.

I unlace my boots at the threshold. Somewhere further inside music's playing, a soft, synthetic sound I recognize immediately. This is what Mom listens to when she's in one of her moods.

I make my way toward the music, my socks sliding a bit on the floor. Mom keeps it set to an old-fashioned hardwood theme, but its texture is smooth as glass.

Mom's in the den. The walls are on gray glow as usual,

and as usual I find my mother on the silver couch, feet propped up on the cushions, knees close to her chest. Her doctor uniform hangs over the back, and she's wearing gym shorts and a tank top. Her hair is pulled back into a ponytail. It's dark brown, almost black, similar to the color mine would be naturally. Right now mine's auburn with streaks of copper in it, something Laney and I experimented with.

Mom doesn't notice me until I settle into the couch across from her. She's looking out the window. The next building over almost completely obscures the view, but at the right angle you can see a sliver of Cobalt Park.

"Hey, sweetie," she says, tearing her gaze from the view. One hand reaches out to tap the wall, silencing the music.

"Hey, Mom."

"How was school?" The sure fire conversation starter.

"Fine. We're doing lots of review for finals. And Laney and I are heading to the park after school tomorrow to talk about her Amora."

Mom winces. It's slight, but she's done it before. I know better than to mention it. She's told me that sometimes she just gets this way, and she never offers further explanation. "Sounds like fun."

"Mm hm. How are you?"

She turns to the window again. Then, as if she's forcing herself, she pulls her gaze back to me and smiles. "I'm good. We should do something," she says, more to herself than to me. "Let's bake, or...something."

"Bake," I say appreciatively. Mom's one of the few mothers I know who still makes food sometimes. And always with me, because she knows I enjoy helping her. Somehow, cookies in the vacuum bags from the Grocery Store aren't the same.

"Okay, then." She kicks her feet down from the couch and wiggles them into the slippers resting on the floor. I stand and hold out a hand to help her up.

A voice calls out, "Rachel!"

I drop my hand. Mom's face goes blank, then composes

itself into a smile. "Ross."

My mom's Like walks across the room. He's tall, with wavy blond hair, a wide nose, and gray eyes. I have those eyes, and a hint of his chin, but mostly I'm built like Mom: thick hair, straight nose, full lips, a bit lacking in curves. I surpassed her in height two years ago, which doesn't say much since Mom's about as tall as Thumbelina, the fairytale girl who gets a Like despite being as tall as, well, a thumb. Cute story.

Ross grins at me, then at Mom. "I heated tea for you. You seemed tired, so it's ginseng, very rejuvenating."

Mom exhales through her nose. "Thank you."

Ross smiles again, adoration written in his expression, as always. He sits beside Mom and wraps his arm around her shoulders. She rests the tea bottle on her knee. "Morgan..."

"No big deal," I say. "I have homework. And Laney's expecting me to message her. Besides, I showered this morning, and I'd have to shower again if we baked because I'd probably get flour in my hair."

"Bake?" Ross glances from me to Mom. "Honey, do you want me to run out and get some cookies from the store? I can go now if–"

"No," Mom says quietly. "That's not necessary." She turns to me and makes a motion with her hand, as if to wave away our plans. "Go do your homework."

I leave and head for my room. The walls glow blue; the floor has a grass theme and feels smooth like all floors, but looks like a stretch of earth from the park. My bed is in the corner opposite the door, and my desk stands across from it. I pull out my Personal World, also dubbed a Pow. The curved screen lights up at my touch and I scroll to the CommBox. There's a message from Laney. *CHECK UR WALL*, it reads.

I clip the Pow back onto the thin metal band at my wrist and sit in front of the empty wall facing my bed. I tap it and a box pops up, telling me I have new messages. I scroll through them until I find Laney's. It's titled *colors*. Upon opening it, boxes of colors fly across my screen and settle in order from lightest to darkest. They're all shades of blonde; Laney insists it'll go best with her stunning green Amora dress.

Using my finger I scrawl a message: *the third one*. Then I wave away the images and the subtle blue glow returns.

Homework doesn't take long. I'm done by nine. I flop back on my bed and the blanket fibers light up around me, shimmering in the creases. I close my eyes.

Laney's Amora is the day after tomorrow. And as the mayor said, my seventeenth birthday, and my Amora, arrives in less than three months. I bite down on my cheek, stomach heavy with excitement and anticipation that's been building for sixteen-plus years. I mean, your Amora's only the biggest event of your life, or so you would gather from the way the older women talk about it.

And there's *so* much to be excited about. Dresses, food, décor, and then the obvious. I bet Laney's ripping her hair out with anticipation—not especially good for the prospective color job. I've already started planning my own event.

After all, it's when you get your Like. The Amora is the party to end all parties, and at the event, you get your soul mate, the Like who's perfect for you. Tailor made.

Dream come true.

CHAPTER 2
Neil

The sound of the mill is deafening, even with the so-called "noise canceling" earmuffs clamped on my head. Probably a good thing they don't work, otherwise I wouldn't be able to hear the shouts of the other boys.

"Hey," a boy yells. "It's jammed again!"

I turn to face the machine to my left, which vibrates uncontrollably. It's supposed to slice large chunks of tree trunk into boards before the boards are moved to refinement. This isn't the first time it's gotten stuck. A few boys rush in and push on the log coming through. The conveyor belt starts to rattle with the pressure.

With a loud snap, boards fly out of the machine, clattering onto the conveyor belt and skidding toward the side.

"Neil," someone shouts. "Catch them!"

I lunge forward, throwing out my arms to stop the boards. The wood slides through my hands; three fresh splinters sink into my fingers. The corners of the boards bite into my shoulder and I brace myself against them, slowly shoving them back onto the conveyor. When they're balanced again, more boys adjust the stacks and remove the slices too small to use. Some of these are shoved into my arms and I back away, dropping them by the brick wall nearest the machine. There's already a day's worth of scraps there.

I pause and shake out my throbbing fingers. But there's no time to attend to them; there never is. I move back to the conveyor, exhausted back and shoulders telling me it's almost the end of the workday.

As soon as the stacks from that log disappear, more fill their place, and we fall back into routine: two boys working the slicing machine, four tying off the logs, and me and another boy, Omri, disposing of the scraps.

It's another ten logs before the buzzer sounds. The roar of metal grinding together and saws whirring through wood peters down. I gingerly remove my earmuffs, hanging them on one of the racks standing against the wall.

There's the usual sound of shuffling as the other boys hang up their own earmuffs and make their way to the doors. Before I join I glance at the piles of scraps, seeing if there are any I can use. Most are too big, but a few smaller pieces poke out. One catches my eye: a sawed-off end. I step out of the line and pick it up, turning it over in my hand, and decide I can use this. I tuck the rough piece in the waistband of my jeans, arranging the hems of my brown work shirt and jacket over it. Then I make my way back to the dwindling number of boys streaming to the street.

The lumber mill is a large building, cluttered with machines and, during the daytime, boys. It's one of the more rigorous jobs assigned. Trees from woods off in some vague location–I don't know where, I've never worked in deforestation, and since I only have about two seasons left, I doubt I will–are brought to mills in the Number Cities, and we refine them into usable material for the Color Cities. City 4 exports to the Blue City. The lumber mill has been my longest shift, almost two seasons so far.

We pass the woman at the doorway. She looks bored and taps at the remote on her wrist absentmindedly. The air outside hangs thick with smog from other factories in the work area, quite normal for spring. Gray smoke spirals across the darkening sky, visible above brick and stone walls of buildings standing sentry to a long, fissured street.

Boys call to one another, forming groups. Typical after-work behavior, which elicits a typical after-work reaction from the forewoman; she steps outside to glare at us. I turn away, a glare burning behind my own eyes.

The activity settles down and the boys disperse. The cracked street makes for an uneven pace, but I'm used to it. My dorm building is only a ten-minute walk from the lumber mill. I've lived in this building for about four months, since the beginning of the year, when Group N became the Year 17's.

Room 302 is at the end of the third-floor hallway, to the right of the stairwell. Convenient, as I avoid walking past the other boys' rooms, except when I use the bathrooms down the hall. At this time of day someone's always itching to start a fight. I can't blame them, because what else is there to do? Eat dinner, maybe nap for a minute, and then go to class at seven are about the only options. It's a mandate that Year 17's attend at least six times a week. I've heard teachers refer to it as 'preparation.' I can figure out the rest from there.

I close my door, then shed my coat on the nearest bed, which is mine. The room contains two beds, a desk, a chair with fraying cushions, and a dresser. Taking a seat by the desk, I flip on the light above it. A yellow glow from the bulb casts shadows of my hands as I pick up a bent piece of wire, something Han made for me a while ago, and study my smarting fingers.

I take the wire and pinch the ends together. The first splinter comes out easily, as does the next. The last one sunk in deep, though, and when I finally pry it out, a bead of blood wells to the surface. I press the finger to my mouth. The skin is dry and rough, and the metallic taste of blood seeps over my tongue, making me grimace.

Having taken care of the splinters, I pull out the scrap of wood I'd taken from the mill. It's about the right size. In addition to wire, Han brings flattened metal from the factory where he does inventory. They work as blades and I use them to shape the wood scraps I scavenge. If I can concentrate on carving, I can almost forget work and pain and frustration.

I form the basic cylindrical shape in thirty minutes. I'm just starting on holes when someone says, "Another one?"

I freeze to keep myself from jumping. Then I set down the blade and wood and rotate in my chair. "Han."

"That would be me." My roommate walks to our dresser and pulls open the top drawer. "The one and only." He takes a small bottle from beneath a bundle of white shirts. Amber liquid sloshes inside as he pops the cap off. "Want some?"

"You always ask that." I turn back to the wood, picking up the blade.

"And you always decline." Han tips some of the drink into his mouth and sits down. Boys aren't supposed to have alcohol, even though we produce it in the distilleries. All of it is supposed to go to the Color Cities and the security women working in Number Cities. I've seen them gather at their large apartment building in the City Center, exchanging bottles of wine and other liquors with long, fancy names.

I worked in a distillery as a Year 14; I know how the underground trade runs. Some of the boys at distilleries or wineries manage to smuggle out alcohol before the bottles get fancy labels and are officially accounted for. Han knows people in the network, so he always has access to a bottle. He says it relaxes him, makes him feel better. I don't judge him too much about his drinking; I know at one point it helped him deal with his burn. But I refuse to take part, because I've seen the drinks drive boys out of their minds, and I know I don't have much time left in my own mind as it is.

Han stretches out across his bed, takes off his glasses, and rubs his eyes. He's been in the inventory department of the Metal Factory for two months, and every day he complains about headaches and eyestrain from staring at a computer screen for hours. Han is always verbal, just another way we're different. He says what he thinks, especially about the system of life here. I'm quiet, silently hating work and women for the life I live, and the one I know is coming.

I find it easiest to just follow the rules, even though I loathe them. Han likes to test them; he tries to see how much longer than regulation he can grow his blond hair before the women notice. He's happiest when it's long; it helps hide the burn on his neck. My dark hair is cut short to stay below the radar. Han socializes with other boys, but I keep to myself, with Han as an exception. Even our eyes contrast. Behind the glasses his are an intense gray while mine are dark brown.

16

A half hour later, a whistle takes shape from the wood. When I'm fairly satisfied, I raise the instrument to my lips. The sound it makes is low and a bit breathy, but different from the two I've already made this season.

Han, who'd been dozing, stirs and cracks one eye open. "Another one?"

"You already said that."

"You never replied." He yawns and sits up, fumbling for his glasses and shoving them back on his nose.

"Yes, another one."

"Why? You already have two."

"Because." I don't really know why. It's almost as if I can make something unique, even if it is only a sound that disappears in a moment. I test the whistle, changing the pitch by moving my fingers over the holes whittled down the rod.

"They're neat and all." Han stands up. "But not especially...useful, to be making multiples of."

"You have multiple lock pick sets."

"Yes, but lock picks... Now, *they're* useful." Han is something of an artist with locks. He has three sets of picks assembled from wire and metal scraps. With his skill we found out what happens to Year 18's; with his skill, we'll also find out when we're supposed to disappear as well.

"Mm." I let him win. He's the kind of person that never loses, plain and simple.

"Are you going to class tonight?"

I put down the whistle and glance at the clock set in the plaster walls; it blinks 6:30. My stomach rumbles. "I have to. I have maintenance tomorrow night."

"Ah, right. I guess I should too."

"No, you should rest. You already had maintenance this week."

"But I skipped the night before," he says through a yawn and yanks open the dresser. After replacing the alcohol bottle, he removes two white class shirts and tosses one to me. I catch it. Han also pulls out a standard black knit hat.

We stop in the dinner room on our way to the

classrooms, quickly eating whatever meal the Year 10's prepared and a caffeinated drink, somewhat fighting my drowsiness. Class runs from seven to eleven, which doesn't leave much time between falling asleep and when the alarms go off at 4:30 in the morning. Work begins at 5:30 and ends twelve hours later, allowing us an hour and a half to eat dinner and get extra work done before class, where we go to learn language and math and skills to help us in the future. Because our futures are so bright to begin with.

Han and I sit near the back of classroom 17. Each classroom's number corresponds to the year of the students in it. Our residential section has about twenty-three boys in Year 17. I try to pay attention to the opening lecture, but it's not easy. Beside me Han rests his chin on his hand and his eyes glaze over. He's slept about sixty minutes in the past twenty-four hours. I take notes for him.

History lectures are usually brief and repetitive, reiterating stories of the Wars, where nuclear warfare wiped out more than half the world. That and rising sea levels explain why there's so little land left in North America, and as per the treaty that ended the Wars, there has been no contact between continents for almost two centuries. In addition to some inventions here and there, that's the extent of what we're taught, so my mind already feels numb.

By ten Han's head is in his arms, hair falling out of the hat and hiding his forehead from view. The burn, though, is visible, deep scarring spread across the left side of his neck and shoulder. I swallow. Every time I see the scar, or think about Kellan, or the future, I just hate women even more.

Eleven finally comes, and the boys start to pack up. I kick Han's shoe and he raises his head, blinking, mouth falling open.

"Up," I hiss. "Get up. Class is over."

We stand and join the line filing out of the room. Our teacher, Ms. Rayelle, a short, dark woman, watches us leave with arms crossed. As Han and I pass her, she speaks.

"Nathan."

Han stops and turns. "Ma'am?"

Her arms uncross, and the next moment the back of her hand cracks against his cheek. "Pay attention in class, or next time you'll be disciplined properly."

Han looks steadily at her, then turns and strides out of the room. I fall into step beside him. A red mark darkens on his face.

"Do you need…?"

"I don't need anything." He shrugs off any further conversation, gray eyes flashing. We make our way back to the dorms in silence.

CHAPTER 3
Morgan

I can almost feel Laney's excitement, as if it's something tangible rolling off her shoulders. She keeps fidgeting next to me, glancing at the walls, currently set to a world map. A clock blinks in the corner; we have ten minutes left.

The class couch makes a U in the center of the large room, opening toward the wall with the map. All twenty-three girls in Cobalt Academy class 15 sit on the cushions with our history instructor, Ms. Heron, settled in the middle.

"What are we doing?" Laney's voice is soft.

"Review." Ugh, review. We've had this history drilled into our heads since class 1. I hardly want to be thinking about studying when Laney's Amora is *tomorrow*. I still don't have my dress, even. A few weeks ago my grandma told me not to pick out a dress yet because she has a surprise for me. Well, I can only assume the surprise is a dress, but hello, Grandma, running low on time here. Laney's already upset because she doesn't know what I'm wearing.

"Where is Europe?" Ms. Heron's voice calls me back to class. Seffa's Pow lights up a bright blue color. "Seffa?"

Sef swirls her finger across her Pow's surface, and a circle appears around Europe.

"Yes," Ms. Heron says. "This mass of land, and the few islands surrounding it. Asia?"

Shannon circles Asia.

"The smaller mass, across the sea," Ms. Heron says in clarification. "And then, of course, Africa is below Europe, and Australia is the island way down south." The map zooms out to show America as well. "What brought about the Communications Wall? Mia?"

Hermia McAllister glances up, as if surprised to hear her name. She doesn't volunteer much, though she knows all the answers. "The Treaties."

"And what did they do?"

"Decreed the CommWall. The continents wanted to avoid more nuclear warfare after the Wars, so they created the CommWall to stop communications among them, and therefore prevent conflict. It's been in place for nearly two centuries. Nothing has breached it." Hermia appears distant as usual, twisting a lock of brownish-gold hair around her finger. She doesn't dye it different colors like the rest of us.

"Nice summary," Ms. Heron says. "On the test I'd mention how there was no clear winner of the war, though the women on all continents believed they were victorious."

The map closes just as the clock starts to blink.

"Yes!" Laney jumps up and pulls me to my feet. We start grinning at each other, silently acknowledging this as the last time she'll walk out of class without a Like to meet her at the entrance.

"Hey, Laney! Morgan! Heading to the park?" Seffa calls after us.

"Yeah, in a bit. Morg and I are gonna stop by my place first," Laney calls back. "Come on," she says, grabbing my elbow and steering me out the door and down the street, as if I don't know the way. We arrive at her apartment building within five minutes and climb five flights of stairs to her number.

"You showing me the room?" All residential units—apartments, townhouses, et cetera—have at least four bedrooms. One for the woman and her Like, one for the daughter, one for when the daughter gets her Like, and one extra. Of course, girls usually get their own places during their first year of career training, so the whole separate-rooms thing is temporary.

"Yeah, I put on the final touches." Laney opens the door and beckons me along. Her mom's not home from work yet, but her mom's Like, Evan, is polishing items, mostly Laney's football trophies, on the display shelves in the living room. Laney looks a lot like her mom's Like, same button nose and rounded chin and natural light hair color.

"Hi, girls." He looks over at us. "Elena's still at work."

"I know." Laney waves at him before dragging me down the hall. Her room's near the end, blue-themed, with floors that send out light ripples where you step. She stops at the door and throws it open. "What do you think?"

The dark blue walls cast a hazy glow over diamond-patterned floors, different from the dots she originally chose. The bed is simple, but seems comfortable, and there's a dresser and closet as well.

"I think your Like will think it's just fine," I assure her. "Did you notice one of the walls was dim on the outside of your building?"

She ignores my random question; she's used to them. She twists a strand of coppery hair around her finger. "Fine? Is that enough?"

"I don't know." I say it more to myself than to her, then see the alarm on her face. Laney obviously needs pacification, not random thoughts from the back of my mind. "Hey, Lane, stop freaking. You haven't even met him yet."

She blinks at me. "But...what do you mean?"

What do I mean? "I mean, of course he'll like it. And once he gets here, you guys can work together to make it something he'll love."

She considers this. "Or maybe I'll just stand in the middle of the room all day," she decides finally, muffling a giggle. "Don't think he could ask for better decoration."

"There's a plan." I roll my eyes.

"So...approved?" Laney reaches out to close the door.

"Approved. Let's hit the park."

Cobalt Park is the only place near Cobalt Residential Area with more than two trees within two blocks of each other. There's a walkway through an open, grassy area, and trees line the path and clump together by the lake. Benches stand to the side, some occupied by other academy girls who come here after school. And, when the weather's nice, a few birds can even be seen flying above.

Right now it's the middle of spring, so it's a chilly sixty degrees. I have a light jacket on, and I have a bag of workout clothes from Laney's room slung over my shoulder because Laney wants to go to the gym later.

Despite the chill, Laney and I purchase ice cream cones from the parlor near the park. I have a napkin tucked in my pocket; Laney refuses to wrap napkins around her cone like normal girls do and insists I don't either, because, according to her, it's annoying.

After we've finished our ice cream Laney practically dances circles around me on the path, tugging at her hair and fiddling with her Pow wrist clip in agitation. "Tomorrow," she keeps repeating, not stopping even when I point out that saying *tomorrow* over and over won't make it come any faster. By the time Daye and Jeanne, their Likes, and Seffa find us, we're in hysterics.

Jeanne continues what she was saying before we joined up, something about her career plan. "I'm having severe second thoughts. I mean, I don't know if being a biologist is for me. There's the special test you have to take after basic career training, and only a few make it into the last year of study. Those who aren't selected become researchers for medicine and stuff. I don't know if I want that."

"I'm sure you would do just fine on the test." James, her Like, runs one hand soothingly down the length of her spine.

"There's the same test for doctor," I point out, naming my career choice. "No one knows what it is, but I'm willing to risk it."

"There's no secret test for lawyer," Laney says happily. "Only a test of wits against your opponent."

Lawyers deal with disputes in court. For example, if someone repeatedly breaks curfew and takes the matter to court, Laney would be appointed to defend or oppose any claims the accused might make. If you're a lawyer long enough you can be promoted to Judge. But as there are few disputes, there isn't a high demand for lawyers. Therefore

Laney will have to get a good reputation to get many assignments, even if there isn't the special test.

Of course, we can't stay off the subject of the Amora for long. Soon the chatter turns to dresses, hair, and makeup, everyone talking at once until Seffa claims our attention.

"You've finalized your guest list, right?" Seffa runs her fingers through her glinty gold hair. It looks superb against her dark skin, especially in this light.

"Pretty much," Laney responds. "Still trying to decide about some girls Morgan and I know from the gym."

It's customary to invite your academy class, then honor some younger guests with an invitation, while inviting older friends and moms (and their Likes) to your Amora. Laney's guest list is hovering around two hundred, about the standard.

"Eh, invite them," says Daye. "All the more people to see you in this stunning dress you keep talking about!"

Daryl's arm is around Daye's shoulders. As she speaks he leans in to her ear and murmurs, "And all the more people to see *you*. You're always the most beautiful." Daye grins.

"We'll see about that," Laney says. "Ms. Cori's my favorite seamstress, and the dress is perfect. Brings out the green in my irises, she told me. My eyes look brown, but they're actually hazel."

Laney's confident she'll elicit an incredible reaction with this dress. So am I. I sat there while it was fitted, feeling excitement and jealously zing through me, it looked so pretty.

I bump her shoulder to get her attention. "When are you dying your hair?"

"After we go to the gym," she says. "You're coming."

"I'm coming?"

"Yes. You're getting blonde too."

"Um, news to me." I laugh. "Why?"

"Because it'll make your eyes silvery. I asked my hairdresser, and instead of your eyes just being gray, they'll shine. Though, if you'd tell me what color *dress* you're wearing it'd be a lot simpler."

Oh, of course. "I don't *know* what color dress I'm

wearing," I remind her. We've been over this.

"You don't *know*?" Jeanne untangles herself from James's arms and shakes my shoulders. "Hello! Her Amora's tomorrow! I've had my dress picked out since last *week*!"

"You tell her," Laney says crossly. "She says it's a *surprise*."

"Morgan's always so last minute with dresses," says Daye.

Well, this is true. But I have a reason this time.

"I know," Sef says. "Laney's her best friend. She should make sure it's amazing."

"Hello, guys? Yep, I'm still here," I remind them. "My grandma's getting me a dress. So, I don't know what it looks like yet, but I'm sure it'll be awesome."

Jeanne laughs. "Like in Cinderella. Only instead of a fairy godmother, you have a fairy grandmother."

Cinderella was one of my favorite stories growing up, about a fairy godmother who gives a girl the perfect Amora dress, but it has to be returned by curfew. "Exactly."

The girls consider this.

"You're still getting blonde," Laney decides.

"There's one person you can cross off your guest list." Jeanne's chin jerks toward the occupant of a nearby bench.

It's Hermia McAllister. I don't know much about her, even though she's in my academy class. We used to play together when we were really little, but we haven't spoken since class 9. She's a ballerina, and she doesn't interact with other girls much. The one thing everyone knows about her is that she isn't interested in getting a Like, and doesn't come to many Amoras, invited or not. So therefore, everyone also knows she's just weird. I mean, not going to Amoras? Really.

"What's she doing? Reading?" Jeanne's voice is louder than necessary. James snorts.

"Looks like it," Laney observes. Hermia's head is bowed over her Pow, her finger scrolling through a white projection from the screen.

"Yeah, reading. So her," Daye says. Daye and Seffa take

ballet classes with her, so they probably know Hermia better.

"*I* wouldn't want to read a book," Daryl says. "Not when I have you to be with instead."

This reminds Laney. "*Tomorrow!*"

Seffa scowls. "Lucky."

"Hey, yours isn't too far off." I poke her in the side. "It's closer than mine, so *you're* lucky!"

Her frown lessens. I check the time on my Pow. "Hey, Lane, time to hit the gym." Laney and I go to the gym regularly, to stay in shape and all. She's the only one I work out with, though, because of my breathing. Other girls would try to get me to run on the treadmill or use a spinning machine, and I'd have to make up some excuse as to why I'd rather stick with the dumbbells or leg presses.

"And then, dye time!" Laney bounces on the balls of her feet. We say goodbye to our friends and the Likes and head for the nearest monorail station. When we're seated in the car, Laney seems to lose some of her previous exuberance. A crease forms between her eyebrows.

"Nervous?" I keep my voice low, reading her expression.

She considers, then nods. "Yeah, a bit. I mean...my whole life is about to change. It'll get better–I'll have my Like–but still change."

I nod. "And then is graduation, and career training."

"Career training should be fun. Lawyers argue all day."

"Fun but difficult for me," I tell her. "Only a few doctor trainees are admitted into the field. If I want to be one of them, I'll have to focus."

"Yeah, I still don't get why doctors are so 'specially' selected. I mean, I know they can't let *everyone* stick their hands into other women's guts, but unless you fail career training, shouldn't you be okay?"

I shrug. "You have to have the mentality for it, not just the training, to perform surgery or deliver daughters. A lot of women would get lightheaded at the sight of blood." Not me, thank goodness.

"I just said that. Delivery, ugh." She shudders. "How

26

could you want to do that? You'll see the dead baby, too."

We've had this conversation before. "I know, but that's just how it is." Everyone is born with a twin, dead at birth. Birthing doctors deliver them, so they're the ones who take the dead baby girls away. Even so, I've always wanted to be a doctor, like my mom.

"Speaking of doctors," Laney continues, lowering her voice, "how's your…breathing been?"

I glance around us, then shrug. "No different."

Only Laney knows I have breathing problems. From what I've figured out, exercise or stress induces it. Sometimes during workouts, in crowded halls, or before big tests, my airways tighten. I have to struggle to fill my lungs. Usually, if I can just keep a clear head, I'm fine. But I don't tell anyone, because I wouldn't be admitted into doctor career training if people knew. Even potential doctors can't have such distractions due to safety. And apart from my Amora, being a doctor is what I'm looking forward to the most.

We do a light workout this evening because Laney wants to "preemptively work off some of the food I'm going to eat tomorrow, without getting *too* tired." By the time she decides we're done, we've barely broken a sweat. She pats her forehead with a sweat rag anyway. "Off to the hairdresser's."

We giggle our way through our appointment at the salon, sharing grins in the wide mirrors facing us as hairdressers lather our heads with creams and fine-tune styles with silver scissors and layer our hair with shimmering dyes. Laney looks natural in blonde. I, on the other hand, look different. It's not natural, but that's not exactly the point, is it?

I get off the monorail two hours later at the station near my house. I take the stairs down rather than the elevator; I tend toward claustrophobia, and it affects my breathing. My shadow elongates and shrinks rhythmically as I pass the streetlights and the cracks between shimmering buildings.

All lights will turn off soon, at eleven curfew, saving energy (and really, what would we do between then and five the next morning anyway?) As per a mandate, all women must return home by curfew, because when the lights go off it's dangerous to be outside. It gets so dark you can't see anything out the windows even, except maybe a few stars if you twist your neck funny to catch a glimpse of the sky.

As a little girl I was something of a daredevil. Laney and I used to challenge each other to do these ridiculous things, like crawl across the frozen lake in the middle of winter. Or wear a pair of her mom's stiletto heels all day. One time, we visited the garden on the roof of the monorail station, stories above the ground, and we dared each other to stand on the wall at the edge of the roof. It was just us, not our moms, or their Likes, and the ground looked impossibly far away to our nine-year-old eyes. It took us nearly a half hour to work up the nerve, but finally for a second we were both upright on the ledge, gripping each other's arms, not looking at the ground. Then we tumbled back onto a mulch bed, eyes wide, giggling, amazed at our own bravery.

On the night of my tenth birthday, however, I did the most daring thing yet. I'd had a big party and my grandma gave me this gorgeous sundress. Laney got me a makeup kit and my mom baked a delicious cake. But the best part was the fact that I turned ten, double digits, only seven years from my Amora. I was so buzzed on sugar and excitement I couldn't sleep. My window already went dark and my mom and Ross were asleep when I decided I needed to do something, anything, to let out the excitement. I wished Laney was there to challenge me, but she'd felt sick after three slices of the rich cake and left.

I tiptoed down the stairs, stopping on the bottom step, unsure what to do. The walls glowed faintly, so I could see shadows and stuff, but otherwise it was dark and very quiet, while at the same time familiar and boring.

I ended up in the laundry room, where Ross cared for our clothing. In the back of the room was a small door that led to the fire escape. Laney and I climbed on the fire escape a few times, until Ross exclaimed it was too dangerous and we shouldn't do it anymore. That was in daylight, too.

It was my birthday. I was double digits, wide awake, and, most of all, curious. No one would know if I just peeked outside, right? To see the stars? I opened the door. The darkness was like a wall. I instinctively glanced beside me, to meet Laney's gaze, to find some courage. But I was alone.

I only made it two hesitant steps beyond the door. My feet felt cold on the metal landing, and my hand held tight to the doorway because there was *nothing*, just black, inky nothing, pressing on my eyes and making me dizzy and immobile.

Very slowly, I peeled my fingers from the doorway. Without touching it, I was no longer anchored to my house. I wasn't anchored to anything, as if my city didn't even exist.

I was out there just long enough for my eyes to begin adjusting. Vague shapes appeared, large and looming, and even though I knew they were structures I saw every day, they lost familiarity in the darkness. It was a different city after curfew, and fear zinged through me, making me gasp. I stumbled back, grabbing for the doorway, and pulled myself inside the dim interior that suddenly seemed miraculously bright. I shut the door and leaned against the dryer, chest heaving, feeling awe at what I'd just done.

For a moment, I wanted to go back out. I wanted to see the different city again, taste the adrenaline breaking curfew momentarily caused. I almost did. But then I remembered it was a rule for a reason. It had to be. What if I'd tripped, fallen down the fire escape, and ended up injured on the street below? I would have been stranded in the darkness, unable to escape back into the light of the laundry room.

Realizing that, I put as much distance between the door and myself as I could. I crept back to my room and collapsed on my bed, trembling, grateful for the light shimmering in the creases of the blanket.

I can see why we have curfew.

Mom emerges from the hallway as I arrive home,

closing the townhouse door behind me. "Am I to understand you colored your hair again?" This is her greeting.

"Yes, you understand correctly." I step into the living room and brighten the walls, spinning around for her to get the full effect. It's silvery blonde and straightened, so the hair falls silkily around my shoulders and down my back. New layers on my forehead brush against my eyelids.

"It's a very *Laney* style." Mom's in sweats again, holding a book in one hand, a finger marking her spot. Being a doctor, Mom has special privileges, such as getting to read old paper books with faded color diagrams and such.

"Well, yes, it's Laney's Amora, after all," I reply, grinning. I'm pretty sure Mom wishes I'd wear my hair natural, at least sometimes. She never dyes hers.

"That it is." Mom's gaze drop to study the floor, shoulders rising and falling with a deep breath.

"What?" I step closer and lift Mom's chin so she's looking me in the eye.

She attempts a smile. "Nothing. You're just…growing up."

"That tends to happen," I point out. "You're a doctor, Mom. You should know how life works."

I laugh. She doesn't. "Yes, I do."

Then she gives me a brief hug and walks away, up the stairs, leaving me standing in the living room, shoes still on and newly blonde hair tickling my eyes.

CHAPTER 4
Morgan

If I don't spend Saturday morning doing something I'll be a wreck by the time Laney's Amora actually starts. I've spent the week combating a jittery stomach, thinking about how weird it is that what Lane and I have been planning for is finally happening, and how weird it is that mine isn't far off. And then the thoughts would overwhelm me and I'd stop thinking about it.

In fact, that's what I'd been doing at the library when I got caught with the book. Trying to distract myself, or at least, until I'd been successfully distracted. Then I just wanted to read the book.

Speaking of which, I should probably apologize to the librarian. Ms. Elliott, I think, is her name. She let me read some real paper picture books when I was younger. It only seems fair I go say sorry for breaking into her back room.

The library's not far from the monorail station by the mayor's office. I get off at the station and head to the roof first, to see the gardens. Some gardeners tend to the plants, but otherwise it's peaceful. I can see the other leafy rooftops from here. It's a good place to think. I thought at one point I might want to be a gardener because of the pretty flowers, but once I was old enough to understand my mom's work, I knew I'd be a doctor.

Wait. I'm on a mission. I take one last breath of the cool air up here. It smells like damp earth, not a scent one usually finds on the streets. Then I make my way to ground level.

The Library is quiet, per the Library rules. I wander a bit, through the old magazine section, looking through the glass at covers of issues featuring women in science, and medicine, and who achieved great things, all before paper became obsolete. When I end up in front of the librarian's

Office, I knock.

Someone I don't immediately recognize opens the door. Instead of the thin, dark-haired librarian, a plump, fair woman stands in the doorway.

"Yes?" She smiles. "How may I help you?"

"Oh." I place her in my mind as the secondary librarian, Ms. Northrop. "Um, is the librarian in?"

"That would be me."

I blink. "Where's Ms. Elliott?"

The woman shrugs. "She doesn't work here anymore. But if there's anything I can do for you, please tell me." Her smile widens.

"Ah...no, thanks." I take a step back. I don't really have anything to say to Ms. Northrop. Except, "Do you know where Ms. Elliott went?"

Ms. Northrop looks puzzled. "I think she might have moved to another City. Maybe Green City. I went there once during my class 15 spring trip, it's really pretty. But what does it matter? Are you sure you don't need anything?"

I nod, and walk away. Well, I hope Ms. Elliott enjoys Green City. By the time I get home all questions about the librarian have been replaced by more pressing thoughts, such as how am I supposed to plan a hairstyle if I haven't seen Grandma's dress?

Daye was right, I'm usually last-minute about dresses, but I totally planned on getting something early for Laney's Amora; I mean, she's my *best friend*. But I was waiting until I saved up a bit more money. Lane and I went to this year's Designer Market in Red City, and when trips to other Cities aren't with the school or work, they're expensive. The government, or in other words, the Mayors of the five Cities committee, gives money to girls during their academy years, a certain amount each month, so they can afford to buy things like dresses and dye jobs and maybe a trip or two. The only time we travel in a structured fashion between cities is for our graduation trip, choosing to go to one of the other cities for cultural experience.

Anyway, the trip took a lot of our savings, and before I'd saved enough, Grandma intervened and told me not to get a dress. Grandma assured me her 'surprise' would come closer to the Amora.

Well, it's pretty darn close now.

I slam my feet against the wall in frustration, flopping backward. Ripples of blue expand from the point of impact, glimmering sharply in protest. "Oh, shut up," I tell it.

"Morgan?"

I turn my head and grumble, "Hi, Mom."

Mom crosses the room and stands over me. "What's the matter?"

"I don't have a dress."

Mom raises an eyebrow. "You have multiple dresses," she corrects, as she's done the last seven times I complained about not having a dress this week. She'd then offered to let me borrow one of her dresses, but I'd reminded her I was still waiting on Grandma, and she'd just sighed.

"Do we have any donuts left from breakfast?" I don't bother mentioning Grandma this time.

"Sorry, no." Mom holds out a hand to help me up, and I take it. "I actually came in to tell you Grandma's here."

"Oh, *good*." I follow Mom into the living room. Three figures occupy the couch; Ross, my grandma, and her Like.

My grandma, Annie, grins at me. "Hey, Morgan."

"Hey, Grandma." I lean against the nearest chair, fighting the urge to demand my dress. So curious!

"Looking forward to the Amora tonight?" Grandma crosses her legs, brushing off her jeans. She's sixty, but like every other woman in the age range, her body has hardly aged since thirty. Her hair is in a new style this week, long and straight and blue-black. Her Like, Ari, runs his fingers through it as she speaks.

"Yes." I'm also excited about the dress. Come on, Grandma, show it to me! "I have to leave soon," I hint. "It's my best friend's, and I'm heading over to her apartment early to get ready."

"She must be so excited." Grandma sounds excited herself. "I was invited too, you know, along with some of my coworkers." Grandma is a graphic artist, designing images on walls and Pows.

I've often been amazed at the contrast between my grandma and my mom, who leans against the wall behind me, just watching. Grandma's hair and clothing styles are always changing; Mom always wears her natural color and sweats when she's not in her doctor uniform. Therefore, Grandma's usually my go-to woman for fashion and hair; hence, the dress.

"By the way, I love your hair," Grandma continues.

"Thanks, yours is pretty, too." Dress dress dress...

"I wish I'd known you changed it," she says. "See, I saw this dress a few weeks ago"–*here* we go–"at Ms. Harmony's shop, and it was *gorg*eous. But it was orange, and you had red hair last time I saw you. So...I asked for her to make one in white." Grandma turns to her Like. "Ari, could you get my bag?"

"Of course." Ari jumps to his feet and hurries to the door.

"Surprise," Grandma sings, as Ari comes back, handing over her duffle. She winks at me and unzips it, pulling out a carefully rolled garment packaged with a plastic sheet.

"Mom," Mom protests. "You didn't have to–"

"Oh, please, what are Grandmas for?" Grandma stands up and lets the sheet unroll, then removes the plastic to reveal a short, white dress with one strap and stones glittering down one side.

"It's..." Mom starts, brow furrowing.

"Great!" I step closer to run my hand down the dress, feeling the smooth fabric ripple beneath my fingers. I throw my arms around Grandma. "You're a lifesaver."

"I try," she jokes. "It won't be perfect, because it wasn't fitted, but I had your measurements on my Pow, and how else was it supposed to be a surprise? Besides, think about this. If this dress is so great, just imagine how fabulous the dress for your *own* Amora will have to be to top it."

Mom makes a weird sound. I gaze at her face, which is now carefully emotionless. She lets out a long breath.

"Mom? What is it?"

She looks off to the side. "Nothing."

"Lighten up, Rache," Grandma says. "I know what you're thinking: it's so old and mature and all. I understand. I mean, I'm a mom too. I'm *your* mom, sweetie. But Morgan's getting her Like soon. Give her some more leash."

"It's not that." Mom turns away. "I said, it's nothing."

"Honey." Ross starts to stand, but something about the way Mom's standing, spine stiff, makes him hesitate. "Please come and sit down. Do you want me to get you anything?"

"No." Mom walks away, down the hall, stopping only at the end to glance back at me. "You should go soon, so you're not late to Laney's."

"I will." I'm wishing for the thousandth time that I understood why Mom gets like this. "Mom...love you."

Her voice softens. "Love you too, honey." Then she turns the corner to the den.

"Um." Looking worried, Ross hurries after her.

"Well," Grandma says after a moment. "Let's have you try this on quick, before you run off to Laney's."

I take the dress and leave the room, too.

"Eek! I can't look. No, I have to look." Laney peeks out from between her fingers, then quickly hides her eyes again. "I can't look!"

"Laney, for heaven's sake, it's just the Amora building. Nothing's special about the outside, and besides, you've seen it a million times." I try to reason with her, knowing if I let my inner excitement show it'll just set her off again.

We're standing outside the monorail station, the evening sky turning violet between the buildings above. Women and Likes swarm around us as they exit the station, many stop to wish Laney happy birthday before they run inside the Cobalt Amora building. Laney's wearing a shawl across her shoulders, her shining platinum hair piled on top of her head with shiny black clips. The green dress is spectacular, with a lining of black mesh over the skirt and black and silver stones in patterns. Once we enter the building she'll be the star of the party.

I reach out and pry Laney's hands from her face. Her hazel eyes, lined with black makeup, seem larger than they should in the natural light. When the party lights are in full swing they'll pop out in the intended manner, but for now she looks twelve years old.

"Breathe," I tell her. "Don't want to asphyxiate before you even get inside."

"Oh, stop confusing me with your doctory words." She seems to relax nonetheless. "And fix your skirt, it's twisted."

I glance down and adjust my skirt. The dress ends midway down my thighs, the crystals dotting it match a pair of Laney's low heels.

"Okay." Laney sucks in air. "Ready?"

"Are you asking me, or yourself?" I grin and she rolls her eyes. She grabs my hand, pulling me to the doorway.

The lights inside are dim, and there's the sound of the band warming up in the background. The walls flash *Happy Birthday, Laney*, and show all of her academy class pictures, from age two until now.

"Oh no, they have my class 6 picture," Laney moans. "I had ebony hair then, what was I *thinking*?"

"No one will mind," I assure her. "Look around. Mayor Vee did an especially awesome job setting this up. I think she used all of your suggestions. See? There's a shrimp bar, and the dance floor is checkered green and black. And that's your favorite band, and..."

"Okay, okay." Laney pulls out her Pow. "Ugh! Two hours and ten minutes 'til nine!"

"*Laney!*" I shake her shoulders. "You're here. The party starts in ten minutes. Enjoy yourself!"

Someone nearby repeats my exclamation. "Oh, Laney!" People crowd in. "Hey! Happy birthday," comes the collective chatter. "Omigod! Aren't you just psyched? I love your dress!"

We make our way to the tables set up around the large dance floor. Most of our academy classmates sit near us with their Likes, which many of them already have. I see the older women on the other side, mingling and taking seats and comparing dresses while their Likes stand dutifully by.

The Amora building has one main, open room. Smaller areas on the sides feature bars, games, and other entertainment, couches and beanbag chairs also occupying space. Less used rooms are in the back, like bathrooms and a few utility closets. A tall, sloped ceiling changes to match the theme of the current Amora; right now it's black with green ripples, as Laney's colors are green and black.

There are tables around the edges and on the street side of the building. Further in, there's the large dance floor; the Stage, where the nine o'clock Presentation Ceremony happens, rises from its center. The band sets up on the other side of the dance floor. Multiple pillars stand on either side of the band's spot, casting crisscrossing shadows when the dance lights are on and conveniently blocking the bathroom and closet doors from view.

When the clocks floating across the walls tell us it's 7:00 p.m., the roar of voices settles to a hush as everyone waits. Laney practically bounces in her seat. All attention focuses on Mayor Vee ascending the stairs to the top of the Stage. Her blue dress sparkles, and her hair shines green in the overhead lighting. She never repeats a dress, but I wonder if she's used this one in another district. She has to attend every Amora in Blue City. Thankfully, other districts have their Amoras at different times, so Mayor Vee can go to multiple celebrations in one day. I went to one in the Azure district last year, and they all start at four there.

When the mayor speaks, the transmitter linked to her Pow sends her voice through the walls, so she sounds like she's standing by each and every table. "Welcome to Lanora Hill's Amora."

There's cheering, and Laney gnaws on her lip, eyes wide.

"The featured band playing tonight is her favorite, Rainbow Eyes, alternating at times with Superwoman. There's a shrimp bar, and a lot of other delicious food at the buffet tables and cuisine stands, and a small wine bar for everyone of age. Laney, don't go crazy there," Mayor Vee jokes, pretending to scold in Laney's direction. "Now. This is the official commencement," she continues, winking at everyone who laughs at her formal speech, "of the celebration. In two hours, we'll convene again for the Presentation Ceremony. But for now…have at it."

Soon as she's done, the building is flung into a dark ambiance. Green and silver swirls spin and burst on the walls, while the ceiling is checkered to mirror the dance floor, lighting up with the music thundering through the building. The strong beat of the music pounds in my head and reverberates through my bones.

Laney pulls me to my feet shouting something, and my ears, unadjusted, don't catch it.

"*What?*" I have to yell.

"Let's *dance*," she screams, and we plunge into the mass of bodies swarming onto the smooth dance surface. Laney maneuvers through the crowd, pulling me along until we reach a suitable spot. In the dark the people around us look more like shadows, randomly illuminated by flashing and spinning lights. The smell of a hundred different perfumes fills the thick air. I can see women of all ages are out here. Most dancers have Likes, and cling to them whenever possible.

The music practically regulates my heartbeat, slamming through my body and mind. Minutes run together as I spin around and through women and Likes, dancing to the overall movement of the group. Everyone is part of the mass of glamorous, energized individuals, and therefore all the same. Sometimes I can't even distinguish Laney from the silhouettes until a pulse of light flashes on her green dress or her hand catches my arm. The lights ripple on my dress and the white material glows. Good thing, or I might lose myself in the adrenaline coursing through the room.

Perspiration makes my shoulders prickle and strands of hair cling to my cheeks. My swinging earrings are cold when they brush my jaw, my lungs feel tight, but the sensation of dancing makes it impossible to concentrate. The music changes, becoming darker, sexier, driving the dancers wilder and wilder. The collective energy of the group alternately teeters on exploding and imploding, seeming to press on me from all sides.

Finally, Laney catches my attention and beckons. With some difficulty we find the side of the dance floor. Once out of the crowd I'm acutely aware of the throbbing in my veins, the ringing in my ears, the rawness of where the shoes rub into my feet, and mostly the difficulty I'm having drawing air.

I follow Laney, stumbling slightly, to the other side of the room, where steam rises from buffet tables laden with bowls of seafood and soups and sizzling vegetables. A few women and Likes stand nearby, sampling food and conversing with friends. I guess they can hear each other, since the music isn't as loud back here, but it hardly makes a difference to me as my ears are still ringing.

Some women converge on Laney, congratulations and exclamations poised on their lips. I slip off to the side to the nearest coolers, fumbling for a bottle of mineral water. The outside of the glass is slick with condensation, making my fingers slide as I try to unscrew the cap. I'm successful after a few seconds and drop the cap, pressing the bottleneck to my mouth and gulping down the icy liquid. It takes a minute for my heart to start to calm. Another minute and my breathing grows less frantic.

"Morgan?" Through the ringing in my ears, I hear my name called. I turn to see Laney standing beside me, eyebrows raised. Pieces of hair hang free of her updo, and her cheeks are flushed a deep pink. "You okay?" she mouths.

I nod, then crouch to pick up the bottle cap and screw it back on.

She pats my shoulder when I straighten up. "Want to get some food?" I nod again, and we move up to the shrimp buffet. After we've grazed enough, we stack up our used plates and bottles and wander away from the food. Laney keeps glancing at the clocks, which tell her she has a half hour left.

"I wonder what his name will be," she says, and I can actually hear her now. "Lucas? Leo? Those are cute."

"Lance, Liam," I say automatically. We've had this conversation before.

"Oh." Laney suddenly comes to a halt. A curious expression spreads over her face. "I can go there now."

She's looking at a wine bar, manned by some volunteer Likes. Laney approaches, rocking back and forth as she considers the bottles on display. I stand off to the side as she chooses something. She comes back with a thin, delicate glass full of a deep red liquid.

"Well," she says, mouth twitching, "my mom mentioned this kind is really good. Guess I'll see." She raises the glass to her lips and takes a sip.

"And?"

"Mm," she says approvingly, draining the rest of the glass.

"Watch how much of that you drink. I've been warned of the effects of too much alcohol at a lot of the doctor seminars, and…"

"It's my *Amora*," Laney reminds me, but doesn't return to the bar. Instead, she heads for the dance floor, and I follow. It seems like only a minute later the music dies down with one last reverberating note, the swirling and flashing lights slow, and Mayor Vee once again stands on the stage.

The dancing stops and necks crane to see. I've worked my way to the front, next to the stage, which rises to the height of my chest. Laney climbs the curvy steps, strappy heels stopping level with my eyes.

"Lanora," begins Mayor Vee.

"Laney. Call me Laney."

"Laney," the mayor amends. "Congratulations. Seventeen years ago you were born, and now you're ready to take one of life's largest steps. Following this will be graduation, a career, and a daughter. Are you excited?"

"Yes." Laney's voice trembles. Out of the corner of my eye I see Elena, Laney's mom, gripping her Like's hands and beaming.

"Well." Mayor Vee looks around, and a pathway starts to form in the crowd, leading from the edge of the dance floor to the bottom of the Stage steps. "If that's the case, then no further talk is necessary, now is it?"

Now everyone turns to see the figure walking up the pathway. When he's ten feet from me the light illuminates his face, which is flawless, just like every Like. Curly blond hair covers his head, and light blue eyes blink upwards toward Laney. Laney stands still, hands clapped over her mouth, her own eyes wide. The room is hushed. Then the Like speaks.

"Oh my gosh." His voice is saturated with sweetness. "You are *beautiful*."

Laney lets out a squeal, then spins and dashes down the staircase, straight into the Like's arms. I feel lightheaded, like Laney's exuberance is seeping into me as they stand there, staring at each other, her hands clasped around his neck. It's so incredibly adorable.

"Laney," Mayor Vee says, "meet Lloyd."

With that, the music rockets back into existence. Laney and her new Like are blocked from my vision by people, energy renewed, dancing en masse. It's like the beat is embodied in us, an irresistible movement making it impossible not to dance.

For two hours, I merely glimpse Laney, dancing with Lloyd the entire time. I can't get close enough to speak. When the clocks alert everyone it's 10:45 p.m., the dancing becomes more frenzied. With curfew at eleven, Amoras and any other functions come to an end at 10:50. I wonder if Laney forgot about the whole surprise thing I heard her mom mention to her the other day. She's running out of time.

And then the smoke pours in.

It's the neatest effect, almost pure white fog, pulsing and shimmering with the colors of the walls and ceiling. Cheers rise from the crowd as the smoke engulfs the dance floor, amplifying the scent of perfume. At first, I see what everyone else does, a world of mystery, where lights are tangible and the only people in existence are the ones within three feet of you. After the first few moments' euphoria, however, I start to panic. My lungs constrict, rebelling against the smoke, and I erupt into a coughing fit. Knees trembling, I try to find the edge of the crowd, but I have no idea which way to go.

After a minute, there's a general pull in one direction, toward the door, I'm guessing. But it moves too slowly. I fight it, finally finding a break. My feet are clumsy and I stumble into one of the poles. The back of the room. Maybe the bathrooms aren't as smoky. Anywhere where there's clean air…

I'm fighting to fill my lungs now. I fumble for the Pow on my wrist clasp, but the small device slips through my fingers and clatters to the floor somewhere by the base of a pole. Black spots dot my vision. I find a doorknob and try to open it. The door sticks. My fingers scrabble up the doorframe until they find a bolt. I yank the bolt to an open position and blindly thrust the door open.

The air inside is heavy and stagnant, but not smoky. I push inside and slam the door behind me to block out the smoke. I know I should get outside and get something cold to drink, but I can't make myself go back out.

Where's Laney? She's supposed to look out for me, in case something like this happens. It happened one time before, but Laney extracted me from the holiday crowd and brought me a drink.

She's not looking out for me now, something in the back of my mind decides. My hands feel around as my vision swims. Shelves…boxes… A closet of some sort? It's a struggle to remain standing. Why can't someone find me? Is this door supposed to be closed? Doesn't anyone notice I'm missing? My knees give out and I sink to the floor, automatically lowering my head between my knees.

Then the lights go out. It's as if I've been plunged into a pool of nothing. Nothing is visible. I don't even know where the door is now. No sense of direction. No Pow to illuminate this unnatural blackness. It must be eleven o'clock and everyone's back home. My mom will be worried....

At some point, I'm vaguely aware the absence of light nothing is fading to the nothing of unconsciousness, and then I'm aware of nothing else.

CHAPTER 5
Neil

"You look terrible, man."

"Maybe because I *feel* terrible," I snap at Han while rubbing the back of my neck. "They used remotes to get our attention today...twice."

Han opens his mouth, then closes it again, wincing. "Sorry."

I shake my head. "Don't be." I shuffle backward and wearily lower myself onto the thin mattress of my bed. The springs creak beneath my weight. Evening light filters in through the small window in our room, casting double shadows with the lamplight and elongating Han's shadow, keeping time with his pacing. He weaves around the edges of the beds and dresser and desk, the room being too small to simply walk back and forth.

"Do you want any–"

"No." I lie back on the sheets. "I don't want a drink."

"It would help."

"So would a nap." I fight a yawn. "I have maintenance tonight."

"So no *investigating* before class?"

"I can't. I can't even think about it right now."

Han sighs. "Shame. I fancied playing detective tonight."

"Sorry." I am. Han is just as anxious to find answers as I am, but with as little unsupervised time as we have, opportunities to search for them are few and far between.

Han came up with the idea months ago, when I finally told him about Kellan and how I couldn't stand not knowing where he and the rest of the boys disappeared to. The first time we entered a woman's office, skipping work hours and using Han's original set of lock picks to grant us access, I was so scared it took every bit of resolution not to run from the room. Han and I were punished for being late to work, our excuses about feeling sick falling on unforgiving ears.

It got easier, easier to be brave. We learned the best time to investigate was the half hour before work starts, when the women disperse to the factories. Our trips paid off. The third office we unlocked had information we were looking for: records, on paper, in cabinets. One paper about almost every boy in City 4 who disappeared in the last ten years.

We didn't find Kellan's record where it should have been in the alphabetically-ordered system, but we found enough information to understand. When we read records, and realized what the information meant, I turned out to be the strong one. I'd had a shield separating me from my emotions since I lost a friend named Kellan, and it stayed intact. Han, on the other hand, nearly passed out. I hardly got him out of there undetected.

However, he didn't want to stop there. Now he wants to find our records. He wants to know when we're scheduled to disappear, how long we have. I want to know too, but unlike Han, I don't think the information will give me a brilliant idea for escape. Because I've tried to escape plenty before, and it only ends in disappointment and punishment and frustration.

Han sits on the edge of his bed. "So you're not going to class?"

"I don't know. I should if I want to rest tomorrow night."

"What about resting tonight?"

"What about tomorrow…night?" I stifle a yawn.

Han shakes his head. "Damn it, Neil. Just get some sleep. Start now."

I take a deep breath. "Wake me up before you leave."

Han rolls his eyes before yanking open a desk drawer to pull out an unfinished lock picking set. My eyes slide shut.

It only takes a moment to figure out I can't rest on my back. My shoulder muscles are too tight and my neck aches. I turn over and press my face into the pillow. The dusty, stale smell of the fabric fills my airway and the pain and fatigue seems to crescendo. I squeeze my eyes tight, fighting a burning sensation there. And for that moment, I reconsider Han's offer to get me a drink.

Then fatigue takes over.

A voice tugs at my consciousness. It's Han's, and he sounds exasperated.

"I'm only telling you this because you asked me to and I'm a good friend, but anyway, it's quarter to seven. I personally think you should keep on sleeping and totally ignore me like you are currently doing. However, if you want to be a responsible masochist, I suggest you get up now."

My entire body protests as I open my eyes. "You have to be the most wordy alarm ever."

"Didn't catch that, sorry."

I hear Han moving around, opening drawers and dropping what sounds like a shoe. Suppressing a groan, I roll over and prop myself up in a sitting position.

"You're sure it's quarter to seven?" I squint at the window, and the darkening sky outside.

"Quite. Here." A class shirt thwacks against my head, sliding down the side of my face and into my lap. "You lunatic." He sighs. "The sad thing is, you don't even care about the class part, and you're still doing this to yourself."

"Why would I care about the class part? It's the planning ahead part I'm thinking of."

"You know, if life were different, I'd say education might be important."

"But life isn't different." I pull the shirt over my head.

"I know. But I'm not saying a change isn't possible. Hurry up."

"Hm. I guess you're an idealist."

"I find it helps one to survive. What are you, then?"

"A realist."

"Meaning what?" Han shuts the door behind us as we exit the room.

"Meaning I'm not prone to fantasy."

"I'm not prone to *fantasy*," Han says indignantly. I duck

into the washroom to splash water on my face. When I come out, Han amends, "Except sometimes when I'm drinking."

"Exactly."

On the street we join the crowd of boys walking to the classrooms. Many stop to say hi to Han, or ask him about something. When we're seated in the back of the classroom, Han leans over to whisper, "Perry says he saw a new teacher here this afternoon."

Perry's a group P, a Year 15, so he's two years younger than Han and I. Boys are named alphabetically by the year they're born, meaning Han's and my Year is comprised of boys born seventeen years ago, all of our names starting with the letter N. "And?"

"She's probably our new teacher. It's about time for Ms. Rayelle to be promoted."

"Mm." The low tone sounds, signaling the start of class.

Yep, Han was right. The woman who walks in isn't Ms. Rayelle, but a tall, thin woman with dark hair.

She clears her throat. "Hello." Her voice is quieter than Ms. Rayelle's, as though she's used to speaking softly.

The boys stare back at her, silent.

"Um…" The woman fiddles with the remote cuff on her wrist like she's not used to having it there. "Ms. Rayelle's been promoted. I'm Ms. Elliott, your new teacher."

Not for the first time, I wonder where these teachers come from. I assume from the Blue City, or another Color City, where women live. But why would anyone volunteer to come here when they could live in a fantasy world instead?

Ms Elliot excuses boys with maintenance duty twenty minutes early. Han shoots me a look that's both sympathetic and exasperated. I just turn away.

After running to the dorms and changing into a black maintenance shirt, I make my way to the station. An underground subway links City 4 with the Blue City. It might run to other cities as well, but I wouldn't know. It's on the list of Things to Find Out.

When I board, I have to skirt through a crowd of boys already in the car to find an empty seat. The maintenance group on any given night is comprised of a few Year 16's or 17's from all seven Residential Areas, making about forty of us total. We work on the same part of the Blue City, every Saturday night. Sometimes Year 15's will be sent on other days to patch things up, but Saturday is the main maintenance day. The women tell us we do maintenance to become accustomed to Color Cities. I tell myself that's ridiculous.

The subway lurches before the smooth sensation of speed replaces it. I lean my head against the wall, eyes closing. Stupid, lucky Han is probably already asleep. Most nights after class Han and I return to our dorm, and I don't even remember what happens after because I fall asleep within a minute. The next thing I know alarms are sounding, telling us to wake up and start the process all over again.

It's about a fifteen minute ride at this speed to the Blue City. The station here is similar to the one in City 4, underground, with dark tunnels looming on all sides. The major difference is the walls. These are Color City walls; they look like brick, but feel smoother than glass when I brush my fingertips against them.

As usual, the boys grow quiet, clumped together at the base of the stairs leading up and out of the station. This building is down the block from the women's monorail station. The mayor uses that to get here. She's watched us arrive a few times.

Also as usual, one of the women supervisors stands at the top of the stairs to regurgitate the routine warnings. "Pick up your assignment on the way out. Report directly to your assigned location. Handle the maintenance materials and *only* the maintenance materials. Do not make noise. Do not wander anywhere. And even though the women are inside as per curfew, do not attract attention. *It will be your fault.* There will be consequences." She fingers the remote strapped to her wrist to get the point across. I rub my neck automatically.

Seeming satisfied, she turns and walks across the upper floor, out of sight. After a moment, the boys climb the stairs and file past the machine dispensing assignments. The slip of paper I receive is labeled *Amora building, Founder Road*.

That word–*Amora*–causes my teeth to clench until my jaw aches. Usually when Year 15's are sent to the Color Cities on random nights it's to clean up after one of those. And I know why.

Chilly air causes goosebumps to rise on my arm. The streets outside are dark, and I catch sight of a few stars blinking down between buildings. We never see stars in City 4; too much smog. But the Blue City has air-cleansing gardens on the rooftops, energy efficient devices, and most helpfully, no factories.

I let my eyes adjust a moment, dusky shapes of structures coming into view. We're not supposed to carry a light, so I rely on the almost unnoticeable street signs for direction. Their glow only extends a few feet, but I don't need much direction. The subway station lies right across the street from my destination.

About five other boys also have this assignment. One opens the door, and we follow. On my way in glass crunches beneath my shoes; I make a note to come back out and sweep it up. Once inside, we turn on the walls. They radiate a soft light equally on the room, illuminating the smoky, waste-strewn interior. My stomach curdles. Yes, there was another one tonight.

The smoke smells sickeningly sweet. Other boys grumble and spread out, grabbing the brooms propped against a few tables near the entrance. I reach for one, but a boy looks up and says, "Can you go get some trash bags? I have a feeling we'll need them."

I fight back a sarcastic comment and just nod before making my way to the utility closet. The door is closed, but unlocked. The bolts on closets are usually secure.

It's dark inside. There are portable lights on a shelf to my left, so I feel around for one, shutting the door in the process to give me room to maneuver. As soon as I can see, I step back, then trip over something. I stop, confused. My beam of light lands on a shoe. And that shoe is attached to a leg.

I stumble backward. The light catches the rest of her. Yes, her. A woman. A girl, even. Out cold on the floor, maybe even dead. Good grief, I found a dead girl. An image bursts into my mind, of the supervisor fingering her remote. *It will be your fault.*

I clench my teeth. What do I do? Tell someone? Pretend I didn't notice? Not that the women would care. If I'm even remotely affiliated with this, I'll get blamed. And what if she's not dead? Shouldn't some sort of medical action be taken?

As if to answer my question, the girl stirs and starts to cough. I drop the light and twist the doorknob, planning to just get out of here. But then she sits up and clutches her throat, shoulders rigid.

I don't know what, but something innate reacts in me, buckling my knees so I'm kneeling next to her, and my hand rests between her shoulder blades so she doesn't fall while she struggles to breath. That's where my gut reaction ends, though, and I'm left panicking, not knowing how to proceed.

It takes a moment, but the girl gasps, taking in a long, shaky breath. The beam from the dropped light shines right in her face and she squints against it, hands clutching her knees. It seems like she's okay. I still should probably run. Or should I? This isn't covered in our weekly *or else* lectures. We're just told to have no contact whatsoever. But wouldn't the women want me to help her? What is she doing here, anyway?

The girl's shoulders slump, halting my racing mind. For a second, I think she's passing out again, but she's just relaxing. And inevitably, her head turns, and she looks at me.

My first thought is, her eyes are gray. And my second thought is she's looking at me, and that is most definitely considered contact. So my third thought is, I'm dead.

CHAPTER 6
Morgan

I drift in and out of awareness. I'm aware of time passing, but I don't try to wake up because when I slip into nothingness I no longer have to fight to breathe.

But then a noise tugs at my consciousness, and something catches on my foot. I start to drift upwards, like floating through water, and my surroundings rush in on me. When I break the surface of awareness, the first thing I notice is my lungs are still. Immediately my body panics. I cough, yanking myself upright, hands over my throat, frantically sucking in air. My vision spins, my balance spinning with it, as if I am falling backward or sideways, but I'm not sure which.

Then there's a hand on my back, anchoring me in place. My vision stops spinning and I can focus. Finally, my lungs expand; relief makes me dizzy. I squeeze tears out of the corners of my eyes and slowly slide them open. A bright light attacks me. I cringe, breathing hard.

Now I remember the hand on my back and turn my head. Someone's there, looking like a silhouette in the glare of whatever light is on the ground. Maybe it's a Pow light, the emergency setting, though it seems too white, too harsh.

The hand falls from my back and the person backs up, kicking the light away. It faces the corner, reflecting back and casting a dim glow around the closet. I can sort of see the features now; it's a Like. Probably one the mayor sent out to find me if Ross called in that I'm missing. He's young, though, Lloyd's age or close to it. And this Like glares at me like he's almost...repulsed.

"Whose are you?" I try to speak, voice hoarse.

The Like's spine stiffens, and I see his shadowy hands clench. "Damn you. I'm no one's. I don't belong to *anyone*."

51

I stare at him. I've never heard a Like use that tone. It's angry, resentful, the total opposite of the adoration usually coming out of their mouths. Maybe I'm hallucinating.

"When did I pass out?" I grope at the shelves, searching for something to help me stand.

"I don't know. Dammit!" The Like slams a fist into his thigh.

"Would you cut that out?" I sound irritated. "Here, help me up." I hold out a hand. The Like presses himself harder against the shelves across from me, hands staying balled up at his sides, and I frown. "What's going on?"

"Nothing good," he hisses. "I shouldn't have helped you. Just for talking to you...do you know what they're going to *do* to me?" His voice shakes, but I can't tell if it's with fear or fury.

I manage to pull myself up, but I just stand there, facing the Like, trying not to lose my balance and blatantly staring at the same time. Likes don't act this way. Ever. They don't even raise their voices unless they get into arguments over whose woman is prettier.

"What do you mean, *they*? *They* who? Why? Who *are* you?"

He grinds his teeth, seeming to talk more to himself than to me. "When you tell them, they're going to think I broke the rules, and..."

He kneels suddenly, scooping up the light. The beam swings around illuminating his face. His hair is brown and messy, and his eyes are shadowed and dark, glaring out at me. Something about the expression causes me to shiver. I've never seen a Like glare. And on his skin there are marks, odd marks and discolorations. "What are those?" I blurt out. I blurt out questions often.

It's his turn to stare. He doesn't say anything, though. "On your face," I explain, touching my own. "The marks."

"They're called scars. Not that you'd have any, with your charmed life."

Scars? I know what scars are. They happen after

52

surgeries, but there's treatment and lotions to get rid of them. No Like I've seen has scars anywhere, let alone on his face. I voice a ridiculous question. "You're not a Like?"

He shudders. "No. I'm *not*."

Good grief. I probe my temple with my fingers. I must be hallucinating. "Who are you, then?"

The look he–it?–gives me is weird, confused. "You should be running off to report me."

To what? "I must be dreaming. The smoke and...I have to get home."

I wait for him to reply, but he doesn't. He just turns off the light and I hear something brush through the doorway.

He left? I trip forward, hands finding the door, and stumble out as well. That's it. He's not a Like. Or he's just *not*. *Not* as in, I'm not thinking straight. My foot hits something. I see it skitter away a few feet, glowing faintly in protest. My Pow. I drop to my knees and pick it up, instantly relieved.

There are more figures in the room, moving around. Some appear to be sweeping. Only Likes sweep and clean homes. Except my mom, she insists on doing a lot of her own cleaning. I see her sweeping sometimes, which seems to make Ross feel uncomfortable.

Ack. I have to get out of here. I have to get home. I back up, reaching the wall behind the bathrooms, and find the small back exit. No one calls after me. I burst out onto the street, the utterly dark street. Just like I've always been warned. Except, there are signs. Faintly glowing street names. Oh, good. I stagger toward one, hands outstretched in case a structure jumps out in front of me.

Chilly air invades my lungs, which actually feels good. I light up my Pow and open a map, not trusting myself to navigate dark streets without help. It takes me ten minutes to reach my townhouse. I'm about to grasp the doorknob when the door flies open. It's Ross. He pulls me inside and quickly shuts the door behind me. Then I'm smothered by a hug.

"Mom." Her hair thickens my voice. After a moment she lets me go and steps back, eyes rising to meet mine.

"Where—"

"Were you?" another voice finishes. I peer over Mom's head, my tired eyes focusing on Mayor Vee. She's watching me from the living room, her expression concerned. Her Like, Vaughn, stands beside her. "Why did you break curfew?"

"Can't she sit down first?" My mom's voice is short. The mayor glances at her sharply, but I think I imagined it because then she smiles.

"Good idea. Sorry, dear. Come on." She ushers me to the couch, settling next to me, while Mom lowers herself into the armchair. She tries again, her voice gentler. "Why are you home so late?"

I open my mouth, and a voice plays through my head. *I shouldn't have helped you. Just for talking to you...do you know what they're going to* do *to me?*

"I hung back to wait for Laney," I say, then wonder wildly what I'm doing. Lying. But lying is what you do when you tell someone their dye job looks great even when it's totally not their color. Lying *isn't* what you do when you're asked a question by the mayor. I've only ever *really* lied about my breathing before. "But she wasn't there. So I left, and the monorail station, it was so crowded I...I decided to walk a little ways to the next one. But then it got dark."

Why didn't I mention about the not-Like? Probably because I don't know what I saw. Or because I can't tell her about my breathing. Or because I'm afraid I'll get in trouble, when I got off easily on the *Romeo and Juliet* thing. Or maybe because I don't even know if it was real.

"When it got dark I was...afraid." Truth. "I waited, I wasn't really sure where I was, and I thought someone would come looking for me. But then I decided to try to find my way back. The street signs were glowing, and my Pow has the map, so why not?" I glance at the plain wall of the living room. The clock in the corner reads 11:34. "I'm not too terribly late, am I?"

Mayor Vee is nodding along now. "I'm sorry this happened. You should have come straight home when the

Amora ended, though."

"I'm sorry," I mumble.

The mayor nods, her pale blue eyes hold my gaze. "Did you see anyone?"

I swallow. My face slips into a confused expression, covering the moment of surprise and panic I feel. Does she know? Does she know what I saw? I don't even know what I saw! If I say no, and she knows, she'll know I'm lying. But if she does know, then she knows I'm lying already. No. Play along, I tell myself. "No," I say as steadily as I can. "Should I have?" Maybe she'll explain, clear up my confusion.

The mayor lets out a breath, shaking her head. "No. I mean, there were some Likes looking for you."

"Oh. I didn't see them. And it won't happen again."

Mayor Vee smiles now. "Well, you gave us a little scare. But that's okay, as long as you're all right." She pats my leg and stands up. Vaughn stands as well. "Enjoy your day tomorrow," she says to my Mom, and they leave.

Now I turn to my mom. Her hands are in fists, pressed against the cushions of the armchair. "I was worried," she tells me, her voice low.

"I'm sorry," I whisper, for the second time. Mom shakes her head, almost to herself. Ross comes up behind her and puts his hands soothingly on her shoulders. Mom shakes them off and stands up. I stand as well. "Wash your face," she says. "The makeup is smudged. Then please get some rest."

"Okay." I back away to the stairs, then turn and run straight into my room.

On Sunday afternoons Laney goes to the indoor sports complex. She played defense on the academy's football team, and even though her last season's over she continues this part of her exercise routine. She claims it helps her get rid of the cobwebs Church service gives her. I go to Synagogue sometimes, but Mom and I aren't particularly religious, so I don't have a regular cobweb-clearing routine like Laney does.

I wasn't sure she'd be here today, after the party, but she

surprises me. I'm waiting by the railing separating the tracks from the stretching areas. The walls are light blue, swirls pulsing with the energetic music filling the room. Other women work out, most accompanied by their Likes, on weight machines and the gymnastics floor and basketball courts visible through windows to other rooms. Further away in this building are pools, an indoor driving range, ice rink, batting cages, and other sport facilities.

Laney circles around the far end of the track and sees me on her way back. After crossing a white line she slows to a jog and heads over.

"Whew!" She props her elbows on the railing. Pink spots darken the apples of her cheeks, somehow color-coordinated with her pink shorts and white tee. "That was fun. I needed to let out some excess energy."

I grin. "I still think you should play football for a career team. At least try out for Blue City's."

Laney breathes hard, shaking her head. "Nah. I'll be too busy."

"Busy with career training?"

"And Lloyd." She winks at me as I hear her name called from behind me.

I turn around. "Speaking of whom..."

The curly blond head bounds forward across the stretching mats. Lloyd stops, catching the railing, eyes wide. "Laney, you're amazing! Better than you told me!"

Laney grins. "Am not."

"Are so. I got you some water. Mixed berry flavored, your favorite." Lloyd hikes a leg onto the railing and hops over, handing Laney the water before throwing his arm over her shoulder.

Laney laughs and uncaps the bottle. "It's my favorite. How'd you know?"

Lloyd kisses her forehead. "It felt right."

I hear myself say the routine *aww*. Laney's lucky. Lloyd is absolutely adorable. Laney asks Lloyd to get her a towel, and he scurries off to do so. As soon as he's gone I lean over the railing and catch Laney's eye. "I passed out last night," I say, chewing on my lower lip.

Laney's eyes widen. "Oh, no! Oh my gosh, I'm so sorry. It was the smoke, wasn't it."

I nod. "Did you...?"

Laney shakes her head. "I didn't know about it, I swear. I knew there'd be something, but I didn't know what, Mom making it a surprise and all." She frowns. "How did you get back home?"

"I found my way. Used my Pow map." I told her about the breathing, so why did a lie just tumble out of my mouth?

Do you know what they're going to do *to me?*

"Who helped you? Did someone find you? God, I feel terrible." She wraps her arms around her torso.

"I...no." I shake my head, more at myself, trying to get his–its?–*voice* out of my mind.

"I should have thought about that," Laney moans, hands over her eyes now. "I was preoccupied, I didn't..."

Automatically I shake my head again. "No, no, it's understandable."

"What's wrong?" Lloyd runs up and pulls Laney's hands from her face, taking them in his. "What's the matter?"

"Oh," Laney says. "It's nothing much. I just made a mistake yesterday."

"A mistake?" Lloyd sounds skeptical. "You're too perfect to make a mistake."

Well, point for consolation. "It's no big deal," I assure both of them.

"Morg just has some br–" Laney starts, lowering her voice. My eyebrows fly up.

"Breakfast plans," I say quickly, cutting her off. They both stare at me. "I just have some breakfast plans."

"It's nearly four in the afternoon," Lloyd feels the need to point out.

"Yes," I agree. "Um. The plans are for tomorrow. With my mom."

"Doesn't your mom work early shifts this week?" Laney

raises an eyebrow.

"My mom's friend," I say. "Actually, my grandma. Er, Laney, can I talk to you?"

When Laney steps aside with me I hiss, "What the hell, Lane? Were you going to tell him?"

"It was an accident," she insists. "But what does it matter? He's my Like. He's trustworthy."

"So are you, right? Please, don't tell anyone, remember?"

Laney nods. "Okay. Sorry. My mistake." She glances back toward where Lloyd waits and sighs. "But just wait 'til you get your Like, Morg. Then you'll understand."

CHAPTER 7
Neil

I'm a mess. I try to stay lost in the crowd of the subway, and reach the dorms without outwardly panicking. Once I'm inside my room I shut the door tight, wishing it could lock. Then my knees give way and I'm sitting on the edge of my bed, elbows digging into my knees, fingers twisting and ripping at my hair.

I stay here, eyes wide and locked on a stain in the wooden floor, for the hour until the alarm sounds. For once I don't even jump.

Han stirs in the bed across the cramped room. After a moment I hear his voice. "You're already up?" he asks, voice thick with fatigue. "Or did you even go to sleep? You probably didn't. I'm pretty sure you have some sort of death wish involving you making yourself so tired you just fall into that slicer machine at your factory one of these days."

"I don't need a death wish," I say, voice oddly steady. "I'm dead on my feet already."

"You see my point." Han flops back on his mattress. "You're like a zombie from one of the living dead myths we learned about last year."

"No, Han, I really am dead." I stand, gripping the corner of the desk. I watch Han sit up again and raise an eyebrow.

"Did you go the poison route, then? I've always found that unnecessarily painful and melodramatic. And where'd you get the poison, anyway?"

"It's naturally made and easy to find. It's called *stupidity*." I kick the bottom of the desk. It's almost satisfying, so I do it again, ignoring the protests of my toes when they connect with the hard wood.

Now Han is silent. He knows how much stupidity can cost a boy. I feel him watching, waiting for an explanation.

59

I've already decided to tell him, so if/when *or else* happens Han will at least know why.

"My assignment was the Amora building. I went to get trash bags from the closet. And inside was this...girl."

Han stills, eyebrows rising. "There was a girl. In the closet."

"Yes, unconscious. *Unconscious.* What was I supposed to *do*?" My hands twist in my hair again, as if the pain of roots separating from my scalp can possibly distract me.

"Get out of there?" Han suggests.

"I would have. But then she started to cough, or choke, and I don't know. Something made me try to help."

He closes his eyes. "Define *help*."

"I knelt down and put a hand on her back. Some idiotic part of my brain thought it was being smart, but I don't think I did anything useful."

"You *touched* her."

I swallow. "Then she looked up."

"She *saw* you."

"The light was shining in her eyes," I say defensively. "And she seemed really confused. She kept thinking I was a *Like*. She asked about my *scars*. And when I said she should be reporting me, she didn't know what I–"

"You *talked* to her." Han stands up, scoops up the pillow on his bed, and flings it at me. It smacks against my shoulder and drops to the floor, sending a puff of dust across my feet.

"Yeah," I mutter. "I am so stupid."

"I have to agree. You know, if you weren't such an idiot, I'd be kind of in awe of you right now."

"There's nothing to be awed by. Except maybe the method in which the women choose to carry out *or else*. I'm sure it'll be interesting." My stomach clenches.

Han inhales deeply. "Well. Maybe *or else* won't happen. You said this girl seemed confused. She was probably drunk, and won't remember what happened."

"I bet she already reported it. While she was drunk."

"How would you know? Have the women come to drag

you away yet?"

"No."

"Well. There's still a chance *you* can escape the consequences of your idiocy."

Han's hand brushes across the burn on his neck.

"Unlikely. Listen, when I'm carted off to *or else* land–"

Han cuts me off, waving a hand. "I'll make sure your whistles stay hidden, put out a flower in your memory, et cetera. In the meanwhile, try not to give yourself away by wearing a sign saying, *'I'm an idiot, ask me how!'*"

I blink, then sigh. "Fine. Okay. I'll stop griping. I'll act like nothing happened. Play dumb or something."

Han gives me an exaggerated wink. "Good idea! Why didn't I think of that?"

I shake my head and turn away. Holding my hands in front of me, I see they're shaking, so I cross my arms. "We should get ready."

"Nah." Han flops back down on his bed. "It's Sunday, remember?"

Oh. Relief washes over me. On Sundays work starts late, at noon, even though the alarms still go off at the normal time. It's mostly for the women's benefit, so they all have concurrent free time to discuss the running of the city. Boys are supposed to study or clean their dorms or, when it's nice out, there's the option to be outside exercising.

"Are you going to rest?" Han stares up at the ceiling. "We could, you know, play detective, but I think you'd stumble into walls in your current state. Which would be something of a hindrance. So you should get some sleep."

I shake my head. "You go ahead. I couldn't sleep anyway." When we're not breaking into offices, we take turns sleeping in on Sundays, one of us always staying awake to wake the other if a surprise inspection takes place.

"Are you sure?" Han squints at me. "Your face looks like oatmeal, you're so gray. Do you feel nauseous, or is this really just from exhaustion?"

"Now that you mention it, Han, yes, I do feel a bit

nauseous. Can't imagine why."

"Rest would help."

I reach across the desk for the blade and wooden whistle I'm working on. "Go to sleep, before I change my mind."

"I wish you would," Han mutters, but rolls over anyway and is out in five minutes.

I spend the time whittling, trying to make my whistle better, but my vision keeps doubling and my fingers slip, slicing the blade across my own skin. It's impossible to focus. Everything comes back to either that girl, *or else*, or life.

I don't ever recall not hating women. At one point, though, I didn't hate them as much. That was before Kellan, and before I found out what happens to the disappeared.

I've always been kind of a loner. From Year 12 and up many of the boys got involved in drinking and fighting during the few off-work hours, and I just wasn't interested. No one really took an interest in being my friend, either, and I didn't care. I only wanted more sleep.

When I was a Year 14 working in a distillery, another boy working there, Kellan who was a Year 17 at the time, made an effort to get to know me. He could make off-work time fun sometimes, like showing me where to swim in the artificial lake near the residential area. He's the one who taught me to make whistles. That year he earned my trust.

But the next year Kellan became a Year 18, the year they all disappear. And it happened. One day Kellan was gone. I spent the rest of my Year 15 and all of Year 16 hardly speaking to anyone. I made a lot of whistles then, destroying most of them afterwards. Rooming with Han this year is some weird stroke of luck, because I doubt anyone else would have been my friend again. Only, it's not a matter of *would* have, it's *could* have. Han could, because he forced me to trust him by figuring out what really happens. I guess I have a sort of understanding with him, too, because of his burn.

My fingers slip and I glance down. I've been whittling absentmindedly; the whistle is deformed. Useless. I clench my teeth and run the blade down the length of the wood.

Shavings drop into my lap until there isn't enough of the whistle left to fit the blade across. By the time Han stirs, the sky is light and I have shallow cuts crisscrossing my fingers.

"Whattimeissit," he mumbles.

"Ten. Give or take a few minutes."

Han rubs his eyes. "Oh. Okay. Hey, I've been thinking."

"No, you weren't. You were sleeping."

"And thinking," he insists. "Anyway, you said this girl seemed confused. How so?"

My hands shake, so I set the blade down. "I told you. She kept thinking I was a Like, and didn't understand me when I kind of snapped at her that I wasn't. She asked about my scars. She didn't know why she should report me."

"She didn't understand you," Han muses. "That's what I was thinking about. Maybe she really didn't understand."

"What do you mean?"

"Maybe she doesn't know about us, or maintenance, or whatnot."

"That's stupid."

"Maybe it's not just her. Maybe a lot of them don't know. I've been wondering for a while, ever since we figured out what happens to us."

I consider, but only for a moment. "That's stupid. "What, do they think their buildings clean themselves? Alcohol refines itself? Their *Likes* appear out of midair?"

Han shrugs. "Maybe they're the stupid ones, then."

"Now that," I say, "I can believe."

Chapter 8
Morgan

My window automatically darkens at 10:50 p.m. At eleven, the faint glow permeating the tinted window dims, and I finish lacing my boot over the black jeans I'm wearing. I feel more alert now than I have all day. All week, actually.

I quietly make my way downstairs, past my Mom's room and Ross's room where both are asleep, and cross through the laundry room. I had this idea Monday evening, after I'd spent two days worrying I was crazy or I accidentally drank some of Laney's wine or something. Or, worse, I wasn't crazy and I hadn't consumed alcohol and I really saw a not-Like. Then what? What was he? *It*?

Anyway, I was pretty sure I needed to figure out what happened, or I really *would* go nuts, so I'd waited until Mom and Ross retired to their rooms before I dressed in a black jacket and jeans, quite a cute outfit actually, and crept to the fire escape. I'd stopped there, rocking back and forth in my boots, too nervous to step outside into the pitch-black city, memories of my tenth birthday trembling in my fingertips.

I knew bringing my Pow, using it out there, wasn't going to work. The small light from its screen would pretty much put me in a spotlight for anyone looking outside. Also, I wasn't eager to get caught and questioned by Mayor Vee for the third time in less than a week.

After several unsuccessful attempts to step into the wall of black, I retreated to my room and dropped my black clothing on the closet floor. But the next day I pulled them back out. I got a block from my house before anxiety clawed at my organs, making my airway tight and drawing me back.

On Wednesday I wised up and realized silvery blonde hair glowed more in the light of the faint street markers than my natural hair color, so I un-dyed it. I could tell it shocked my mom, but she didn't say anything. Laney, of course, had a lot to say on the subject, and so did the girls at academy, when they got around to noticing after they were done exclaiming over Laney and Lloyd.

By Thursday night I made it all the way to the Amora building. There wasn't anyone around when I quickly opened the door and peered inside. The eerie stillness freaked me out. I ran back home, able to find my way because I'd memorized the street names leading to and from the Amora building.

I was constantly tired during the days, but got adrenaline rushes at night, like mental coffee. Yesterday, Friday, I stayed out long enough to even look in some buildings around the Amora building. But the city, like all the other nights, was still and silent; there were no not-Likes, imaginary or not.

I'd pretty much given up, but today, Saturday, Laney reminded me excitedly that it's been a whole week since her Amora. Therefore I decided to extend my prowling one more night, just in case. And, oddly, I kind of enjoy the rush of exhilaration breaking curfew gives me. It's something out of the ordinary, pushing me toward some edge of excitement I hadn't even known existed.

I hesitantly make my way through the streets, darkness pressing on my eyes. I guide myself by the small street signs on the corner of each block. I didn't even know they lit up until I came out the first time. I can't see them from inside.

My mind flashes back to a week ago, trying to pull any useful information from the images. The not-Like's silhouette is burned in my memory, but is it enough for recognition?

I guess it'll have to be.

Perhaps there won't be anyone here. That's the likeliest outcome. If so, I'll stop breaking curfew. I'll just wonder the rest of my life what the hell I drank at Laney's Amora.

But as it turns out, I don't have to wait long. For the first time, I see it. Movement. A shadow darkens the faint glow around a street name sign. I spin around, searching for more, for any way to see them. And then my gaze lands right on it. That same silhouette from a week ago flits past the *Frasier*

Street sign. I propel forward, after the form, catching a faint glimpse every few seconds. The wider I open my eyes, the greater the light entering them, the better I can see, and the more the whole thing feels like a dream.

The not-Like enters the career ballet studio three blocks away. I wait a minute, then slip through the door myself. The doorway opens into a luxurious waiting room, the outlines of sofas and poufs and coffee tables visible. Though the walls and floors are mostly darkened, some sections are lowly lit to allow objects to be distinguishable. I've been here before, meeting Seffa and Daye after their ballet practices.

The hallway is right in front of me. Faint noises, like doors opening or objects being shuffled around, float into the lobby from the otherwise quiet interior. After a moment's hesitation during which excitement and nerves make my stomach quiver, I follow the sound deeper into the building.

I hear a brushing sound like sweeping coming from the room labeled *Practice A*. I peek inside the doorway. It's dimly lit via one of the poles in the middle of a wall, but the mirrors lining the long room magnify the light. And on the right side of the room, holding a broom, is the not-Like. I'm 99% sure it's the one from the closet at the Amora building. He wears a black polo shirt and loose jeans, and even from here I can see his hair is messier than any Like would keep his.

For minutes I just watch, mouth half open, mind working, trying to put puzzle pieces together as if watching will make what I'm seeing make sense. But even as a child I was too impatient, and I'd try to jam pieces into the wrong shaped spaces. That's how it feels now.

I take a deep breath. Well, here it is. The moment. The fruit of my nightly excursions. I've ruled out the *what the hell did I drink* theory. Now I'm just crazy or…not crazy.

I guess the least I can do is say hi.

The not-Like must be distracted, because he doesn't notice me approach. In his defense, I'm being quiet on purpose, and my boots don't squeak. He seems pretty immersed in sweeping, eyes cast down, not watching the mirrors. I'm about five feet away when I stop.

"Umm…"

The not-Like freezes, shoulders going rigid, head snapping up. When he sees me his mouth drops open and he jumps back, tripping over the broom which clatters to the floor. The not-Like presses his hands against the mirrors, eyes staring. *Déjà vu,* I think.

"Hi."

He puts a hand to his ear, like he doesn't think he can hear correctly.

"Do you remember me?"

The not-Like keeps staring.

"We met about a week ago," I prompt. "Actually, exactly a week ago."

Now he speaks. "What is this, some sort of trick? Or a test? I don't want anything to do with you!"

I blink once again, shocked such a tone could come from something so similar to a Like. "No, it's not a…what do you mean, *test?*"

He shakes his head, pressing further against the wall. "I figured it out. Why they didn't punish me yet. Because they're testing me. You're testing me. Well, I'm not talking to you. I'm not supposed to. I didn't want to in the first place."

"You're talking to me now," I point out.

He glares, removing his hands from the mirror and glancing down at the smudges they left behind. "I have to clean that now," he mutters, but he's talking to himself.

"And who's going to punish you? For *what?*" I practically beg for an answer. "Who are you?"

"As if you don't know."

If words could be venomous, then his would be lethal.

"But I don't."

"I have a better question. Why are *you* here?" The not-Like picks up the broom and grips it in his hand. A vision flies through my head of him swinging the thing at me, fracturing my skull, or crushing my carotid artery, or snapping a rib. I take a step back.

"Because I want to know." My voice sounds too high, too young. "Because you're not...imaginary, okay? And I want to understand. Why are you cleaning? What are you? Where did you come from?"

"That's what the mayor told you to ask me," he replies acidly. "To see if I'd answer."

"The mayor?" I shake my head. "The mayor doesn't know about you. I didn't tell anyone."

Now he pauses. "Why in the world didn't you tell?"

I shrug. "I thought I was crazy. And you seemed scared."

He doesn't say anything, but he gives me a *look*, like I just said something as stupid and obvious as "It's dark out."

"Stop." Annoyance sparks inside of me. "Stop acting like I'm an idiot and know everything at the same time. I don't understand, okay? And I've lost sleep for a week sneaking out to try and figure out what's going on."

"Poor thing. Losing a few minutes of beauty sleep *all week*. Your life just *sucks*, doesn't it." His dark eyes narrow, looking at me, then down to the broom, as if he can't bear the sight of me standing here for more than a second.

I grind my teeth. "No, but why are you talking to me like that? How can you say if my life sucks or doesn't suck? You don't even know me."

"I don't need to." The not-Like is sweeping again. "You're a woman."

"And what are you, making you act so superior?"

The not-Like pauses. "Superior? *Me?* No. Quite the opposite. I'm a *man*. A boy, even. But you knew that. Of course you did. Otherwise, you wouldn't be here."

Now my mouth drops open. *Man?* As in *Romeo and Juliet?* What did Mayor Vee say those were? Some old form of Like? "How many are there? Of you. Men, I mean."

"Would you *stop* asking stupid questions?"

"They're not stupid questions!"

The not-Like jumps, startled. "Keep your voice down," he hisses.

"No." In three steps I cross the floor until I'm standing

inches away, arms crossed, glaring up at him. A faint pine scent tickles my nose. From this angle I can see if he's about to hit me with the broom, and I can glare quite effectively too. "Listen closely. I have no idea what's going on, who you are, where you come from, or what I'm supposed to be *testing* you on. I didn't *tell* anyone about you. Are you at all grateful? I'm not even supposed to be here. If a woman walked into the room, I'd be screwed. I'd have to go to court or something, have privileges taken away. And I'm already in some hot water for accidentally breaking curfew last week and not giving a good enough reason, thank you very much."

The not-Like's eyes are dark and indiscernible due to the shadows falling across his face. In a small patch of light I see those scars across his jaw line, which is tight, like he's clenching his teeth. But finally he is listening to what I'm saying. It's quiet, just the sound of my breathing and my heartbeat pounding in my head. I'm struck by how odd this is. The closeness, I mean. I've hardly ever been alone with my friends' Likes, let alone this close to one.

Then the not-Like–the *man*, or *boy*–steps back. "You really don't know?" His tone is dubious, but no longer acidic.

"I really don't know."

He shakes his head, looking away. "How could you not?" he asks, almost too quietly for me to hear.

"I don't know how. I mean, you look so similar to a Like, except..."

The boy glances at me sharply. I hesitate, afraid of losing whatever progress I might have made, but too curious to stop. "Except for the scars, the ones on your jaw, and how you talk, it's just so different, and the fact that you're here. I don't even know what you're doing here, either."

The boy just blinks. Then he says, hesitantly, "The scars are from work. And accidents, and..."

"You work? What do you do?"

That annoyed expression returns. I quickly say, "I mean, we, um, us, well, we don't start working until after career training, which takes a year or so after we graduate the

69

academy. Is this your work?"

"No, this is maintenance. Extra," the boy says shortly. "Usually we're in factories. So yes, we work. Always have."

"Maintenance?" I almost miss what the boy says because I'm shocked he's actually answering.

"Yes. Once a week. Shifts rotate, one day per residential area. You can thank us for your city being so clean."

"And you're here at night because you work in factories all day?" Factories are something I've learned about from old times, before the Wars, when women were more oppressed because of international pressure. They're kind of like mass manufacturing houses.

"Yes. And we're here at this time because all the women are asleep, so we don't *inconvenience* you."

I frown. "When do you go to an academy, then?"

"We don't. We have classes. At night."

My mind tries to put this information together, to make sense of it. It's not working so well. "Factories. And classes at night? Where…where do you come from?"

The boy stares at his hands gripping the broom handle. "A city. But, not one like this. A city with factories and dirt and smog. And it's crowded, and everything is regulated. The walls are real, not surfaces with fancy images."

"I…" I close my eyes for a second. "I've never heard of a city like that. I've only been out of Blue City twice before, but I don't remember seeing a dirty, crowded city outside."

"It's miles away. But close enough for a subway to get here in fifteen minutes." The boy shakes his head. "Each of your Color Cities has one. A Number City, like mine."

"How many of you *are* there?" My voice is soft, unable to be loud and confident while my head spins like a top.

"I don't know. I don't go outside my residential area much. The women don't like it. But I estimated once, based on class numbers and residential areas, that there's a little under three thousand of us, all ages, in City 4 and–" He stops abruptly, seeming surprised to find he's talking out loud.

"Three thousand," I repeat, my voice oddly empty. Three

thousand. About how many academy age and below girls there are in Blue City. That's a lot of men that aren't supposed to exist anymore. And there are *more* cities. "Show me."

The boy stares at me with a guarded expression. "No."

"Why? I want to understand."

He rolls his eyes. Likes don't roll their eyes unless they're teasing. But this boy is definitely not going for humor. "Even if you aren't going to report everything back to your mayor—which I'm expecting you to, so it won't be a big shock or anything—you couldn't come to City 4."

"Why not?" I resist the urge to cross my arms again.

"Think about it. You're a girl. You'd be noticed."

"What if I cut my hair and got some of whatever you're wearing, a black shirt and baggy jeans. If I made myself look like a Li—like you, would I be noticed?"

"If anyone really *looked* at you, yes. But it's a far cry from your perfect utopian life here. You couldn't handle it."

I do cross my arms now, feeling the blow to my pride sting. "Like I said, you don't even know me."

"And *you*," he replies, "don't know anything."

Another pause. The soft light from the support pole illuminates his face and scars, but since it's coming from behind me, it leaves my face in shadow. The boy twists the broom back and forth. The bristles swish as they rotate.

"But I will," I say finally. "I'm going to find out. I want to know what's real. Do you understand? Do you know why no one knows about you? About men?"

"I thought women did know. I'm still not convinced you don't. And besides, I'm positive your mayor knows, and the women who work in City 4."

Mayor Vee knows. He's said that, but I only now realize what he means. She *lied* to me about *Romeo and Juliet,* about men not existing anymore. Maybe she called me into her office not because I read the book, but because the book referenced men, and for some reason they're a secret. And women *work* in these other cities? "How—"

I stop as I hear a low tone echo through the building.

71

"What's that?" I take a step back, head jerking toward the door. "Is it an alarm?"

"It's the hour marker," the boy tells me. "It's midnight now. An hour wasted. I still have to clean this place."

"Midnight," I repeat, feeling my stomach roll over. I'm an hour past curfew. I am in so, so much trouble if I get caught now. "I should get back."

"It would be best if you just forgot about this," the boy says. I blink. Forget? I can't just *forget* when what I thought I hallucinated is not only real, but way more confusing than an apparition. "Go back to your picture perfect world."

I shake my head. "I can't. That's like I'm wading in the park pond and you tell me there's a shark in there, but to forget about it and keep wading." We've learned about sharks, carnivorous fish living in the ocean. They're why we don't go to the shores. "Not going to happen. I'm coming back next time. Are you here every Saturday night?"

The boy pauses, then nods slowly.

"How will I find you? Do you know where you'll be?"

"No."

"Do you have a hat? Can you wear one next time?"

He raises an eyebrow. "I suppose."

"Okay. Good. I'll look for a hat."

"A few other boys wear hats."

"Well, at least this way I can eliminate anyone not wearing a hat," I explain.

"Ah, okay. But I don't think it'll matter."

"Why?"

"Because either I'll be in punishment, or recovering from it, or you won't show up."

"No. No, none of those will happen. Because I will show up. And I promise, I'm not going to tell anyone."

"You promise," he says doubtfully.

"I haven't told anyone yet," I point out. "And as for punishment, that's if the women at your city find out, right? And if I don't tell, they won't find out, right?"

"Presumably."

"Well, then, they won't find out. And what exactly is punishment?"

The boy just looks at me. I can't read his expression.

"Okay. I'm leaving." I take a step back to prove my point. But then I stop. "Um..." My brow furrows. "Do you have a name?"

His expression is wary, but after a few seconds he nods once. "It's Neil."

"Hi, Neil," I murmur, thinking it sounds like a Like name. "I'm Morgan."

"Hi, Morgan," he says quietly, then turns away, moving the broom to the other hand and starting to sweep again. I leave without another word.

Chapter 9
Neil

This time I'm not frantic; I'm disconnected. I move through work and class like routine, but I steel myself to not care about the outcome of what happened during maintenance. If women barged through the doors of the lumber mill and dragged me off to administer punishment, I would probably just blink.

In between class and work I manage to tell Han what happened. He nearly flips out again, until I explain how the girl, Morgan, insisted she knew nothing about us.

"Well," he says smugly once the initial awe wears away. "I was right."

"What?"

"Remember when I said they probably didn't know?"

"No, you were half asleep, incoherent, and said *what if*."

"Details." Han waves his hand dismissively.

Wednesday morning Han wakes me up minutes before the alarm goes off. "My inner detective is getting lazy," he informs me. "Just because you're trying to get yourself punished until forever doesn't mean we have to call off the information hunt."

I fight a groan and force my eyes open. If I didn't know how much Han wants to know when we're scheduled to disappear, and if I didn't want it so badly myself, I'd let my heavy eyelids slide shut again and refuse to move until the alarm actually does ring.

But I pull myself upright. Han takes this as agreement and tosses me a brown work shirt. I pull it on and stumble to the bathroom, trying to shake cobwebs from my mind. Cobwebs caused by the *girl*, Morgan, the one who's making everything complicated. Who insists I wear a hat next time.

Am I going to?

I don't even know. I splash water over my face, trying to wake myself up. There's a small, dirty mirror above the sink, and when I raise my face I see a cracked, wavy image of myself. Water drips off my chin, hair clings to my forehead, and the scars that Morgan found so shocking line my jaw.

Most scars result from work related accidents, a nick from a protruding nail or a line from broken glass. All boys have them. Occupational hazards, Han says.

It's interesting Morgan mentioned the scars on my jaw in particular, because they aren't from random accidents. They're from women, from the punishment I got the first time Han and I were late to work after investigating. But they had the opposite effect. Instead of just scaring me, the punishment spawned resolve, resolve to make it worth the scars.

Han and I take off before most boys have emerged into the hallway, soon arriving at our destination, the office building by the women's apartments. The brick building is silent. We figured out the offices are used on Mondays and Fridays, and the rest of the time they're empty.

I make sure no women are in sight. Han whips out his lock picks and opens a side door. We enter a polished room with cushy-looking furniture. Boys are sent here to clean, and I've dealt with enough offices in Blue City to know even women's work spaces are more comfortable than boys' dorms.

There are two offices we haven't searched yet. We found two Years so far, 5 and 9. Each set of files was in a different office in a different place. Han says there must be a master list of locations somewhere, because there's no way the records would be kept in such random order.

Han gets to work opening today's office. By now we only have fifteen minutes to get back to work, which gives us about five minutes to find files, if there are any in here. We work fast, opening closets and pulling out drawers and peering under desks. Most of what the women use for office work is electronic, so we're basically looking for any paper.

We don't find any. If I weren't already numb, I might be disappointed. Han keeps glancing at the digital clock hanging over the desk; it's time to leave.

Voices stop us. Han pulls me away from the door, even though it's closed, and we press our backs against the wall. Two women are outside. Their voices aren't immediately familiar to me.

"Can you imagine?" one woman asks. "This girl just happens to stumble across *Romeo and Juliet*. You know, one of those love stories by Shakespeare."

"Is that why the new teacher's here," the other woman asks. "Marcia Elliott?"

"Mmhm. An ex-librarian. She left a Library closet door open, and the girl looked inside. So Mayor Vee had to talk to the girl and convince her to forget about it."

"Did she believe her?"

"Yes, of course. Why would a girl question the mayor?"

"Of course," the second woman repeats. It sounds like her tone is sarcastic, but that doesn't make sense.

"But," the first woman continues, "the next night this girl broke curfew. So, of course, Mayor Vee rushed to her house, just to make sure it wasn't connected."

"Was it?"

"Mayor Vee doesn't think so. The girl claimed she just left an Amora too late and got lost." The voices are getting faint now, as the women move away.

"Sounds like she drank too much, if you ask me. Probably didn't notice anything."

"Yeah. The mayor just seemed exasperated when she informed us about it yesterday."

"I see. So what about Marcia?" The voice is almost too faint for me to hear. "Think she might be a candidate?"

The other woman's reply is inaudible. I glance at Han. His eyebrows are raised, but otherwise his face doesn't register the same shock I feel.

"Morgan," I whisper.

"Beg pardon?"

"Morgan, the girl they were talking about. Morgan. I found her after an Amora."

Han cocks his head. "How interesting."

I open my mouth to say something else, but my words are lost as more and more thoughts jumble my mind. Morgan really didn't tell the mayor about me. She claimed she simply got lost, and let them guess she was drunk.

She told me the truth?

I don't associate women with the truth, especially not girls who seem intent on making me do something *or else*-worthy. And obviously Morgan *can* lie, if she fed that story to the mayor. So she could have lied to me, easily.

But she didn't.

When Han decides the coast is clear, he leads me from the room and we run. I barely make it to work on time. I don't know if Han did, but I do know the punishment for being just a bit late is a shock from the remotes, which he doesn't have to worry about.

Today I hardly notice the fresh splinters. My mind is busy thinking about hats, ballet studios, and lies.

CHAPTER 10
Morgan

Mom can tell I'm tired, she could tell all week. But when she asks me why I tell her I stayed up late studying for finals. She doesn't believe me, of course she doesn't. It's another lie. Is this becoming a habit now? Why am I lying when I have my Amora to prepare for?

I spend most of the morning in my room, reading over the *Doctor Career: Introductory to First Aid* pamphlet on my Pow. I emerge at one point and ask Mom if I can read her real books. She has a few: a biology textbook, a handbook on responding to injuries, a chemistry and medicine reference book. All are printed on paper. She says no, I can't read them, which is always the answer.

"You can talk to me, though. I'm better than a textbook."

I sigh. "That wasn't...I mean, yes, of course. What's up in Rachel Waters' World?"

She smiles. It's one of those times when she's sitting in the den playing music and her smile is like sunshine peeking out behind a layer of clouds. She pats the spot on the couch next to her; I sit down. She puts an arm around me and proceeds to talk about the one girl she's checking up on, Reece, who is seven months pregnant. "She studied ballet until she decided to be pregnant. She's in great health."

"And her Like is looking out for her, of course," I say. Our conversation is still on the awkward side, considering Mom's showing all of her routine depression symptoms.

"Of course." Mom frowns again, pretty much ending the conversation.

Around two I meet Laney and Lloyd at the ice cream parlor, just a few blocks from my house and the park. The tabletops and floor are set to a soft blue and the walls have images of different ice creams floating around on them. I sit on one side of a booth table with Laney and Lloyd across from me, his arm encircling her shoulders. They're both wearing green, and Lloyd keeps making commenting about how Laney's shirt makes her eyes gorgeous. But, he clarifies, they're *always* gorgeous.

"I still can't get over your *hair*," Laney says, one hand raking through her own bangs. Her hair is still platinum, but she got the ends frosted green and added a black streak on one side to commemorate her amazing Amora. "It's so pretty. You should wear it natural more often."

"It's nice," I agree, willing myself to be hungry. "And dark."

"Yeah, and the darkness of it totally frames your face and makes your eyes stand out, like, they're glowing."

Well, it'll be interesting if my eyes start glowing in the dark street next Saturday. No. Wait. Not interesting. Not good. I'm already having second thoughts about sneaking out again without having to worry about my eyes glowing. What if I *do* get caught, and discipline conflicts with Amora prep?

"Glad you like it," I reply anyway. Because I am, of course, glad she likes it.

"I prefer green and black hair myself." Lloyd winks at Laney. She catches my eye and grins, like *isn't he amazing?*

I blink back. *Adorable.*

"Come on, Morgan, finish," Laney says. "We're done and waiting on you."

"Nah. Not hungry." I push the bowl away, letting out a long breath.

Laney eyes the dish. "What's wrong?"

"Nothing." Except for the fact that I apparently don't know *anything,* and I really, really want to know what *anything* is. Because part of *anything* are these things called *men* that show up past curfew once a week. And they really don't like women. Or at least the one I met, Neil, doesn't. And now I'm lying all the time. "I'm just tired."

"Well, take a nap or something, you're being no fun." The table brings up a message, requesting we pay. "I got it,"

Laney says as I reach for my Pow.

"Thanks."

"Yeah, yeah." Laney pulls up the screen on her Pow and moves her finger through it, transferring a few dollars from her account to the ice cream parlor's. "I know you're saving up to buy embroidered lab coats for the doctor-y career."

"Yeah," I say, rolling my eyes. "The doctor-y career."

"That's interesting," Lloyd says.

I nod. "Would you ever want to be a doctor?"

"No way," Laney says. "I mean, if I *had* to be, I'd consider being a nurse or sports trainer. But not birthing, like you want to. Eww, too much blood and gore."

"One," I say, "don't give me the 'too much blood and gore' thing. You're the one who gives other girls bloody noses during football drills. And two, I wasn't asking you."

Laney glances at Lloyd. "You were asking Lloyd?"

"I was."

Lloyd looks surprised, then confused as well. "I don't understand."

"What don't you understand? I said, if you had the option, would you want to be a doctor?"

Lloyd's brow furrows. "I don't take a career."

"If you did," I repeat.

"But I don't." Seeing I'm still waiting for an answer, Lloyd adds smoothly, "But I have to agree with Laney. Some fields of medicine are too bloody."

Now I feel a bit outnumbered. I switch topics. "So, Lloyd, where do you...where are you from?" Maybe I can scope him out and see just what kind of Like Laney was given. How Best of a Friend would I be if I didn't?

Laney and Lloyd both stare at me.

I stare back. "What?"

Laney shrugs, then glances at Lloyd, seeming a bit curious. The crease in Lloyd's brow depends and he frowns.

"What's your story?" I prompt, feeling like I'm becoming an expert at digging for answers.

"My story?"

"Yeah. You know, your past."

He smiles, turning a mushy expression on Laney. "What past do I need? Everything except Laney is completely irrelevant."

I bite back an *aww* and try to remain on topic. "Yeah, but..."

I trail off as Laney, grinning, sits up and kisses Lloyd on the mouth. I wait for another chance to speak, but after a minute Laney shows no sign of surfacing. I stand up and say goodbye. One of her hands waves me away.

I almost get Laney to go with me to get my hair cut Thursday, but I don't want her asking why. This way I don't have to lie, and besides, she's busy all week spending quality time with Lloyd.

Even though Laney is the language of hair expert, I consider myself to be fluent as well. "I want it short," I tell Ms. Kenji, my hairdresser, when I'm seated in the cushy chair for my appointment, inhaling scents and smells of various waxes and oils.

"Short?" In the wide mirror I see her fingers touch the end of my braid.

The smooth fabric wrapped around me seems a bit too hot. I nod quickly, not letting myself second-guess. Yeah, I've been growing my hair since class 11. But my plan requires my hair to be shorter, so it will be.

"How short?" Ms. Kenji starts to braid my hair back.

I give a prepared response. "Chin length. Some layers."

"Is this a graduation style?" She wraps a ponytail holder around the end of the braid.

"Kind of." I repeat the same rationalization I used to convince myself. "It's more of a jumpstart on the summer season. You know, get in the habit of having my hair short. Then I can dye it and wear it in style when the really warm weather arrives."

Now Ms. Kenji smiles approvingly and picks up a large pair of scissors. The next moment my head feels lighter and I hear the thump of my braid hitting the floor, which is patterned with silver and blue polka dots. Sorry, hair. I'm going to miss you. But I'm too curious not to try this plan.

Ms. Kenji starts to work, humming along to the song playing through the walls. Smaller, more delicate scissors fly around my ears. A half an hour later she spreads smoothing oil across my head and uses her hands to shape my hair.

"What do you think?" She adjusts a strand over my forehead. "*I* think this is adorable! And the ends are perfect, if you ever want to frost them."

I nod along with her. I still have bangs, but they're shorter, resting over my eyebrows on one side instead of dangling in my eyes, and my hair curls around my ear to tickle my jawbone. Feathery layers form the rest, which, when smoothing oil's not inhibiting them, will make my natural curls stand out. At least, that's what Laney would say.

"Thanks." After assuring Ms. Kenji I'll consider frosting options, I grab my bag and leave the store.

In the bag are the four items I bought today. The first is a hat, a generic, knit black hat. The second item is a black polo shirt, which resembles the one Neil wore. The third and fourth are a pair of Like's jeans and a pair of generic brown shoes I got from a shop near the Azure district. I told the seamstress my friend asked me to pick them up for her Like, and the seamstress happily assisted me.

I get home at around six. Ross welcomes me, beaming as he comments on how wonderful my hair looks. He has a nice smile. The apples of his cheeks stand out, and the skin around his gray eyes crinkles. Mom once said I have the same smile.

"What's in your bag?"

"Oh," I reply, one hand gripping the strap. "Just a shirt I picked up."

"Lovely. I got dinner from the supermarket, it's on the table. It's steak, London broil."

"Cool." I set my bag on one of the stools by our counter. "Why's it called that?"

"Why's what called that?" Ross peers around the wall of

our kitchen, down the hallway to the den. "Rachel, sweetie? Morgan's home. I have dinner all set out."

"London Broil." I slid into my seat. "Why's it called London broil?"

"Well," Ross replies, sitting down across from me, "London was a major city in Europe. I suppose they named the steak after it."

"But before the Wars, right? Nuclear weapons destroyed London."

Ross nods. "The whole area is below sea level now."

I trace my finger across the tabletop. "How do you know all this?" When I was little I'd ask my mom for help with homework, but Ross stepped in to assist on occasions when he insisted Mom needed a break. Mom never seemed to appreciate this, but Ross adequately provided knowledge.

"It's basic history." He looks over his shoulder for Mom.

"I know, but where did you learn it?" I feel like I'm repeating the ice cream parlor scene. But, that was when talking to Lloyd. This is Ross, my mom's Like, who I've known my entire life. And, I mean, I have some of his genes.

Ross glances at me sideways. "Why? Do you need help reviewing for finals? They're coming up soon."

"No, I just wondered how you knew about London." I try to sound detached, like I'm not as curious as I actually am.

Ross hesitates, confused, then he shakes his head. "Why aren't you eating? It's been a long week, you– Hi, Rachel."

Mom appears in the kitchen doorway, dressed in sweats. Ross beams at her, as if he hasn't seen her in days. "Come on over, honey, I got dinner."

Mom stares at me. Ross's gaze follows her line of vision, and he says, "I know. Isn't her hair pretty?"

Mom nods slowly, her gaze finding mine. I shrug.

Ross keeps up a running chatter about my finals and graduation and how he thinks he and Mom should save up for a trip to the Red City so they have something exciting going on once I'm occupied with career training. "And your *Like,*" he adds. "Your Amora's coming up in only two and a half months. Are you..." He pauses, glancing down at his wrist, where his Messenger is. Likes don't have Pows, but they have a messaging device to contact Pows and receive news.

"Morgan!"

"What?"

"Your eval was scheduled for today at three. You've missed it."

My eyes widen. "My eval! " In the mess of things, I'd completely forgotten. How could I? I've been planning for months! "Can you reschedule it, please?"

Ross swirls his finger through the projected screen, typing. "Okay, it's set for Wednesday after academy hours."

"Thanks," I say, relieved.

We're done eating by now. Ross stands and takes our plates. "I'm going to go straighten up the bathroom," he tells us and disappears upstairs.

Then Mom stands, walking around to lean against the counter. She faces me. "Why?"

"I wanted something different." Not entirely a lie, right?

"Blonde wasn't different enough? Natural wasn't different enough?"

"Do you not like it?" I evade her question.

Mom lets out a long breath. "I don't not *like* it, I just don't *understand* it. I thought you were growing your hair."

"I needed it shorter. It's more practical."

Mom blinks. "Who are you, and what have you done with my daughter?"

"Mom," I grumble.

Mom sighs. Straightening up, she notices the bag on the stool. "Don't–" I start, but she's already reached inside. She pulls out the polo and hat and sees the jeans and shoes inside. Her expression freezes, no emotion, gazing at the items.

"They're for Lloyd," I say lamely. Her gaze flicks from my hair to the clothes. Then she shakes her head.

"I'm going to take a shower," she says. And then she walks out of the kitchen, leaving my bag sitting on the stool.

* * *

My mom and Ross go to bed at ten on Saturday. I spend the evening pacing, thinking, trying to come up with excuses why I shouldn't and reasons why I should. When I'm pretty sure no one's going to walk in on me, I assemble the outfit I've been planning all week. Sports bra to flatten my (not considerably large to begin with) chest, hat to hide my hair, shoes, jeans and shirt.

It works, in a way. The jeans are loose, turning my legs into ambiguously straight denim tubes. The shirt has no definition, and the blackness smoothes out any curves. The shoes are clunky and the hat only lets a few strands of dark hair peek out.

I have no makeup on, but my skin is still clear and smooth. If anything I'm more similar to a Like than to the boy. But what can I do?

I'm sick of pacing. I topple back on my bed as all the ways this could go wrong crowd my brain. Can I do it? Can I really sneak out, in these clothes, and not just go out in the dark in my city, but maybe go to a whole other city as well?

I don't come up with an answer. As I lie there, minutes slipping away, the only thought I have is how I wish my Amora was once again the most pressing thing on my mind.

CHAPTER 11
Neil

Saturday arrives and I haven't been dragged away, so tonight I sit in class bent over a math worksheet.

Ms. Elliott weaves through desks to check on our work. I'm staring at my paper, vision unfocused, when she taps on my arm.

"Excuse me?"

I jump. "Sorry," I say quickly, flinching automatically.

"Are you okay?" Ms. Elliott's voice is quiet. I stare at her and she frowns. "I mean, why aren't you working?"

"I am. Right now." I put the tip of my pencil against the paper, not sure how to proceed.

Ms. Elliott kneels by my desk. "Turn the radical into a fractional exponent," she says, sketching the proper method.

"Oh," I mumble.

"I think Nathan understands this concept." She glances at Han, who looks up at the sound of his name. "If you have trouble, you should ask him."

I just nod, numbers swimming in front of me. Ms. Elliott raises her wrist, peering at the all-purpose device women have the *privilege* of wearing. "Oh," she says, surprised. "It's time for those with maintenance Duty to leave."

I drop my pencil and stand, shoving the wrinkled math worksheet in my pocket.

"Neil," Han hisses as I walk away.

I look over my shoulder. "What?"

"Don't do anything stupid," he mouths while twisting his pencil through his bangs.

"Too late," I tell him, and turn away.

Once at my dorm, I pull on the black maintenance polo. Then I hesitate, staring at a hat squashed into the corner of the drawer. We have black hats and jackets and gloves for winter when fingers go numb. Some boys still wear their hats in April. It won't be conspicuous. After a moment of hesitation I snatch it up and jam it on my head. I have to run to make it to the subway on time, but I avoid the glares of the women.

My assignment tonight is the second floor of the Medical building, private offices. Boys are sent here to clean and sterilize the emergency wing, first floor. I'm the only one working the offices tonight. Every noise makes me jump.

Fifteen minutes into cleaning and I'm done with two offices. It's close to eleven thirty and I feel little satisfaction in knowing I was right when I said she wouldn't show. But I can't keep from watching the hallway out of the corner of my eye, as I polish desk tops. No figures appear in the doorway, but at quarter to twelve I see a shadow move, ripple across my own. I'm in the process of emptying the trash, facing the door, and the light's coming from behind me. I spin around.

At first I think it's another boy, features in shadow by the light strip on the wall directly behind. But then she turns, and I see the gray eyes.

"Sorry I'm late," she says a bit breathlessly. Her hands knead something between them, a cut of black fabric. "It took me a while to find you. You know, you guys are really absorbed in your work here. No one noticed me."

Once the shock ebbs away I say, "You don't have one of those devices on your wrist."

"Oh, yeah. I left my Pow at home. You don't have them."

Interesting response. And, "Why are you wearing that?"

She looks down, one hand touching the stomach of her black polo shirt. "It's what you're wearing," she says, as if I'm unaware of my clothes.

Her jeans are straight and loose, unlike the tight jeans women wear. In fact, they're like my jeans. And her dark hair is shorter than last week. A lot shorter. Good thing her eyes seem familiar or I'd be wondering if it's the same girl.

My attention refocuses. "You didn't come through the door. How'd you get in here?"

Morgan jerks her thumb over her shoulder, toward the closet in the corner. Every room has one filled with filing cabinets and extra lab coats.

"This closet has a shared door with the office on the other side of the wall. I came through there because I went up the back way. Didn't know where you'd be, though. Purely coincidental." She sits on the edge of a chair by the desk.

I slowly tie up the garbage bag I'm holding. "How did you know about the closet?"

Morgan sweeps her hand, as if to indicate the room. "I've been here before. This is my mom's office." She flicks on the wall panel above the desk. My eyes widen. "Look." I glance at the now lit wall. A single picture appears on the surface showing a woman with dark hair like Morgan's standing on a rooftop garden, a little girl sitting on her shoulders. They're laughing. The girl has gray eyes. "We took this years ago."

I'm distracted by the picture and the feeling of happiness that seems to jump from it, like a spark leaping from metal to my finger. Then I toss the garbage bag by the door and face Morgan. "Turn it off. They can track those walls, and I'm not supposed to touch anything except what I need to clean."

She jumps, but quickly turns off the wall lights. "It's interesting," she says. "Even though I know how, I almost never turn off walls or floors. Just gray is weird."

I shake my head, turning away.

"Well, I guess it makes sense to turn them off in office buildings and such," she continues. "Everything goes off after curfew. It saves energy." The chair creaks as she leans back. "I'm just saying, my mom's office looks very different now."

"So, your mom's a doctor."

"Yep. Just like I want to be."

"Hm."

I use a rag to dust off the filing cabinets and take care of the grit in the corners. The rag's dotted with dark spots, one from every office I've been through. It's a minute before Morgan speaks again. "So, what exactly what are you doing?"

I stop and just frown. Han's diagnosed this expression as

a symptom of my "rebellious nature," but I prefer to see it as "choosing not to answer asinine questions." And then I like to remind Han which one of us grows his hair past restriction and smuggles alcohol into our room.

Morgan lets out her breath in a huff. "Cut it out. I mean, I know you're cleaning. But *why* are you cleaning?"

I shrug, tucking the rag into my waistband and grabbing the broom leaning against the wall. "Because they tell us to. I'm moving to the next office now."

She follows me across the hallway, thankfully being quiet, even though as far as I know we're the only ones on this floor. I get to work on the new office. Morgan hovers behind the closed door, finally deciding to lean against the wall. Now I notice how rigid her shoulders are, and how she constantly fidgets with the cloth in her hands. So she's actually is worried about getting caught, however minor her punishment would be in comparison to mine. Though, maybe she doesn't even understand the proportion.

"Do you do *everything* the women say?"

I nod.

"Why?"

"Because that's how it works."

Morgan doesn't seem to comprehend this. "What if you just refused?"

"That would go against the concept of self-preservation." I'll just leave it there.

She cocks her head, then frowns. I turn away and set down the rag. But before I can pick up the broom I hear a noise like a door handle turning. If someone's heart could exit their ribcage, mine would. I whirl around, fighting to control my panic, taking a step away from the door at the same time.

A woman stands there, but I can only see her silhouette as she's wielding a flashlight. The beam catches my eyes and I flinch, my heart pounds wildly somewhere in my esophagus. Sometimes the women check on us, but my mind frantically decides this is different. Morgan probably tipped her off. And even if she didn't, there's no way the woman supervisor will be able to skim over the other occupant of this room, a girl.

The beam leaves my face and travels around the room. I blink rapidly, trying to clear the spots from my vision. I can vaguely see the flashlight beam cut across the walls and pass right over the spot where Morgan...was.

Somehow she's not there anymore. I stop myself from looking around, a small spark of hope flashing somewhere in the back of my mind. The woman at the door moves the flashlight back to me as she checks something on the all-purpose device clasped to her wrist. "Neil 17?"

"Yes," I say, trying to swallow.

"What the hell are you doing?"

My mind goes blank. I look down at myself. Oh. I'd set the rag down, but haven't picked anything back up, so my hands are empty. "I was just about to sweep," I say, knowing she won't care what my answer is.

"You don't have enough time to slack off," the woman snaps. There's a remote clutched in her hand, and her fingers twitch. My eyes squeeze shut.

"Keep working," she adds as she leaves, but I hardly hear her as a shock jolts through my body. I can't keep from gasping in pain, and my fingers knead the back of my neck. Eight, nine, ten seconds later I open my eyes. My knees feel weak, something I've learned to ignore. I reach out and find the broom handle and half-dazedly start to sweep.

A minute passes before the door closes of its own accord. Morgan steps out from behind it, eyes wide.

"That was..." she says, one hand spinning in front of her, searching for a word to describe what happened. "Yeah," she finishes. She has an excited, awed expression on her face. "I can't believe she didn't see me. Incredible. I was so freaked out." Then she frowns. "But, why did the woman sound so mean? I didn't recognize her. And why did you gasp?"

I don't respond, concentrating on keeping my shaking hands from dropping the broom. I feel her staring at me, and turn to say she should just leave now, please, and not push my luck, but her expression stops me. It's drawn, confused, and almost concerned, a face I've only seen directed at me from Kellan and Han before. Maybe that's why it seems familiar. And at the same time, foreign.

I take a deep breath, then shake my head. This time Morgan doesn't press it, just stands in silence until we move to the next office.

She speaks after a while. "So this is how everything stays clean?"

"You're welcome," I mutter.

"What's your favorite color?"

Her tone doesn't change, which is the most bizarre part. I'm reaching across a tall cabinet to dust the back, and I look over my shoulder, blinking.

Morgan shrugs. "I'm curious."

So am I. I've never really thought about it before. Maybe… "The color the sky is right before it storms." Which is a ridiculous answer. "Gray," I amend, trying to backtrack. Why did she ask?

"I like that color, too." Morgan doesn't seem to find it a weird response. "I also like the storms themselves, and the sound of rain. I don't turn on neutralizers like others."

"Neutralizers?" That sounds threatening.

"Yeah. The wall app. It creates white noise so weather doesn't disturb your sleep."

Well, her walls are different than mine, so that makes little sense to me. "What about you?" I hear myself say. "What's your favorite color?"

"Hmm." Morgan leans against the wall. "Black."

Interesting. I'd expected pink. "Why black?"

Morgan waves her hand around. "Black is such a mysterious color. It's the color of the night women aren't allowed out in. And I like the darkness."

Definitely not the answer I'd expected.

I finish the last office with twenty minutes to go. For a moment, I let myself pause, standing in front of the utility closet after putting away the carpet cleaner and broom. The dusting rag still dangles from my waistband.

Morgan seems to sense the shift in my mood, from working to hesitation. She moves from her half-dozing position sitting against the wall and pushes to her feet. We had on and off conversation until a half an hour ago, when Morgan slipped into a tired, distant state. I'm not even sure why she's stayed out here so long.

She clears her throat. "Are you done?"

I nod.

"So you're going back to your city now?"

I nod again. "You should probably go back to..." I trail off as she picks up the cloth she's been carrying around. Only when she puts it on do I realize it's a hat.

"Does this work?" She tucks loose stands of hair into the hat. I blink. It could pass for a boy's haircut. "Neil, Does it?"

"Does it what?"

"Does it, you know, make me look like one of you?"

"I..." I frown. "Yeah, I guess it does."

"Good. I got my hair cut just for this."

I tilt my head. I'd assumed she'd gotten her hair cut because that's what women do; they change their hair every two days. "Why does it matter?"

She raises her eyebrows. "Well, if I want to blend in, it matters."

"Blend in? I–" My jaw drops. She was serious. Really serious about wanting to see City 4, and about the outfit and trying to blend in. "No. No, it can't work."

"Why not?" She crosses her arms and leans on one leg more so than on the other.

"For one, just that *pose* gives you away."

Morgan glances down, then slowly uncrosses her arms and centers her weight.

"And two, aren't you pushing your luck as it is?"

"Well, duh," she says. "But this isn't enough. I need to really understand."

"And I need to stay alive past tomorrow," I counter.

She ignores my argument. "I have it all arranged. I told my mom I'm getting up early and leaving to go to the gym, and then I'll be touring facilities all day. To see if maybe I want to be a sports trainer. Which I don't, by the way, but I don't think she knows. So I'm good for a while."

"You need a firmer grip on reality. And a dictionary so you can look up the definition of *good*."

We stare at each other for a moment. Then Morgan glances away, biting her lip. She takes a deep breath.

"Listen," she says, "if I get caught, I will swear in court, even, that I found out about you maintenance workers by myself, and no man was involved. I'll do everything I can not to implicate you, okay?" She steps closer, glaring at me now. "But if you *don't* help me out here, I'll go straight to whatever authority I can and tell them...I don't know...something about you they won't like. You talked to me, or waved at me, or whatever else you're forbidden to do here."

My eyes widen. "You wouldn't."

"I *would.* I have to know. And I need you to help me. So there."

I'm speechless, futilely searching for a loophole. She senses this, and her lips press together in satisfaction.

"Give me the rag," she says.

Beyond arguing at this point, and seeing the steely expression on her face, I yank the soiled rag out of my waistband and hand it over. Morgan takes the cloth and studies it. Then, warily, she holds it up and disappears behind it for a moment.

When she lowers the cloth I see what she's done. There are smudges of filth across her face, effectively camouflaging the unmarked skin Color City residents have. Her hand twitches, as if she's resisting the instinct to wipe her face clean.

"Well," she says. "How do I look now?"

CHAPTER 12
Morgan

The anxiety writhing in my gut is twice as strong as the first night I tried to sneak out past curfew. But the curiosity and stubbornness is three times as strong, so I follow Neil's shadowy form through the streets. We walk in silence, hurrying, and I try to remember names of streets we pass.

Earlier, when the woman almost walked in on us, I felt a wave of fear crash over me. But almost instantly that fear turned into energy and I disappeared behind the door. Now the adrenaline lingers, tingling in my fingertips and making my breathing shaky. It's like I'm on a Pow charger, energy constantly being pumped through my veins.

Neil slows and stops next to a barely visible door on the side of a building. "Are you positive?"

I nod, then remember he can't see me. "Yeah." Before he enters the building I speak again, voicing a worry I'd thought of on the walk over. "Do they do a head count?"

"No, they'd know if one of us wasn't there."

I want to ask how, but I don't think there's time. "But they won't know if someone extra is there?"

"Not if you do a good job blending in." Now, in the strip of light cast by the barely open door, I see him frown at me. "Don't make eye contact. Keep your face down. Don't talk. Follow me, quickly." He pulls open the door and slips inside.

I follow, but have to force myself not to come to a halt in surprise. It's a room, just a regular room, filled with large shapes. I blink furiously, eyes adjusting to the dim light inside. The shapes are desks and boxes stacked on top of each other. They create a vague pathway across the room that leads to another doorway. A woman stands by it, arms crossed. The best word I can think of to describe her expression is sullen, sullen like a girl who wants to go to parties but is too young.

Neil walks purposefully forward, looking straight ahead as we pass the woman. I shuffle behind him, staring at the floor as Neil instructed, reminding myself to breathe. Nothing happens. She doesn't shout for me to stop, or pull off my hat, or cry into her Pow for Mayor Vee. I don't think she even glances at us. We proceed onward, down the flight of stairs.

The air becomes cooler as we descend until the stairs stop and open up into a large room. It's like a monorail station, except the stairs lead down and not up, and the overall appearance is dirtier. I try not to gawk at the crowd of boys in black. Instead, I continue to keep my eyes down, and see Neil's hands clenching and unclenching by his sides. Guilt flickers in the back of my mind. Then I suppress it. I was honest; if I'm caught, I'll pretend I don't even *know* Neil. What does he have to worry about?

There's a rushing noise, and the crowd pushes forward. It takes me a moment to distinguish what comes hurtling through a hole in the wall and stops smoothly in front of us. As the boys herd inside I get a better view. It's like a black monorail, but I realize as I step inside, the interior is far more crowded with seats and bodies.

Then the doors close, and I fully understand three things. One, I'm actually on my way to see what I've been thinking about for a week. Two, I can't change my mind. And three, there is very, very little space in here.

Neil darts through the crowd to a back corner. I stumble after, keeping my face down, cold energy zinging through me in waves. Neil finds two vacant seats. He indicates for me to sit at the one closest to the wall. I quickly drop in, gripping the bottom of the seat as the underground monorail's engine thunders to life again and instantly shoots forward. Neil teeters for a moment before collapsing into his own seat.

After a few seconds, the engine and speed seem to smooth out, and if it weren't for lights flashing through the small windows inside, I'd hardly be able to tell we're hurtling along to who-knows-where. I clutch the seat, trying to breathe normally. I can't panic and pass out here. I'd screw everything up. No. Look at something else. Don't think about it.

From what I can tell, the boys all seem to have their eyes closed and heads back, maybe napping, which would explain the relative silence in the car. Except for, well, the thundering engine. At least none of the boys are looking at me.

My lungs are almost shaking, but I don't collapse, a good sign so far. As another flash of light from the window illuminates Neil's face, I see him glance at me.

Neil. He does this all the time, I tell myself. Okay, not all the time. Once a week. Which is practically all the time. It's just a monorail, a very crowded monorail. Underground. And not breathing won't help. At all.

I spend the ride concentrating on *not* not breathing. I'm not sure how long it takes, because it seems endless to me. When the underground monorail slows down, relief spills through me. The boys stir, all except for Neil, who sat rigid the entire ride and merely stands when the monorail is still.

The boys shuffle up the stairs leading off the platform. Women stand there, expressions stony, almost like Neil's. Each time I pass one a shiver of anxiety races up my spine, but none look twice. Next thing I know, Neil and I are stepping out into the chilly air.

My shoes, already heavy and awkward, land on rough, uneven material. Tall lights line the street, casting patches of yellow and patches of shadow. There's a general flow of movement to the right, but Neil veers the other way, leading me down an empty street. I try to keep up with his pace, a combination of the shoes and the rough street causing me to stumble more than once.

It's not a long walk. Neil turns and approaches a tall, boxy building, and I realize he took a detour to avoid prying eyes. The building he stops at is just like all the other structures on this street. The walls have a weird pattern, kind of a reddish brownish and uneven looking. As we pass through the door I hold out my hand to touch it, to make sure it's real, to make sure I'm not imagining everything. When my hand connects with the wall, I gasp. Instead of being smooth, the material is just as rough as it appears, and jagged material tears at the skin of my palm. I jerk my hand back and stare at the beads of blood welling from the scratches.

Neil grabs my elbow and drags me along. My feet climb more stairs. In the back of my mind I know I should be exhausted, but the energy still fizzles in my veins and I'm more alert than ever, noticing every time I trip in these shoes and each prick of pain in my hand.

Finally, we stop. I blink in shock at the room as Neil shuts the door. It's tiny, utterly tiny. Blank white walls border a space that would classify as a closet in Blue City. There are two beds with thin mattresses and only one blanket on each, a dresser, a desk, and what may be a trunk in one corner. The one light source, an old fashioned lamp, glows dimly on the desk. As I take in the scene I see a form sprawled across the bed farthest from the door.

"What is this?" I whisper, speaking for the first time since entering the underground subway station in Blue City.

"My dorm." Neil sinks down on the edge of the unoccupied bed. "Han's and my dorm."

"Han?" I repeat. Neil waves a hand at the sleeping form in response. I nod, then hesitantly sit on the corner of the mattress near Neil. "Is this where you live?"

"Home, sweet home." Neil leans back, resting his head against the bare white wall, and his eyes slide closed.

"Tired?" Suddenly, I feel more awkward than my clunky shoes.

"I haven't slept in almost twenty-four hours."

My eyes widen. How many more surprises can these men and this city throw at me? Speaking of which... "I'm sorry. Er, really quickly, do you have any antiseptic? I scraped my hand on the outside of the building." I desperately want to know what the walls are, but I don't ask.

"No. You'll live," is Neil's response. I frown, but don't feel like pressing it. He's leaning forward now, elbows on his knees and chin resting in his hands. The yellowy glow of the room throws the shadows under his eyes into sharp relief.

97

"Did you want to sleep or something?" I wonder how much rest men need.

"Can't."

"Is it normal for you to go this long without sleep?"

"On maintenance nights."

"When do you usually get up, on non-maintenance nights?"

"The alarm goes off at four-thirty."

My eyebrows fly up. "Four-thirty? That's hours before I usually..." I trail off, seeing him roll his eyes. "This really is different," I say quietly. "Okay. I get it. I'm just trying to figure out *how* different."

"You'd have better luck trying to figure out how it's not different," Neil murmurs. "Much smaller list."

I see a clock protruding from the wall at the head of the beds. It tells me it's 4:03. "Do you go to bed earlier?"

"Eleven. Or as close to as possible."

"Eleven to four-thirty is just over five hours of sleep." I frown. "Six nights a week. That *can't* be healthy."

"It's routine."

"Do you ever get holidays or breaks?"

"No. Only the women practice religion. We're not introduced, or allowed, or whatever. And there are different religions practiced by the women here, so there are always supervisors on duty."

My hand yanks the hat off my head, freeing my hair and allowing me to rub at the itchy parts. As I do, I can't help staring around, differences leaping out. "None of you go to churches, or synagogues, or mosques, or anything?"

"Women only." Neil stares back at me, as if not sure how to react to my hair being free.

"Are there any breaks not related to religion?"

"Kind of. Such as today. The first half of Sundays women are in meetings, and we're off work."

"So you catch up on sleep now?"

"No. Only sometimes. We're not supposed to sleep."

Not supposed to, not allowed to, can't. Everything Neil

says is negative. "What do you do, then?"

He shrugs. "We're told to exercise or study or do something productive. Sometimes I run to the edge of the city. But usually I carve."

It seems like there should be more to the sentence, but he trails off. I scan the room again. My gaze lands on the sleeping form; Han, Neil called him. "Should I hide when he wakes?"

Neil slowly looks over, like moving his eyes is an effort. "Han. No. You won't have to hide."

"Han can know?"

"Han knows." Neil says *knows* like he means knowing about more than just my presence. His words are heavy, too, encompassing the darkness that seems to surround him. It's as if he's a shadow behind everything I thought I knew; dark features, dark attitude, dark waking hours, hiding secrets in the negative space of the bright, cheerful world I live in.

Minutes of silence fly by as I attempt to sort through all this new information. Neil stares unfocusedly at the ground. I sit across from the foot of Neil's bed until a loud buzzing noise causes me to leap up, gasping. Neil jumps, but seems unfazed. "The alarm," he says simply.

I remind myself to breathe, leaning back against the wall. Han sits up. Blond hair catches the light. He reaches over to the desk and fumbles for a pair of glasses. I watch curiously as the boy shoves them on his nose. I was told glasses haven't been used since the 2100s, before doctors perfected vision correction surgery.

"You're already up," Han says to Neil. Neil nods. "Or did you even go to sleep?"

Neil doesn't seem to be eager to introduce me, or do anything, for that matter. Han, oblivious to my presence, stretches, the thin white blanket falling away from his rumpled T-shirt. He's in mid-yawn when he notices me. I know as soon as he does, because he freezes, mouth open, and his eyebrows jump upwards an inch. Then he settles his hands back down on the mattress and stares at me for a few seconds, his expression one of mild interest.

Then he says, "Neil."

Neil looks up, still sitting hunched over. "Han."

"Remember when I said that thing about not doing anything stupid?"

"Yes."

"You screwed up."

Neil lets out a long breath in response.

"Nothing personal," Han assures me. "Neil here just has some issues in the smart department."

"Yes, he does," Neil mutters.

"Mind if I ask what the hell is going on?" Han's tone is pleasant enough, but he's obviously shocked.

Neil looks sideways at me as if to say, *this was* your *idea.* I press my lips together and glance at Han, who waits expectantly.

"I wanted to see your city." I wish Neil would explain. I'm not sure what he wants me to tell Han.

"And you are?" Han inquires.

"Morgan," I say, lowering my voice and glancing at the door. "Waters. Morgan Waters." As I'm speaking I see Han meet Neil's gaze. Neil nods once.

"Well, Morgan Waters," Han says, brushing hair out of his eyes. In some places I think his hair is nearly as long as mine now. I've never seen a Like with hair like his, since they keep their styles short and groomed. But, I remind myself, these are men, not Likes. "I'd say it's nice to meet you, but I'm not really sure if it is yet. No offense, of course. And you met Neil two weeks ago?"

"By accident."

"Why?" Han's tone doesn't change, but I can tell it's not so casual a question.

I look from Han to Neil. "Um," I say, stalling for time. "My friend had her Amora. Do you know what an Am–"

"Yes," Neil says sharply.

I blink, a bit startled. "Well. At the end there was a white smoke machine and I got confused and I ended up in the closet. And then I couldn't find the door in the darkness." It sounds lame and unbelievable, but I can't use the same excuse I gave Mayor Vee; Neil obviously knows he found me.

"You were unconscious," Neil states.

I could say I tripped and hit my head, and they might buy it, but dignity in my medical knowledge prevents it. If I'd hit my head that hard I probably would have been bleeding, unresponsive, or dead, not so lightly passed out. So I just nod.

"So you want to see the city," Han says after a while.

"I do." I'm grappling to gain back some of the respect the terrible excuse cost me. "I'm curious. I had no idea any of this existed, and I *need* to understand." I might have put too much emphasis on *need*, but I do. I need to, or I won't be able to function. I'm so confused.

"Told you so," Han says to Neil, who rolls his eyes in response. He seems to do that a lot.

"Told you so?" I repeat, alarmed now. What did he tell him? I wonder if I've walked into a trap. What kind of trap I don't know, but still a trap.

Han swings his legs off his bed. He's wearing boxer shorts with his T-shirt and when he stands he stretches, yawning again. He steps to the dresser and opens a drawer. "I told Neil I thought maybe you women didn't know about us, and he thought that was absurd. Didn't you, buddy."

"I still think so," Neil replies.

"Isn't he just impossible?" Han shakes his head.

"So," I say, "all of you men know about Blue City? And the other Color Cities? And women? And everything?"

"Men know about women and Color Cities, and the other Number Cities. But do all men know *everything…*"

"No," Neil finishes.

Know everything? "What don't they know?"

"Hmm?" Han acts like he didn't hear me, shaking out a pair of jeans and another polo. Before I can repeat myself he heads to the door and cracks it open. I immediately jam my hat back on my head and tuck up my hair.

"Relax," Han says. "I'm just heading for the bathroom.

I'll even close the door behind me." He slips out and the door clicks shut.

After a moment I say, "May I?"

Neil turns his head, propping his cheek on his hand, dark hair spilling across his knuckles. "May you what."

I know it has to be a question, even though there's minimal emotion behind the words. "May I see the city?"

"Seeing the whole city would take hours, which we don't have, and there's a much higher chance of you being noticed."

"That's why I came here. Not to get noticed, I mean, but I want to know what this place is like. It doesn't have to be the whole city."

Neil sighs. "*You* can go."

"By myself?" I sound whiny, but I can't help it.

"Yes, if you want to risk going out there. I'm too tired."

I close my eyes. "I will if I have to. But I'll probably–no, I *will*–get lost."

"Maybe Han will give you the grand tour."

My incisors gnaw at my lower lip. I used to bite my nails, but I broke that habit last year and this is the replacement. "Maybe. You really trust him?"

"Yes."

"He didn't seem too…disconcerted by my being here."

Neil shrugs. "That's Han for you."

My lip is starting to hurt. I force my teeth to release it. "All right." I glance at the door. I'm already waist-deep in whatever is going on here. Why not take the plunge and figure out more?

Except for the obvious repercussions of getting caught. Would discipline affect my Amora? I've never heard of one being postponed, but it seems like it could be a plausible disciplinary action. Oh, no. I can't risk postponement.

Except I already am risking it, by being here. *Just do it*, I command myself.

My hand turns the doorknob and the door swings open. I hear sounds of movement from behind the doors lining the hallway. I step outside, feeling exhilaration start to pound through the chambers of my heart again.

I haven't moved two feet before something closes around my wrist. I spin around.

The skin on Neil's hand is rough. Not uncomfortable, but noticeably dry and scratched. He's staring at my hand the same way I'm staring at his. I finally catch his eye, my own eyebrows raised as I take in the sight of him standing in the doorway to his room, one hand pressing against the doorframe, the other gripping my wrist.

He lets go within a second, arm dropping to his side. "Okay," he says. "I'll show you."

CHAPTER 13
Morgan

It takes almost four hours of questions and differences and knowledge being slammed through my head before I finally stop and drop to my knees in a narrow alley. My hands press against the bricks, feeling the roughness. So much roughness.

"What is this?" I'd asked as we entered the first alley.

"What?" Neil glanced at the wall I'd touched. The reddish brown color of the material was visible in the light from the streetlamp. Neil's face was half illuminated, the other half in shadow.

"This. The wall. What's it made of?"

Neil's face twitched, as if he was resisting the urge to scowl. "Brick."

"Brick," I repeated. It seemed so dirty, up close, and why would walls have such an uneven surface? "Does it change?"

"Brick is *real*. It doesn't change."

It just got worse after that, walking through the back alleys of the city clustered with brick buildings, avoiding the eyes of its inhabitants. I saw factories, and Neil explained them as places where the boys work every day, all day, without pay. He said they don't have a choice, but he didn't say why. I asked why they worked in the factories.

"All for you, of course." Bitterness laced his words. "The women. You've never wondered where wood comes from for your furniture? Or where the material in your clothing is made? Or where wheat is grown for your food? During agriculture seasons we work in fields, growing your crops. Everything we make gets shipped to you. Every raw material, every commercial food in your stores, comes from here."

It was the longest speech I'd heard Neil make, and the worst. It tore apart my world at the foundations. Why had I

104

never wondered where everything came from? Why had I never asked? It was a struggle to rein in my racing mind after that.

And I can't anymore. I'm in a spot hidden from the mouth of the alley by a large metal container that Neil calls a Dumpster. I'm fighting to breathe again, but I'm losing. The air here is thick and has a faint, omnipresent scent to it. Neil calls it smog. Well, smog doesn't agree with my breathing condition very much.

I've only been on my knees for a second when Neil, walking ahead, stops and glances back. His eyebrows jump upwards. I open my mouth to speak, but end up closing it and pressing my lips together, the alley becoming blurry. Neil's shoes appear at the edge of my swimming vision.

"I'm fine." I choke the words out, mentally berating myself for being such a crybaby.

He steps back, then hesitantly crouches down. "You don't look fine."

"I know," I snap before wiping my eyes with the shoulder of my T-shirt.

"What..."

"It's just a lot, okay?" I feel defensive and utterly defenseless at the same time. "I didn't know about factories or the food or anything. And now I feel like everything's a lie, so I need to sort that out for a moment."

"You're crying."

"*I know!*" My voice rises to a near scream. It echoes off the high walls, off the *bricks*, amplifying my emotion. Neil falls back, startled, hands slamming against the ground.

"I know," I repeat, burying my face in my hands. "I know I know I know." *I know*. Such a familiar phrase. It implies power, power of knowledge, over something concrete, a fact. Knowing something. But do I? Do I really know something? No. "I don't know anything," I whisper.

Now would be the perfect time for Neil to say, "I told you; I said you wouldn't be able to handle coming here." But he doesn't. He just stares at me.

I don't speak for a while, concentrating on breathing past the lump in my throat. Then I say, quietly, "Do you know how I can get home?"

I raise my head to see him nodding.

"Subway trains go back and forth between here and Blue City three times during the day. For cargo."

"When?"

"Soon. They come at nine, twelve, and three. It'll be close to nine by now."

I take a deep breath, letting it out slowly. "Okay. I should go on it."

Neil nods and stands up. Then he holds out his hand. I blink, taking it. He helps me up.

We walk to the subway station. Even in the light of the sun it's the same as every other brick building. Just a few stories shorter. Standing outside, I pause, realizing I'll be on it alone. Less claustrophobia, but still, alone. As in, Neil won't be there.

"It will be the cargo subway," Neil says in a low voice. "Not the passenger one you rode here on. A car is up front for the women, if any go along, but it could be that none do."

"Cargo subway?"

Neil nods again, once. "It's been sitting down there for an hour already. Some Year 14 or 15 boys are always chosen to load up cargo in there, so no women really need to ride it." Neil glances up. I do too, and see a clock overhead. It reads 8:45. "The barriers will be up by now."

"Barriers?" All I do here is ask questions.

"Barriers. They detect and report if a boy crosses them."

"Won't they detect me, then?"

"Boy," Neil repeats. "If a boy crosses them."

"But I look like a boy."

He shakes his head. "They won't detect you."

"How can they tell the difference?" I demand. "We're just walking through a door."

Neil winces, but doesn't answer. He rubs the back of his neck.

"Are the Year 14 or 15 boys gone, because the barriers are up?" I see him nod. The Year reference raises yet another question. It's actually been nagging at me all day, but I haven't had the strength to ask it yet. "Where are all the adults? Where do they work?" I haven't seen a single man older than eighteen, yet I assume they continue to age like women and Likes do, right?

Neil averts his eyes. "You've obviously learned enough today. Don't push it." He looks back at the clock. "You should go." And he starts to walk away.

"Neil," I say, kneading my hands together. His head turns. "I'm going to come back." The street is empty, but I feel a need to tell him this, and loudly, so he is sure to hear me. But I keep my voice quiet enough. "I'm going to."

I can't read his expression now. There's a beat of silence before he says, "I believe you."

"But you don't trust me."

"No."

"You will," I promise. How else am I going to learn about this place? About the men?

Neil's dark eyes connect with mine for a moment, just a moment. Then he turns away. And I disappear into the station.

CHAPTER 14
Neil

"I'm going to come back. I'm going to."

I reflexively glance over my shoulder, then jerk my head forward, telling myself to focus. Focus on tying strips of lumber together, even though my fingers are dry and starting to chafe against the rope. Her voice has been running through my head since yesterday, saying she's coming back, and it makes me jittery. Because for some reason I could see her appearing behind me while I'm working in the mill or something. And who wouldn't be nervous, being caught up in all this?

"But you don't trust me?"

"No."

"You will."

And there's that, too, constantly repeating in my mind. What did she mean? How am I supposed to trust her? I try to figure out what will occur if she follows me here again, but I can't. The only scenario coming to mind is a woman eventually finding out. And then the *or else*, which would probably surpass any punishment I've heard of to date.

The buzzer sounds, and I immediately clench my fingers around the fabric of my shirtfront, willing them to stop stinging. And now it's time to go back to the dorms, to sleep for half an hour before class, unless Han convinces me to investigate. He's insistent we'll find something in the next office, the last office of the building.

Han's already back at the dorm when I arrive.

"I have a question," he says as I shut the door.

The metal frame of the bed scrapes against my pants as I sit down and untie my shoelaces. "I'm not sure if I have an answer."

"Is she coming back?"

"As I said," I grunt, tugging off my too-small shoe, "I don't have an answer." If I did, I probably wouldn't be obsessing over the fact that she *might.*

"So you don't know."

"Well, yeah. Kind of what I meant."

"Hm. You so rudely ran off last time. I didn't get to really meet her."

"How horrible."

"I'm curious, Neil. I want to know what she knows. And I want to know what kind of a woman would—"

"Risk a perfect life to figure out reality?" I finish. "Just a guess. You haven't already stated your curiosity five times this morning or anything."

"Bingo," Han says. "You get a prize."

I raise an eyebrow.

"For being the number-one smartass," he clarifies.

"Number two."

"Sorry?"

"Number two. You, obviously, are number one."

Han throws his pillow at me. As I unlace my other shoe there's a knock at the door. I sit up, I can hear my heart pounding in my head.

A soft voice reaches my ears. "Hello?" For a wild moment I think it's Morgan, it's gotta be Morgan, who somehow found her way here on her own. But then the door opens further and I see it's not Morgan, it's Ms. Elliott, the new Year 17 teacher. I should have known, anyway. Morgan probably would have barged right in.

"Salutations," Han says from across the room, where he's perched on the edge of his bed. He appears relaxed, but I can see his hands tighten around each other. Me, on the other hand; my shoulders lock, nerves running like electrical currents through my body.

Ms. Elliott nods to him, then turns to me. "Neil, may I talk to you for a moment?"

I force myself to nod. She beckons me out into the hallway. I quickly grab my other shoe and shove it on before

109

I follow.

The hallway, previously rowdy, has hushed. Ms. Elliott's presence was detected and the word quickly spread over the floor, causing boys to retreat into their rooms. Ms. Elliott seems oblivious of her impact and just opens the folder she's carrying and pulls out a sheet of paper.

"Your math test." She hands it to me. As I take it, I can almost feel the relief tingling in my sore fingertips. The math test. She wants to talk about the math test.

On top of the test, in a dark red color, is the number 53.

"Um, that's your percent," Ms. Elliott explains. I nod slowly, wondering if there's a repercussion for such a low grade. I had a teacher one year, Year 13, who especially enjoyed repercussions for anything lower than an eighty.

"None of your previous math scores have been low."

I purse my lips, not looking up, waiting for her to go on.

"I was wondering," she continues, "is it this unit? Do you not understand the concept, or were you distracted?"

The latter, most definitely. I just shrug, unable to explain.

"Is there any way," Ms. Elliott says, "I can help you?"

Now I look up, searching her face for a hint of a smirk or a patronizing expression. But I don't see anything but, possibly, concern. Concern?

"I'm not sure," I finally answer.

"Maybe I could meet with you at some point to go over the concepts. We can pinpoint what you don't understand."

Go over the concepts? She really is new. Generally the method for getting us to understand is more along the lines of *do better next time* with a clear *or else* inflection.

"Why?"

It takes me a moment to realize the word came out of my mouth. My gaze darts around, as if searching for a way to take it back, but Ms. Elliott is already frowning at me.

"What do you mean, why," she asks. Not demands, asks.

I don't say anything. I don't trust myself to.

"Do you mean, why might that help? Or do you mean..."

And here her voice falters, grows distant. "...why does it matter at all?"

It must be a trick, something about how sound bounces off the walls in this hall. Those words should have been said with a hint of gloating, superiority, not uncertainty.

I still say nothing.

Her all-purpose device on the wrist opposite her shiny, new-looking remote chirps. She glances down. "Oh," she says, as if emerging from deep in thought. "I'm supposed to be teaching the Year 5s and Year 6s in a few minutes."

I nod, because it seems like I should do *something*.

"I'll come back." She frowns, and my mind immediately reminds me, *I'm going to come back. I'm going to.* "Later this week, we can discuss this again then, okay?"

Of course, there's no other option except to nod again.

She's still frowning, even as she starts to turn away. "And get some rest."

She says it like a question. One I can't answer without my eyes narrowing and face falling into that *look* Han says is my gut reaction to idiocy. So I don't answer.

Ms. Elliott walks to the stairwell. I gather my thoughts for a moment before reentering my dorm room, where I know Han is hovering by the door, waiting to rant about something he just heard. Probably the *Get some rest* question.

I want to laugh. But it's not the kind of laugh that feels good. It's the laugh that comes when nothing makes sense anymore and you know nothing you do will make difference in the long run, whether you understand it or not, so as things fall apart you just watch and laugh an empty laugh. Because if you don't laugh, you cry.

CHAPTER 15
Morgan

"*Mor*gan!"

The squeal is familiar enough. So is Laney's tackling hug Monday morning as I'm walking up the academy steps. I normally wouldn't lose my balance, but I'm so dazed today I can't stop from pitching sideways. I throw out my hands to stop myself and wince, because even though the steps are smooth, my palms are still sore from scraping across bricks.

Laney, surprised, tumbles down too, landing on her butt. "Sheesh!" She glances down to make sure her outfit is in place. "Walk much?"

"Tackle much?" I press my hands to my stomach. "You're a bit out of practice."

Laney's about to reply when Lloyd bounds up the stairs, capturing her attention. "Oh no, are you okay?" He takes her hand and helps her up. "I was worried for a second."

"Aww," she says.

I stand awkwardly trying not to use my hands to push myself up. "I'm fine," I say pointedly. My point misses, however, as Laney grins and pulls on one of Lloyd's curls. One of his green curls. My eyebrows inch upwards as I see Lloyd has dyed one curl green and another black to match Laney's hair. I'm surprised she's kept her style for this long. Usually she changes her hair on the weekends; until recently, I'd change mine, too.

Then Laney remembers her reason for tackle hugging me. "Oh!" She draws away from Lloyd to face me. The sun glints off the dye in her hair, and she raises her voice to speak over the girls walking around us. "I feel *terrible* because I totally forgot your eval happened Thursday. And then I forgot to ask you Friday, and then I was busy on Saturday–Lloyd and I went swimming in the Azure district, and then we shopped at their Design expo–and Sunday I couldn't find you and your mom said you were touring some facilities or something and then later I tried to call your Pow but Ross picked up and said you were napping, so I didn't see you again until just now."

I blink a few times. "Did you have a question in there?"

Laney laughs. "No. Sorry. I was just trying to explain why I forgot. But anyway, how did it go?"

"Oh, don't worry about it." We start to walk inside. "I didn't have it Thursday."

Laney stares at me. "You didn't? Why?"

"I forgot about it."

"You *forgot?* How did you *forget?* Are you *insane?*"

"Yes, I don't know, maybe?" We enter the building, blue light dances around the lobby.

"She forgot what?" Someone else runs up. It's Seffa, with newly frosted hair and shimmering makeup around her eyes.

"About her *eval*," Laney says.

"Why don't you get a megaphone," I mutter. I hadn't been planning on sharing with anyone else. I mean, who forgets her eval? They're going to think I'm weird.

"How did you *forget?*" Seffa cries, proving my point. "I was, like, an hour early for mine last month. You must be crazy!"

"Just a bit tired." I am tired. I fell asleep yesterday afternoon, but woke up early in the morning, wide awake. I stared at the dark ceiling for a while, thinking about the fact that, as Neil explained, somewhere in Blue City another shift of maintenance workers was arriving. And how lucky I was to return to Blue City undetected on the cargo subway. And how, in a sense, lucky I am to live in Blue City and not be a boy in City 4. And by the same token, how sheltered I am– how sheltered *everyone* is–and how more makes sense now, and at the same time less makes sense. And by then I was way too confused to form another coherent thought, so jumbled images and voices sloshed around my mind, keeping me awake for hours.

I find myself only half-listening as Seffa gushes about her eval, describing the features she chose: tall, black hair, yada, yada, and yada. Or at least, that's what I hear.

Then, while looking at the clocks floating around on the walls, Lloyd says, "It's time for me to go." I turn and walk away, nearly making it to our classroom before Laney appears next to me again.

"He's so *sweet.*"

Girls immediately gravitate inwards as we head for the couches. I find myself squashed in the middle of the group, pressed against Laney on my left and Ellie on my right. The rest of the girls crane their necks around or lean over the back of the classroom couch, waiting to get a word in.

Daye smiles. "Lloyd?"

"Yeah," Laney gushes. "Did you see his hair?"

"Ohmygosh, yes," Jeanne exclaims. "I want to get matching stripes with James, but, would you be upset? I totally don't want you to think I'm copying."

I don't point out that she kind of would be copying. I let Laney answer.

"Well," she says, frowning slightly, "it *is* kind of our thing. At least for now."

"I'll wait a week," Jeanne decides.

"And now," Daye says, "we've got something else to look forward to. Sef!"

I glance at Seffa, who smiles broadly. "Omigod, guys. You're being silly. There's still over a *month*!" She ends with a squeal. "Just over a month!"

The volume increases, grating on my tired mind. I shut my eyes against it, but it doesn't help, so I feel myself wriggling out of the group. Reaching the floor, I crack one eye open. Whatever hole my absence made is already filled, my friends not even noticing. So I cross the room and sit on the other side of the couch. A small clump of girls sits a few cushions up, and then me. And, I realize, one other person to my right, Hermia McAllister, who's reading on her Pow with a faintly disgusted expression on her face.

She glances over and sees me, and her expression changes to confusion. Then she just shakes her head and turns away. Slightly offended, I open my mouth to speak, then think better of it. Then I think better of it and decide I didn't do anything wrong by coming over here, right?

"What are you reading?" I want to see her reaction.

"Nothing good."

"Who's the author?"

She glances over, raising an eyebrow. "It's a description, not a title."

Oh. "Why are you reading it if it's not good?"

"I'm looking for something." She closes the book.

"I've read a lot of books," I say. "I mean, yeah, many of them are medical stories and accounts, but I like fiction too. Maybe I can help you find what you're looking for."

Hermia tugs at a strand of her hair, twisting it back behind her ear. It's a pretty golden color, as always, natural. "I don't think you can."

The way she says it puts emphasis on *you*. So, it's me. Again. What is it lately? Neil makes me feel like I'm an idiot, telling me I can't understand everything. And now Hermia, a girl I hardly know, is tells me I can't even help her find a book because I'm *me*.

"Well, what are you looking for?" I try one more time to make conversation with her.

She looks sideways at me, mouth twisting into a half-scowl. "Something that doesn't end with a sappy romance story about a Like and an Amora."

I blink. "Oh." I think she's right, I can't help her with this. I don't remember reading anything lacking those elements. "Um, maybe a medical pamphlet?"

She just shakes her head.

Whatever. I drop my gaze, watching my fingers trace the material of the couch. It's smooth, dyed fabric stretched over padding and attached to a wooden frame. I haven't really noticed the design before.

You've never wondered where wood comes from for your furniture? Or where the material in your clothing is made?

It's like Neil's sitting next to me, saying those words in my ear, tone just as high on the bitterness scale as when he said it originally. I jump slightly, mouth dropping open. My fingers jerk away from the fabric and I stare at them, then the couch. This couch, the fabric, the wood, everything. It's all a product of those *factories*. That's what Neil said.

"Are you okay?"

I blink. Hermia looks at me again, brow furrowed. I realize my expression is shocked, or maybe horrified, and I quickly rearrange it.

"Fine." I hear myself lying again. Hermia just shakes her head a second time.

"Hey-*y*, girls." Ms. Heron's voice rings through the classroom. Our teacher walks to the couch and settles herself in. "Who's ready for more review?"

There's a collective groan. Ms. Heron looks sympathetic. "Yeah, I know, but in just three weeks you'll be graduating. You want to leave with flying colors, right?"

There's a mumble of assent, and Ms. Heron launches into our lesson. "Pull up your Wars textbook," she instructs, and girls reach for their Pows. "We're onto chapter eleven. Go ahead and read silently. It's a good chapter." She winks at us.

This section focuses on Lavinia Mahon, a woman instrumental in establishing peace after the Wars. I skim my finger through the curved colored surface of light, scrolling through the text. We've already read about the beginning of the Wars, so it jumps right into a dramatic moment.

Lavinia's lower lip began to shake as she read the message. This happened to her friends, but she never thought it could happen to her.

"Darling?" Lukas called, concern evident in his voice, as he entered the kitchen.

Lavinia looked up, gazing at her Like with teary eyes.

Lukas gasped, dashing to her side. "What's wrong?" She buried her face in his shoulder, his soft black hair tickling her cheek.

"You've been drafted," she told him. "Into the Army[15]."

My gaze flicks to the bottom of the screen and find footnote 15.

[15]*Army: (n) in this context, a regimented, government-organized international defense group comprised of brave women officers and drafted Likes.*

Oh, I knew that. We've learned about those. But the topic isn't brought up much, so maybe the footnote is for women who don't remember.

A tearful goodbye follows. I keep skimming, reading briefly about Lavinia making her plan to restore peace and yearning for her Like to come home. It's very emotional when he does.

The station was packed, and Lavinia could hardly see the monorail car bringing the Likes and Officers back from the sea-port. Her friends, standing next to her, exclaimed over the crowd. But Lavinia was more level-headed and kept silent. She wore her favorite afternoon outfit. It was…

And it goes on for about a page to describe her outfit, which includes color-coordinated dye and pants with shades of blue changing and glowing on the sides. All of it came from somewhere, I realize, swallowing. The dye, the fabrics, the material. All from number cities.

There! She saw him. He saw her too, and he smiled with affection. He was limping, probably hurt, but she threw her arms around him anyway.

Well, that probably wasn't very smart, considering his injuries.

She immediately felt better. He wrapped her in a strong embrace. "You look beautiful," he exclaimed, and Lavinia knew everything would work out.

I finish this part in time to catch Hermia's disgusted snort. I glance at her and see she's closed her book. She catches my eye, then taps her Pow as if to say, *see?*

I nod, only half paying attention. She's right. Even the history books have Likes and glamorous clothing and romance. But it makes them fun to read, even as we're learning. So why does she care?

After everyone's done, and my classmates gush about how adorable the chapter was, Ms. Heron clasps her hands together. "Get a partner."

Partner? Oh, no. Partner means one-on-one conversation and I so, *so* do not want to have to deal with that right now. Every other second my thoughts are pulled back to City 4 and Neil and Han. Do I have to think of lies at the same time, too?

"Hermia," I hear myself say, turning quickly to the girl next to me. "Be my partner?"

"No."

What? "Why?"

"Because I want a good grade."

And here we are again. Why does everyone assume I'm such an airhead? Shrieks and giggles emanate from the other side of the couch, where I should be. Oh. Hermia's not into the shrieking and giggling, I guess, which doesn't bode well for me. And in Neil's case, it's probably because compared to his lifestyle mine is really soft, so it'd be natural to assume I'm incompetent and soft as well.

"Morgan and Mia?" Ms. Heron stops in front of us. "Are you two partners?"

"I–" Hermia starts.

"Okay, good! We're all set." Ms. Heron describes an assignment where we should make a review game about the consequences and outcomes directly following the Wars and the innovations following, up until recently, the early 2200s. Next to me, Hermia sighs. She obviously isn't going to want much friendly conversation. So, perfect.

Academy takes forever today. By dismissal I feel like I'm being pulled in different directions. One is toward the hidden subway station and the secrets, and the other is toward my friends and wanting to be able to think about my eval and hair dye as if they're the most important things in the world.

And then there's a third direction, which is just away. If I choose the away direction, I think I'll just keep running, going until I pass out or reach the levies that keep the sea from flooding the land. And maybe I'll climb over them and jump into the ocean. Then the sharks would come after me, but at least I'll know their purpose; they want to eat me.

Or maybe sharks are a myth. Or maybe they don't actually eat people who go in the ocean. Maybe they're gentle, misunderstood herbivores that eat seaweed. I could never know, just continuing to take the word of what we've been taught. And I don't even know whose word I'm taking.

Laney walks with me until we reach the lobby, saying something about how she didn't understand why I wasn't her partner or why I moved to the other side of the couch, and oh, by the way, everyone's meeting at the nearest ice cream parlor to start planning for Seffa's Amora, until she sees Lloyd waiting for her outside and she dashes off to greet him.

I look around. As I do, Hermia passes me. "Hey."

She stops and nods to me, then walks on.

"No, wait," I say. "Wait a sec. We'll have to work on this project some time outside of class. When are you free?"

"I don't know," she says tonelessly. "I have ballet every day. And I'm sure you'll be incredibly busy choosing between amaranth and Persian pink for the lace on the tablecloths at Seffa's Amora."

"Um, I honestly don't know the difference."

"Oh. Well, either way."

"But what if I'm not busy? I don't feel like planning an Amora right now. After Laney's, I'm all Amora-d out." This isn't even a lie. I *want* to feel like planning, but I just *don't*.

"Hmm."

"Hey," I say, my voice sounding sharp even to me. But I'm sick of this. "Stop *judging* me, okay? Why do you insist on thinking you understand me? You don't even *know* me. Maybe I'm not a typical airhead girl. Well, I was, but now that I know, maybe I just want to understand. Or help."

I shake my head and find Hermia staring at me. Quickly I replay what I just said. Wow. For a moment, my tired mind

119

slipped, and I was speaking to Neil, not Hermia.

"I don't need your help." Hermia sounds confused now.

"Sorry," I mumble. "I didn't mean to say that to you."

She stares at me, one eyebrow slowly rising. "Who–?"

"Morgan! Morgan Waters," someone behind me says. I turn around, avoiding Mia's gaze. It's Ms. Cai, one of the counselors here. She nods to Hermia before turning back to me. "Is your Pow not on?"

I glance down. Oh. "It's sleeping."

She cocks her head. "Well, the mayor's office has been trying to get a hold of you." The counselor glances down at the lightly illuminated screen of her Pow. "She just would like you to pay her a visit, to follow up on the issue previously discussed."

Which one? I almost say, but don't. That would raise questions I'd rather not explain, or lie about. "When?"

"When?" I ask instead.

"Now, if you can."

"Okay." A twist of anxiety grips my lower abdomen.

Ms. Cai walks away. I feel Hermia's gaze still on me and sense the curiosity behind it. But when I look at her, her face is calm.

"I guess I have to go now."

"I guess so." She glances sideways, then back at me. "I'll…"

"Talk to you later," I finish, and she nods. Then I walk out of the building and to the monorail, taking the short ride into the city center and to Mayor Vee's office.

She ushers me in immediately. "Hi!"

"Hi." I try not to sound how I feel, which is like I just swallowed a black hole.

"Sit, sit." She directs me to the still very purple couch in the middle of her purple office. "Don't worry, you're not in trouble. I just want to talk. I only have a minute, or we could have done your eval now! But you have to wait two more days, I'm afraid.

I take a moment to regain my internal organs and figure

out if I need to respond. But she continues speaking, so I'm spared.

"Anyway." She sits down. Her hair is still blonde, but it's a bit more layered now, and has silver streaks. "I just want to make sure of a few things. One, we're smoothly over the whole book thing, right?"

The book thing? *Romeo and Juliet*? That seems like ages ago.

"Yeah." I don't add how, now that she brings it up, part of me still wants to read the end.

She grins. "And no more getting lost in the dark?"

"Ha. Nope." Lost, no. I have a guide now.

"Oh good! One more thing." She drums her shiny nails on the table between us. "I'm a bit curious as to how you missed your eval last week. I thought you'd be excited for it."

"Excited. Yeah, I was excited," I say quickly. "I, um, I just decided to get my hair cut, and go shopping, and I totally lost track of time. It kind of felt like a Friday, you know, shopping and all, almost the weekend, and I, well, totally forgot it *was* Thursday, so I wasn't thinking about the eval."

Mayor Vee nods along. I can tell she still doesn't get how it completely slipped my mind, but at least she doesn't seem outright suspicious.

"All righty," she says cheerfully. "I have a meeting now, a conference with the other Mayors. You know, politicky stuff. Then I must attend an Amora in the Aqua district. You know I get to do Amoras almost every day? It's a treat. Also, they have delicious food. I can't wait to hear what you'll pick out for yours." She winks. I stand up, taking my cue to leave.

"Oh, and Morgan," she says as I'm walking out. "The book and the accidental curfew thing, it's all behind us." Her tone, meant to be reassuring, makes me cringe.

"Thanks," I manage to say, before escaping the office.

CHAPTER 16
Neil

Days pass in a sort of haze, the only things penetrating it being Han's sarcastic comments, Morgan's words, and the desire for more sleep. The realization that it's Saturday again sends a jolt through me, the only thing effectively clearing the fog wrapped around my confused mind.

It's Saturday. It's Saturday. I have maintenance tonight. Morgan promised she'd find me again. Tonight.

The thought causes a pang of something to flash through my stomach. Not sure what. Though my money—what a weird expression, I have no money—would be on anxiety. That feeling is enough to occupy me as I walk across the uneven road to my dorm building and climb the stairs to room 302. I almost don't notice the figure hovering outside.

I try not to show how startled I am when I see Ms. Elliott. She appears uncomfortable, standing by my dorm door clutching the same folder as last week. Is she here to interrogate me? To order me away to *or else* because the women have finally figured it out?

I shake my head. Last time she came here she wanted to talk about a math test. I can't afford to overreact.

"Hi," she says.

I nod back. She glances once, then twice, at her wrist, checking the time.

"I had an idea. Ms. Yu is usually my assistant when I'm teaching the Year 5's and 6's, but she's taking a break. Would you be willing to help me for a while? We can discuss some options there, if you want any help with math."

Slowly I let out my breath. All I want to do is close my eyes for at least thirty minutes, since this would be my last chance in twenty-four hours. But I can't say 'no' to a woman. It's just not done. "Yes."

"Are you sure?"

Is this a trick question? "Yes."

There's a ghost of a smile on her face now. "I appreciate it. We're reviewing addition today, and the alphabet."

I nod, hardly listening. As she starts down the hallway, I turn and duck my head around the doorframe.

"Han," I say in surprise. Han is closer than I expected he'd be, sitting on the edge of my bed by the door. He must have been listening.

"You're going with Ms. Elliott," he says, since he already knows.

"Yeah. Not sure for how long. See you in class, at least."

"Deal." Han's gaze follows me out.

I run a few steps to catch up to Ms. Elliott then slow down when I'm a half step behind her. She's quiet, flipping through papers in her folder, as we walk. She wears jeans and a blue shirt, like all the women here do, and her face has lines around the eyes. But she doesn't carry herself like many of the other women. They almost strut, like their power of status creates sunbeams for them to walk on. Unlike the others, Ms. Elliott seems almost timid, hesitant to use her power.

The Year 5 and 6 classroom is larger than the higher grades. Instead of desks, there are piles of lapboards and blocks used to learn arithmetic and numbers. Years 5 and 6 were probably the happiest of my life. Probably because up until Year 6, we only did simple work during the day, like snipping loose threads off shirtsleeves in garment factories and carrying baskets to older boys in the agriculture fields during harvesting season. Also, the class ended at seven, so we got more sleep.

I probably was happier as a baby, too, in the years I don't remember. Or maybe not. I have no idea what it's like in the childcare facilities; they're in a different part of the city.

The kids arrive only a minute after we walk in. Ms. Elliott sits in a corner, spreading out papers on the lone desk there, and I'm left standing, unsure, by the door. I hear their voices from down the hallway, and the angry sound of a woman shushing them.

I vaguely recognize the red-haired woman leading the kids in as Ms. Meryl, the forewoman at the lumber mill. She has a perpetually annoyed expression, more severe now as she regards the little boys filing through the door. She's one women who really seems to take pleasure in the enforcement part of her job; in other words, her remote is busier than most. I turn away, hoping she'll leave quickly.

"They're all yours," she says. Out of the corner of my eye I see her look around and realize Ms. Elliott's at her desk and I'm the one standing by the door. Her expression deepens to one of disgust. "Hey."

I raise my eyes to acknowledge her, and I see her tap her wrist. I can't do anything except cry out as a shock emanates from the back of my neck.

"I'm talking to you," Ms. Meryl says crossly. My eyes are watery, so I can't read her expression, but I force myself to stand still, not drop to my knees like I want to.

"Hey," I hear from behind me. There's a shuffling sound and Ms. Elliott appears at the edge of my vision. "What are you doing?"

"Disciplining the impetuous." Ms. Meryl gestures in my general direction. "It's something we do here in City 4."

"I know," Ms. Elliott says. "But Neil's here to help me. I'd appreciate it if you didn't discipline my assistant, Lydia."

Ms. Meryl raises one eyebrow diapprovingly. "I gotta go anyway. Ferrah's having a wine and cheese buffet at her apartment and I'm in the mood for some delicacies." Shooting me a look of superiority, she leaves.

"Er," Ms. Elliott says after a moment. "Sorry I didn't see her sooner."

I turn away, shaking my head. Only when I'm not facing her do I let myself grimace.

Ms. Elliott shuts the classroom door. Then she says to the kids seated on the floor, "Okay, everyone. We're going to be reviewing addition today. Sounds like fun, right? Could everyone get a lapboard?"

The boys scramble up and each one grabs a lapboard. Ms. Elliott passes out paper. On the large chalkboard in front of the class she writes down a few simple addition problems. "Everyone please give these a try. Work quietly for a few minutes." She turns to me. "Could you just walk around, maybe? And help those who need it?"

I walk to the nearest boy. He seems to be doing fine, so I move on. The next little kid has his lower lip stuck out and his pencil gripped hard in his hand, almost breaking the tip on the lapboard.

"Hold on," I say in a low voice, kneeling next to him. Gently, I loosen his grip, showing him how to hold the pencil.

"I don't know what to do," he whispers, shoulders drooping. I see the $3 + 2$ written on his paper. Above the numbers is his name, Zaire.

"It's a hard one." I settle down next to him. "Can I see your hand?"

Zaire holds out his hand. I'm surprised at how smooth it is. It's the same surprise I felt at Morgan's hand when I grabbed it almost a week ago.

"So, hold out three fingers." He obediently extends them, and as he does, I notice another woman enter the room. She walks toward Ms. Elliott. I refocus. "Good job, now, add two more." I pull out his thumb and forefinger. "That's like adding three plus two. How many are there?"

Zaire's eyes widen. "Five," he whispers excitedly.

I pretend to count his fingers. Out of the corner of my eye I see the new woman write something down on a piece of paper for Ms. Elliott. Before they've exchanged more than a few words the woman leaves.

"You're right," I tell Zaire and give him a high five.

After the kids complete the problems on the board, Ms. Elliott talks for a bit, then writes up new problems. This time she beckons me over.

"So, Neil, would you want any help with the math concepts? Maybe we could see if you can retake this test and try to get a better score."

"I could probably ask Han." I don't want to have to fake concentration right now. "See if he can help."

"Oh, good idea." Ms. Elliott flips a pencil between her fingers. I glance down at the paper in front of her. In the corner, in different, squashed handwriting is what looks like a name and *noon*. Probably some appointment to learn how to properly discipline us impetuous boys.

"Sorry for the confusion," she says. "I'm trying to get used to the teaching role. I was a librarian before I came here, so I knew enough to teach, but I'm not the teaching-type I guess. I liked the quiet library environment."

Knew enough to teach. Does that mean she knew about men before? "Why did you come here?"

Ms. Elliott's mouth tugs downward, half thoughtfully, half sadly. "I didn't do my job well enough. So the mayor *offered* me a position here."

I'm silent. She seems to take that as a cue to continue. "I mean, when I say I didn't do my job well enough, I mean I left a door open, and it wasn't supposed to be." A door open? In a library? My eyebrows inch upward, making the connection. This is what Han and I overheard when we were in the offices. "There's information, books and such, the women in Color Cities can't see, and a girl did see it because I left the door open."

A girl. *Morgan.* So… "This is punishment," I say.

"In a way," she replies quietly. "It hardly matters, though. I didn't leave anyone behind. My Like came with me, but I only see him after work. He stays at the apartment otherwise, same as the rest of them."

Ms. Elliott looks like she's about forty. I thought all the women in the Color Cities have a kid around twenty or something. "You didn't have a daughter."

She shakes her head. "I gave birth to one, but she was dead upon delivery. Really dead, I mean. And the boy… Well, obviously I never saw him again. I thought they both died, for about a year, until I became the librarian and, well, found out. It hardly matters," she says again.

"The...boy."

Ms. Elliott hesitates. "Women are given medication, so we give birth to a boy and a girl, twins. This is where the boy goes, as you know. The girls are raised in the Color Cities."

A boy and a girl. Twins. I feel my fingers dig into my knees as I digest this. I knew the boys were born in the Color Cities. But I didn't know we were *engineered* to be born at the same time as a girl. I guess that's how they make sure there's an equal number.

"I'm confused," Ms. Elliott is saying. "Did you know about twins already? Maybe I shouldn't have told you. I'm so unclear as to what I'm allowed to say or not say."

I just stare at her.

She sighs. "Um, okay. Sorry. I mean..." She lets out a long breath. The kids on the floor are getting restless. "I'm going to teach now," she says, more to herself than to me. I just nod.

I stay at the class building after the younger class ends and walk down the hallway to Year 17's room. I'm already sitting in the back when boys start to enter, finding their own seats. I wait for Han, tapping my pencil distractedly against the metal leg of the desk. But by the time Ms. Elliott walks into this classroom to get started, Han hasn't shown up. He doesn't walk in during the next few hours, and by the time Ms. Elliott tells those on maintenance to go, my mind has created a dozen scenarios explaining why he didn't show up, none of them particularly cheerful.

I sprint back to the dorms and take the stairs two-by-two. I don't knock, just shove the door to 302 open. "Han," I call out, before I even see if he's inside.

He is. He's sitting on his bed, head turned to face me. I take a breath of relief. "Why–"

Then I really look around. And my mouth falls open. My hand unconsciously closes the door as I stare.

"Oh," Morgan says, standing up from her seat at the desk. "Hi."

CHAPTER 17
Morgan

It seems like I spend the entire week watching the clocks, not paying attention, willing it to be Saturday. Not much new happens. Seffa launches fully into Amora prep, having daily meetings after school at the nearest café. I attend one before I decide I can't handle it, not right now, when I already have to pretend nothing's different and life's just as carefree as it used to be.

Funny how it didn't seem so pointless when it actually was pointless. Three weeks ago, my biggest problem was finding a dress to wear to Laney's Amora. Now the foremost thing on my mind is figuring out how I'm going to pull off sneaking back to a hidden city.

I have my eval Wednesday afternoon, and I make sure to be there. Mayor Vee is smiley and cordial, like always, and I try to act as excited as possible. All I have to do is sit down and describe my perfect Like. How I'd want mine to be. I've known the answers since class 5.

She starts with eyes. My mind is so lost elsewhere, it's a good thing I have an autopilot filling in babble for me. It's only when we're starting in on hair that I replay my own answers in my head and realize I haven't been giving the answers I'd already formed. Instead, absentmindedly, I've been describing Neil. Oh, no. This can't be good. Since Mayor Vee knows about the men, she might recognize Neil from what I'm saying and start to wonder. I'm not sure how much she interacts with the men.

"Hair color," she prompts.

"Light," I say quickly. "Light brown. Blond, even." There. The opposite of dark. Behold, I am a genius.

Except I'm not. By the end of the eval my teeth have chewed raw patches in my lip and the metallic taste of blood coats my tongue.

The entirety of Saturday morning is spent in nervousness, distraction, and impatience. How am I supposed to make it until tonight? I want to go back now. I want to know more. I'm ready to know more.

I try to study in the afternoon. I almost wish Laney would message me or something, asking if I want to shoot hoops at the park like we did when the weather was warmer, just to provide some sort of break in the monotony of *waiting*. But she doesn't.

So around five-twenty in the evening I remember what Neil said about the cargo subways, and how on Sundays they arrive at nine, noon, and three. Well, they might run on Saturdays too, and six is the next number in the pattern of threes. If a cargo subway pulls into the hidden, underground station near the Amora building, I could sneak on it.

Okay. I'm going to try that, I decide, instead of waiting another five hours, and then another four while maintenance is going on, to get back to City 4. I put on the jeans and black shirt and pull on a pink sweatshirt to hide the polo. I put the hat in the pocket of the sweatshirt and head for the door.

"Mom!" I glance into the den where she's sitting on the couch. "I'm going out. I probably won't be back until late." I'll figure the return part out later.

Mom peers back at me, but I don't think she can see me clearly. "Where are you going?"

"To find Seffa and help her with Amora prep. And then maybe hit the gym with Laney." I duck backward and almost make it to the door before someone else calls my name.

"Hey, Morgan." Ross's voice is jovial as he steps out of the kitchen. "Where are you off to?"

I repeat the answer I just told Mom. He cocks his head, eyeing my jeans.

"Are those new? They look different."

I look down at my legs. "They're loose."

"Yes." He blinks at me, gray eyes wide and blank.

"Loose," I say, "like the instructors at the gym wear when they practice Tai Chi, which Laney and I might try. These are Lloyd's. Laney let me borrow them. If we do Tai Chi today I want to be comfortable, but not wear a real Tai Chi uniform on the first day, because that would be weird."

Yes. There's a good one. *A good one.* I'm feeling pride now? Over my lying ability?

"Oh," Ross says. Then, "What do you want me to buy for dinner?"

"Nothing. I mean, I think I'll grab something with Laney. See you later." And I walk out the door.

CHAPTER 18
Morgan

I stop in the Cobalt News office building on the corner by the Amora building and go into the restroom. There I take off my sweatshirt, leave it in the hamper meant for towels, and walk out a side exit. Now I'm in the narrower street between two buildings, where the entrance to the subway station is. In my hand is the hat, but I don't put it on yet.

I hesitate as I reach for the handle in the wall, then I force myself to grab it and pull the door open. The room is empty of people. Slowly I make my way to the second door in the back of the cluttered room and down the staircase.

The dimly lit area is still. Goosebumps rise on my arms; I rub my hands over them. When I snuck off the subway last Sunday, I'd run out of the car and hid under the stairwell while women came to unload the cargo into storage rooms above. Only when the subway left again and everything was silent had I torn up the stairs and out into the street.

I thought I'd been scared *then*. Now I jump at every noise. The stillness is more unnatural, telling me I could be surprised at any second.

It's almost six. I duck under the stairway. More dirt and cobwebs line this space than I've probably seen in my life. I didn't even know cobwebs existed indoors; aren't they only meant to be the pretty patterns in the grass, holding beads of dew so little girls can *ooh* and *ahh* over them at the park? The cobwebs here, in the corners, are just masses of shadowy threads with–yikes!–spiders resting in the centers or scurrying around the edges weaving more web. Ross always removes spiders before I have to see them up close. I try to position myself as far away from them as possible.

Five unnaturally long minutes pass before I hear a faint screech and see lights cutting through the dark tunnel. I press myself against the wall and am covered by shadow. Same as last time, voices echo down the stairwell, accompanied by footsteps.

"No big shipment on this one, right?" one woman asks.

"Just a few boxes. I think a seamstress needs fabric."

Something brushes my arm. I shiver and hear the subway doors open. The women move back and forth, stacking up the few boxes. "I'll get this larger one. You grab the small bins," one woman says, and the other agrees. My arm tickles again. I glance down in time to see a shape disappearing behind my elbow. A spider. A spider on my elbow.

I can't stop the yelp as I fling my arm away from my body, my other hand frantically brushing away the creature. Oh no, oh no. From my left, the bottom of the stairs, I hear a woman say, "Did you hear that? Was that the subway?"

"Probably."

More footsteps grow louder through the echoes. A woman reaches the bottom of the stairs and suddenly I can see her, not looking at me, but walking by the cobwebby space where I'm crouched. I lean back, shrinking against the wall, feeling cobwebs stick to my forehead.

"Marin," the other woman calls. "I actually don't think I can get this box by myself. Come help."

She's right in front of me. I try not to breathe. I try not to think about the cobwebs in my hair or how I'm suddenly convinced spiders are crawling all over me. I try not to exist.

She walks back up the stairs.

I want to run out of this dirty space and jump in a large, bubble-filled bathtub, but I don't. I stay curled against spiders until the door at the top of the stairs slams shut and the only sound is the idling subway.

Only now do I tear myself away and risk a peek.

There's no one in the station. The front doors of the subway are shut while the back ones of empty cargo cars are still open. I take a deep breath and dash.

The doors close just a second behind me. I fall into a

corner and start wiping frantically at my hair, my shirt, and anywhere I think I feel a tickle. Only when I'm on the verge of hyperventilating do I slow down and rest my forehead against a pole a foot away, welcoming the coolness now. My heart is audible in my ears, even over the engine, which roars now. I lift my head from the pole and put on my hat, tucking up my hair.

I spend the fifteen-minute ride focusing on breathing. When we pull into the station I repeat the same procedure I used to get into the subway in reverse. And as soon as this station is quiet I climb the stairs, stepping out onto the hard, uneven material of the City 4 road.

My feet move quickly, getting me away from the subway as fast as possible. I rack my brains to remember the route Neil took. The streets are empty now. Neil told me they get off work at five-thirty, and around me are the work factories, large and ugly. So the boys aren't here now, which is why it's so quiet.

After turning down more than a couple wrong streets, I finally find the right path. A few minutes later I see them, the row of brick buildings with square windows lining every floor. Where Neil and the boys live.

I almost stumble–okay, I *do* stumble–when I also see the boys outside, some sitting, some eating, some tossing around what looks like a rolled-up shirt. What do I do now? They're going to know I'm not a boy. Holy crap. I'm so, so busted now. Do I run? I have a feeling they're faster than I. *No*, I tell myself. *Wait.* I've already come this far. I didn't almost go into cardiac arrest on the subway for nothing, right? I should just keep walking, confident; they'll never know.

Okay, pep talk not working. I scrap the confidence idea, because if I tried that, I'd probably end up looking like I'm made of wood, walking stiffly around trying to be brave. So I settle for shoving my hands in my pockets and dropping my shoulders, the front of my shirt ballooning out into an ambiguous mass, keeping my gaze on the ground as I walk. It's almost a skulk, and yet it draws no attention. Maybe this is normal. It seems familiar to me.

As I walk through the doorway of the building, I realize who it reminds me of: Neil.

His dorm is room 302. I remember that much. And lucky for me it's right outside the stairwell. I tap lightly on the wood, the soft surface on my knuckles. There's no answer, so I try the handle. It turns, and I slowly push it open.

The room's empty. I debate, *what now*, and then I just tell myself to shut up and step inside. I close the door behind me.

So. Now what to do? There are two beds in this room, one desk, one dresser, and one chair. I sit in the chair, then feel too exposed, too *right in plain sight of the door*, and stand back up. I move the chair to the side of the desk opposite the doorway and curl up on top, feeling slightly more concealed.

And again, I wait. It's not long before the door opens. The boy who walks in is blond. I almost throw my hands over my face to hold off recognition for even a second before I realize it's Han, Neil's roommate.

He sees me immediately. Guess my 'concealment' didn't work so well. Staring at me, Han shuts the door and steps inside, arms dangling by his sides, eyebrows raised behind his glasses. His gray polo is wrinkled, and dirt coats the bottoms of his jeans and shoes.

He speaks after a moment. "Morgan, right?"

"Han, right?" I shift in the seat. The toes of my shoes brush real tiles.

"Technically, it's Nathan," Han says, walking toward me. I watch as he reaches over the desk and flips on a light. "But I'm a bit of a non-conformist, so I prefer Han."

"How is a nickname non-conformist?"

Han adjusts his glasses. In the light I can see his irises are gray and tired-looking. Kind of like Ross's, only more animated, even in fatigue. "Well, boys are named according to their year of birth. And the boys born in my year, which I guess is seventeen years ago, so 2221ish, they gave us all names starting with *N*."

I twist a loose strand of my bangs around my finger, too roughly, feeling hair snap. "Why?"

Han waves his hand in a small circle. "It's a method of grouping, I guess. It goes alphabetically. Why are you here?"

"I need to know more."

"Oh, good. Me too. What is it you want to know?"

"I want to know why..." I look around, searching for a starting point. Then the obvious dawns on me. "Where's Neil?"

"Interesting question. I think the response you're looking for is: he's helping a new teacher with a Year 5 and 6 class. I just checked, to make sure he really *was* there. Because when Ms. Elliott came and asked him to go with her, I wasn't entirely comfortable with that, given the recent events. But he's fine."

I sit up straighter. "Ms. Elliott?"

"Our new teacher."

"What does she look like?"

Han cocks his head. "Thin, dark hair, kind of timid."

I don't believe this. "She's the old librarian. When did she come *here*?"

"Circa two weeks before you first did."

My mouth drops open. "That's when it happened! When I read the book."

"When you what?"

"When I... Never mind. So, wait, Neil's okay?"

"Neil is not in trouble at this particular moment. As to the 'okay' part, I don't know. I never do."

I settle my chin on my fist, elbow resting on the desk. "What do you mean?"

"I mean," Han says, folding his hands together, "Neil's hard to figure out. Now, it's my turn to ask you a question."

"When did that become a rule?"

"Right now. It's like a trade. I assume you know how those work. My question is, of all the women in your city, how many do you think know about this? About men?"

I let my breath out in a huff. "None. Except the mayor, apparently. But then again, I haven't taken a poll. And I don't trust my knowledge anymore. My turn. What do you mean about Neil being hard to figure out? And why did he hate me right away? I mean, I understand about the hostility toward women and everything, but, for example, you don't seem to hate me as much, and I know you less."

"That," Han informs me, "was two questions." He stands up and walks to the dresser, pulling open the top drawer.

"Fine. Ask another one, then answer mine."

He closes the drawer. When he returns to sit on the edge of his bed he has a bottle of alcohol in his hand. "Want any?"

"No, thanks. And there goes your one question."

Han narrows his eyes. "Well played." He seems to think, taking a slow sip from the bottle. "Neil isn't an open person. He doesn't *offer* much. Especially about his feelings. I can hardly tell what he's thinking half the time, and I'm his closest friend. Plus, I'm entirely too good at reading people. So therefore, Neil must be very difficult to read if my prowess in the area isn't sufficient."

"Incredible," I say with a snort.

"I know, I am." Han waves his hand dismissively. "As for your other question, I can only guess. But, luckily, I'm superb at guessing, too."

"So tell me."

"Was that an order?" Han's expression dares me to say yes.

"No. A request."

"Really. Well, then, I think I can oblige." He kicks off his shoes and leans back, resting against the wall. "A few years ago, before he really knew me, Neil had a friend, Kellan, a Year 18, meaning he was a year older than Neil and I are now. But anyway, Kellan was Neil's role model. He taught him how to carve those whistle things Neil's always making. Check in the drawer." Han nods at the desk.

I pull open the nearest drawer. Inside are three wooden cylinders dotted with strategically placed holes. I carefully pick one up. It resembles the recorders all the girls learned how to play in our early academy years, but smaller. I was never any good at the recorder, so I didn't pay much attention. But I can tell, while the shape is similar, there's something very different about this whistle. I think it's the groove marks, the lines and fissures from whatever blade carved this. It's like he made each stroke carefully, thoughtfully. I quickly place the whistle back in the drawer.

"Anyway," Han says, "like all Year 18's, Kellan disappeared. Poof. That happened right before I met Neil. And once we trusted each other, I helped Neil figure out where Kellan and the rest of the Year 18's go. Where we all go. And when we found out, I think it was too much for him."

"What did you find out?" I mean to say it, but my voice comes out as kind of a cracked whisper. I clear my throat, preparing to repeat myself, but Han heard me. He doesn't demand his own question. He just answers.

"We found out, we go to your cities."

This doesn't process for a moment. "But there aren't any men, not in Blue City, and I've never heard about them from other cities, and…" I trail off, suddenly dreading what Han's going to say next.

"We're called Likes," he says simply.

And there it is. The final pillar of the constructed reality I'd been living in, crumbled. My airway starts to feel tight. "No." I want to fight it, not believe it, but it makes too much sense. Why there are no men older than academy-age girls here. Why Likes appear out of nowhere. Why everything.

"The Likes, they don't talk about their past," I say, knowing I'm grasping at straws. "I tried to ask some and they just don't…I mean, wouldn't they tell someone…?"

Han continues. "I'm a bit of a pro at picking locks, so Neil and I know a lot of things we're not supposed to. And so we know the answer. We, the men, undergo something called a *Conversion*. It alters our image and implants artificial intelligence into our minds. So, basically, we just don't exist anymore. The *Likes* take our place in our own minds."

My vision is fuzzy. The last strand of hair breaks off of the lock I was twisting and I drop my hand. The tip of my finger tingles, the hair wrapped tightly around it cutting off circulation. But that's kind of a moot point when I can't breathe. I grip the edges of the seat, hard enough to make my palms sting. *I had no idea*, I want to shout, but I'm afraid if I speak I'll release a lot more than words.

"I guess you really didn't know."

I shake my head, staring at the floor. It's a minute before I can say anything.

"How did I not notice?"

"That's what *I* want to know."

My gaze moves to my hands as they slowly release the chair and open in front of me. I tug the loop of hair off my finger, wondering if it's even real. If my hands are even real. Maybe *I'm* not even real.

"Did I really go through almost seventeen years of life just *accepting* it?" Did I really go through almost seventeen years planning for the party where the *shell* of a *boy* would become mine, as in a possession, and did I do it with a grin on my face? Because I didn't know any better?

"Did you?" Han sounds curious.

"I was an idiot."

"Were you?"

I take a deep breath. "I *am* an idiot!"

"Hmm. You do, however, know now. Sounds like that's more than the rest of your city can say. And you're the one who took the initiative to find out."

"I'm *blind*."

"And," Han says, "I believe you now."

"Believe me?"

"Yes. I believe you now. You're telling me the truth. You look like you're going to pass out. Or throw up. Please don't, by the way. Anyhow, I don't think you'd seem this revolted if you already knew."

I open my mouth, close it, and shake my head. "It…the Likes…that's disgusting."

"I would have to agree."

"And I don't think many things are disgusting. I want to be a doctor. I've watched a surgery before, at my mom's office, with no problem."

"Well, I commend you. We don't have surgeons here, or emergency medical staff. Just first aid doctors for the boys."

"What do you do if you need surgery, though? Or emergency treatment?" I try to steer the conversation on a track I better understand.

"No idea. I've never needed surgery. And I guess there is an emergency doctor, but mostly she's here in case a woman needs something, or it really *is* serious."

"Serious like what?"

"Serious like more serious than a burn. A third-degree burn."

"That's the most serious classification of burn there is. What's above third degree?"

"Dead." Han stands and turns toward the dresser.

Maybe it's because he mentioned burns, but I notice it. Peeking out above the collar of his shirt, on the strip of skin between the fabric and his hair, is scarring, mottled red and white in color.

"*You* have a burn." I stand as well.

Han drops the bottle in the drawer. "Quite the detective, you are."

"Let me see."

"I don't think so."

I cross my arms. "I think so. Take off your shirt."

"No."

"Yes."

"I don't want to."

I almost say, *Do it, I'm a doctor,* but I remind myself I'm not a doctor yet.

I glare at him. "Please."

Han lets out his breath in a huff, then tugs the shirt over his head. I almost gasp, but stop myself. I've never seen a burn scar so bad. It stretches from the center of his left shoulder and disappears under his hair.

"What caused that?" I feel myself slipping into my doctor-to-be mode. Where my voice is calm because I *am* calm. Because I can handle it.

"Welding torch."

"What was a welding torch doing next to your head?" I step closer and run my fingers across the area. Han doesn't twitch or pull back, and I realize the nerves there are dead. I once heard my mom say, when discussing medical situations with an Emergency doctor, "Burns are the worst."

"I tried to stop a fight," he says, in an offhand way. "Years ago. In a tool-making factory. One boy had a welding torch. Enough said."

"And no one…it wasn't…fixed?" In Blue City, the rare times someone receives a burn, medical technology has the ability to grow new skin in the area.

"The women were angry. Leaving it was my punishment. Oh, they made sure it didn't get so infected that I *died*, but I felt pretty sick for a while."

Now he pulls away and yanks the shirt back on. I stare at him, thinking this shouldn't even surprise me by now.

"Besides," Han says with a shrug, "it turned out to be a blessing in disguise. I can no longer feel a shock when the women use remotes."

"Remotes?" I ask dizzily.

"At birth, boys have a chip, or implant, put into the base of their neck. It can give us a shock when activated by one of the women's remotes. It's the main method of keeping order. When I got the burn, I think something melted in mine. It still tracks me, but the women don't know the shock is ineffective, and I haven't informed them otherwise."

"That's why Neil gasped," I say quietly.

"Pardon?"

"Neil, last week. Before we got on the subway, a woman almost saw me, but I hid. I couldn't see but I could hear her scolding Neil for not working. Then she left, and he gasped, but he didn't tell me why."

Han nods. "Yeah. Sounds like a remote. Neil doesn't like to talk about those, either. I think it frustrates him. No matter what scenario he could think of, the remotes could always thwart it."

"Scenario?" I sit down again, wondering if there's anything Neil *does* like talking about.

Han settles back on his bed. "For a while, before we found out about Conversions, Neil would try to come up with ways to get to the Color Cities or make contact with Kellan or the other boys who'd 'left' City 4. But he gave up. Now he calls himself a realist. Which is code for pessimist, I think."

"What about the rest of you? What are the other boys like?" I peer around, as if I can see through the walls and watch the other boys of the city.

Han considers my question. "Well, they don't know exactly what happens when they're a Year 18, so in a way they're a bit naïve. But none of them really buy what the women tell us, about how we'll go live happily in a Color City. No one's really rebellious, but a lot of the boys are violent and start fights with each other. Just to have some sort of excitement, I think. Some drink. And some are already lost, just doing whatever they're told. I think those are the boys who simply accept how the women treat us, like we're the human equivalent of sheep. They actually believe we are."

I voice one of the few clear thoughts in my head. "Why?"

"Well, that's how they've been treated since birth, and–"

I interrupt. "No, I mean *why*. Why is this system in place? It doesn't make sense. Was it always like this?"

"The history we're taught is vague in that respect. It implies this system was always in place, but never says specifically when or why. I wonder, before the Wars..."

"I wondered about the Wars, too. I mean, I found this book, which I think is kind of how this all started, me finding out, but anyway, this book was written a *long* time ago, and it's called *Romeo and Juliet*. By–"

"Shakespeare."

"You've read it?" I lean forward.

"No. Well, we've read some of it. We did a Shakespeare unit in Year 15, studying a few of his major works."

"His?"

Han glances at me. "Shakespeare."

"Shakespeare was a woman."

"Um, not according to what we've learned."

I should just keep my mouth shut. Han glances around and sees the clock.

"Oh, hell," he mutters.

"What?" I glance at the clock, too. It's just after eight.

"I'm missing class. Neil's there; he expected me."

"Can we go to your class? I want to see what it's like," I say excitedly, already half-standing. But Han shakes his head and I lower myself back down.

"One, we're already late, so you'd draw attention. And two, I think Ms. Elliott would notice you. Didn't you say she was your librarian?"

"Oh, right." I pause, frowning. "When is class over?" I have a feeling I know this, or I should.

"Eleven."

"Is that when Neil will be back?" Eleven's after curfew.

"He'll be back a bit sooner. He has to be at the subway by eleven. He has—"

"Maintenance." It's my turn to finish the sentence. "Does a subway run earlier than eleven?"

"'Fraid not."

I clench my hands, trying to figure out how I'll get past breaking curfew again. The thought makes my stomach squirm, but not as badly as it would have two weeks ago. The idea of an Amora postponement doesn't seem so awful now.

Han and I talk on and off for the next two and a half hours. Half the time I'm trying to absorb everything I learn, and the other half it's almost idle chatter. From what I can tell, Han's something of a mutual friend to everyone, part of all circles, but the way he squares his jaw when he talks about Neil shows me where Han's loyalty lies.

At quarter to eleven, when Han and I are talking about walls and how theirs never change, the doorknob turns. I snap my mouth shut and my hand flies to my hat to make sure it's still on. Han's face is calm as the door swings open. Instantly I recognize Neil's dark form standing there.

"Han," he says, voice relieved. "Why–"

His gaze swings around, jerking to a halt on me. We stare at each other for a moment.

Then I quickly stand up. "Hi," I stammer.

More staring, then thankfully Han intervenes. "Morgan and I were having a little chat."

"Were you." Neil doesn't take his gaze off my face. His leg moves, kicking the dorm door shut. "How," he says, directing his words at me now, "did you get here?"

"Subway."

"You actually took the subway here, on your own, and you didn't get caught."

"Not to my knowledge."

"And you and Han just decided to hang out a while?" Now he tears his eyes away from me and turns to Han. "Damn it." He speaks in a low voice I don't think I'm supposed to hear because it trembles slightly.

"That's not very nice," Han says mildly.

"You could have been in trouble." Neil's teeth clench together. "For all I knew, anyway. You could have been...gone."

"The circumstances were pretty extraordinary, you must admit."

"I don't care." Neil pivots and grabs a black shirt from the dresser. "I don't care," he repeats as he leaves the room.

My mouth falls open, and I step toward the door. "Where–?"

"Bathroom." Han stands up, stretching. The ceiling is low enough for his fingers to brush across it. "He'll be back."

Han's right. Neil reappears within a minute, now wearing the black maintenance shirt. "Are you coming," he asks.

"On the subway?" I walk toward the open door. "Yeah."

"Hurry, then." He disappears into the hallway.

"That's my Neil," Han remarks with theatrical adoration. "Ever the pinnacle of manners, he is."

I'm about to leave the room when I stop, and glance back. Han still stands inside, watching me.

"Thanks."

"Gratitude accepted." He gives me a small wave and I nod and run after Neil.

CHAPTER 19
Neil

She doesn't catch up until I'm outside. "What," she says, "is wrong?"

"Shh, just follow me. We're running late." I glance at her before breaking into a jog.

Running, especially to and from the subway station, is routine for me. It only takes a few minutes, and I'm hardly winded upon arrival. Morgan, however, seems to be having a hard time catching her breath. Figures; she probably doesn't do much exercise in her charmed Color City life, and all they have to breathe there is fresh, pollutant-free air.

In the subway car we find seats in a back corner as the other boys crowd on. As soon as the subway starts moving, Morgan tucks her knees to her chest, still not breathing right.

"Can't handle the smog?" My voice is hardly audible.

She looks sideways at me. I press my lips together, fighting the urge to shrug. I knew it would affect her.

"Sure," she mumbles. Her gaze darts back and forth, finally landing near my shoes. "Why are you so angry?"

"I'm not angry."

"Yes, you are."

"Okay. But I'm always angry."

"Why are you especially angry at me right now? You practically stormed out of your dorm building." She fiddles with the bottom of her jeans, which are spattered with mud. It rained earlier, while I was at class, and streams of murky water ran down the sides of the streets.

"I'm not especially angry with you," I say. "I think you were careless in coming here alone."

"Sorry. But I still think you're mad."

"Perhaps."

"At me."

"No."

"Yes." Her breathing seems to be getting easier as we talk.

"I was upset," I allow.

"With me."

"*No*. Stop being so annoying. I was upset because I thought Han might be in trouble when he didn't show up for class." I stare at my shoes, avoiding eye contact. She wouldn't understand how Han is the only one I trust and how people can just disappear in Number Cities. She *couldn't* understand.

"Sorry," she murmurs. "That was my fault."

I grunt. *Yeah, figured it out for myself.*

Morgan lets out a long breath, then the words burst out. "Han told me. About Likes."

I actually look at her now. "And..."

"And I still feel like throwing up."

I open my mouth, but I realize I have nothing to say.

"And he told me about the remotes," she whispers. "So I feel like I'm going to throw up *and* pass out."

I still have nothing to say, not yet. After a few minutes, I finally speak. "Han nearly did pass out, when we found out about Likes. You're not doing any worse, at least."

"Wow. Your reply consisted of two whole sentences. I feel somewhat accomplished."

Morgan sounds impressed and I frown. "Oh."

"So Han nearly fainted. Did you tell him to put his head down, between his knees?"

She acts like she wants me to continue, so I do. "No. I dragged him out of the office."

"Next time make him put his head between his knees. It helps blood flow to the brain," she says, like she's rattling off medical notes.

"Huh." Her comment reminds me of Ms. Elliott. "So," I say in a sharp tone, "you want to be a doctor in your city?"

"I do."

"Would you work with..." I gesture, trying to come up with the right phrase. "...women who give birth?"

146

She nods. Out of the corner of my eye I see her sit up straighter. "My mom does. It's the career path I want to take."

I put a hand to my forehead, resting my palm there while my fingers curl around my bangs. "Is it true everyone is born with a twin?"

"Yes," Morgan says. "One always dies, though."

I take a deep breath. "No."

There's a pause, then, "No?"

"No. One doesn't always die. Ms. Elliott let slip today how those twins are engineered. A girl is always born along with a boy." Now I can't help looking at her, to see her expression, to see if she's shocked.

It's like her features have frozen. Then, slowly, her eyes close. "Oh. That makes sense. I suppose you aren't grown in greenhouses. And then there's an equal number. Boys and girls. Everyone can have a Like."

"The boy is taken to a Number City."

"So everyone...every girl...her twin is alive," she whispers. "Why don't I feel more surprised?"

I almost say, "Maybe you're getting smarter," but don't. She speaks before I come up with anything else.

"Neil! *My* twin is alive." She squeezes her eyes shut even tighter. "Somewhere in one of these cities, these Number Cities, is my twin. Right?"

The way she says my name makes me hesitate. "Presumably. Sometimes boys do die, in accidents. It's rare, but it happens."

"But then, how is there an equal number?" The obvious answer follows. "Ahh. I've heard stories about times when both of a woman's daughters have died. But, if it's engineered so a girl and a boy are born, it could be planned for two boys, right? So it's all manipulated, isn't it."

"Everything is controlled."

Her eyes slide open. "Neil, there have to be more women who know. People who decide how all this works and who spend time figuring out this messed up system."

"I'd imagine so."

"And others, some others would obvi–" She stops, then says quietly. "My mom must know. She has to know. She's a birthing doctor."

Her expression doesn't change, as if the idea is having trouble registering. It registers for me fine. I don't see how her mom *can't* know. I start to say this, but Morgan cuts me off.

"No, my mom wouldn't." She bites her lip, eyes narrowing. "My mom's too…she's not…into the system. She doesn't get all excited over dresses and hair and even her Like, so how could she?"

The subway suddenly slows, throwing us forward. My feet slam against the floor, keeping me from sliding off the seat. Moments later the machine stops and boys get up. I do too, Morgan stands shakily beside me. She stays behind me as we exit onto the platform.

As usual, we're hushed, heads turned expectantly and reluctantly toward the steps. A woman stands on them, arms crossed. Morgan shoots an uneasy glance my way as she tilts her face down. I keep my expression calm, trying to tell her this is routine.

Once she is sure she has everyone's attention, the woman on the steps unfolds her arms and speaks. "The usual," she announces. "Pick up your assignment on the way out. Report directly to your assigned location. Handle the maintenance materials and *only* the maintenance materials. Do not make noise. Do not wander anywhere. Though the women are inside as per curfew, do not attract attention. *It will be your fault.* There will be consequences." Then, as if bored, she walks back up the stairs.

The boys move for the stairs. Morgan stands still, gaping. I put a hand on her shoulder and steer her forward.

"No wonder you freaked out," she hisses, trying to catch my eye. I keep my gaze locked in front of us. "When you found me. The whole consequences thing."

"Shh."

Morgan slips by the machine dispensing assignments as I take mine. Almost too soon, it seems, we're walking down an empty street. Her form is shadowy beside me and silent until we pass under a street sign near the Amora building.

"I have to go. I can find the way back now. I'd stay and go back to your city, but I never went home earlier, so they'll think I–"

In the faint blue glow I can see how wide her eyes are. "All right," I murmur, starting to walk away.

"Neil." I feel fingers wrap around my arm. Her fingers, just as I caught her wrist last week. "See you soon." Her fingers slip away, as if she was as surprised as me to find them there in the first place. "Next week. Promise."

I pause for just a moment. "See you." And then I keep walking.

CHAPTER 20
Morgan

I try to open the door to my townhouse as quietly as possible. I feel I do a good job, but it's a moot point. Mom is waiting in the living room.

"Come here," she says as soon as I walk in. She takes my arm, pulling me to the bathroom and closing the door behind us. I notice the shower is running. I'm about to ask why when she yanks back the curtain and, gripping the back of my neck, bows my head so the water soaks my hair.

"Mom?" I splutter, pulling back.

She hands me a towel and I wrap it around my head. Then she hands me another one and turns around, saying through her teeth, "You just stepped out of the shower. Make it look like it."

Wordlessly, I strip off my clothes and wrap the towel around me. Then I shut off the water and Mom turns back.

"I covered for you," she says, teeth still clenched. "Ross asked where you were, and when the wall said 10:55 I started running the water down here just in case, because I knew you weren't back yet. So I told him you're showering."

I'm speechless for a minute. Then I hug her. "Why?"

"Because he would have called the mayor. You *know* that, Morgan," she hisses. "And you *know* another infraction would not be good. Now, go say good-night to Ross."

I nod quickly and scoop up my clothes before exiting the room. I walk upstairs and toss them in my bedroom before stopping in the doorway to Ross's room. Most women share a room with their Like, but my mom has always claimed she rests better alone. Until now, I've never thought to question it.

Ross is inside, pacing. His room is plain and gray-themed. His eyes are, like mine, gray, so I think he keeps his room this way to make them, as Laney would put it, 'pop' and be more appealing to my mom.

"Hey, Ross," I say, as cheerfully as I can muster.

He glances up, mouth cracking open in surprise. "Morgan. Hi. Did you have a nice evening?"

He steps closer, smiling. The smile that's also my smile. But now his smile brings a flood of questions. Who was he, before? Is there any part of a man inside? Is he thinking anything, anything at all, when he kisses my mom on the forehead? When he sweeps our kitchen? Or is his mind just empty, like his eyes?

"Yep. I just took a shower." I try to stem the inevitable flow of questions. "Why are you still awake?"

Ross shrugs. "I'm waiting to say goodnight to Rachel. Why are you up so late?"

"Lost track of time. Mom already told me off. I'm going to bed. Night!"

"Night." He kisses my forehead. I retreat back to my room, where I hide my boy-clothes in my closet and change into pajamas, drying off my head as much as I can, not feeling like using an electric dryer. As I do, something keeps flashing through my mind. Not an image, but a feeling. Of my hand wrapping around Neil's arm. It isn't until that image clears that I remember about Mom, and how she knows. Knew. Always has. She has to. As the nausea starts to curdle in my stomach she appears in the doorway.

"So," she says.

"Thanks again." Should I bring it up? Maybe she doesn't... No, that's ridiculous. What can I say?

"Where were you?"

I swallow. "I can't tell you." Would she tell the mayor?

Mom looks at me for a long time. Then she shakes her head. "I can't do this for you every time. Let me know when you *can* tell me." The way she emphasizes *can* makes it clear she knows the proper words there should be *want to*.

"I will," I promise, not sure if this is a lie or not. Then I roll over, away from her, and don't fall asleep for a long time.

* * *

My lack of rest shows when I'm at Academy, and Laney or Daye or Hermia or whomever I'm sitting by has to poke my arm and remind me to pay attention. Or, at least, make it seem like I'm paying attention. I can't help it, though. Academy doesn't hold my interest. I don't even notice my mind slipping until I'm thinking about something else, and by then I'm too zoned out to care.

Particularly when the something else I'm thinking about is Neil.

What kind of life *is* that? The one he has to live? It's awful. Horrible. I admit I couldn't do it, I honestly couldn't. And I don't consider myself weak or anything. Or, at least, I didn't use to. Now, in comparison to Neil and Han and probably every other boy, I know I am. Even physically, I'm weaker. I saw the muscles in Han's back, and I felt them in Neil's arm when I touched him Saturday.

My train of thought always comes back to the moment when I grabbed his wrist. It makes something tingle below my ribcage, remembering when I held onto him in the dark and, for a second, he was the only other thing in the world.

I could replay it in my mind a thousand times.

I do have to spend some time in the real world, though. Such as when I'm working on the game board project with Hermia, who tells me to call her Mia the second time we work together. We'll be at her house, or mine, or even the park, and she'll call me out when my eyes go unfocused.

I don't mind as much, though. Mia seems to be the only girl capable of talking about anything other than Seffa's upcoming Amora, which is fine with me because every time anyone even mentions the word *Like* my insides twist into knots. Instead, Mia talks about ballet and her upcoming graduation recital and how relieved she'll be to get out of Academy. On Wednesday, after stopping for milkshakes, she brings the topic around to my friends for the first time.

"How's Laney?" she asks, sipping her milkshake. I take a gulp of my own. The sun warms my arms and legs, and I take a moment to enjoy wearing a T-shirt and shorts. Mia is dressed similarly, except she's wearing sandals and I'm wearing my blue boots with the laces.

I shrug, then frown. "I've only seen her a few times, mostly in school. She's busy."

"With Lloyd?" Mia fiddles with her straw. "Her Like? Is he why she's so busy?"

My lips compress into a thin line. *Like*. "Probably," I say, forcing my face to relax.

"What do you think of him?"

The frown returns. "I don't...um..." Great, now my voice sounds strangled. Finally, I mutter, "I don't want to talk about Likes."

Her eyebrows shoot up, but she doesn't complain. If she pressed the subject I'd have to make up more excuses and maybe leave. But she doesn't, and I'm glad. I actually enjoy her company, and I think she might enjoy mine.

Mia and I plan to go rock climbing at the Cyan District indoor sports complex Saturday morning. They have the best rock wall.

"Thanks for coming," I say as I secure my harness. Behind us the harness machines blink green, saying they're ready to go.

"Should be fun," she says. "I haven't gone rock climbing in about a year."

"Yeah, me neither. I need the distraction, though." I wonder if Neil's ever been rock climbing. Probably not. "Okay. Let's climb this mountain."

"Yes," Mia says in a mock-grave voice. "We must reach the summit by sundown or risk hypothermia."

"Don't forget lack of oxygen. Can't risk altitude sickness."

"Fine. Be technical with your doctory talk."

"No, really," I say seriously. "Seek help if you find yourself coughing up blood, or if you notice cyanosis or loss of consciousness."

"All right. If I lose consciousness, I'll be sure to tell

you." Mia finds a foothold and hoists herself up. "Coming?" She feigns impatience.

"Yes, yes, as soon as I fix this strap thing."

"For someone so technical…"

"As soon as I weave this strip of fabric through this plastic securing device in order to finalize the fastening of my harness…"

"Well, hurry," Mia says. "By the way, what are you up to tomorrow?"

"Ah, I'm busy tomorrow."

"Oh. Okay. With what?"

"Um…studying. But not really. Er, I'm…" I look around. "Actually, I'm observing at my mom's office tomorrow." As I say this I feel myself wince.

"Huh. I just wondered if you wanted to study with me. But since you're busy with something, never mind."

"Sorry," I reply meekly. "I would if I could."

"No big deal," she assures me, but her expression tells me she's curious.

And then a cry resounds toward us. "There you are!"

Mia jumps. I glance around, recognizing the voice.

"Laney?"

It is Laney, bounding into the rock wall area accompanied by (of course) Lloyd and also Daye and her Like, Daryl. Laney's hair is carroty today, one of Lloyd's curls dyed to match.

"What are you doing here?" I try to avoid looking at the Likes.

"Trying to find you, silly," Laney answers. "I messaged you fifty thousand times. I even called!"

"It's inactive." I point to the dim device on my wrist.

"And Ross told us you were here," Laney goes on, "so we came to get you. Seffa and Jeanne are back in Cobalt, at the ice cream parlor. We're working on décor plans for Sef's Amora. You gotta come."

I shake my head. Seeing this, Laney adds, "Seffa's upset you haven't been to our other planning sessions. She really wants your input!"

"I have plans right now." I nod to Mia.

Daye glances at her. "Oh. With your *friend*, Hermia."

I notice the inflection. "What do you mean?"

Daye shrugs. "It's just interesting, how you'd rather be rock climbing with her than planning with us."

My nerves must be really worn, because I say, sharply, "Well, maybe it says something about you."

Daryl steps in front of Daye, whose mouth drops open indignantly. "Don't talk to her like that," Daryl says.

"Morgan," Laney pleads. "Come on. Please? I haven't seen you in forever."

"Sorry, but Sef'll just have to deal without me." My hand reaches out, getting a grip on the wall. "And Lane? You had all week to see me. And you didn't."

"That's not fair," Laney argues. "You know I've been busy."

"You can't blame Laney." Lloyd wraps his arms around her.

"Have fun, guys." I turn around and pull myself up. "Come on, Mia. Let's shoot for the summit."

My third trip to City 4 takes place this weekend. Both Neil and Han accompany me, venturing to the edge of the city. The outskirts of Blue City are composed of a few acres of neatly-mowed grass and a couple trees, and if you look closely enough you can see a place where a strip of grass and sky shimmer in the sunlight. It's the perimeter wall, and we're told it's there for our safety, like curfew, so we don't keep wandering and get lost, because the next city is far, far away.

Well, the next Color City, that is.

However, City 4 just ends with a wall. Not a big, impressive wall, either, just one stretching a few feet above my head, made of brick, across a lot with scraggly weeds facing the back of a factory.

"I want to climb up." I motion for Neil or Han to help me.

They exchange glances. Then Han shrugs. "*She* can."

"I can if you *help* me."

For some reason I want it to be Neil who reaches out, but it's Han whose fingers lace together to lift my shoe. I push off, stretching my arms up, clamping them on the edge above me. The rough brick bites into my skin, but I ignore it as Han lets go and I press my feet into the vertical surface. They catch on the texture, and I push myself up. It's kind of like the rock climbing Mia and I did yesterday.

Soon enough I've hoisted myself to the flat top of the wall. It's about three feet across. I stand up, feeling my legs shake a bit. I turn, away from the city, to see what's outside.

The view is almost more dizzying than the height. The wall is at the top of a hill, a gentle, rolling slope, more dirt than plant. But beyond the hill it's green. So, so green.

Grass taller than any I've ever seen, probably taller than me, rolls outward. It has a golden glow as it ripples in the overhead sun, and I want to dive in, jump off the wall and run down into the expanse and be lost. Other plant life dots the mass, colorful flowers poking up and small trees growing into large patches, branches stretching toward the sky, which is unobscured. I've almost never seen the sky like this, so clear, eye-wateringly blue, and not framed by buildings or windowpanes.

There's nothing artificial about it. It's just *there*, just *natural*.

In the distance, on the line where the grass meets the sky, I think I see a ripple. Is it Blue City? I can't tell, and I don't care.

"Have you seen this?" My voice sounds too small and I don't think my eyes can open any wider.

The boys don't respond, so I tear my eyes from the view to look down, blinking hard. Below me Han shakes his head, and Neil looks away.

"You need to come up here. Now."

"No can do." Han's voice is sad despite his wry grin. In response to my unasked question he taps the back of his neck.

"It tracks us. One step and we'd be reported. Not to mention poor Neil here would be fried."

I drop my gaze and realize, of course. The chips. They keep the boys from crossing over the wall, from escaping. So they can't climb the wall. They can't ever see this.

"The only times the barriers don't hurt are when we take the subway or are on the bus to do deforestation," Han says.

I don't even ask what a bus is. I just stare out at the view. I *want* them to see it. I want them to see it so much something between my ribs hurts. But they can't, because of the wall, the thing I'm standing on.

No, not because of the wall. Because of the system. Because of the women.

I climb down in silence, and this time it's Neil who reaches out. He hasn't said a word, but I know he understands. He pulls me down and steadies me when my feet hit the ground, one arm around my waist. And even though he lets go after just a second, a feeling not unlike the one I got looking past the wall rides through my veins and tingles in my fingertips.

The next week is crazy, with finals and graduation prep and visiting City 4. Mia and I turn in our history project and end up getting a decent grade. Sometime in there I manage to get tickets to Mia's graduation recital on Friday evening.

And then Friday, our last academy class comes to pass. It's mostly a party day, celebrating the end of finals and the start of a weeklong break before career training schedules are issued. I feel the impact–the end of academy classes, and the commencement of career training, and how my Amora is hurtling full speed ahead at me with the arrival of summer– but then I shake it off and don't think. I just put one foot in front of the other.

The official graduation ceremony is Sunday, June 4th, after the graduation trips Saturday. And since tonight is Mia's ballet, plus the fact that I'll be sneaking off to City 4 again, I have a busy weekend ahead.

When time is up on the last academy day, most girls collapse into each other's arms, bawling. Even Laney looks a bit teary. We're on speaking terms as she chose to attribute my behavior at the rock wall to 'stress,' but I still feel a coolness, a detachment in me when I'm around her and the other girls. Except for Mia.

Mia is amazing in her performance. The ballet is *Nancy Drew*, and Mia's cast as Bess. She partners with Daye's Like, Daryl. A while ago I heard Daye complaining about how she'd auditioned for Bess and volunteered Daryl for Bess's partner, and then Daye got the part of Hannah the Cook instead. When the show ends I make my way backstage, clutching a few roses in my hand. I find Seffa and Daye first and give them their roses, then wade deeper through the crowd until I see Mia.

She's hugging an older girl with gorgeous chocolate colored skin and a very pregnant belly. "Fabulous," the girl says, pulling away. "Really awesome, I'm so glad I saw it."

"I'm glad you did, too," Mia tells her, then sees me and waves me over. "Hi, Morgan. This is Reece. We used to do ballet together. Reece, this is my friend, Morgan."

Reece, I remember that name. "My mom mentioned you once."

She laughs. "Who is your mom?"

"Rachel Waters."

"Oh, yeah." Reece rubs her stomach. "She's an awesome doctor. I can't tell you how excited I am for my daughter to arrive."

A Like appears behind Reece, dropping his hands onto her shoulder. "We should get going," he tells her, his thumbs rubbing the back of her neck. "You need to rest, darling."

"I do," Reece agrees. "Ryan, this is Morgan, Mia's friend."

"Nice to meet you," Ryan says. I just nod. With a last one-armed hug and a few more gushing compliments for Mia, Reece and Ryan make their way out of the area.

"She was my best friend," Mia tells me, as if explaining something. "Until she got her Like."

The weekend flies by. I go with a portion of class 15 to Orange City for my graduation trip, but while everyone else *ooh*s and *ahh*s, pressing their faces to the monorail windows, I am disappointed. I almost wish we were touring City 4 instead, even though I know it's not an option, because at least there's something new there. Something I haven't already seen.

And Neil is there. And Han.

At some point I find Mia and drop into the empty seat beside her. Mia glances at me. "What's wrong?"

She must see the frown tugging at my lips. "It's not special," I say. My voice sounds resigned, even to me.

She nods. "I was thinking the same thing. It's just like Blue City. Except, orange. Not amazing enough for all the enthusing the teachers did."

I slowly shake my head, looking at my hands. "Is *everything* fake?" My words are not directed at Mia.

"What?"

"I feel..." I search for words. For a way to explain my emotions without explaining everything else, without saying how I know Likes are fake and I want to scream but I can't because I can't tell anyone, not even Mom, because she knows and I'm still sick over that. But no words fit, so I sink lower in my seat. Just as I do the monorail slows to a stop. Smiling guides encourage everyone to stand and quickly make their way off the monorail, because we have exciting, exciting sites to see!

In the crowd, I lose Mia.

I'm starting to feel more comfortable in City 4, with Neil and Han, than in Blue City with all the women and Likes. I stay through Sunday morning, even after they both have to go to work at noon. I just wander through empty alleys, letting the bricks surround me, shield me.

159

But at three I catch the subway back to Blue City, race home to put on a proper outfit, and make my way to the Academy Building. The graduation ceremony starts at 3:30. I would gladly skip it, but people would notice, and I don't want to be noticed.

I slip through the doors right before the teachers finish calling roll. *W* being near the end of the alphabet, I'm able to call, "Here," as I run up the aisle.

Ms. Keeler, the head teacher at academy, pauses on the stage. "Have a seat, Morgan," she says perplexedly.

I nod, my gaze darting around. Moms, Likes, and friends of other ages fill the plush seats behind the graduates. My mom catches my eye, hers full of questions. Beside her, Ross's expression is blank.

Mia waves at me from the back row. I slip in beside her.

"Why are you late?" She keeps her voice low. I don't answer at first, just focus on breathing deeply.

"I was…somewhere," I mutter while tucking hair behind my ears.

"You're not wearing your Pow,"

I glance at my wrist. "Damn. I forgot to put it back on."

"When did you take it off?"

"Earlier." Graduation starts and everything speeds up from there. I'm summoned to the stage near the end, after almost everyone has received their diplomas. Emotional teachers talk about how after only a week's break we'll be getting career training assignments and going off to help the community in our own special ways. Moms in the audience scrub at their eyes. After Ms. Heron ends her speech with, "This isn't just a step, it's a *leap* toward adulthood, because after this comes careers and a family," I realize I'd seen graduation as a barrier between me and my Amora.

And now this barrier is gone. The next event on my horizon, is my Amora on the thirtieth. The realization presses down on me, filling me with dread. As everyone else celebrates, running to hug their Likes and moms, I stand alone in the chaos.

CHAPTER 21
Neil

June is a sweltering month. I start looking forward to nighttime even more because the temperature lowers and the sun isn't around to bounce off the smog in the air and give me a headache. Also, at night I can be indoors, instead of working at this season's location, agricultural fields.

The second Sunday of June, the eleventh, is no exception to the heat. However, it's not so bad early in the morning when Morgan and I sit in my dorm waiting for Han to wake up. I have the window cracked open, hoping a breeze might float in, and Morgan perches on the desk.

I seem to be getting used to this, though I still have a weird feeling, somewhere in my gut, each time she finds me during maintenance. And the feeling never really leaves until she leaves as well. Right now she's telling me about her graduation a week ago, keeping her voice low so Han can rest uninterrupted.

"...almost late." She swings her feet. "Well, I *was* late. But everyone just forgot. I had to wait until the end for my diploma, which I didn't mind. It gave me a chance to catch my breath. And then I graduated. Just like that."

"We never graduate." I don't mention how if I arrived late for anything no woman would just 'forget' about it.

Morgan tugs at her hat. "Never? You never stop classes?"

"No. They're every night, and you can only miss one a week."

"No summer vacation."

It's not a question, so I can tell she doesn't expect an answer. "No vacation," I say anyway.

She breathes out slowly. "You should do something about your arms."

161

"Um" is all I say, not sure what she means. Her rapid subject changes still throw me.

"And your forehead." She studies me, squinting in the dim light. I have the lamp on, but it doesn't do much to combat the early morning. "And your nose, and I'm guessing the back of your neck."

I don't speak, waiting for her to go on.

Seeming to be done with her assessment, she explains, "You have sunburn."

I nod.

"Wish I had some aloe," she muses. "Do you have access to any lotion?"

I shake my head.

"Cucumber? Baking soda?"

"No."

"Yarrow?"

"Uh, no."

"What about ice?"

I shake my head again. "No."

She frowns. "Where did you get the sunburn?"

"I'm guessing from the sun."

"Sarcasm noted. Were you outside, then?"

My eyelids are closing. I stand up to try and keep myself awake. "It's a new season. I'm working in agriculture now."

"Oh," Morgan says, but the alarm sounds right as she speaks. And like normal, Han's hand reaches out and grabs his glasses off the corner of the desk. He sits up, one arm across his mouth to stifle a yawn, the other extended toward the ceiling, stretching.

When he opens his eyes, he nods to Morgan, and then to me. "Good morning, my clockwork companions," he says cheerfully. "I do believe I'm experiencing déjà vu from last Sunday. Morgan, your hat looks extra black this week. And Neil, the bags under your eyes are exquisitely purple today."

"I'm so glad."

Morgan jumps off the desk as Han slips out of bed. "You said you'd show me today."

"Ah." He rubs his forehead. "I did say that."

Morgan grins. I glance first at her, then at Han. "What?"

"Han promised to show me his lock-picking thingies."

"Tools." Han shakes his head in mock disgust and pulls open a desk drawer, the one holding my whistles. He removes the false bottom to retrieve one of his sets. "Objects so eloquent as these cannot be referred to as 'thingies.'"

Morgan laughs. "You sound like me defending medical terms."

Han replaces the fake bottom, but leaves the drawer open. I step forward to close it. Before I do, I pick up a whistle, contemplate it, then pocket it.

"We'll have to go somewhere with a lock." Han sticks the set in his waistband and folds his shirt over it. "I like to practice on the factory two blocks behind us. It's down for refurbishing, but none of the boys will be assigned to work repair on it right now."

He leads the way out of the dorm building, walking ahead of me with Morgan, discussing something. It amazes me how quickly they formed a bond. I'm still unclear what they talked about the second time Morgan came to City 4, but she got Han to trust her.

Also, Morgan acts like she's comfortable here. Something must appeal to her as she keeps coming back. Last week I was ready to walk her to the subway at noon, but she declined, saying she wanted to explore the city alone. I know from experience she's incredibly stubborn, so I didn't argue.

Han's lock-picking lesson lasts a while, as Morgan insists on trying herself until she can successfully unlock the back entrance.

"No door I've seen in Blue City is ever locked," she says. "Except the one door in the library, but I used it when it was open. Han, did you know you smell like fish?"

"Lovely, isn't it?" Han carefully inserts his tools back into the fabric pouch he made for this set. "This season I'm working at the hatchery. For seafood, you know. And even after I shower the scent clings to me. What can I say? It can't get enough of me, I guess."

Then we walk around, like usual. Morgan talks about seeing another Color City, and how she starts career training tomorrow.

"I was unsure if I still wanted to go into birthing after what you told me, Neil. But I do, because if I know more, maybe I can figure out a way to help. I really want to help."

"I don't know if you can," I say bluntly.

"I can. I have to believe that."

At ten o'clock, when the sun is high enough to heat the asphalt and make the temperature rise sharply, Han announces he has to head back to the dorms and finish some accounts for work. "I'll catch up with you guys soon. Where will you be?"

Morgan turns to me for an answer and I shrug. "Swimming pond." It's hot enough.

Han makes the *okay* symbol with his hand and exits the scene. Morgan and I walk slowly away.

"What's the swimming pond?" Morgan scratches under her hat. "I hate this thing. It's too warm and itchy and ridiculous in summer."

I brush my own bangs off my damp forehead, grateful I'm not the one wearing the hat. "A pond on the edge of the next residential district in City 4. There's lots of shade."

"Sounds nice. On days like this in Blue City, everyone's usually inside with air on."

"There's no air conditioning in the dorms."

"To the swimming pond, then."

I lead the way down the next street. We're both quiet for a little while, keeping our eyes down to take in as little sun as possible. We don't encounter any other boys. They must be trying to entertain themselves in the dorms or the shadows of nearby buildings.

Then I remark, "We can sit by the pond for a little while, but then we need to get you to the subway."

"Oh," she says. "I thought I'd just stay again, until three."

Again. She'd rather be here, in this heat, than in her city's precious AC? And aren't there adults in Blue City who actually miss girls? "Why?"

Out of the corner of my eye I see her shrug. "I don't know. Actually, that's a lie. I do know. It's a bit silly, though."

"What." It doesn't come out as a question. I forget the inflection a lot. I don't correct myself, though.

She looks over at me as we walk. Strands of hair stick to the sides of her face, and her cheeks are turning pink with sun. Like me, her hands are in her pockets, though hers rest easily while mine are jammed in so hard the whistle in my right pocket digs into my fingers.

"I feel alone in Blue City." Her gaze wanders away, to the side. "No else one knows about men. Or, at least, no one else that I trust, except my mom, and I don't even know what she knows, if anything. And if she does, I don't know what she thinks about it. That was confusing. I just mean, I feel like I have to lie because I know I'm living a lie. And I'm the only one who feels that way. Except there's my friend, Mia, who isn't obsessed with Likes like everyone else is, but she doesn't...*know*."

That's interesting. I want to ponder this information, but something gets in the way. It's me, frowning. And feeling bad. Bad? As in, sympathy? I'm feeling sympathy for a woman?

The sun must be getting to me.

"I know," Morgan says hastily, seeing my frown. "It's silly. But I can't help wishing everyone knew. And I'm trying to figure out how to change it. Make it dif–"

I cut her off in mid-sentence. "I'm sorry."

"Sorry? *You're* sorry?"

"Yeah. Sorry you feel that way."

"Oh." She blinks rapidly. "Um, well, thanks."

I nod, avoiding eye contact by staring at the opposite wall. "We're almost there."

The pond is just around the next street corner. It's artificially made, a hole dug in the ground and filled with drained rainwater, hidden behind an old factory. I don't notice

Morgan has stopped until she hisses, "Neil!"

I start to look over, and as I do my gaze flicks across the mouth of the alley. My first thought is nothing, just blank surprise. My second thought is, *damn*. I stop too, but it's too late to backtrack. They've already seen us.

It's a group of three boys. I recognize them. They're all from this district: Year 18's Mac and Misael, and Noah, who's my Year and also worked in the lumber mill. I also recognize them as boys who like to spend free time picking fistfights.

"Neil," one of them calls. I don't hear any movement behind me and realize Morgan is frozen in place. I tilt my chin up, a loose nod. They come closer. The skinnier of the Year 18's says, "What are you up to?"

I'm silent, gaze darting around, trying to think my way out. It's a narrow alley.

Misael jabs two fingers at my shoulder, his rounded head blocking the sun. I twitch away, but don't back up. "Mac asked you a question, man."

"Oh, forget it." Noah says, off to one side. "Neil doesn't speak. He doesn't even curse when the stupid slicer machine breaks for the millionth time."

Well, I don't curse out loud.

"Who's your friend?" Mac looks in Morgan's direction. I glance over my shoulder. She's standing still, eyes down, shoulders hunched forward. Unrecognizable.

"Neil also doesn't have friends," Noah feels the need to add. "Except Han, which I really don't get."

"Han's cool," remarks Misael. "He once covered my section of the conveyor belt at the garment factory, just as a favor."

"Han's not here," Mac points out.

Morgan and I shouldn't be here, either. Now I step back and turn, signaling to Morgan we should get out of here. Before I've taken two steps Misael's hand catches my shoulder and roughly spins me around. The next second, his fist flies square at my face. I manage to dodge so his knuckles only connect with my lower jaw, but it's enough to cause liquid to well up in my mouth. I shake my head, spitting, wiping blood from my lips with the back of my hand. Ow, dammit!

"Don't walk *away*, man," he complains. "We're bored."

I've backed up enough that we're only two feet from Morgan, whose expression is both petrified and indignant. Like she's not just afraid, but angry.

"His friend is speechless, too," Mac remarks.

"I'm *telling* you," Noah insists. "They can't be friends." He turns to Morgan. "What are you, a Year 14? You're short. Are you from the next district over?"

She glares at him in response, but I don't think he sees she also twists away from him. Misael moves in my peripheral vision, slamming me sideways against the wall. I gasp as pain jolts through my shoulder.

"You're bleeding," he tells me, as if I didn't know. Scowling, I sink my elbow into his ribs. He loosens his grip and I twist away, turning to Noah. I freeze when I see he's got Morgan in a chokehold. He's saying, "He won't retaliate. This is boring."

What shocks me are Morgan's eyes. They're unfocused as she gasps, a vision of complete and utter panic. It only lasts a moment, but it's enough for me to start running and shout, "*Noah!*"

He's only feet away, but before I reach him Morgan bends her knees, then extends and slams the top of her head into Noah's face. He howls, letting go of her to clamp his hands over his nose. Morgan stumbles back, one hand on her throat, the other on her head. Misael pushes me aside and advances.

"Oh," he says. "*Now* it's interesting."

He stops, though, when he sees the blood dripping from beneath Noah's fingers. "*Damn* you," Noah says, glaring at Morgan who faces away. Misael and Mac hold themselves awkwardly, as if they don't know what to do.

"Hey," Noah says thickly, starting forward again. "You. Are you afraid? Because you should be. Turn around."

I've stepped in front of him before he gets another foot, shielding Morgan behind me. "Noah, back off."

"Neil," Noah growls. But I remain where I am, my only thought to stay between him and Morgan. Noah's eyes narrow; I brace myself to fight him off.

Then a shout of "*Oi,*" rolls through the alley. A figure runs up, blond hair and gray eyes unmistakable even in the bright sun.

"Han," Mac says uncomfortably.

"Mac," Han acknowledges, then turns to me and Morgan. "Are you all right?"

"Fine," I say.

"What happened?" His tone makes it obvious he knows just what happened.

"We were just leaving." Mac retreats around the corner. After a pause, Misael follows. Noah spares one last glower from behind his fingers, then hurries after his buddies.

I turn to look at Morgan, but my gaze meets air. Dropping my gaze, I see Morgan sinking to the ground, leaning against the wall, arms wrapped around her torso as she gasps for air.

My mouth hangs open. She's kind of done this before, breathing hard or struggling to breathe, but I'd assumed she was just being dramatic. Now, though, she seems scared, fingers digging into her sides, eyes wide, not unlike the first time I saw her.

"Morgan." I kneel beside her. She glances at me, her desperate expression not changing. Han steps closer.

"What's happening?"

"I–I don't know," I stutter. Morgan seems incapable of answering.

She tries to speak. "It's…the…the panic," she manages between gasps. "Distract me…please."

The panic? My mind flashes back to the expression on her face when Noah held her in a chokehold. That panic? And how am I supposed to distract her?

"Should I launch into a humorous narrative?" Han rocks

back and forth on his heels, as if he wants to pace but hasn't quite taken the initiative to walk yet. "Or perhaps perform an acrobatic sequence?"

I tune Han out and feel the form of the whistle pressing into my leg, trapped in my pocket. I tug it out and start to play without thinking, generating random melodies I've come up with on other days. Despite the throbbing in my mouth I try to focus on the sound the whistle makes and not my confusion, but it's only a minute until I lower the whistle and look at Morgan again.

She's looking at me, face calmer now, hands resting in her lap. While her breathing is shaky, she's no longer gasping.

"You're okay?" I murmur.

"I am now."

I spin the whistle between my fingers, chewing on my lower lip. I stop when I taste the blood again. Misael's punch sliced my lip against my teeth.

Morgan points at it. "Ice."

"Don't have any."

"Water, at least," she insists. "Let's get to the pond thing."

"Wait." I put my hand on her shoulder as she starts to stand up. "What was that?"

She knows I'm talking about the panic and the gasping. She sits back down. "It's a breathing problem," she whispers. Han crouches down to better hear. "I've always had it. When I feel panic, or claustrophobia, or something in the air aggravates my lungs, my airways constrict."

"Don't you get treatment? Or at least have an inhaler?" One year, I worked with a boy with breathing problems, a substitute from another residential area, and he carried around an inhaler.

"I never told anyone, so I never got treatment. I'm not allowed to be a birthing doctor if I have breathing problems, especially not if it's triggered by panic or stress."

I consider this. She must really want to be a doctor. "I'm sorry this happened," I say quietly. "And that it made you panic."

"It's not your fault. I don't blame Noah either. I mean, I hate that the boy punched you. But still, I don't understand how you *all* haven't gone whacko with your schedules and lifestyles."

"I think we all have," Han says. "Just in different ways. Neil, for example, is Exhibit A in the hall of Detached Introvert Whackos with Whistles in Their Pockets."

"And Han is number-one smartass," I mutter.

"I'm going to do something," Morgan says. "I'm just not sure what. But when I want to make something happen, I make it happen."

"Sounds like a nice skill to have," comments Han.

Morgan blinks up at him, then her gaze moves over me, flicking to my hand, which is still on her shoulder. She bites her lip and I quickly drop my arm. She stands; I do the same.

"At least the blood doesn't show up on your black shirt," she says, changing the subject in her signature style. "It's all over your chin, though. Don't you want to wash it off, at least? Also, I need to look at your shoulder."

"My shoulder's fine."

"You're rubbing it, so it obviously doesn't feel fine."

I shake my head, pocketing the whistle. Han beckons us along. By the time we get to the pond, there's only a half hour left until Han and I have to report to work. We sit in the shade, talking about random things—after Morgan's satisfied that I've sufficiently washed my face and she's given me a long list of instructions on how not to potentially injure my shoulder more (all of them void because of work), of course.

Morgan's face falls when we get ready to leave. I ask, "Are you sure you don't want to take the noon subway."

"I don't want to go home yet."

"Well, either way, 'tis time to bid adieu." Han holds out his hand. He and Morgan shake, like they always do.

"Good day, Han," Morgan says in a theatrical tone.

Han salutes. "Fare thee well, Morgan."

Then Morgan turns to me.

170

"You're positive you're okay?" I repeat for the third time, frowning.

She nods. "Thanks, Neil." She hesitates, then steps forward and wraps her arms around me, giving me a quick hug. I'm so shocked I hardly hear her say, "For stopping him. And for playing your whistle."

Then Han tugs my arm, saying we're going to be late, and leads me away. We've turned the corner by the time I can think enough to look back.

CHAPTER 22
Morgan

Before Laney's Amora—before I met Neil—I thought doctor career training would be a hundred times more fun than school. Sure, I wouldn't get to see Laney and my other friends for hours every day, but we'd have afternoons to hang out and tell each other about training. I'd travel to the Doctor Career Training building in the Cyan District every day and meet other girls with the same interest. And speaking of interest, I'd get to spend my days studying the one topic that truly does capture my attention.

After Han told me about Likes, and especially after Neil told me about the twins, I was apprehensive to start training, but curious. How would the teachers explain the twins? Would they tell us about boys, or try to cover the fact with a lie? It was a morbid curiosity though, as I felt almost afraid to know the answers.

After the first week I decide training is not terrible. It's an introductory week, reviewing the schedule for the year as well as discussing some emergency procedures in case of accidents. My teacher, Dr. Iltchenko, went through career training with my mom, so she shares side stories with me about 'way back when' twenty years ago.

I see Mia after training on Friday. We meet in the park, the sun beating down and causing my hair to stick to my cheeks and neck. I need to trim it. Mia's cheeks are flushed and strands of hair stick to her forehead. Her ballet bag digs into her shoulder. This is the first time I've seen her since training started. Apparently career ballet is incredibly intense, but Mia can't stop grinning when she talks about it.

"I hope Reece starts soon," she says after describing the training session at the fitness center. "She'd love it, too."

"Reece is your friend who graduated academy a few

172

years ago?"

"Yeah." Mia's foot scuffs the ground, sending a pebble skittering across the smooth walkway. It must have been tracked up from the edge of the pond. There are a lot of waders down there in this heat. The younger girls, the academy-aged girls, take part-time internships in the summer to explore career options and have more free time to hang out. "Reece got her Like right before she graduated. She used to be more like me, as in, she wasn't obsessed with getting a Like. But once Ryan entered her life, he *became* her life. She postponed career training to spend time with him. He doted on her and made her feel pretty like they all do. She took a job helping my mom put together clothing designs to make a little extra money, and now she's pregnant."

Two words in her sentence–*Like* and *pregnant*–jump out at me, making me shudder. And I'm the only one who knows it. I look away to gaze at the pond. Little girls crouch by the edge, splashing with their feet or playing with the round pebbles surrounding the water. Their mothers and their mothers' Likes watch them. Older girls sunbathe on the opposite side, watching videos on the curved screens of their Pows or chatting with each other. Everyone is smiling. Everyone has a happy-go-lucky, carefree expression as they enjoy a summer day without any concerns or dark thoughts constantly lurking at the edges of their minds.

I haven't worn a happy-go-lucky expression since I laid awake all night, having just found out what, rather *who,* Likes really were. And that I have a twin, somewhere, and he's going to be one of them someday.

That night I promised myself I would do something. It was the only way to lessen the almost overpowering sense of being sucked down a huge drain, a drain made of all the truths causing the world I thought I knew to disappear.

And I made a silent promise to my twin: wherever he is, I'll find him. Before he is turned into a Like.

I felt slightly better once I resolved to do something. Resolve got me through the last few weeks, even helping me come up with a potential step in figuring this all out. Resolve hasn't, however, rid me of the sudden isolation I feel.

More than once a week, I want to be able to talk to someone about something *important*. But more and more the only important thing on my mind is doing something about Likes. Helping Han and Neil. Finding my twin. At the same time, Neil constantly flits in and out of my thoughts. He won't go away.

And I don't think I want him to. Tingles race up and down my spine when Thought-Neil makes appearances. Especially if my mind is replaying the time when he played the whistle for me, and the moments before, when he dove in front of me to stop Noah.

Why did he do that?

"*Morgan.*"

I blink. Mia looks ready to say something else, but then she glances at me and her frown deepens. "What is it?"

The first word in my mind now tumbles out of my mouth. "Neil." Realizing this, I press my fist over my lips, chiding myself. I've been so careful about not saying what I'm thinking out loud. It's automatic; when I'm looking at a woman's omni-happy expression, my real thoughts lock up. The only times I have trouble are when I'm around my mom and Mia. They never wear the omni-happy expression. Like now, for example, Mia has a crease above the bridge of her nose and one eyebrow is raised. Inquisitive, like she's really thinking something. And I have no doubt she *is* really thinking something. Such as, *who is Neil?* Which I don't want her to be thinking.

Actually, I do want her to think. I want her to *know*. But she can't know. Can she? I can't risk it.

"What?"

"Nothing," I reply quickly, and something inside me pangs in protest. Neil is not *nothing*.

Then I tell myself he is nothing to Mia.

"Are you sure?" Mia clearly knows I am not sure.

I nod, not trusting myself to speak.

"All right," she says when I don't expand on the subject. "Anyway, I was going to tell you to look behind you."

I turn slowly, putting up a hand to shade my eyes. Someone waves as she sprints up the walkway. In a few seconds, Laney's skidded to a halt next to me.

"*Morgan!*" She throws her arms around my neck. I stumble backward, drawing in a sharp breath. "It's been way too long! I haven't seen you since last *week*." She steps back. "I *miss* you."

"I...miss you, too." Well, I do. Or at least, I miss the Laney minus the Lloyd.

Laney smiles. "Oh, quick, did you notice anything different about me?"

I blink. "Um."

"My *hair*. I got a summer cut."

Her hair is now a more golden color, with coppery highlights reflecting the sunlight. It's also shoulder-length. "Oh. Of course." I hadn't noticed. "It's nice."

"Nice?" She seems surprised with this adjective. Then, shrugging it off, she barrels on. "I saw you here when I arrived at the ice cream parlor with Lloyd. He's getting ice cream now. He's gonna bring it out. Anyway. How's doctor career training? How have you been?"

"Good. Good," I reply. "Um, how about you? How's lawyer training?"

"Great." Laney grins in an almost wicked way. "I get to argue all day. And I'm beastly at it."

I chuckle, then glance at Mia. She stands off to the side, expression disinterested. Laney glances at her too, then back at me.

I hear footsteps behind us, and the next moment Lloyd strides into view. "Banana," he says, holding a waffle cone topped with yellow ice cream. Already beads of thick cream are sliding down the cone, so Lloyd wraps a napkin around it before handing it to Laney. "Your favorite."

I wait for Laney to object. This is the girl who hates napkins wrapped around her ice cream cones. The one who used to claim that if I couldn't handle a bit of ice cream on my fingers, then I couldn't handle eating the ice cream either. Then she would take my cone.

But the girl in front of me only puts on a smile gooier than her melting ice cream and goes, "Aww, how sweet of you."

I tear my gaze away for two reasons. One is every time I see Lloyd, unanswerable questions pop into my head. What Number City is he from? Where did he work? Who *was* he? It drives me nuts. And the second reason is, I don't want Laney to see me roll my eyes. "I need to go."

"Me too," Mia mutters.

"But I just got here," Laney protests.

Yeah, and so did Lloyd. "Sorry. I have stuff to do before tomorrow."

Laney's expression brightens. "Tomorrow! Sef's Amora. Can you believe it's also on a Saturday? *Exactly* seven weeks after mine."

"Happy almost seven weeks." Lloyd kisses Laney on the cheek. Momentarily distracted, her sugary smile returns. I share a *look* with Mia and start to walk away.

"No, wait, Morg," Laney insists. I glance back, catching her eye. "You'll be there, right?"

I hesitate before responding. I already know what my answer is, I just don't like it.

Laney senses my reluctance. "Please. It'll be fun. The theme colors are gold and blue. It's going to be fabulous. She's having a whole seafood buffet, not just shrimp. Oysters and calamari and salmon. You love that stuff."

That stuff. From the hatchery. *Where Han works,* my mind supplies. "Yes," I say, feeling myself shiver even as the heat rises around me. "I'll be there." The first Amora since I learned the truth.

"I'm glad." Laney seems sincere. I start to back away again. "By the way," she adds, "you're the one leaving this time. *I* came over to you."

"See you, Laney." I turn and walk as fast as I can until

I'm out of the park and in the shadow of a tall building. Then I stop, stretching my hands out in front of me, staring at them. Everything else is a blur for a moment.

Until someone says, "Yeah, your hands are still there."

I blink. Mia stands only a few feet away, out of the shadow. Her naturally golden hair glows more than Laney's artificial coloring. I hadn't realized she'd followed me.

"I thought you, being a prospective doctor, would know hands don't usually fall off spontaneously." Then she gasps theatrically. "Unless...Oh my gosh. *Do* they? Is that a doctors-only secret? Should I start putting duct tape around my wrists from now on?"

I laugh weakly. "I don't think you're in any danger. It's not a doctor secret."

"Aha. So there *are* some doctor secrets! Let's hear one. I'm curious."

I don't reply.

She blinks, then shrugs. "Okay. Never mind. I actually wanted to ask if you're really going to Seffa's Amora."

"I am." I've had a plan forming in the back of my mind for a few days, ever since Seffa sent out a message reading *OMG ONLY A WEEK TIL MY AMORA!!!!!!* And, unfortunately, this plan requires my presence at the event. "Are you?"

Mia makes a face. "I was certainly not planning on it."

"Could you?" Mia would be like a breath of fresh air when I'm surrounded by the other academy girls and women and Likes at the ceremony. I feel as if before meeting Neil, I looked at Amoras in a fun house mirror, and they appeared completely normal. But now that I've turned around and am looking at an Amora clearly, it is most definitely not normal.

Mia takes a few seconds to respond, allowing all these thoughts to run their course through my mind. Then she says, "We could do something else instead. You could come over to my apartment. We could have a sleepover, play some video games, whatever."

I shake my head. I can't sleep over on a Saturday.

"Sounds like fun. More fun than the Amora. But I have to be at the Amora."

"And you're not going to say why," Mia observes. "Well. Maybe. Maybe I could come for a little while. It would make my mom happy, anyway."

I let out a breath I hadn't realized I'd been holding.

CHAPTER 23
Morgan

Saturday evening arrives faster than normal, probably because I spend the day pretending to do career homework while really my mind is churning, thinking about my plan. My plan to find Seffa's Like before he's revealed. I'm assuming he'll be in the Amora building somehow. And maybe I can find out…something. Anything.

Around six I'm lying on my floor, staring at the ceiling. When the door opens I hurriedly sit up, afraid to be caught with my thoughts. Mom enters and closes the door behind her. "So, you're going tonight."

"Yeah. I kind of owe it to Seffa."

"And your Amora is in two weeks." Mom's voice is so tight I have to glance up at her to make sure she's not asphyxiating.

"Yeah. With all the excitement for Seffa's, no one's really been thinking about mine." Not to mention I haven't brought it up, like other girls would have.

"Have *you* been thinking about it?" Mom walks past me to sit on my bed. Bags underline her eyes like puffy half moons. She hasn't covered them with makeup like other women would.

"Yes." I fight to keep my tone normal. I have to pretend, even to her. It's incredibly hard, especially when all I want to do is take Mom's shoulders, look her in the eye, and demand to know what she knows, and why, if she knows anything, she never *told* me. And at the same time, I want to hug her.

Mom sees through my attempt. "Then why haven't you mentioned it lately?"

I hesitate. "Nerves?"

Mom studies me some more. "Morgan," she says quietly. She rubs her knees as she speaks, an anxious habit of hers.

"Where do you go Sunday mornings?"

"Um...out," I stammer. I curse the trouble I have lying to people I care about. Sometimes I'm positive Mom knows about my breathing problems. But if she does, she hasn't said anything. "I like the early morning."

"Please don't lie to me," Mom whispers, and I cringe. "I know you. You have a reason for breaking curfew."

"Breaking curfew? I don't...I don't leave earlier than five. When curfew ends."

"I woke up at four last week. You weren't here. Please, honey, tell me." She doesn't sound angry, but her eyes implore me to explain. And I want to. I almost do.

But then I remember; she also has some explaining to do. "What about you?" I keep my voice equally quiet. "What about you, and what *you* do? What can you say about *that*?"

"What I do?" She sits up straighter.

"Yes. What you're *part* of. Maybe you should tell *me* first."

Mom looks confused at first, then a new expression dawns on her face. Hurt. And something like grief.

"I didn't..." She trails off, taking a deep breath. My bedroom door opens and Ross sticks his head in.

"Someone's here to see Mor– Honey! What's wrong?"

Mom shakes her head. "Nothing's wrong. Who's here?"

Face drawn in concern, Ross says, "Hermia McAllister. She's here to–"

"Let her in," I say, turning away from Mom to face my closet. I hear Mom leave. A few seconds later my door opens again and Mia is standing over me.

"Hello." I try to speak normally past the lump in my throat. "What's up?"

Mia tosses something on my bed. A dress. "I figured I'd come over early."

"I see. Why?"

"So you can try again to explain why you really, really have to be at Seffa's Amora."

I flop backward, lying down again on the bed. I can

almost feel frustration pushing through my veins. It's thick and hot, like syrup, making me clench my teeth against the words that want to come out in a torrent.

Neil, I tell myself. *Think about Neil, playing the whistle. Stepping in front of you.*

And then, slowly, I ease my teeth apart, the tingles zinging to my fingertips. "I want to find her Like."

Mia drops to the floor, settling in a cross-legged position. "Find her Like," she repeats. "Seffa's Like?"

"Yes. Before they present him."

"And why do you want to find him?" She doesn't sound averse to the idea. Instead, she sounds intrigued.

"Because I want to know what they're like. *Before* they get googly eyed." A lie and a truth at the same time, easier to say.

Mia is nodding. "Me too. Let's do it."

Let's? As in, us?

I only consider this for a moment. I like the way it sounds. "Let's," I agree.

I wear my blue dress, one I've worn for other Amoras. Mia's in a simple brown dress, her hair pulled back in a bun. We arrive somewhat on time.

I can tell Mia's distinctly uncomfortable as Mayor Vee gives her usual commencement speech. As soon as the dancing starts Mia and I head for the side of the room. The music borders on deafening.

"Where do we start?" she shouts, but she might as well have whispered. I make her repeat it so I can read her lips.

"I don't know," I admit. I've been trying to recall from which way Lloyd walked onto the stage, but the events of Laney's Amora are fuzzy in my memory. We make our way around the perimeter, trying not to appear conspicuous. We stop to eat when we catch women looking at us. At times I can hardly choke down the featured dishes of seafood, wondering if Han's hands harvested the fish.

By eight-thirty we've nearly circled the area, having

battled through crowds and entertainment. My anxiety increases; only a half an hour until the Ceremony.

We're on the side of the building that borders an alley. I close my eyes for a moment to picture it in my mind. This alley would open right across from the one leading to the subway station. I'm not sure if that has anything to do with it, but for a moment I feel a bit more hopeful.

Mia follows as I slip behind a woman leading a game of cards. We slide along the wall and edge behind a curtain into an area slightly sheltered from view. And then something smacks against my side. I look down. It's a doorknob, glowing the same blue color as the rest of the wall. I try to turn the knob, but it sticks.

I'm certain this is it. But of course, it's locked. My earlier frustration starts to build again. I kneel to peer at the doorknob, then gasp. The keyhole resembles the mechanism on the factory door where Han taught me how to pick; a pin and tumbler lock. The kind I spent hours on.

Damn it, Han, where are you and your lock-picking tools when I need them? I rock back on my heels, thinking. Maybe I could substitute... I meet Mia's gaze. "Do you have any bobby pins?"

She nods, reaching into her hair. She yanks out two and hands them to me. "Occupational hazard of being a ballerina," she shouts back.

I contemplate the lock, then yell again, "Can you get me a butter knife? One of the tiny ones, used for crackers."

She raises her eyebrows before slipping away. Soon she's back with a flat knife. I press the end to the ground, then take the heel of my shoe and push against it. The metal doesn't give way at first. I grunt and continue grinding down until I have it bent in a ninety-degree angle. Then I straighten the bobby pins and yank off the plastic on the ends. On one I bend the end up until I have another square angle.

Just like Han showed me, I insert the butter knife into the bottom of the keyhole. Holding it there, I stick the straight bobby pin in the top and push it all the way in. Then I quickly yank it back out, raking the pins in the lock. I do this a few times, then set it down and pick up the pin with an angle.

I turn the butter knife counter-clockwise, the way with more give. Keeping it held at the point where the resistance stops me from continuing, I insert the angled end of the second bobby pin into the lock and feel around for the pins. Upon locating them, I start trying to push them into place.

It takes seven tries, nine minutes, and lots of cursing (not that anyone can hear me), but I finally manage it: the knob turns. I gape for a moment at my success. I think Mia's gaping, too. I hand her my tools, since her dress has a pocket on one side, and slowly peek into the small room.

It's dim, but I can make out one occupant. A Like—or a boy?—sits on a chair. I step inside and Mia follows, pulling the door closed behind her. The sound from outside is dulled.

The Like looks up. I can't see his features clearly.

"Hello?"

He sounds confused. My brow furrows as I move closer. "Hello," I say slowly.

"Is it time?" He starts to stand, his face breaking into a smile. A Like smile with a wide grin and flat eyes.

"No, it's not time," Mia says behind me. I hardly hear her. There's a new buzzing in my ears. I recognize that smile. I saw it last week, right before I slammed my head into his nose. And I recognize the black hair. And the height.

"*Noah.*" My voice is shrill.

Noah blinks, looking at me. "I beg your pardon?"

I stare at him, thinking he should recognize me. Less than a week ago his eyes were glaring at me around Neil before he turned and fled from the alleyway.

But now his eyes are blank. Detached. Like's eyes. Framed by flawless skin. Like's skin. And a dress shirt and tie and shining black shoes. Like's clothing.

Han's voice floats through my head. *Basically, we just don't exist anymore. The Likes take our place in our own minds.*

"Noah," I beg, my mind balking against the realization

that I know him. *Knew* him, however briefly, and now he's gone.

I feel Mia staring at me. Noah stares as well. "Who?" His tone is still level, cordial, courteous.

"Noah. Is. Your. Name," I say, trying to make my words clear. Trying to slam them through his skull.

Noah shakes his head. "My name is Salvatore. You can call me Sal, though, if you want. When do I get to see Seffa?"

Mia grips my arm, hissing in my ear. "We need to leave. It's almost time."

I don't seem capable of independent motion, so she drags me out of the space and closes the door. I reach out, try to open it; it's locked again. Mia pulls me over behind a shellfish bar, where the music is not quite as loud.

"What," she yells, "was that?"

I just shake my head, feeling like my blood is boiling. I know it's impossible, but I could swear my insides are squirming as well.

Noah is, or *was*, a group N. Same as Han and Neil. So he's their age, their Year, 17, so *what is he doing as a Like?*

Is it not just Year 18? Can someone in Year 17 disappear too? Obviously it's possible. Which means it's possible that Neil…that Neil and Han…

"Morgan," Mia calls out to me again. I try to swallow, but I can't move. Then someone else runs up. Two someones. Dizzy as I am, I recognize Laney in her light purple dress. The other someone is, of course, Lloyd, sporting a matching tie and a halo of blond hair.

"Hey, come on, Morg!" Laney's voice is loud enough to reach my ears over the music. "They're starting the ceremony any minute."

The ceremony. I open my mouth. I'm not sure what I'm going to say, but I need to protest. But as soon as my lips part, the world lurches and I double over, vomiting onto Laney's dress.

She stumbles back and my knees slam into the floor. I press a hand over my mouth, fighting the nausea roiling in my stomach. I watch Lloyd's feet rush off, probably to get napkins, while Laney's feet stay put. I hear her exclaim over her dress, and how is she supposed to hide this, and did I do it on purpose, because if I did she didn't understand why I'd be such a bitch because I walked away from *her* yesterday, or didn't I remember?

Mia's crouching next to me, holding out a glass of water. I start to tell her you're only supposed to take a sip two hours after you've been sick, but the shellfish threaten to come up again if I speak. My mouth tastes terrible, so I take a sip.

I'm vaguely aware of Mia leading me out the door. I stumble about a block before I sink down against a wall, hugging my knees against my chest. The fresh air helps. We stay like this for a while. Mia doesn't speak, just sits and watches me. The street is empty. Everyone who's not at home is at the Amora. I still hear the music, even at this distance.

Finally, Mia whispers, "Why?"

I look at her, then away, then back again. I'm fighting the urge to cry. I want someone to understand. I need someone to understand. "I knew him." Past the lump in my throat, I force out the words.

Mia's eyes widen, but don't move from my face.

"Before he was a Like," I babble. "His name is Noah. He tried to choke me last Sunday."

Mia continues to stare. "Choke you," she repeats.

I nod. "But I don't blame him, because he was just trying to get some excitement, and anyway, he didn't know me."

"Morgan," Mia says quietly, "who did he think you were?"

It's my turn to stare at her, my train of out-of-control emotion crashing to a stop. What am I doing? I can't tell *anyone*.

"I need to go home," I whisper.

"But—"

"Please." I hold out my hand. Mia silently helps me up. We walk to my house without speaking.

Chapter 24
Morgan

Mom is surprised to see me, but Mia quickly explains how I got sick at the Amora. Mom thanks her for bringing me home, then takes me to my room and gives me ginger ale to sip like she does if I get a rare stomach bug, or eat too much sugar and feel sick. Swaddled in blankets on my familiar bed, I close my eyes and pretend I'm ten years younger, seven again, and my biggest worry is the skinned knee I got playing tennis might show if I wear my new capris tomorrow.

But before I know it the lights are dimming, telling me it's now eleven, past curfew, and I'm slammed back into my almost-seventeen-year-old mindframe, which feels almost too unstable to hold me.

My stomach doesn't feel as horrible as it did two hours ago. I flinch, thinking Mia must be really confused and kind of mad right now. And I really, really don't want her to be mad at me.

But that has to be remedied later. I sit up and slide out of bed as quietly as I can, change into the black polo and jeans and grab my hat. This is routine to me by now. Before I leave, I tuck some aloe cream from Mom's bathroom into my pocket.

As I slip through the hallway and down the stairs, I hear voices. I peek around the corner into the living room. Mom and Mia are sitting on the couch, talking in low tones. Mia has changed out of her dress and now wears sweatpants with one of my mom's boxy T-shirts. As I watch, my mom stands up, yawning, and climbs the stairs to bed, telling Mia she's free to stay in the guest room and thanks again for getting me home.

Mia's staying here?

I push away the complication. I have to talk to Neil. I

continue to the laundry room and out the fire escape. I trace the familiar path to the subway station; I'm right on time.

I pick out Neil's silhouette immediately. I follow him down the street to where I see forms heading into the Amora building. I force myself to concentrate so I'm not sick again.

Neil ends up a few blocks away, at the gym. I enter quietly, looking around to make sure he's the only one there. Then I run over to where he's holding his portable light–a flashlight, he called it–and peering into a cleaning supply closet. He jumps when he hears me, relaxing when the light washes over my face.

"Hey," he says.

I nod, taking deep breaths. His eyebrows draw together, shadows on his face in stark contrast with the features thrown into light. His eyes look almost black. I can tell he's still sunburned, and for a moment, characteristic of me and my rapid changes in topic, I forget about Noah and feeling sick. I step closer, pulling the cream out of my pocket.

"I brought this for you." I uncap the tube. He watches as I squeeze a bead of lotion onto my finger. Hesitantly, I run it over his nose, rubbing the cream in.

"Feel okay?" I bite on my lip.

"Yes," he mumbles, eyes cast downward. I press the tube of lotion into his hands.

"Use it, then. Doctor's orders."

He slides the tube into his pocket, meeting my gaze. All I see is the darkness of his eyes. "How was your week," he asks, his voice low.

And I remember again. As Neil pulls a rag and cleaning solution out of the closet, I say, "Not good. I mean, today. Today was not good."

He stops, looking at me, eyes questioning.

"It's Noah."

Neil's hand touches his throat. "The fight?"

"No. It's *Noah*. He's gone, Neil."

For a moment, Neil's face doesn't change. Then the meaning registers and his eyes go slightly unfocused. "The

Amora today."

"Seffa's," I murmur. "I found her Like beforehand. I went inside this room, and there was Noah."

"He was absent from class today," Neil says, his expression frozen in shock.

"He thought his name was Salvatore. He didn't recognize me. Neil, he's an *N*. A Year 17, right? I thought it was Year 18."

"It is," Neil says. "Usually. There have been a few times, a few, otherwise."

"So," I say, queasiness creeping back as I voice my fear, "*you* could potentially become a...one of them. Or Han."

"Potentially." Neil's expression is back to stony, his default face. I feel like a door has just been shut, one I hadn't realized was open until it closed. He walks to a row of cardio equipment.

"Why? I thought everything was even. Because of the twins."

"Like I said, sometimes there are accidents."

Right. *My* twin could be dead. Or worse, he could become a Like any day now for some girl in another Color City, and I'd never know. I feel my eyes burn.

"I hate this."

"Join the club." Neil scrubs the damp rag over an elliptical machine. Then he glances up, his expression softening for a moment, like the door has cracked open again. "Sorry."

"Don't say *sorry*," I tell him. "It's just that *my* birthday is in two weeks. *Two*. I need to stop it. I can't stand the thought that...well, duh." I close my eyes tight.

I feel a hand on my elbow, then arms wrap around me. Surprised, I lean into them, my head pressing against Neil's shoulder. The pine scent that clung to him when we first met is gone, replaced by a grassy smell. It's not unpleasant.

After a moment I feel something stirring inside me, and I lock my arms around his back, holding him tighter. I don't want to let go. I don't want to let him go back to City 4 where he's miserable and overworked and overtired and could be taken away and *gone* any day. I take another deep breath, letting the smell and the feel fill my senses, as if he's the only thing anchoring me to the world.

He doesn't let go like I thought he would. He always jerks away from me, as if I burn, but this time he stays. I want him to stay. I want him to stay here, with me, and be real and smell like grass and make my vision go dark with his eyes.

The stirring feeling is now writhing. Holding him tighter seems to make it worse. I open my eyes and look up, wondering if something's twisting in his chest, too. His eyes are so close to mine at this point, and in the nearness I'm struck by how *deep* they are. I've always noticed they're not the same as Like's eyes–flat and unchanging–and instead are animated and flash with emotion. Now that the door has reopened, they seem endless, like I could walk into them and just keep going forever.

Like the view over the wall in City 4.

Our faces are almost touching. There has to be a reason. Whenever Laney and Lloyd are this close they end up kissing. My mind plays the image of Laney and Lloyd at the ice cream parlor, kissing for minutes and minutes and not even noticing when I leave. But somewhere in the muddled memory my mind replaces Laney and Lloyd with me and Neil. Kissing. In an ice cream parlor.

Just the idea makes me inhale sharply, startling me, as if I'm suddenly waking up. What does that mean? Do I want to kiss him? Right now? In the gym, where a woman could walk in and find us and then what would *they* think it meant? It can't be good.

It's Neil who pulls away, dropping his arms while those thoughts are still spinning through my head. "I don't normally hug," he mumbles, reaching for the rag again. I blink, staring at his hand, because it seems to be shaking. Kind of like my knees.

"You should." At least, hug me. It does something. It causes the stirring feeling. As if I want something. Really want something. Something more.

He glances up. Our gazes lock and hold for a few seconds before the darkness tumbles back. I feel lost, but safe, as if being lost is okay.

Then there's a shuffling noise. We both whirl to face the row of treadmills and the darkness breaks. My vision returns and I find myself breathing hard.

"Who's there?" Neil's voice is rough.

A form rises and slips gracefully between two machines. I recognize her even before she steps into the light.

"Mia," I say dazedly. She's standing there, still wearing my mom's T-shirt and sweatpants. My gut reaction should be shock or anger, but instead I feel relief, because I was right, someone could walk in, and so I didn't kiss Neil.

Mia squints a little in the glare of the light, her expression mimicking that of a little girl caught trying on one of her mom's dresses. Sheepish, but not repentant. "Hi," she says as I clench my fists and wish for her to disappear. "So. I'm guessing this has something to do with the Like today."

"You *followed* me." My voice doesn't come out angry like I intend. Instead, it's confused.

She nods. "Sorry. But I watched you leave on the fire escape, and I was curious."

Neil is looking at me, eyes sharp. "Who is this?"

"This is Mia." I take a step back. "My friend." I put my hands over my face. "Mia, you don't understand–"

"I knew there was something *more* going on with you. Something different."

"No! Please," I beg. "You can't tell anyone about this. This is my fault. Neil doesn't even know who I am, I swear."

Crap.

"Right," Mia says slowly.

"Morgan," Neil mutters, "you are a horrible liar."

Which isn't even true. I've gotten quite good at lying. "You can't tell anyone."

"I *won't*," she says. "I swear, I swear, I swear. But please tell me what's going on."

Neil picks up his rag and cleaning solution. "I have to go clean." His voice is flat; the door has slammed shut again. "And then go die a probably painful death." Sparing me an unreadable expression, he crosses the fitness center to where the dumbbells are stacked.

For a long time I just stare at Mia while she stares back. Then I tell her, something inside me feeling a sense of relief as I finally explain everything that's been rattling around inside my head for the last seven weeks, desperate to get out.

When I'm done, her sickened expression probably mirrors my own. She's sitting by now, me with her, on the edge of a treadmill. She could have said any number of things, but her only words are, "You're right."

"I am?" I'm not sure what she's referring to.

"We have to do something. Pronto."

Through my anxiety, I actually smile. Minutes of silence pass before she speaks again. "Should we go back to your house?"

"You should. I'm staying here."

"Oh yeah. You go to his city on Sundays." She stands up, rocking back and forth on her heels. "I'll cover for you," she says before I can ask.

"Thanks." Seeing the look on her face, I add, "I'm sorry. That you know."

She cocks her head. "Everything's different now, isn't it."

I nod.

"At least I'm not alone, like you were." She shakes her head. "You should have told me sooner. You wouldn't have been lonely."

I make no comment, and she takes a step back. "I'm leaving now. Don't worry. I'm already working on a cover story. Fresh air makes you feel better, okay?"

I nod again and watch her leave. A few minutes later Neil appears behind me.

"Well," he says in an emotionless tone.

I turn to face him. "I trust her."

He looks at me for a while. Then he says, "All right. If

you trust her."

I want to ask, *Neil, do you trust me yet?* But I don't. I don't think I'd get the answer I want, not after what just happened. So instead I point to the extra rag hanging over the cleaning solution he carries. "Give me that."

My change of subject confuses him. "Why?"

"Because," I say, crouching and snatching up the rag myself, "I'm going to help you."

He doesn't agree, but he doesn't object either. And as he walks off to the machines he's working on next, I swear I see a hint of a smile on his face.

CHAPTER 25
Neil

The whole situation is so out of hand, I tell myself to not even waste time grinding my teeth or ripping out my hair. So another girl, someone Morgan says she trusts, followed her to where she met me during maintenance. So what if she knows. So what if I should be incredibly worried right now.

So why aren't I?

I don't know. I can't even concentrate. Instead, I just push the thoughts to the back of my mind and try to pretend it's a normal Sunday. Or, as normal as any Sunday has been the last few weeks.

Morgan and I head down to the swimming pond again, not encountering any trouble along the way. I think most of the boys in my year are still shaken by Noah's disappearance. His absence in classes is noticeable, and even though they don't really know what happened to him, they know he's gone, and that's enough.

As for Han, he's finishing invoices back at the dorm, like last week. He says he'll meet us "in time to heroically save you from any insubordinate thugs out and about today."

The pond sits on the edge of the district and the city, framed by the backs of two brick factories and the brick wall that is probably capable of shocking a boy if he even thinks about climbing over it. The water in the pond is drainage channeled from the streets. It last rained on Wednesday, so the muck has settled and the water is relatively clear.

It's not really a swimming pond today, as neither Morgan nor I are actually swimming. Morgan has her shoes off and her feet rest in the water's edge. One of the factories casts a shadow where we sit, sparing us from some of the sun's heat.

Right now I'm playing a few simple melodies on one of my whistles, which Morgan insisted I bring along. She lies back on the ground, which is as close to grass as one can find in City 4. It's really half gravel, with patches of grass and weeds sticking up here and there.

Once I notice myself repeating sequences of notes, I stop playing and set the whistle down before glancing at Morgan. "You must be bored."

"I'm not. What have I told you about assuming?"

More than once she's told me off for "jumping to conclusions." I shrug. Her hand reaches to the side, fingers closing around the whistle.

"Is there a trick to this?" She raises the wooden cylinder to her lips. "I mean, there must be. You have to cover different holes to get different sounds. Like a recorder, right?"

"You're assuming," I point out. "And I don't know what a recorder is."

"But I'm assuming correctly. A recorder is a stupid plastic thing that somehow passes for an instrument. All the girls have to learn them in early academy years." Furrowing her brow in concentration, she blows into the mouthpiece. A breathy sound results. She holds the whistle above her eyes, frowning. I hide a grin by pressing my lips together, hard.

"What did I do wrong?" She sighs and tries again. There's a faint whistle now. She glances at me and, seeing my expression, scowls before making one more attempt.

As much fun as this is to watch, I intervene. "Your upper lip is covering the first hole. And you're not exhaling sharply enough."

Morgan's expression reflects deep concentration as she inhales. The next moment, a high-pitched squeak emanates around the pond. Morgan's eyes widen and she yanks the whistle away from her mouth.

"Goodness," someone yelps. "Are you trying to shatter my eardrums?"

"Shush, Han," Morgan snaps, twisting around to give the new arrival the evil eye. "You'd be in no danger until 150 decibels. That was probably only ninety."

I can't help it. I start laughing, leaning back until my

shoulders hit the ground. As I laugh I'm struck by the difference, the difference between this and how I usually laugh. This time the only feelings I have are *good* ones. It's like the emptiness that fills my normal laugh has been filled.

After a minute I crack one eye open, still grinning. Han stands over me, glancing from my face to Morgan's. Then he points down at me, eyes narrowing.

"You are not scowling." He turns to Morgan. "He is not scowling," he repeats.

Morgan rolls her head to the side, meeting my gaze. "He's not scowling," she agrees.

"It's impossible!" Han clasps his hands on his head theatrically. "Unfathomable! Unheard of! Inconceivable!"

Morgan chuckles. "Okay, Mr. Thesaurus."

But Han's not done. "What did you *do* to him?" He clutches his heart.

"I failed at playing a whistle. By the way, you can have this back." She throws the sculpted piece of wood at me. It bounces off my stomach. I sit up and grab it, tucking it in my pocket. Han is still pretending to be in the middle of a coronary. I'd expect Morgan to whip out instructions on how he should react to save himself, but she ignores him, sitting up and crawling over to me instead.

"You've got gravel all over you." She reaches out and swipes her hand across the back of my shirt. I shiver.

"You do, too." I brush off her shoulders. As usual I feel the instinct to shy away from touching her. But I also feel an urge to move closer. I try to ignore both.

Off to the side, Han says indignantly, "Hello. I have gravel on me, too. On my knees. From when I keeled over in shock. Which is completely your fault."

"Get it yourself." Morgan stands and holds out a hand. I take it, and she pulls me to my feet.

"Well, fine," Han mutters. "I see how it is." He makes a point of groaning as he clambers to his feet as well.

Even though the grin has faded from my face, I still feel like I'm smiling.

* * *

Morgan says she's taking the noon subway back, to get a head start on smoothing recent events over with Mia. Only after she's gone does the sense of smiling disappear.

Even though the workday is hours shorter, it feels days longer. Maybe it's the heat, or maybe it's just because it seems so much duller in comparison to the morning. Maybe it's because I keep checking the time in between thoughts, thoughts that drift back to the swimming pond and gravel on her shoulders and a high-pitched whistle.

Either way, it takes ages for five-thirty to arrive. I'm so distracted by then that I walk right by Ms. Elliott, who's waiting outside the Year 17 dorm building.

"Neil?" She catches my arm. I stop, swaying slightly, and face her.

"Oh," I say. "Sorry."

She waves away my apology, letting go of my arm as she does. "I'm wondering if I could ask you a favor. Would you be willing to assist me in teaching the Year 5's and 6's again? You really helped them understand last time."

My eyelids are sticking together when I blink, and I have a headache that feels like a metal band is wrapped around my skull. But I nod. Just like last time, I can't refuse. In City 4, a woman's request is synonymous with an order.

"Are you sure?" She looks concerned. "Only if you want to."

What? "Yes," I say, rubbing my forehead.

"Thanks." She sounds sincere as she starts walking toward the class building. I follow a half-step behind.

Guiding the younger boys through arithmetic and spelling is easier this time, and Ms. Elliott really seems to appreciate it. Perhaps because she's busy while the kids are working; after her initial lesson, she retreats to her corner, and soon two other women come in. They huddle there, talking almost the entire class time, breaking up only after a long discussion.

At the end of this class Ms. Elliott pulls out a waxy sheet

with paper cutouts on it called stickers. I've used those before for labeling work. These are shiny, though, and star-shaped. She tells me to put one on each of the boys' notebooks.

Their eyes light up as I do so. When I pass Zaire, the boy I helped last week, he beckons for me to come closer. I crouch down.

"What is it, buddy?" I stick a silver star on his notebook.

He glances around, then whispers, "You're my favorite teacher I ever had, Neil."

I hesitate, at a loss for what to say. "Thanks, Zaire," I finally stammer.

"Will you be here next class?" He grips his notebook with both hands.

"I might be."

"Please?"

"I'll try."

He nods, then starts babbling about how he's working at the hatchery, carrying fish food to the older boys so they can feed the lots and lots of fish. A moment later Ms. Elliott escorts the boys out and back to their dorms. I cross the hallway to my classroom and wait for Han.

Over the next week I use my free time carving, making another whistle from the nicest piece of scrap wood I have. I concentrate harder on this one, making it as smooth as I can and trying to pitch the sound just right. By the time it's Saturday again it's done, or as done as I can possibly make it.

During maintenance I'm assigned to the ballet studio. Morgan shows up on time, accompanied by Mia. They're both dressed in jeans and polos, but only Morgan's wearing a hat.

Whatever, I tell myself, attributing my urge to scowl to the apprehension I feel about Mia. I don't know anything about her. It's like meeting Morgan all over again. Except I suppose it's not. Morgan trusts her.

Both of them help me sweep and wipe down the mirrors. I'm uncomfortable, having assistance. So I just listen to them as they talk, mostly to me. Morgan explains how she and Mia are trying to think of ways to delay her Amora and see other Number Cities. Mia mentions her ballet practice takes place in this studio.

At one point Morgan and I are both wiping dust from the space where the mirrors meet the floor, and we find ourselves in the same corner.

"Mia needed to be here," she whispers, swiping the last of the dust. "She needed to see again, for herself. I understand. But she's not coming to City 4."

After that my scowl lessens.

Back at City 4, the Sunday progresses like usual with us going to the swimming pond, except Morgan keeps getting distracted, her expression slipping into one of deep concentration, like when she tried to play the whistle last week. Each time I remember that I feel myself grin, but then I'll frown, wondering what she's concentrating on now.

Finally, around midmorning, she explains. "This is the last time I'll be here."

I turn sharply, facing her. She's sitting next to me with her knees tucked up, one arm wrapped around them, the other lying loosely by her side as her fingers absentmindedly explore a patch of grass.

"What do you mean?" Something like panic flashing through me.

"The last time I'll be here while I'm still sixteen," she says, and my head stops spinning. "Before my Amora." She almost has to choke the word out. "It's Friday."

"I know." I let out a long, slow breath, trying to make myself calm down. Her Amora's been on my mind all week.

"I'm going to appeal to the mayor. Ask to postpone it. Mia gave me the excuse of needing to focus on my career studies. But I'm sure the mayor won't buy it. I'm on thin ice with her anyway."

I don't respond, choosing to study the pond instead. Half of it is black from the shadow of the factory and half is gray, reflecting the steely clouds overhead.

"I don't know how I'll handle it, having one of them

constantly close to me. I can hardly stand the other girls' Likes, and they don't even pay attention to me."

Can't say I'll ever have that problem.

"What a terrible birthday present," she mutters. At the same moment a warm drop of water splashes off my nose. Another one follows. The surface of the pond ripples as a steady drizzle begins. Morgan doesn't move. Neither do I.

"Speaking of your birthday," I say after a while.

"I'd rather not." She stares at her jeans, which are splotched with dark blue now.

"Well." I reach into my pocket and pull out the whistle I carved this week. I hold it out, resting my arm on my bent knee, staring at it. Raindrops dot the wood. "Quickly, then."

She glances over, first at the whistle, then at my face. I hold the whistle out to her. "I made it this week," I say, in as much of an offhand voice as I can manage. "It's some sort of approximation of a birthday present." Boys don't get birthday presents, largely due to our having no idea when our birthdays are. But I've seen the women talking about gifts and exchanging festively wrapped items over the years, so I'm familiar with the idea.

She takes it, slowly turning it over in her palm. "It's…"

"I know. Not much." I look away.

"There you go again. Assuming."

I turn my head back, watching her fingers fold over the wooden piece.

"I was going to say, it's beautiful."

I stare at her. Strands of hair stick to her forehead and cheeks as she examines the whistle. Her expression isn't joking or sarcastic, though. She means it. She really means it.

She unfolds her knees and one leg settles against mine. She's looking back at me now, eyes so close I can't even focus on them both. A raindrop splashes off her nose and the spatter hits my cheek.

"Neil?" she whispers.

"Yeah?"

"Do you trust me yet?"

199

No words come. Do I? Do I trust her? I don't know. How I feel about Morgan is so foreign to me, so complicated, so *different*, I can't imagine words encompassing it.

Before I can try to explain this, she's so close her features are blurry and I can only freeze, my thoughts scattering, leaving nothing coherent behind.

Her lips brush mine, almost curiously. That's all it is, at first, and just the touch makes my breath stutter.

"Morgan?" I try to speak, but she kisses me again. This time her lips stay, pressing harder, and my hands are on her face and her hat falls off and her lips part as she sighs and it's like the world is spinning backward as rain streams down our faces like tears.

CHAPTER 26
Morgan

That's what it was, the stirring, the writhing inside of me, when I hugged Neil. I've never felt anything like that before, nothing as strong as the desire to kiss Neil, to bring him closer. And it happened again at the pond today, when he gave me the whistle and it was so smooth yet slightly uneven and I could feel where the blade made each line and edge, and those imperfections made it even more perfect.

Just like Neil. I'd studied him, taking in each of the scars and flaws making him Neil. Making him so different from a Like, because Likes don't have scars and they definitely don't have flaws. Which, I realized, is their biggest flaw of all.

It's almost a blur in my memory, what happened, before we heard footsteps and pulled apart, before Han came around the corner. But that blur carried me through the day, and now, sprawled on my bed in my dark room with an even darker window, a smile still hovers around my mouth.

I'd do it again. I'd do it a million times again. And I will. Even if I get a Like, even if I start career and grow old, I'll still meet him, every night. We can keep a secret, I know we can. We'll talk about it once I'm done with my Amora.

Oh.

No.

The smile is gone, scared away, and my shoulders are rigid as I clench my fists. I forgot. In the wake of this morning I forgot the whole scare of Seffa's Amora and how it was Noah, which means Neil could disappear any day to be turned into a Like.

For someone else.

For a girl who wouldn't know him, and never could, because Neil won't even exist.

Why? I want to scream. My blanket glows sharply as I

grip the fabric, twisting. Who decided we can't be together? Who decided I belong in the soft, artificial world and he's forced to be in the cruel, too-real world, and we can't coexist? Who made it this way? Because I hate them. I truly hate them.

I hadn't realized it was possible to feel two such opposing emotions with the intensity I do, and in close proximity to each other. The intense happiness, the extreme anger. Emotions this deep aren't part of my side of the world, the cushioned one. There's never a need for them.

And now they're so real they feel raw inside me.

All week I'm wracked with nerves and anxiety and dread. The appointment I make with Mayor Vee on Monday doesn't help at all.

"Honey, your big day's on *Friday*," she says, as if I need reminding. The walls of her office match the frosted tips of her hair today. "This request you have, to *postpone* it, it's a little last minute, don't you think?"

"Sorry." I rub the bottom of my shirt between my fingers. "But I just…I have a lot going on right now. I really feel that to be the best doctor I can be I need to be able to focus, and to do so I'd prefer to get my Like at a later date." I've practiced this speech with Mia.

"No one's ever asked for something like this before." The mayor's tone is polite, but her eyes are sharp as they rake over me.

I force myself to smile. "There's a first time for everything?"

She returns the smile thinly. "I suppose. However," she says, and I feel my stomach plummet past the purple floor, "I don't see how a postponement could work out. Everyone gets their Likes on their seventeenth. I'm sure you've been busy planning, and your friends, too. I'd hate to disappoint them, wouldn't you?"

"Um, yes, but–"

"Also, your Like is so incredibly excited to meet you.

We shouldn't disappoint him, either."

The room seems to freeze, waves of sound creating a buzzing noise in my mind. My Like. Is excited. To meet me. How could she know? "He–he's–" I stammer.

Probably mistaking that for excitement, Mayor Vee says, "I know, isn't it sweet?"

"You've talked to him?" Please say no.

"Yes," she says. I swallow. "But that'll be our little secret." She winks. "I know I'm not supposed to mention anything beforehand, as per tradition and all, but between you and me, he's adorable."

My mind still buzzes, at a standstill and going a thousand miles per hour all at once. I don't trust myself to speak.

"So, even though I admire your tenacity, I don't think postponing your Amora would be a good idea." Mayor Vee's tone that tells me this settles the matter.

There's no way I'm falling asleep tonight, which is probably for the best since there's something I need to do. Something I need to check, and it's causing a gnawing sensation to grow in my abdomen. Panic.

It's a Monday night, but around one in the morning I pull on my jeans and polo and hat and sneak down the fire escape. Neil explained once how the maintenance schedule runs, and from what I remember, Monday nights there are boys in the Aqua district. Aqua is next to Cobalt. Going by street names I manage to find my way to the district.

Now I just have to wait until the boys come out from where they're working. Then I can follow them and find the subway station here. Wherever it is I have to be on it.

It's half an hour before I catch a break. In a small building, which I think is a coffee shop, I see a glimmer of light. I quietly slip inside, something I'm good at now, and make my way around the edge of the room. A boy is wiping drips of dried coffee off the counter in the dim light.

The light also illuminates his black shirt, jeans, and

blond hair. It only takes me a moment to recognize him and take in the impact of the coincidence. When he turns his head and his glasses reflect a flash of light, I'm positive.

"Han."

Han looks up, not jumping or exclaiming or doing anything theatrical. I guess when he's serious he leaves that stuff out of his act.

"Morgan."

I stride over and he stands so we're face to face. Well, face to neck. He's taller.

"How did you–?"

I cut him off. "Is Neil okay?"

He nods before speaking. Relief washes through me, creating more buzzing in my ears, but I welcome this noise.

"Why wouldn't he be?" Something like concern is clouding Han's already shadowy face.

"I wasn't sure, I thought maybe he...my Amora...the mayor said..."

"One sentence at a time," Han suggests.

My hands are on my forehead, kneading, getting caught in my bangs. "I was so stupid, Han. At my evaluation, I started giving characteristics like Neil's, and I didn't mean to, but then I wasn't worried because you said Year 18's were the ones turned into Likes, but Noah got turned and so I realized, because of what I said, they might choose Neil, and when the mayor said she'd talked to my Like today, I thought it could be too late, which is why I felt so guilty I don't even know what I would have done if Neil wasn't okay."

Han is silent for a moment. Then he says, "When I said, 'one sentence,' I didn't mean you had to make everything into *one sentence*."

I hear myself laugh weakly. It's okay. It's okay. It's not Neil.

"Neil is fine. I saw him right before maintenance. I mean, his back is sore and all from bending over in the fields all day, but other than an impending spinal disorder and a new inclination to smile, he's his normal self."

I breathe deeply, something I haven't done all day. I feel like hugging Han, I'm so relieved. "There's more time," I say to myself as much as to Han. "I wasn't able to postpone my Amora, but at least it's not Neil who's…gone."

"Neil better not be gone," Han says. "Or he'll have to answer to me."

I search to meet his gaze. "Keep an eye on him, okay? Please?"

Han lets out a long-suffering sigh. "I always do. It's my second full-time job." Then he meets my gaze and says, seriously, "I will."

Han refuses my offer to help him clean and tells me I should go home, not get in trouble, and preferably get some sleep because I'll, in his words, need my wits about me. Can't say I disagree. And now that I've spoken to Han and know Neil's not the Like Mayor Vee talked to, I don't need to travel to City 4. So I return to the Cobalt district and reenter my townhouse.

There I spend the rest of the night assessing my life. The imminent Amora. Making sure Han and Neil stay safe. Keeping up the appearance of normality and my studies in doctor career training. Juggling it all while thinking of a way to locate my twin before it's too late.

It's like trying to think my way out of a locked trunk, and the best tool I have is the Power of Positive Thinking. Which is not so plausible in this case.

On Wednesday I try to focus during career training. Take a break and think solely about what we're learning, which are still the basics of first aid, because it's the one part of my Blue City schedule I actually look forward to.

After training I'm spread out on my room's floor with my Pow propped up in front of me, giving the appearance of studying. My mind is actually as far away as, maybe, the cirrus clouds in the sky today. Some menacing clouds hover on the horizon, but directly above the Cobalt district the sky is bright, eye-watering blue, causing sunlight to stream in my windows and fall across my stomach.

Mia and I have discussed ways to get to other Number Cities, but we haven't figured out a plan that doesn't involve first traveling to another Color City. And then we have the issue of curfew and, primarily, how to even find the subway station, which could take a week, by which time I'll have a Like and he'll insist on coming.

How am I going to endure the proximity to a Like? *My* Like?

I push the unproductive thought away and continue my previous train of thought. In order for Mia to generate ideas on this topic, I had to first explain to her how I got to the Number Cities and then the way I got to Neil and Han's dorm and every complication surrounding it. She asked if she could go to City 4 sometime soon, her expression nervous but determined. I'd told her I didn't know. It would be a huge risk, and maybe too much for the women not to notice two extra people on the subway.

My thoughts are interrupted by an incessant knocking on the door. Then it's flung open. Laney walks in and towers over me, arms crossed.

"Look. I'm willing to put the whole thing at Sef's Amora behind us. Ross told me you just felt sick and of course it wasn't anything personal. I didn't doubt you, of course. Well, maybe I did a little, because you've been acting weird lately. Really, really weird. But I'm sorry I called you a bitch. So, let's talk."

"You're already talking," I point out.

"Yes, I am, because you aren't. Now say you forgive me."

"Does it count as forgiveness if it's a mandate?"

"Yes. Say it."

"I forgive you."

"Good. I forgive you too." She drops down and settles cross-legged next to me. "So, here I am. You have my undivided attention. Your Amora is the day after tomorrow and I don't even know what your color scheme is. I feel like a crappy best friend and I really don't like feeling that way. So tell me."

"I don't have one yet."

"You don't have one yet?" She reaches up to grab a fistful of her hair, which is now platinum. "Gah! I don't understand. They're *due* today!"

"I didn't like anything I came up with." Not a lie.

"Morgan, what are you going to *do*?"

"I don't know. Black and white, maybe."

Laney opens her mouth to protest, then looks thoughtful. "Interesting. Yeah. I like it. I mean, *everyone* goes for color, right? Monochromatic is…mysterious. Sexy. Kind of has…*je ne sais quoi*."

"Yeah."

"You could send out messages to everyone telling them to wear black and white only." She pulls out her Pow.

"Tell you what," I say. "Why don't you do it?"

"*I* do it?" She blinks.

I nod. "Why don't you put it together? You like planning. You're good at it."

"Can I do whatever I want?"

"Yes. Surprise me. Just not too over the top."

"No smoke," she promises, jumping to her feet. "Great! Okay. If that's the case, I should go. Lloyd's in your living room, waiting. He and I can run over to meet with your friend Mia's mom who's a designer and discuss shades and all." She starts for the door.

"Shades?" I stare after her. "It's black and white. There *are* no shades."

"And I'll need a different *dress*," Laney adds to herself. Before she leaves she says, "Don't worry. This is going to be *awesome*."

Somehow, I doubt it.

CHAPTER 27
Neil

"Guess what today is?"

Han's voice intrudes on my sleep. Well, it's not exactly sleep. I'm floating in a half-conscious state of mind, watching disjointed images roll across my eyelids. I've been this way for a while.

"Oi."

I ignore him. This–the images, the not sleeping–has been happening all week. But I don't mind, so I also don't see why I should have to open my eyes until the alarm sounds. What could be more important?

"I am patiently awaiting your guess."

She isn't like any of the women here. I've known that for a while. She doesn't treat us like we're anything less than she is. She actually seems to care, too, and she is so insistent on doing the right thing, even if none of us can decide what the right thing is.

And she makes me laugh.

Han's voice interrupts again. "All right, I lied, I am actually not patiently waiting. I am very impatiently waiting."

The images are already blurry and fading. I try to hold onto them, but they trickle away like sawdust through my fingers. Next thing I know my eyes are open, nothing but the dim ceiling and Han's disgruntled expression to fill the gap.

"Usually I'm the one who takes a while to wake up," Han remarks. "This may be a historic occasion. Shall we record it?"

I mumble something along the lines of "no." I squint against the lamplight as I pull myself up. Thin sheets twist around my ankles, and my fingers fumble to free myself.

Han studies the knots. "Sweet dreams?"

"Just trouble sleeping."

"Ah." He gives me a knowing glance, though I'm not sure what he thinks he knows. However, he wastes no further time before clapping his hands together. "All right, back to my question."

"What question?"

"The question in which I inquired what day today is."

I blink hard, trying to clear the leftover haze from my eyes. "It's Thursday."

"Correct!" Han claps again. "And what does that mean?"

The only thing I can think of is it's two days from Saturday, but somehow I doubt Han would wake me up just to tell me that. "I give up."

Han shakes his head, too-long hair smacking his face. "You are no fun. It's–"

I sit up straight. "It's the day before Morgan's Amora." Something clenches in my gut. How did I not remember that first? It's consumed my waking thoughts for days. I must still be half asleep.

Han frowns. "You're right." He's not looking surprised; instead, he appears concerned. "But–"

"Are we going to do something? Is that why you woke me up?" I know this is irrational. What *can* we do? "Nothing" is the logical response. But there's an illogical part of me that doesn't agree, that hates the idea of a handsome, *perfect* Like wrapping his arms around Morgan. She says she can't stand the Likes and their sappy attitudes, but who knows what will happen when one turns relentless adoration on her?

Stop, I tell myself. I'm being ridiculous. It can't possibly change her, can it? She won't stop caring, will she?

"Neil. *Neil.*" Han sounds exasperated at having to call my attention back again. "No. That's not what I'm saying." Then he adds quickly, "I'm saying we can use this morning to investigate, because it's Thursday and the office building is empty."

"Oh." My brow furrows. "I almost forgot."

"I know." Han sighs. "Where do you think I've been going these past Sunday mornings?"

I look up. "I thought you were doing invoices. Stuff for work."

"Please. That's computer stuff. I could do it in my sleep. If I had a computer here while I slept, I mean. I've been trying to find other places to search, in case this last office turns out to be nothing."

"Why didn't you go in the last office?"

He shakes his head. "I thought you should be with me when I do."

"Oh."

"Oh." Han mimics my reply, then pulls open our dresser. I stand before he can throw a shirt at me, so he just hands it over instead.

The streets are quiet and sky is dark as we leave our dorms and steal through City 4. Streetlamps are our main source of light, and even as the sky turns from inky to indigo there are still shadows around the yellow glow. It's good to know we can disappear if we need to.

Han and his lock picks grant us access once again. He must have picked that lock a dozen or more times, but today he pauses as he does, giving me what I'm sure is a meaningful look. I can't see it clearly, though. I'm casting a shadow across his face.

"Last office," he whispers unnecessarily as we enter. I know it's the last office. I've kept track as carefully as he has, and I hear the double meaning in his words; it's our last shot here.

Han picks the inside lock with relative speed. He works better when under pressure, using nerves as a stimulant rather than a hindrance. In half a minute he's pushing open the door, revealing a dim interior, but not so dim that we can't make out the shapes of a desk and a couch.

Our minutes run down and my frustration runs up as we check drawers and cabinets and under the couch. Han insists on peering behind it too, but I've already given up on anything being contained in the furniture. Anxiety chases itself through my gut, and standing still doesn't help.

I force myself to move, not to check any more furniture, just move. I walk around the edge of the room, fingers trailing against the walls. They're smooth, but not in the way the Color Cities' walls are. These walls are coated with slick paint, the work of boys. I spent a few days in Year 14 painting offices.

A ridge passes beneath my hands. I blink, and actually look where my fingers are. I have to squint, because the corner I've walked to is darker than the rest of the room. But I can make it out. It's a door, a closet we overlooked because the light doesn't reach it.

"Can I theorize, since you've ceased pacing, that you have sighted something of interest?"

I don't look at Han "If you're asking if I've found something, I think so."

He's beside me in a second. "Does it require lock picks?"

I reach out and fumble for the handle. When I find it I close my fingers around it, the cold, metallic shape turning easily. "No."

"Shame." Han sighs, but leans in as well to peer into the space. It's so dark I can hardly make out any shapes, and I can't locate a light switch. Han shoulders me aside and steps into the closet. "Definitely crates. And if I can just find the handle– Here." He pauses. Then, "Neil."

I already know. "They're in there."

"A lot of paperwork." He's unable to maintain his light tone. It wobbles, slipping into something unrecognizable. It might be apprehension, or even fear, but I'm unfamiliar with these emotions coming from Han, so I'm not sure.

He steps out of the closet, clutching a few cream-colored folders, moving them to catch the light. He opens one, showing the two papers inside. There's a little information on each one, just short, abbreviated text.

"This is the first one," Han whispers. We both lean closer to read.

NAME/ NAJEH
BY/2221

BD/0103
STAT/NONE
EYE/ BR, HAI/BLK, RAC/AFR.

The second paper is similar, with a list of places worked dating to the beginning of this year, and an added *CD/0321.*

"*CD*," Han murmurs. "That has to be it."

"What?"

"Conversion Date." Han meets my gaze now. "This is Najeh's file. Remember him? He hardly talked, but I worked with him in textiles one year. He disappeared in March." Han jabs a finger at the number. "0321 has to be the date. March 21st."

I vaguely remember. "So these are ours," I say, my voice sounding distant even to my ears.

Han takes the file and ducks back into the closet. I hear a scraping noise, and he drags the crate out and kneels beside it, flipping through the folders as soon as he has enough light.

"N-a-t…N-a-t…"

I hang back, suddenly afraid to know. It's what we've been looking for, and now that it's right in front of me I can hardly bring myself to look at the box.

I wish Morgan was here; I'd be braver.

A folder is shoved into my hand. "Mine," Han says and turns resolutely away, continuing to paw through the files while muttering, "N-e-i…"

I raise the folder so I can see it. On the tab is *NATHAN 17.* He should have opened this right away. His curiosity has to be eating at him like it is at me, but also like me, he has to be scared.

"Open it," Han commands, still not glancing up. "I'll find yours. Just open it."

I do. There's only one sheet in it, the shorter one.

NAME/ NATHAN
BY/2221
BD/0630
STAT/ULTIMATUM
EYE/ GR, HAI/BLN, RAC/CAU.

"There's no *CD* on here." I force the words out. There's a mix of relief and disappointment gathering in my throat, making it hard to talk. "Just the one sheet."

Han silently holds out a hand. I pass the folder to him and he takes it, keeping one finger in the crate to mark his spot.

He doesn't speak at first, gaze flicking back and forth across the page. Then he says, "What does *STAT* mean?"

"Let me go get my dictionary," I say, nerves translating into sarcasm. I almost apologize, but the words die in my throat, somewhere below the blockage.

Han ignores my comment. "I think it must mean *status*. I thought that's what it was on Najeh's file, because it said *none*, and of course a baby boy wouldn't have any status. Because I presume these are our original files, from birth." Han's speech is getting slower, calmer, like it does when he's trying to think and not get upset at the same time. When he's just upset he talks faster. "But mine is different. It says 'ultimatum.' You know what 'ultimatum' means, right?"

"Vaguely." I know he'll tell me anyway.

"It's basically a threat. *Or else* is an ultimatum. We have to cooperate, or else. But how can *I* be an ultimatum?"

Now he looks up, chewing on his lower lip, face both sharp and thoughtful.

"Wouldn't that mean," I say hesitantly, "you're the ultimatum? If *Ultimatum* is your status?"

"Well, yes, but while that makes sense, it also *doesn't*." Han speaks as if he's explaining something obvious. "Because who would care enough about *me* for me to be used as one?"

This stumps me, too. "And if it's from when you were *born*…"

Han nods, his expression now distant. "Exactly. Why would I, just a *dead* baby, matter?"

"I–"

Before I can continue–not that I have any idea what to say–Han holds up a hand. "Wait. We can think about this later. We're almost out of time."

He slips his file back into its alphabetical spot, then frowns at the crate. I glance at the clock. It's 5:26. We're going to be late, but we haven't found my file yet.

"Han, hurry," I murmur, though I'm sure he knows.

Han flips two files back and forth, frown deepening. "I am." He thumbs over more tags, checking the end and the beginning again. Dread settles heavily in my stomach. "But Neil, it's not here."

"It's not there." I repeat the words because I can't think of anything else to say.

"It's not. It should be right between *Nehemiah* and *Nell*, but it's not even in the box."

I blink, taking longer than necessary, not wanting to leave the darkness behind my eyelids. "Like Kellan's."

"Yeah. Just like we couldn't find Kellan's."

Now Han glances at the clock. "Neil–"

"Let's go."

Han shoves the crate back into the closet and we run. Outside, the patchy sky creates new kinds of shadows as the rising sun filters through the clouds. I reach the fields late again, get shocked and threatened and glared at again, and start working again.

Disappointment and confusion threaten to overwhelm me. Why wasn't my file there? Kellan's was missing, but he still disappeared. It must just be a mistake, a misfile, a lost paper.

At least we found Han's.

I try not to think about it. I try to think about something else, something like Morgan. That helps, having the opposite effect of thinking about the file. But when I do remember the file, my mood plummets again.

I work for hours, wanting and dreading the end of the day, the last day before Morgan's Amora, tired and wide-awake, hopelessly sad and impossibly happy, the alternating shadows and sunlight from the sky changing as rapidly as my emotions.

CHAPTER 28
Morgan

Thursday's and Friday's doctor career training lessons are fun. Mostly because they're distracting, as I'm doing something I can focus my entire mind on, which means I'm not think about Neil and not feeling a disorienting mix of joy, relief, and hopelessness.

During Friday's lesson Dr. Iltchenko sets up a demonstration, simulating a house call where we act as the first responders. Her Like is used as the model, and Ms. Iltchenko has each of us perform a walkthrough of the first aid required for whatever scenario she gives us.

When it is my turn she says, "He dropped a table leg on his foot. It's swollen and he says it hurts too much to move it or to stand on it."

Her Like obediently sits and removes one of his shoes. I kneel and start the preliminary tests to see if it's broken, asking questions, pretending to feel for swelling and anything out of place.

"Now assume you think it's a sprain, doesn't require emergency medical care, and the woman of the house would rather self-treat him. What would you do?"

"Splint it with a pillow until I can get a professional splint, elevate, and instruct to ice occasionally."

Dr. Iltchenko grins. "Brava. By the way, happy birthday!"

Hearing this, there's a chorus of "happy birthday," from the other girls. I try to smile back, try to appear somewhat grateful. I really do. But I can't.

My hands start to shake on the way home. It's time. The evening I thought wouldn't ever happen is happening. My desperate-hour options seem to be to run away or break my own leg to get a postponement. Considering I can't risk drawing attention to myself, the former is nixed. It's probably impossible anyway. Where would I run to?

Jury's still out on the latter, though.

My Pow alerts me multiple times as I walk. I see three messages and one call from Laney, a message each from Jeanne and Seffa, and one call from my mom. I ignore them all, shuffling home as slowly as possible.

I pass an office building in its closing hours. It doesn't look like there's anyone in the lobby. I walk in for no good reason. The stairwell's propped open. No Good Reason still leading me, I climb it and keep climbing fourteen stories, slowly, until I reach the top and walk out onto the roof garden.

The gardeners and career gardener trainees are all gone from here by now. It's just me and the many plants swaying in the slight breeze. My feet take me to the edge. I lean against the wall lining the roof, gazing out at the dizzying drop beneath me. Well, a detached thought says, here's one way to break my leg.

I'm not sure how long I stay here, just staring out at the city. The people walking on the street are tiny, and at times my vision tilts from vertigo as I think about how high up I am. Then those thoughts slip away and I feel like one of the plants. As though I should just stay here, and be watered, and turned toward the sun in the morning. What a nice life.

But finally the heat from my Pow becomes constant, telling me multiple people are trying to message or call, and I snap back to my semi-reality.

I arrive home around 6:15. Ross ambushes me inside the door, exclaiming over how I need to hurry, or I'll be late. How horrible *that* would be! He ushers me to my room where four women are crowded around the door: Mom, my grandma, Mia, and Laney. Mom wears a simple white gown, Grandma's decked out in a silvery black number, Mia's dressed in a black and white dress, and Laney is in sweats with silky white material flung over her shoulder. They're all standing around, not talking, the feeling in the room distinctly awkward. As soon as I enter, though, they snap to attention, rushing over, all of them speaking at once.

Mom: Are you okay? Where were you?

Mia: What is it? *Who* is it? Do you know? I mean, what took you so long?

Laney: Omigod, this is going to be spectacular. The décor is all set up, black and white like you said, and I found a *perfect* white dress for me. What dress are you wearing? It better be fabulous. You never get a second chance at a first impression, you know, and by the way, your hair really needs to be pulled back or *something*.

Mom: Do you need anything?

Grandma: I've never thought it a bad thing to be fashionably late, but you might be pushing your luck here.

Laney: Maybe a clip or headband, and definitely dangly earrings. But what are you *wearing*? I can't proceed until I know.

Mia: [Signals with eyes for me to signal back if I suddenly found out who the Like is.]

Laney: I demand that you tell me.

Mom: I can't believe this is happening. Today. Your Amora.

Mia: [Looks relieved when I shake my head.]

Grandma: Hon, go drink some chamomile tea or light an incense candle. You're bloodless.

Laney: *I* can't believe you are this late. Just saying.

Once I tell them, without lying, I'm late because I took a stroll to collect my thoughts, they back off a little.

"Mom," I say, "do you have a dress I can borrow?"

Mom nods and goes to retrieve one, coming back with a black empire waist. I spend the next half hour putting on the dress, ignoring Laney's objections that it's not as uber-flattering as another style might be, ignoring Mom when she asks again if I'm okay, ignoring Mia's expressions of concern because they only increase the dread in my stomach, ignoring Grandma's attempts to "jazz up" my hairstyle, and most difficult of all, ignoring the anxiety tightening my airway and turning my stomach to a ball of jelly.

Therefore, when Laney says a slightly disgruntled but still excited, "Tada," and pushes me in front of a mirror, I don't feel like looking. When I was little I always imagined this moment, how I'd look like a princess out of a fairytale. I also imagined I would smile confidently and give myself a thumbs-up. But as I meet my own gaze right now, all I see is me in an old dress and a petrified expression.

Laney's in her dress by now. She leads the way down the hallway. I trail behind, stopping at the top of the stairs. All it would take is a little shift in my center of balance and bam! No Amora tonight.

Mia, two steps down, pauses and turns her head. With an agile twist she's leapt back up those steps and is next to me, gripping my arms.

"What are you thinking?" Her look telling me she knows exactly what I am thinking. "You can't, Morgan. You'd only be delaying the inevitable."

"I might have thought of something by then."

"You'll be incapacitated. You won't be able to go to City 4. Or do anything, for that matter."

I briefly weigh this option against walking down the stairs and to the Amora that will inevitably follow. Sensing I'm not convinced, Mia goes on, "You can't hurt yourself. The Like has already been converted. He's been a Like since Monday, at least. There's nothing you can do for him now." Her gaze locks on mine, pleading. I squeeze mine shut.

"Morgan." Mom's voice calls to me softly, and I let Mia lead me down the stairs.

The welcome speech from Mayor Vee starts as soon as we arrive. I tune out her voice, trying to focus elsewhere, studying the black and white lights glowing dimly and the checkerboard dance floor. The speech ends and the loud music starts and monochromatic swirls spin around the walls. The dance floor fills immediately.

I want to go back to that little room and pick the lock again. I need to see who it is. Despite Han's promise, the thing I've lost the most sleep over is the possibility they converted Neil to be my Like, because of what I said at my eval.

I forgot that, as the birthday girl, I'd be constantly surrounded by people wishing me happy seventeenth and exclaiming over how darn exciting this is and how they remember me from when I was in only my second academy year and they taught me how to recite the visible color spectrum. I try to slip away on multiple occasions but never succeed. I can't send Mia to the room because she is unable to pick the lock. And I like having her near me, so I can shoot her panicked expressions and she'll actually understand.

As nine o'clock draws nearer, my airway draws tighter. I'm already feeling lightheaded when the music slows down and my name reverberates around the walls. Hands buffet me toward the stage. I've done this so many times in my mind. When I was younger I'd literally dream about walking up these few stairs to the platform, standing above everyone in a spectacular dress to hear the mayor say the words of the Presentation Ceremony.

Maybe that's why, as the mayor starts to speak, I feel like I'm trapped in a nightmare.

"Morgan Waters," Mayor Vee says, taking a step closer to me. One of her hands reaches out and rests on my shoulder. Lights glint off of her long black dress, and thick lines of makeup circle her eyes, making them bulge, intensifying the way her gaze bores into mine. "Congratulations. Seventeen years ago you were born, and now you're ready to take one of life's largest steps. Following this will be a career and a daughter. Are you excited?"

I stare at her, then force myself to nod, feeling my tight neck muscles shake as I command them into motion.

"Well," she says, half of her mouth curving upwards. "Without further ado, then…"

The crowd turns expectantly. I turn too and peer into the mass of bodies. Most are facing the path being formed from the edge of the floor to the stairs. But a few people face me. I see Mia and my grandma and Ross, who's beaming and hugging my mom close. And I see my mom's face, looking back at me. Streaks run down the side of her face. Tears. Her gaze meets mine.

I hear, "Morgan, meet Mitchell." And I finally look at the figure walking up the path, who stops at the bottom of the stairs, and says, "Wow, you're gorgeous," and I feel my knees turn to gelatin and all I want to do is sink down and cry with relief, because it's not Neil.

I remain standing, swaying slightly. It's not Neil, I repeat, it's not him. Thank goodness. I don't know who it is. I don't recognize him. But it's not Neil.

The Like named Mitchell hesitates on the steps. I know I'm supposed to run down there, into his arms. It's not a rule, it's just what's *done*, and my not moving seems to confuse him and the crowd. But Mitchell recovers smoothly, bounding up onto the platform.

Up close I'm more positive Neil's where Han said, back in City 4 with a sore back. The features are similar to Neil's and what I said at my eval. But while Mitchell's eyes are dark, they're not as dark as Neil's, his hair is lighter, he's built wider, and I see he's about an inch too tall when he's close enough for me to tell the difference.

And once he is close enough, his arms reach out and encircle me. My face presses against the shoulder of his white dress shirt, the collar of it scratching my forehead. He smells like soap and new clothes.

"It's so nice to meet you," he whispers. I remain silent as I hear the collective, "Aww," rising from the crowd. I want to get out of the spotlight and go somewhere alone and quiet, where I can think. But as I walk to the steps with Mitchell and he takes my elbow to *help* me down the steps, I realize time alone is going to be so much more difficult to come by from now on. I've seen how my mom has to practically order Ross to leave her alone. It'll be like that for me, too.

The music starts again, way too loud for comfort. It's like the first half of the Amora all over again, people converging on us to exclaim their congratulations. For once I don't blame myself for having trouble breathing or feeling claustrophobic. In fact, I can use it. After half an hour I've had enough. I want away from Mitchell and the mob. Claiming I need a drink, I wrench myself away and push through the crowd, ducking around people until I'm sure I'm no longer in the line of vision of the ones who saw me leave.

I make it to the drink counter, keeping my eyes low. "Happy birthday," the Like making the drinks says as he hands me a glass. I look at it. Red wine. I guess he assumed I wanted to try alcohol, since I'm legally allowed to now.

What the heck. I tip my head back and take a long sip. The liquid burns slightly as it slides down my throat. Must be strong wine. Feeling only dizzier, I set the glass down and get water from the nearby table, draining it in only a few seconds.

"*There* you are," I hear Laney exclaim. She runs up to me, expression glowing. Lloyd is a half step behind, gripping her hand. "Isn't it amazing?" She's babbling. "Mitchell is such a cute name. He's so adorable, too, the way he hugged you." Then she blinks, looking around. "Hey. Where is he?"

"I needed space." I clutch my water glass with two hands. Laney sees it, and her mouth forms an 'O.'

"Breathing?" she asks. Right in front of Lloyd.

"No," I say sharply, looking at him.

"Relax," she says. "He figured it out on his own."

I take a step back. "He *what*? When?"

"Don't get upset." Laney tries to sound gentle. "Last night. When I explained how there wasn't going to be smoke or anything."

"It's okay if you have breathing problems, Morgan." Lloyd's blond curls are a white halo in the pulsing lights. "I don't mind."

"*I* mind." I squeeze my glass too hard and the next second it slips, crashing to the floor and shattering. I feel cold ice cubes land on my feet.

Lloyd immediately pulls Laney away. "Be careful! The glass is sharp."

"She's not stupid," I tell him.

"He's just being cautious," Laney says.

Mia appears over Laney's shoulder. "What happened?" She glances down at the floor and steps lightly around shards of glass and ice, like the ballerina she is, to stand by me.

"Dropped a glass," I mutter. Not that anyone can hear. What I can hear, however, is a shout of "Morgan," as Mitchell, in his white shirt, runs up, wraps his arm around my waist, and tugs me away from the mess on the floor.

"That could cut you," he says, like I don't know.

"I am aware of the dangers of sharp objects."

He smiles. "I know you are. You're going to make an amazing doctor."

"How do you know I'm going to be a doctor?"

"It's obvious by the way you treat other people. You have such compassion, of course you'd want to be a doctor."

My hands are on his side, pushing, creating space between us. "You don't even know me," I say shakily.

Laney, Lloyd, and Mia stare at me. Mitchell only blinks.

"Forgive her," Laney interjects. "She's just nervous."

"I understand," Mitchell assures her.

No. No, he doesn't.

I glance at Mia, meet her gaze, and then look away, out at the crowd, and my vision blurs until all I'm seeing is a throbbing mass of motion. It's nauseating. I close my eyes, wishing myself away, back to my room, to doctor career training, the park, somewhere as far from here as I can be.

I'm wishing for City 4.

CHAPTER 29
Morgan

Mitchell knows the way back to my townhouse, as if there's a map of the entire city inside his head, which, I remind myself, is possible. I feel fatigue wearing at me, making my feet heavy as we climb the few steps to the front door. Now that what I've been dreading all week is over, my body remembers what sleep is and how nice it sounds right now. Like an escape.

Mom and Ross are inside, having just arrived as well. I share a long, unreadable look with Mom as Mitchell and Ross exchange cordial greetings. They met each other already; Mitchell introduced himself earlier this evening, of course.

Ross asks if anyone wants something to drink, and maybe we could sit in the living room and chat. I decline, announcing I'm too tired.

"Oh." Ross winks at me. "Why don't you show Mitchell his room before you get some rest?"

I nod and turn to walk up the stairs. Mitchell follows. I stop in front of the door next to my room and push it open. The space inside has generic black furniture and walls set to glow with a grayish light.

"You can buy different furniture, if you'd like." My voice is toneless. "I didn't know what you'd want." And maybe I didn't want to think about the fact that you'd exist.

"What I'd want?" He sounds confused.

I rub my eyes with the backs of my hands. "You can also change the wall settings. Now, I'm really going to get some re-re-rest," I say, stuttering through a yawn. I start to turn and retreat, but Mitchell's voice stops me.

"Wait. Morgan?"

I slowly look over. He's biting his lip, but he's not chewing on it, like I do. He's just holding it, as if he wants me to *think* he's biting it. "What you said, about me not knowing you. I'm sorry about whatever I did to make you upset."

I suppress another yawn. "Oh," I mumble. "Forget it." What can I say? What he did was get turned into a mindless nothing. And that, no matter how annoying he is, isn't and wasn't his doing.

"I want to make it up to you," he insists, and steps closer. *Déjà vu.* Except this time, instead of hugging me, he cradles my chin in one hand and places the other on the small of my back, tipping my head up and pressing my torso against his. The outer fabric of my dress catches on his shirt, feeling scratchy.

When he kisses me I'm too surprised to move away. The closeness is what shocks me first, then the distance, because there's no connection except, obviously, the physical one.

He opens his mouth to deepen the kiss, and now all I feel is the urge to keep my own mouth shut. Because as he's kissing me, Mitchell, right here, in front of me, all I can see is Neil and rain and my hand interlocked with his. A pain, a *desire*, tugs at my heart, and I sigh, but it's not for Mitchell. It's to be back in the memory.

Mitchell pulls away before I've thought to do so myself. He looks at me expectantly, starting to smile. I take a step back and his hand slides off of my waist, dropping to his side.

"Night, Mitchell," I whisper, and turn around for real this time, entering my own room and closing the door.

Once inside I pull off the dress and put on pajamas that feel amazingly comfortable compared to the dress. I wash all the makeup off of my face in my bathroom and finally fall back against my pillows.

But I can't fall asleep. It's like the fairytale I read in my early academy years, the Princess and the Pea. Where the princess can't sleep because of a pea under many mattresses, and then her Like comes and finds her. I'm not sure what the pea ever had to do with it, but that's not the point.

Then I realize what it is. I turn over, onto my stomach, and reach under my pillow. From between the soft fabrics of my sheets and pillowcase I pull out the whistle. I put it under my pillow the night after I got it. It hasn't bothered me until now, or maybe I just didn't notice it nagging at my mind because there was so much else to think about.

I kick my legs off the bed and stand up. Not sure what I'm doing, I go to my closet and feel around the floor until I find my boots, the unique ones with the laces. My hands fumble with one boot, pulling at the laces, finally yanking one free. Then I thread the cord through the last hole in the whistle and tie it securely around my neck.

Now, when I fall back on my mattress, I am able to drift off to sleep almost immediately.

Even before I open my eyes I can tell it's raining. The light is softer than if the sun was shining into my window. Also, I don't have the white noise neutralizers turned on, so I can hear raindrops falling against the glass.

The rain gives me a warm feeling, a shiver. The last time it rained I was in City 4.

My door creaks. I open my eyes slowly, fighting a yawn as I hug my blanket around me. A cord, rougher than the soft fabric, rubs against my neck. It's the shoelace. I vaguely remember tying it around my neck last night.

Mitchell steps in, his face glowing. "Good morning."

"Not really," I mumble. Mitchell's appearance is all I need to remember yesterday and how everything is even more complicated now.

He walks to the window. "But you love the rain."

"No, I don't." I contradict him, lying through my teeth. I prefer rainy days to sunny ones, but there's no way Mitchell should know that already.

His face takes on a confused expression. "Okay," he says, not sounding like he believes me. Not sounding like anything. "Tint the window, then?" Without waiting for a response he slides his finger across the dial by my window. The pane darkens to black, eliminating my view of the street.

I wipe the glare from my face as he turns back to face

me, smiling again. "Someone's here to see you."

"Who?"

"Dr. Iltchenko. She's talking to your mom right now."

I blink. He continues to smile at me. It's distracting. "I'll be out in a few minutes." I nod pointedly toward the door.

Getting the hint, he leaves. I heave myself out of bed and change. One advantage of short hair is, some days, it doesn't need attention to be presentable. I pat my hands over it in the bathroom mirror before I head downstairs.

Mom and Dr. Iltchenko and her Like are sitting in the living room, sipping coffee and talking in low voices. As soon as I walk in I know I'm in trouble. I stand at the edge of the room, watching the two women turn their heads to see me. Dr. Iltchenko looks sad, and Mom just has a guarded expression. Dr. Iltchenko's Like politely studies his coffee.

There's a moment where I debate turning around and dashing away. But instead I just walk in and stand in front of both of them, wondering how much more I can handle before I just start running and don't stop until I pass out.

Dr. Iltchenko clears her throat, looking distinctly uncomfortable now, much different than the confidence she exudes when standing in front of our training class. "Hi, Morgan."

"Hi, Dr. Iltchenko." My voice is flat. I'm just waiting now for bad news.

Dr. Iltchenko clears her throat again. "I have something to talk about."

For some reason I imagine what Han would say in response. *Really? I'm disappointed. I thought we were going to have a staring contest.* And Neil would give her that look he gives me sometimes, when I ask what he thinks is a stupid question. My mouth twists into a wry grin. At least, it feels wry.

"Go ahead."

She nods. "Well, the thing is, Mayor Vee talked with me this morning. And she told me you have been hiding something. That something being a breathing problem. Er, is this true?"

My silence seems to be taken as a *yes*.

Dr. Iltchenko purses her lips, looking down, before saying, "I'm so sorry, Morgan, but if that's the case you can't be a doctor. You could be a physical therapist, if you want, or biologist, but you know the rule. Conditions like breathing problems can come on at any time, and they're real issues if they distract you from an emergency. I'm surprised you haven't seen a doctor about this. Actually, you really should."

I hold up my hand to stop her, my throat feeling unnaturally thick. "I know."

Mom catches my eye, then turns away. Someone puts a protective arm around my shoulders. Mitchell. I shrug him off and step away. Dr. Iltchenko stands, looking as if she's about to hug me, and I step away from her, too. She puts her hands awkwardly by her sides. "Er," she says as her Like rises to his feet as well. "I should go."

Her Like fetches her raincoat from the hanger and helps her into it by the door. Before she leaves Dr. Iltchenko looks back at me. "I'm going to miss you in my class, Morgan."

"Yeah," I say, my voice hollow. "I'll miss it, too."

The door opens. Summer rain falls in torrents outside. Then the door closes, and the room's walls start to close in on me.

"I'm so sorry," Mitchell babbles next to me. "I didn't know you had breathing problems, either. But don't worry, you'll find an equally fun career, there are so many options."

Mom beckons me to her. I stride across the room and sit down beside her on the couch.

"I can see why the rule's in place," she says. I look away, fighting the burning in my eyes. This is the first time we've really spoken since our fight before Seffa's Amora, and she's telling me off.

"I–" I begin, but she keeps talking.

"But it's stupid," she says. I face her now. "You would make an amazing doctor."

"You're not surprised to find out," I mumble. "Did you

know?"

"Of course I knew." She says it quietly, too low for Mitchell to hear. "But I guess I didn't know it was more than an annoyance. Honey, is it a severe problem? You should have an inhaler."

"I don't *want* an inhaler." Now I sound like a little girl. The rational part of my brain seems to be fluctuating between hyperactive and numb, trying its best not to let the news sink in too deeply.

"To be safe," Mom says, and then goes on, "But you never told anyone. How does the mayor know?"

I stare at my hands. How *does* she know? I think back, part of my mind telling me the answer is obvious.

Oh.

Mom's saying, "I'm really sorry. Look, let's spend the day here. I'll take off work and we can make cookies or something. I think we need to talk." She pulls me in for a hug, but my eyes start to blur and I stand up.

"I'm going for a walk," I say, standing up.

Mitchell protests, like I knew he would. "But it's pouring, Morgan!" I hear as I reach the door. His footsteps approach, and in the corner of my vision I see him grab my coat from the closet and hold it out. "Here, take this. I'll hold an umbrella."

"No." I turn the doorknob and open the door. Heavy, damp air washes over me. "You are not coming."

"But–"

"Mitchell, stay here," I say sharply. "Please." Then I step outside and shut the door.

I'm soaked within a minute of walking, but I like the feeling. My hair sticks to my cheeks as water streams down my face, and my sandals squelch when I take a step. I walk for ten minutes, hands in my pockets, not stopping to duck underneath shelter once.

I reach my destination and buzz up to the correct apartment instead of going inside the building. It's another two minutes before someone comes to the door.

228

Laney stands inside, in a T-shirt and shorts. "You buzzed?" She squints at me, then smiles. "Hey! You're soaked. How are you? Where's Mitchell?" She steps aside to let me in.

I don't move. "Why did you have to tell?"

She raises an eyebrow, still holding the door wide. I brush strings of dripping hair out of my eyes, damp shirt feeling cool against my skin.

"What do you mean? Morg, you're shivering. Come in. Lloyd's at the store, getting icing. We're going to stay home and decorate cookies because it's so icky out. Want to join us?"

"No, I don't want to ice cookies or watch you and Lloyd make out and stare at each other for hours. But I *do* want to know why Dr. Iltchenko is telling me I can't be a doctor."

Laney's mouth falls open. "Oh my gosh! Morg, I'm so, so sorry." She steps out of the doorway and into the rain, throwing her arms around me. "Why?"

I push her away. She stumbles back, grabbing the doorframe for support.

"Why do you think?" I grit my teeth. "Someone told Mayor Vee about my breathing."

She blinks. "And Mayor Vee told Dr. Iltchenko?"

"No, Dr. Iltchenko looked in her crystal ball."

Laney's usually the sarcastic one, so my response only throws her more.

"So…so why are you glaring at *me*?"

"Well, *I* didn't tell Mayor Vee."

"And you think I did?"

"You're the only one here I've told," I point out.

"The only one *here*? What does that mean? You told Mia, didn't you? Considering she's your new best friend, why don't you ask *her*?" She fixes me with a defensive stare. "*I* didn't tell. This isn't *my* fault."

I arrange my face in an equally stubborn expression. "I only told you. But *you* told someone."

"Morgan," Laney shouts, now squeezing the doorframe

so hard her knuckles are white. "I. Did. Not. Tell. Mayor. Vee."

"You. Told. Lloyd."

Through the haze of rain I see shock flash across her face. Then she shakes her head once, then again more forcefully. "He wouldn't," she says firmly. "I know him. He wouldn't do that."

This makes me even angrier. "What do you *really* know about him, Lane?" I shake hair off my face. Thick droplets spray outwards and are lost in the torrent. "Anything? Do you know where he's from? What kind of a person he was for the first seventeen or eighteen years of his life? Do you even know his favorite color, or do you only care that he calls you beautiful and puts napkins on your ice cream cones?"

We glare at each other for a few seconds. "You *hate* napkins on your ice cream cones," I add, trying to control my voice.

She tears her gaze away, trying not to let it land on me. "Yeah, well, what do *you* know about him?"

"More than you," I say, control failing and voice shaking. "And I know he betrayed your confidence. How long does it take to get icing, anyway? He could have stopped by the mayor's office, no problem."

Laney steps back, fully inside the building now. "No, I don't believe it."

"Just listen to me, Laney, okay?"

"*I don't believe you.*" She reaches for the door. Before I can say another word, she slams it shut.

I squeeze my eyes closed. Water that's been pooling on my eyelids and lashes spills over. I can't tell if it's rain or saltwater streaming down my cheeks.

CHAPTER 30
Morgan

I stay a while at the park, sitting on a watery bench and watching puddles swell in the grass. I consider going to Mia's, but remember she has career ballet most Saturday mornings. Besides, I really don't want to talk to anyone right now.

Well, that's a lie. I really, really want to talk to Neil. Or even Han. But neither is an option until tonight.

The damp shoelace around my neck rubs against my skin. I tug out the whistle and blow into it. It makes a shrill, wet sound that probably cracked a few windows in the nearest building. If the release of frustration were a noise, this would be it. I do it a few more times, finding it oddly satisfying.

When I finally go home I spend the rest of the day trying to be passive (not difficult) and mollify Mitchell at the same time (quite difficult). I explain to him how Sunday mornings are my alone time, and he should take that time to sleep in so he'll have the energy to hang out in the afternoon. "Maybe we can go rock-climbing," I say, trying to find something to keep him from disagreeing. "Or something."

"Okay." He smiles. "That'll keep you distracted, too."

"Right." I try to minimize the sarcasm in my tone. "Sure it will."

I dress in the black polo, jeans, and hat tonight, like all other Saturdays, and sneak out. As I make my way through the dark streets I let the back of my mind enjoy the routine feeling of this. It's something I know. I know why I'm out here. I know I'm doing something, not just being an ignorant, mindless woman like the rest of them.

I'm sure Mia would have wanted to come, but I didn't

contact her. I think she'll understand. Maybe. I just need the familiarity of sneaking out on my own tonight.

I find Neil in my mom's building again. Of course. The doctors' offices. Irony is having a lot of fun tonight.

He's alone, cleaning the floor my mom's office is on, like last time. And like last time I'm able to slip in through the closet passageway and find Neil a few doors down. The lighting is dim, and he's on his tiptoes, back to me as he reaches up to wipe off a shelf. Suddenly there doesn't seem to be enough oxygen flowing to my brain.

I walk up. "Have any extra rags?"

Neil drops his heels and spins to face me, looking slightly unsteady. "You're here," he says. His gaze meets mine.

"No, I'm not. This is actually my hologram form. The real Morgan is back in her townhouse sleeping. If she could sleep."

"Aren't you in an interesting mood." Neil wipes the back of his hand across his forehead.

I nod and step forward, wrapping my arms around his torso, a week's worth of longing to touch him again coursing through me. His shoulders tighten in surprise, but he immediately pulls me close.

"Here, proof I'm not actually a hologram," I say. "Why are you so surprised I came?" He still smells like grass. And sun, or what I'd imagine the sun to smell like. Not the hydrogen and helium and fiery explosions part. The warm and bright part.

"Um..." I feel Neil swallow. "Your Amora. I thought..."

"You thought I'd want to spend every possible minute with a perfect shell of a former person who annoys the hell out of me," I say sourly. Or, as sourly as I can with half my face resting on Neil's shoulder.

"I was worried."

"Don't be ridiculous."

Neither of us moves for a long time. I feel like my insides are twisting, turning, but on the outside I'm perfectly still, fighting it. Then I back away, before I'm lulled into staying right here forever. We have work to do. Then we can go back to City 4 and walk to the swimming pond and sit down and.... "So. Any extra rags?"

Neil silently hands me one. We start to dust. Once we've moved a few offices over I say, "I'm not going to be a doctor."

I glance at him and see he's raising an eyebrow. "Laney's Like found out about my breathing. He told the mayor. And since it could be a *distraction*, I am demoted to potential Physical Therapist." I let out a long breath. "But you know what? Maybe it was for the better. I thought birthing could be an in or something, and I could see how the messed up system works on the inside and figure out how to stop it. But now that I'm not going to be a doctor, and I don't have that hanging over me, maybe I can do something big."

"Big," Neil repeats, kneeling on the floor to wipe up a spill.

"Big," I say again. "I was thinking, you know, America hasn't had contact with any other continents for over a century because of the–"

"Wars." Neil finishes my sentence.

"Yes. And I'd always assumed their societies are just like ours, except, well, with their own culture and stuff mixed in. But, of course, now I don't know. And if they are different then it's possible someone there could help us."

"Possible," Neil says, "if it weren't for the CommWall."

"I know. That blocks all information from passing between the continents. But what if I could physically get somewhere? Europe, for example. If I could find a way to get there."

Both of Neil's eyebrows rise now. I look away. "I know, it's unlikely. But I need to try *something*. I'm still in the brainstorming process. And by the way, do you have any more ideas about how to get to other Number Cities?"

He shakes his head. "Sorry. I spent the week thinking about your Amora, believe it or not."

"So did I. But I need to get back on track. I'm also trying to figure out how to access birth records." I meet his gaze. "To find my twin, you know."

He nods, then beckons for me to move with him to the next office. My mom's office.

"I'll never work here." My mind plays a memory reel of all the times I've sat in here dreaming about the day when I'd have an office of my own.

Neil glances at me as he starts dusting my mom's desk. I walk over as well, stopping next to him. I wipe off a few of her reference tools, but it becomes difficult when my sight gets blurry from tears.

"Hey," Neil says, and I feel fingers brush across my cheek. "Morgan?"

I turn my head to face him and find myself looking straight into his eyes, even though my vision is swimming. Our noses are almost touching. The closeness doesn't startle me like it did with Mitchell. Well, it does, but in a different way. A way that makes my stomach do acrobatics and goosebumps appear on the back of my neck and reminds me of the last time our faces were this close.

He's the one who leans in this time.

He presses my back against the desk, one hand cupping the back of my neck, tilting my face to meet his. The edge of the desk digs into my back, but I only want him to press harder. Our breath mixes, my eyes close, my heart races.

It's entirely different than when Mitchell kissed me. Something passes between us. I'm not sure which way, but it's there, a connection that makes shivers race up and down my spine. I can feel surprise, fear, confusion, and something else, something so strong it hurts, and I can't tell which emotions are mine and which are his.

His hand trails down my side, leaving tingles blossoming in its wake. Suddenly he pulls me closer, off the desk, and guides me to my mom's chair. The cushions mold around my back and his mouth molds around mine. His knee is next to my hip and his hand is by my shoulder, supporting

234

him as he leans over me. I trace his back and he traces my lips with his tongue and in this moment I can forget Dr. Iltchenko's visit, the fight with Laney, the Amora, and needing a plan of action. I don't have to think about anything. In this moment, I can hear my heart beating in my ears, and I'm short of breath for an entirely new reason.

Minutes, hours, maybe days later Neil speaks, lips moving against mine. "Morgan?"

"Yeah?" I breathe.

"I trust you."

Tingles shoot up my spine and explode in my mind. I clutch his shirt, yanking him down in the chair with me, dizzy with happiness, because he's mine. He is mine, and more importantly, I am *his*.

The women who claim to be in love with their Likes aren't. They can't be. They're just flattered and content with the attention the Likes give them and they don't know anything otherwise, they don't know the feeling of a real person holding her heart in his hands. They don't know what it's like to actually be in love.

But I do.

CHAPTER 31
Morgan

As soon as I get back on Sunday, and as soon as I shake off Mitchell, I hurry to Mia's apartment building. I have to talk to her. She'll make sense of the situation. She's rational. And I have to share. My heart feels so full it could burst. I want Mia to understand that there's more, so much more.

I sprint up the stairs in her building. As soon as I veer around the corner of the eighth floor platform I see someone bounding down the stairs toward me. I try to skid to a stop, but my momentum sends me tripping forward. Mia leaps out of the way.

"Ow," I say as I grab the railing, spinning around and landing on my butt.

"Yeah." Mia holds out a hand to help me up.

"I was coming to find you." I brush off my shorts and the wrinkled shirt I threw on after getting back.

"You found me," she says, and continues down the stairs.

"Where are you going?" I fall into step with her.

"To visit Reece, my friend. You know, you met her at my ballet. I told her I would."

"Can I come?"

She shrugs. "Sure."

Once we're outside, on the street, Mia turns to me. She looks like she has a million questions on her tongue, and I can imagine what at least half of them are. I hold up a hand, indicating for her to let me speak first.

Suddenly, I don't know how to start, to explain. I say the easiest thing. "I got kicked out of doctor training."

Whatever she thought I was going to say, this was clearly not it. "Why?"

My mouth twists into a scowl. "I have breathing

problems. And no one but Laney's known for my entire life, until Laney decided to let her Like in on the act. So guess what? It's not a secret anymore."

"And you can't be a doctor."

"If you have that kind of *distraction*." My voice is like black coffee on the bitterness scale.

Mia doesn't say, "I'm so sorry," like every other girl would, and I'm grateful. "What are you going to do?'"

"I don't know." I tug at the bottom of my shirt, adding to the wrinkles already present. "Maybe I'll just run away."

"To where? From what you've told me, it sounds like you'd inevitably get caught in City 4."

"I know. I would. So I was thinking Europe, maybe."

"Oh," she says. "That makes sense. Except for the part where Europe is across a few thousand miles of saltwater and we have had no contact with them for over a century."

"That's what Neil and Han said. Except Han added, 'But I'm sure those are minor points in the scope of your brilliant plan.'"

"I want to meet Han someday." She's heard about Han from me, but, of course, she's only ever met Neil.

"Maybe you will."

"So what else has been going on? What about Mitchell?"

I brush hair off my damp forehead. "Mitchell is just like every other Like, Mia. There's nothing else to say. I had to promise him we'll go rock climbing later today in order to get him to leave me be now." My foot scuffs against the smooth street. There are other women, Likes, and girls walking on the street, but none of them are close to us.

"And your trip last night?"

"I met Neil in the doctor's offices." I kick at the ground again, adding, "Where I'll never work. Anyway, we talked." Now I feel a hint of a smile tug at my mouth. This is where I should tell her about kissing Neil and how anything we've ever felt is nothing at all in comparison. To something real.

"About what?"

I open my mouth. I'm going to tell her, I really am. But

something stops me. For some reason the words don't come. As if saying it would shatter the bubble of joy surrounding the memory. As if it's a secret, but a good kind of secret. A happy one.

"Europe," I say instead. "But later on I decided to go back to my mom's office, to see if I could figure out what she knows. About anything. I looked in her filing cabinet and at the paper books in her glass case, but I only had a few minutes before I heard a security woman arriving. So I quickly put the books back and slipped through a passage in my mom's closet."

"She didn't find you?"

The answer should be obvious. Still, I wince. "No, she didn't. But apparently opening the case or the cabinets sent out some alert, and she blamed Neil, who was cleaning a few doors down. She used the remote thing, the shock." I wave a hand at my neck. "He didn't tell me, but it was obvious."

Mia shudders visibly. She's more inclined to handle mental distress than physical. I mean, obviously the idea of little chips being planted into boys' necks disturbs me on the psychological level. But the physical level, the level where hands get shaky and internal organs disappear at the thought of blood and surgery other medical procedures, doesn't register for me like it does for her. I told her about Han's burn last week and she looked like her stomach was trying to claw its way up her esophagus. I'm glad I don't feel that, even if I can't be a doctor anyway.

By the time we arrive at Reece's apartment building we're both quiet, lost in thought. Mia knocks on the door. "Ryan's probably going to answer." She makes a face.

But Ryan doesn't answer. No one does.

"She said she was home."

"Maybe she and Ryan went for ice cream," I mutter, staring down the hallway.

Just as I finish speaking I hear it. A scream, from inside. Mia hears it too, and her eyes widen. I only hesitate a second before I grab the handle and push the door open. I dash inside, looking around, baby-pink walls glowing back at me from all sides.

"Down the hallway," Mia says, but I'm already running through the apartment. There's another shriek, and I come to a halt in front of a bedroom.

I hear Mia running up behind me, and my mind snaps into action. "Mia, send a message to my mom and the birthing facility, then bring me towels. Now."

"Reece is having–?"

I don't hear the rest; I've already entered the room.

There's blood. Lots of it, soaking the sheets of Reece's bed. She's moaning now and crying, fingers digging into her mattress. I speak in a low, calm voice. "Reece, it's me, Morgan. We met at Mia's ballet. I'm here to help you. Everything's going to be okay. You just need to listen to me and this will all be fine."

Mia appears with towels. As soon as her gaze falls on Reece, her face turns the color of Laney's green Amora dress, then drains to white. I point for her to turn around. The last thing I need is for her to faint. She turns and squeezes her eyes shut.

I let my calm, rational doctor side take over. I've watched a birthing before with my mom, and I've heard countless stories. The procedures are burned into my mind. I keep talking as I work, keeping Reece from panicking. After a while there's another voice, a tiny one, also crying, and I'm holding a baby in my arms.

"Is there any string?" I demand, knowing Mia can still hear me. "I need to tie the cords."

She spins back around, gaze avoiding the bed. "I don't know."

"Never mind." I use one hand and clumsily untie the shoelace around my neck. When I pull it free I hear the whistle clatter to the floor, but I don't waste time in finding it. I just rip the string in half with my teeth and start working, speaking soothingly again as I make sure there's nothing blocking the baby's airway.

239

As I do, I realize this is the boy.

Thinking about that, though, would not be good. I shove the knowledge to the back of my mind. It's easy. I have a job to do. I know what to do. I can focus.

Reece starts to whimper again. "Mia, go wait by the door for my mom," I tell her, giving her an escape. She takes it, disappearing from the room.

When my mom arrives I step back and let her take over. I'm breathing hard, but not with difficulty. Can't they see that I don't panic during situations like this? How well I can handle it? Then I shake my head. No. It's all an illusion anyway. I have more important things to worry about than not being a doctor.

After a while my mom presses two bundles into my arms: the babies, blankets wrapped loosely around them. They're both screaming, thank goodness, so their lungs are healthy. I busy myself with wrapping the blankets more securely around them, and I know I let myself think about how I know. I know which one should be dead, the boy.

Mia stumbles back into the room and pulls her gaze to Reece, who isn't crying anymore. She's just lying there, propped up on a pillow, face shiny with sweat. "Ryan went to get groceries," she whispers, eyes closed. "I'm not due for two weeks. I was having contractions, but I thought that was normal for this time period. After he left, though, it just started to happen. My Pow's charging and I couldn't reach it."

"Shh," Mom says. "Everything's fine. Sudden labors happen sometimes."

"My daughter?" Reece cracks her eyes open.

"She's fine too," Mom assures her. "The medical staff will be here any moment to get everything in order. You need to relax and let me stop your bleeding."

Reece's eyelids drop again. Mia meets my gaze. I tilt my head to my right, indicating the baby, telling her that's the one.

Mia takes a step toward me, but then there are voices in the hallway, and someone comes up behind her and pushes her to the side. Two women enter with a stretcher, and a third follows, all three dressed in white medical attire like Mom.

Mom starts supervising the transition of Reece from the bed to the stretcher, and the third doctor approaches me. "These are the twins?"

I raise my eyebrows, forcing myself to stay calm. "What else would they be?"

The doctor reaches out to take them. I step back. Only now do my lungs feel tight. Only now am I starting to panic, because I realize what's going on. What'll happen if she gets the babies.

"I need to see them," the doctor tells me. "I need to take the dead baby."

"Both of them are alive," I say, my voice decidedly less steady now than when I administered care to Reece.

The doctor is close enough to me now that she can check the two babies. Then she yanks the child from my right arm. "Correct. But this one will die in a few minutes. You're holding the healthy baby."

She turns and walks toward the door.

"*Wait!*" I lurch forward. "You can't. That child is still alive. If medical care is needed, then start giving it. Don't assume—"

"Don't talk about what you don't understand," the doctor says, looking back at me, the baby still in her grip.

"Morgan," Mom says in a warning voice.

"No." I stare at the wailing child. I know where he's going. Just like Neil, when he was a baby.

I wish I could have saved Neil.

The words come in a rush, without direction or permission from the rational part of my mind. "The baby's not even clinically dead yet. We can save him."

There's a beat of silence. Mom, Mia, and the doctor stare at me. I can tell my expression is just as shocked as theirs are. Then the doctor says smoothly, "Please stop pretending to be a doctor, Morgan. You don't know the processes taken in these situations and, from my understanding, you never will."

She walks out the door.

The other doctors finish loading Reece onto the stretcher and wheel her out of the room as well. Mom stands still, trying to meet my gaze. I'm breathing hard, harder than before, gaze not moving from the baby girl in my arms, who I then hand to Mom.

"Morgan?" Mom sounds lost, like she doesn't know how to feel.

"Go," I say. "You have to take Reece's baby to the Medical building. *Go.*" *Go away.*

Mom blinks, then leaves as well.

I finally look at Mia, and she looks back. It's a while before either of us speaks.

Finally, she says, "It's true."

"Of course it is. And I messed up. I blew it."

"How could you have stopped the doctor from taking the baby?"

"Any number of ways. But that's not what I mean. I said *him.* They all heard it. I'm sure at least my mom and the doctor understood. She has to know I know."

"Morgan, you can't blame yourself for that."

"Who else is there to blame?" My voice rises.

"Everyone," Mia says in frustration. "Whoever created this system, and the rest of the women for going along with it."

I press my hands over my face. "What do we do?"

"We relax. We clean up or do something we would do normally. You're overreacting. In the heat of the moment, I doubt anyone really caught what you said."

What Mia lacks in ability to handle physical duress, she makes up for in handling mental breakdowns. I lower my hands. "Okay," I say, grasping at the hope she's providing. I just hope it's enough.

Mia visits me after her career ballet class Monday. I've been alternately lying on my floor and sitting at my desk doing nothing all day, and I hear when Ross lets her in.

"How nice of you to stop by," he exclaims, his voice carrying up the stairs. "I'm sure your visit will cheer up Morgan."

Right now I sit at my desk chair, which I've wheeled to the window where I can watch the first traces of evening appear in the sky. I have my knees tucked to my chest with my arms wrapped around them. When Mia appears in the doorway I nod at a spot on the floor beside me.

"Reece is doing fine," I tell Mia as she settles down. "So is her daughter. She named her Tesia. Reece is on IV's because she lost a lot of blood, but she'll be okay in another day or so."

"Good." Mia smiles.

"Nothing was really wrong yesterday, either," I continue, still gazing out the window. "Just a freak labor. I mean, she needed medical attention, but it was just fast and early, that's all."

"It's still lucky you were there."

"Yeah, well." I shrug, then rapidly switch topics. "Mia, I have to tell you something."

The words that have been careening through my mind are desperate to get out. I couldn't say them yesterday, but I have to say *something* today.

She nods for me to continue.

"It's Neil." I try to find words that won't break the bubble but still convey the feelings welled up inside me. "I think I might love him."

The expression on Mia's face is more thoughtful than surprised. "So what are you going to do about it?"

It's such a Mia thing to ask. "I don't know," I say, which is *not* such a Morgan thing to reply. I usually know, or at least have an idea, of what I want to do, and therefore what I'm going to do, because they're the same.

But in this case, what I want and what is possible couldn't be more different.

"I had an idea about the rest of the whole thing, though." I chew my lip. "I mean, it's kind of a start of a start. Maybe.

But anyway, tomorrow I'll say I'm going to research different career options. But really I'll get on the subway and just ride it, seeing where it takes me. Maybe it'll get me to a different Number City. Or I could think of a diversion to get Mayor Vee out of her office so I can go in there and see if she has genealogy files in there."

In the window's reflection I see Mia raise her eyebrows.

"Okay, maybe it's not an incredible or decisive plan." I spin to face her. "But I'm going to do *something* now. There's no reason not to try."

"All right," she says agreeably. "May I come?"

"You have ballet."

"I can be too tired one day."

"I don't know. It'd be nice to have company, but I may need you to be the distraction. How do you feel about staging an injury outside the mayor's office?" It's a weak attempt at a joke, but Mia takes it in stride.

"As long as there's no blood involved."

I smile slightly. "Loss of consciousness it is."

She laughs, obviously remembering rock climbing. "I'll let you know when I've fainted." Mia reaches into her pocket and pulls something out. The whistle. It fell onto Reece's floor yesterday. I'd forgotten. How had I forgotten? "I think this is yours," she says, handing it to me.

Relief flashes through me. "Yeah. It is." I walk to my closet and tug the lace off the second boot. Mia watches me thread the whistle back around my neck, but she doesn't ask about it. "Where's Mitchell?"

"At the store, getting me soup. I said soup is comfort food. He believes I'm depressed because of my not being able to be a doctor. And that's not even the half of it."

Mia opens her mouth to say something, but just as she does my Pow, which is lying on the floor, lights up. I bend over and scoop up the device. The name across the screen sends a jolt of panic through my gut. I force it away and answer the call. "Hello?"

"Hi, Morgan," the mayor says cordially. "How are you

today?"

"Fine."

"Glad to hear it." The mayor's tone remains sugary. "Hey, I have some things I'd love to chat with you about. Could you come by my office and discuss them with me?" Even though it's a question, it's clear there is only one correct answer.

"Oh. When should I stop by?"

"Right now," is her pleasant response.

CHAPTER 32
Neil

Han ambushes me as soon as I step into our dorm after work Monday. His arms are crossed and his stance is wide, matching his no-nonsense expression.

"You," he informs me as I duck past him, "are avoiding my questions."

I pull open a dresser drawer and grab a white class shirt. "Maybe because you haven't said *please*."

"Screw pleasantries. I want to know why you've been so *smiley* lately."

"Define *lately*." I tug the shirt over my head, grinning.

Instead of defining it, he says, "What happened with you and Morgan?"

"What makes you think something happened?"

"I have an uncanny sixth sense," Han informs me. "Anyway, I need to talk to you. I've been trying to get your attention since yesterday, but like I said, you're avoiding me."

"I have not been avoiding you. I just haven't had the energy to answer every question you've thrown at me."

"Lies. You're perfectly chipper. And it's not just the questions. I actually need to have a deep and meaningful conversation. You helped Ms. Elliott with the Year 5's and 6's last night and then feel asleep immediately after class, not that I blame you."

"The deep and meaningful conversation will have to wait. Sorry." I stride back across the room and open the door. "I'm helping Ms. Elliott again."

Han scowls. "You're *avoiding me* again."

"See you in class," I say cheerfully, and walk out. Han's right, I have been smiling. Because my day yesterday brought about a mood that overshadows any worries of work and missing files.

The kids have moved on from addition to subtraction. Ms. Elliott gives them new worksheets and we both move around, helping. Zaire waves me over.

"Neil, how do you minus seven from eleven?" He stares down at his ten outstretched fingers.

I sit next to him. "Pretend you have another finger." I hold out one of my own. As I do I see two women walk into the classroom. One of them has red hair: Ms. Meryl. Ms. Elliott hurries over to talk to them. It's not like when other women come in and they have their long discussions, though. Ms. Elliott's expression is one of confusion.

"Then what?" Zaire is asking. I refocus on him.

"Put down seven fingers. Now count how many are left."

Zaire closes one fist and bends down two fingers on his other hand. "Four fingers."

"Right," I say, opening up my hand for a high-five. "So, if you have any more problems like this, just pretend–"

Hands grip my left shoulder, cutting me off. I'm yanked to my feet.

It's Ms. Meryl's nails digging into my arm. "Neil, you're going to have to come with us."

The other woman who entered with her grabs my other arm, flanking me. I'm taller than both of them, but that hardly matters when I have a chip implanted into my neck and they have the remotes.

Ms. Elliott weaves through the kids, who all stare at me. "I still don't understand," she insists, almost sounding angry. "Where are you taking him?"

A good question. One I'd really like to know the answer to. As it is, my knees already feel like gelatin.

"I don't think you have the clearance for us to share that information." Ms. Meryl smirks.

"There's no need for this." Ms. Elliott's face is stony.

"The mayor seems to think there is." Ms. Meryl and the other woman start to pull me away.

Something grabs my leg. "Neil," Zaire pleads, "don't leave."

Ms. Meryl glares down at him, annoyed. I see her reach for her remote. Not stopping to think, I rip my arm out of her grip. She turns to me, and sends the shock jolting through my neck instead of Zaire's.

Tears sting my eyes. I watch Ms. Meryl's blurred form reattach itself to my arm, and hear Zaire's voice, saying, "But—"

"Be quiet," I say harshly, my head spinning. Zaire doesn't speak again. Good. As Ms. Meryl and the other woman push me out of the room my only thought is that I'm Kellan. I'm Kellan and Zaire is me. Who was I to let him look up to me when I knew this would happen, when I know I would inevitably disappear someday?

I don't even wonder where they're taking me, as they lead me to the subway station. If I were going to become a Like, the scene at the classroom should have been avoided. The most likely reason is they've found out, or suspect, about what's been happening for just over two months. With Morgan.

The Blue City subway station is connected to a monorail station. I know that's what it is from what Morgan's described. Ms. Meryl and the other woman hustle me into a private car of the monorail, and when the sleek sky subway stops again they lead me off in the same manner.

Now we go down a flight of stairs in the back of the station. The hidden steps lead to a small room on the ground floor. Ms. Meryl knocks on the only door in the room.

The door opens. On the other side is a woman with short blonde hair and a light purple shirt. I recognize her as the mayor.

"Hi," she says cheerfully. "Is this Neil? Hi, Neil. Come on in."

Ms. Meryl and the other woman shove me forward. I stumble into the mayor's office.

"Why don't you have a seat." She points to a hard, purple chair by the wall. The wall itself glows purple and there are files on it, like on computer screens we use for supply management and information at work. Han talks about computer files all the time. I've never paid much attention.

The mayor leaves the files open long enough for me to see the one in front has my name on it, then she waves her hand across the wall and they fade away. Now it's just purple.

I sit, nails biting into my skin as I clench my fists. The mayor sends Ms. Meryl and the other woman away, insisting she can handle this, whatever *this* is. Then she turns to me.

"Well," she says, running a hand over her hair to make sure it's all in line. "I'm sure you know who I am. And you're Neil 17. So, how long have you been breaking the rules, Neil?"

I don't reply, just look at her. I'm not sure what she knows. Hopefully she'll be more clear.

She sighs, leaning against her very purple couch. "Please answer. I'm so not in the mood for this today. Well, actually, that's a lie. I'm kind of looking forward to this. But still, it would be in your best interest to answer."

I stare at my hands. I knew my good mood was surreal. Too *good* to last. "What do you mean," I finally say.

"I mean, you meeting Morgan. Morgan Waters. Does that name ring a bell? Don't lie, I know it does. I mean, when one of my doctors told me yesterday how Morgan argued over her taking a newborn twin, and Morgan called the twin *him*, it caused me to look extensively at Morgan's recent history. Her mom's Like was able to inform me that lately Morgan's always out of the house Sunday mornings. Those are the mornings right after your maintenance duty, aren't they?"

I nod.

"Also, you were punished for triggering the alarm in Morgan's Mom's office one of these past Saturdays." She leans forward and reaches out, using her fingers to lift my chin so I'm looking at her. "And you know what? I just read through the answers Morgan gave during her Like evaluation. Now that I see you, it's *uncanny* how she somehow managed to describe you almost exactly. Too bad our matchmaker didn't consider you, or you could be her Like right now." Her face moves closer. "Her knowing what you look like...that wasn't a coincidence, was it?"

I don't do anything. I don't even blink. The mayor purses her lips and draws her hand back, to touch her remote. For the second time today a shock courses through me, but this one's stronger than the last, and I hear myself cry out as I slide off the chair. My knees hit the floor, and then my palms, and for a moment all I can hear is my own breathing.

Then I hear the mayor saying, "Get up. I have a better idea. Let's give Morgan a call, shall we?"

CHAPTER 33
Morgan

Mayor Vee bounces out of her office to meet me in the lobby.

"Hi! How are you today?"

"Fine." I can see the lights of her office behind her. She beckons me into the room, which is just as purple as the last few times I've been here.

"I have some things I'd like to discuss with you." She gestures toward the couch.

"If it's about careers–" I start to say, but then Mayor Vee steps aside, and I see what's behind her.

Neil. Sitting on a chair by the wall, shoulders rigid, hands gripping the edges of the seat. When I stop speaking he glances up, then quickly looks away, locking his gaze on the floor.

"What...what is..." My mind goes utterly blank.

"Oh," Mayor Vee says, looking back at Neil. I swear there's a hint of amusement in her expression. "This is nothing to worry about. Just a Like, in preparation for the next Amora. A girl from the Azure district."

No. There's a faint ringing noise in my head as I shake my head. She's going to turn Neil into a Like? "No," I hear myself say. My heart seems to struggle to pump white-hot blood through my body. "That's not possible."

Mayor Vee cocks her head. "Hmm? What's that?"

"He's not–he's not a Like," I stammer. Because I'm sure he's not. Not yet. He still looks just like Neil. He still has his scars.

"Oh." The mayor nods in agreement. "You're right. He's not completely functional yet. Actually, he's been misbehaving." She passes something back and forth between her hands. A remote, like I've seen on the women in City 4.

251

"So I was just taking care of that before you got here."

Taking care of that. "What–" I hesitate as she decides to show me. Catching the remote in one hand, she uses her other to tap a button.

Neil gasps. It's like the first time, right before I went to City 4, when the woman walked in while he cleaned. Except the sound he makes now is sharper, and his eyes squeeze shut, and his hands press against the back of his neck.

"Stop!" My hands grab the couch seat and I push myself upright. The rational part of my mind, the part that says I shouldn't let on that I know this is wrong, is being drowned out by the part of my mind wanting to tackle Mayor Vee. "*Mayor!*"

She doesn't stop, just glances at me, eyebrows raised, and flicks her finger across a scroll bar on the remote. Neil cries out and jerks his knees up to his chest. He curls up on the chair, shuddering.

I lurch forward without consent or direction from the rational part of my mind. My body slams into Mayor Vee and we both topple to the ground. The remote tumbles from her hand and skitters across the floor, lights in the buttons dimming. Neil stops shuddering, but doesn't move.

I don't move either. My elbow stings as I lay on my side where I fell. Mayor Vee pushes herself to a sitting position. The purple glow from the floor gives her the impression of having two black eyes.

She grins. "I see," she says, and stands up. I roll to the side, reaching for her remote, but her yellow shoe gets there first and kicks it away. She stoops down to pick it up. "You should be more careful," she tells me, fastening it back onto the wristband. "It wouldn't be very helpful if this were to break. Now, why don't you go sit on the couch."

I look up at her, but don't stand. She stares back down at me. Her fingers run along the edge of the remote, coming within millimeters of the buttons.

"Once was enough for me," she says, still tracing. "I guess you should decide if once was enough for you."

More than enough. I slowly get to my feet and back up to sit on the edge of the couch. My knees are shaking and I'm trying to hold them with my hands. My lip hurts as my teeth dig into it.

"Awesome." Mayor Vee drops her hands. "Can you see the wall okay?" She waves an arm at the wall across from me, where the curtains are pulled back so the whole thing is in my view. "Good. Now, since you already know about these men, I'm going to give you a history lesson. Can't risk you having some skewed version of reality in your head, can we?"

I glance at Neil. His gaze is focused on his hands, which are shaking. Then he raises his eyes. One second is enough for me to see he's just as stricken as I am.

"I said, *can we?*" Mayor Vee repeats, sighing.

I shake my head to mollify her. She looks pleased. "Right. So listen carefully. And watch carefully, too."

She points her Pow at the wall. An image dissolves onto the screen.

At first I can't make out the picture. It's blurry, and monochromatic. But then I realize what I'm seeing, and I almost choke. It's a picture of bodies. Skinny, emaciated bodies in a heap, their fuzzy skeletal faces locked in what look like screams of terror. I feel shivers running up my spine, totally different shivers than the kind Neil causes in me. Shivers of horror.

I don't have to ask; Mayor Vee explains before I even say the word *what*. "We're starting with some background information. This is a picture from 1943." Her expression shows no shock, just smooth features. She's seen this before. "During the Second World War, the Holocaust took place." She taps her Pow. A new image appears: more bodies, sprawled in pits while Likes, or men, stand on the edges holding guns. "Thousands of people were killed in death camps in Europe. All because of this *man*."

The person in the next image is still black and white, with dark hair and a mustache as severe as his expression.

"This man," Mayor Vee explains, "named Hitler, led

hate groups that rounded up and killed people that were different than him. It is one of the greatest tragedies of history. And it's his fault."

Killed. That word has always been associated with learning about the Wars and history, but I never knew this kind of brutality ever existed. I tear my gaze from the wall and see Neil's also watching, looking nauseated. I want to be gripping his hand, in his arms, anything but alone on the purple couch while we're forced to watch these pictures.

"Morgan, pay attention," Mayor Vee demands, and I pull my gaze back. The image is in color now, grainy color. After a moment it moves. It's a video, a shaky video of two tall towers standing against the skyline of an old-fashioned city. Something emerges in the corner of the screen. It appears to be flying. An airplane. We've learned about those, too, in academy.

The airplane flies straight into a tower. There's an explosion of orange. It happens again, with the other tower. The footage changes, now showing those old vehicles called ambulances and mangled corpses on stretchers. Thousands of injured. Thousands more bodies.

"September eleventh, 2001," Mayor Vee says. "*Men* hijacked airplanes and flew them into the World Trade Center. They were located in a part of America destroyed in the Wars. However, in this incident, thousands of people were killed."

I want to clamp my hands over my ears. But I know the mayor will only pull them away and force me to listen. So I don't. I look at the screen, my eyes unfocused, as she goes on. She describes adultery, domestic violence, rape, serial killings, atom bombs, genocide. I stop keeping track, my mind trying to drown her out with a ringing in my ears. It doesn't work.

"Do you want to know the real story of the Wars, Morgan?" Mayor Vee finally stops the flow of horrifying pictures. "The Wars are, ironically, what brought these terrors to an end."

I don't shake my head, even though I want to. In the corner of my vision I can see Neil, wide eyes still locked on where the last picture dissolved.

She takes my silence as a yes. "For the longest time, the horrible deeds of men went unpunished. No one thought to do anything about the threats they posed to our society. The Wars caused people to realize who was to blame.

"During the second half of the twenty-first century, tension over nuclear warfare and weapons of mass destruction escalated dramatically. In 2068, America elected its first woman president. Her name was Audrey Kessler, and she wanted to make a peace treaty to diffuse the strain, or at least lessen it until a permanent solution could be found.

"While admirable, the idea didn't work. Because at the same time desperation over obtaining oil peaked, and because of the tensions, America's suppliers cut us off.

"President Kessler was willing to negotiate a compromise. But a section of our military, headed by men, was sure force was the right answer. They thought Russia, a country in Eurasia, was behind the Middle Eastern agreements that cut off our oil. These *men* disobeyed a direct order from President Kessler and her women officers and carried out an operation using nuclear weapons to destroy parts of Russia, trying to coerce the country into reversing the ban on oil trade. Russia retaliated soon after, and we lost almost our entire western coastline. Women in America were infuriated. This was an eye-opening example of how truly unruly and horrible men were.

"By the next year, sea levels were rising as the amount of land being nuked and falling into the oceans created an imbalance. Nuclear winter set in, and people everywhere struggled to find shelter and food. A full-scale war was happening, and most of the military was comprised of men. Many of them were dying.

"By 2072 levies were constructed around what remained of the continents in order to keep out the ocean water. President Kessler was reelected and she made sure the men who carried out the operation in Russia were rightfully given the blame. By then women all over America were starting to realize the effect men had on society. During this year some women created a national, undercover organization called LOW. LOW stood for Liberation Of Women."

Mayor Vee pauses to take a breath, and I can't read her expression. I can only feel my fingers clenching around one another and wonder if my hands will break.

The mayor continues. "The country's population had already been reduced by hundreds of thousands. Everywhere, people called for truces. LOW organized operations to utilize new technology in order to give women the societal power they deserved. Women doctors were implanting chips into male babies, chips like the ones we use today for control. Men were being killed on the streets or in their homes. President Kessler was not part of LOW, and she tried to find out what was happening while working to put together potential peace negotiations.

"In 2074 President Kessler was assassinated. The country elected a new woman, one of the founders of LOW, and she made it possible for their operations to continue. She also managed to hold peace negotiations. At those negotiations the CommWall was agreed upon. Because of the CommWall, men from other continents couldn't infiltrate LOW's plans.

"Four years later, the LOW movement went public. Chips were successfully implanted in all newborn boys and almost all men were dead. There were women hunting the remaining land for men who had gone into hiding, or for women who sympathized with the men. There weren't many.

"The technology used for Likes was perfected in the 90's, and our cities were set up in that decade. Well, we use the term cities, but really all of the Color and Number Cities are like sections of a larger city population-wise, and governed by the Mayors of each section. When the cities were constructed the entire areas outside were set on fire, to eliminate any outside threats and fertilize the ground."

I remember the endless grass and the colorful flowers stretching to the horizon. That's the product of destruction?

"By 2110 our society was perfect," Mayor Vee says, "and we raised the newest generation without any knowledge of men. Every woman received a Like and thought that's how life always worked. A few women of certain positions had the necessary information passed to them. There are some women who do not love Likes, and instead love other women. They don't *fit in* well in our society, per se. Most are assigned to work in Number Cities, though some women who work there are volunteers. They may have stumbled across men after curfew–a rare incident, but it does happen. In that case, I'll suggest they're perfect for a job in enforcement. And sometimes women are assigned to Number Cities for compromising information, like the former librarian."

Ms. Elliott. I knew she was in City 4, but I didn't realize it was punishment. I've lost feeling in my fingers.

"You know, Morgan, I was shown this same presentation and told this same story so I could be the mayor. I didn't react this severely, but I'm sure you'll be fine; I was. After I saw the story the now-retired mayor taught me how to be a member of the Mayors of the Cities Committee, and how to keep the system running."

Mayor Vee winds down her story, watching me carefully. My face has slipped into a stony mask.

When I don't say anything, she says, "Do you understand why this system exists? It's so everything I told you about doesn't have to be a part of your life, of any woman's life. Men got what they deserved."

I'm still silent, starting to shake my head. I don't want to believe the things she told me actually happened. Or that it was the men's fault. That what she's saying is true.

"Morgan, look at me." Mayor Vee kneels in front of where I sit and locks my gaze with hers. "Men are terrible. Left to their own devices, they will destroy everything. Remember that book you started? *Romeo and Juliet*? They don't live happily ever after. Romeo drives Juliet to commit suicide. They *die*, in the end."

Now she turns to Neil, and I unwillingly look at him too. He meets my gaze, shaking his head, denying what he knows Mayor Vee is going to say now.

"Neil is one of them," she murmurs sending chills through me. "I bet everything he's told you is a lie. Whatever you've seen, anything he's said, anything he's done, it wasn't real. He's a man, just like the ones who started the Wars. Like the one who killed all those people in the 1900's. Like Romeo, who destroyed Juliet's life. Just like them."

"I'm not," Neil whispers, voice cracking. He puts his feet on the floor, and starts to stand. "I'm not like those people, I didn't even know–"

"Don't move," Mayor Vee hisses. I take a breath, meaning to say something, but I can't. I can't get the images of the skeletal corpses out of my head. Neil and Han. Were they just taking advantage of me the whole time? Using me to cause pain like in history? Is Mayor Vee right? Was anything they told me true?

Did Neil feel what I felt? When we kissed? When he said...when he said he trusted me? I'd been so sure, but what if it was me who misplaced my trust? Because those pictures, and the Wars, and *Romeo and Juliet*...

It's like my world has turned upside down again. Nothing is real. Nothing.

Tears slide down my cheeks and I ignore everything. How Neil protests. How Mayor Vee taps at her Pow, and how two women enter through a door in the back of her office and grab Neil, who sways on his feet. He tries to pull away, but he's trembling. "Morgan," he says. Pleads. His voice is as thick with emotion as when he told me he trusted me. When I thought I could love him.

The women push him back, out of the room. I turn away. Images of his face, so close, mixes with images of death and stories of pain and lies, threatening to overwhelm me. I grab my hair, the short ends slipping through my fingers and snagging in my curled fists, as I'm trying not to feel. I'm trying to turn my heart into a block of ice.

But if my heart is a block of ice, there's a crack running right through the center.

Mayor Vee doesn't speak for almost a minute. Then she says, "Well. I usually give that presentation to the few women who are selected to have jobs with clearance. They know the story of the Wars and all. Sorry about the added drama. Oh, by the way, I'm also sorry how things worked out with your doctor training." The mayor shakes her head. "Though, if you were to become a birthing doctor, you would have had to hear the spiel anyway. It's the special 'Test' a few are selected to take. But guess what this means? You have a whole new array of career options open to you now."

She beams at me. I don't even blink.

Undeterred, she continues. "You could be a matchmaker. That's someone who pairs up boys–*ahem*, potential Likes– with girls approaching their Amora age, who makes sure no pairs are closely related. It's complicated, with the whole twin thing. There's a matchmaker for each Color City, and she has to coordinate with the other cities."

I find my voice. It comes out dry and cracked. "I don't want to."

The mayor shrugs. "I guess it's not for everyone. Obviously. Well, you *could* be in security over in City 4, but I really wouldn't recommend that option. Or..." Mayor Vee smiles, like she's about to let me in on another secret. "I think you're pretty neat, Morgan, so I'll give you this option as well. You could be the next mayor of Blue City. I mean, there's an official election and all, but we really do have to decide who's next in line so we can be sure she knows *everything*, if you understand what I'm saying. I could be your teacher, if you want. I'll have a daughter at some point and when I do, I'll need someone I know I can trust to fill in for a few weeks. How about it?"

Now she looks at me expectantly, as if waiting for me to start jumping up and down.

I don't. "I don't want to think about it." I don't want to

think about anything. I don't.

"I understand," Mayor Vee assures me.

No. I don't think you understand at all. I stand, feeling dizzy. "I want to leave."

"All right." She stands as well and pats me sympathetically on the shoulder. "Why don't you go get some rest. We can discuss career options another time. Remember, though, this is fully confidential. But you've been doing a pretty good job of keeping the secret until now, even though you didn't understand. I commend that. However, you really should have told me."

I don't respond, turning to the door to leave, a cheerful "Good bye!" following me. Then I'm on the street and I'm running, and I don't know where I'm going or how far I run. I just know that a while later I'm stopping, panting, by an office building, and I have a stitch in my side and I can't breathe. I can't breathe, but I don't care. I don't even care.

Fighting for air, I push through the doors of the office building. It's the place I came before my Amora. Same as that night, I climb the stairs, all the way to the top. My lungs feel like they're on fire and circled in metal bands by the time I emerge onto the rooftop garden.

My feet take me to the edge. The view is as dizzying as the lack of oxygen, and I can hardly tell which way the world is spinning. A breeze rustles through the plants, making my hair tickle my cheeks and forehead. Through the dark strands I see women and Likes strolling along on the streets below, their lives flawless, unaffected. Unreal.

I can feel the shoelace rubbing against my neck. I reach back and fumble with the knot, loosening it. I yank it off with a painful tug, and pull the whistle from the string. The wooden piece is the most real thing I own, and yet now I'm told even it can't be real. The intentions it was made with can't be what I'd imagined: right, loving, a truth. They must be wrong, malicious, a lie.

It's a symbol for what I thought I knew.

How many times have I come to this conclusion? I

thought I knew something, and I didn't really, and now I think I know the truth. And again, that truth is a lie. My arm pulls back,I throw the whistle with all the force I can muster. It spins as it arcs through the air, then drops from sight, hurtling toward the street below.

My vision becomes even more disoriented. I feel, rather than see, myself climbing onto the wall at the edge of the garden. My feet have an unsteady grip on the surface, but I stand up.

There's nothing between me and the empty space over the side of the building. An expanse of emptiness swallowing up the truth and the lies and stretching to an unknown fate below. And I want to follow the whistle into it.

CHAPTER 34
Neil

I don't know where the women are taking me, and I can't guess. My head is a confusing mass of colors and indiscernible voices. Sometimes a picture of what the mayor showed us will be distinguishable; death and pain and destruction, and according to the mayor it's because of us. The men.

The clearest image in my mind, though, is Morgan's expression when I was pulled out of the room. In the one moment she looked at me, I could see her repulsion. And hurt. The hurt was the worst. When she turned away I understood; she thought I'd been lying to her, about everything. About kissing her, and trusting her, and being real. And I couldn't tell her no, I haven't, I never lied, because she wouldn't look at me and words clogged my throat and the women closed the door leading into the office and dragged me to the stairs.

We ride the hidden monorail car back to the subway station, and from there to City 4. No one's on the streets by now as it's class time. So they can lead me down the streets without anyone seeing, or stopping them. Not that anyone would.

Some part of me wonders if Han's worried. If Ms. Elliott told him what happened. If she is worried. She seemed to actually like having me help in class.

We reach the apartment building where the women live. At this point I seriously consider running away. But where would I go? One glance at the remotes on the women's wrists is reminder enough; I wouldn't get very far, anyway.

The inside of the building is fifty times fancier than the dorm buildings, though not as luxurious as the buildings in Blue City. Year 11's do maintenance on these residential buildings, and this one is smaller than I remember. But the carpet is still patterned, and animosity is still present for someone like me. A man. A man like the ones in the history lesson.

There's a hallway inside, and a door at the end of the hallway is ajar. "I can handle this," Ms. Meryl tells the other woman. Ms. Meryl shoves me into the room. It's bare except for a couch, a lamp, a sink, and a window where the curtains are drawn.

I hear Ms. Meryl shut the door. The lamp lights up, but dimly against the gray walls, tinting the room pale yellow.

"Did you know," she says behind me, "those chips in your neck can do more than just shock you?"

I didn't know. I don't want to know. I'm done knowing. But something tells me Ms. Meryl will make me know, anyway.

"Security officers don't carry around remotes with other capabilities on a regular basis. It could get confusing. However, since this is a special occasion, the mayor lent me a special remote."

I stare hard at the window, trying to decide if I even care what happens next. Ms. Meryl's footsteps come closer.

"Let me explain."

And then another shock slams through me. Despite the pain, my one, wild thought is that this isn't different. But when the feeling passes and I force my eyes open, something is different. I'm looking at the ceiling now, which is the same color as the walls. The floor is cold and hard against my head and shoulders, which ache from the impact of hitting the ground.

I instinctively reach back to touch my neck. Or, I try to. My arm doesn't respond. Feeling a sudden sense of panic, I look down at it. When I try again to lift my hand, my fingers shake, and rise only a centimeter. The same thing happens with my other arm, and my legs. I can't move at all without a huge effort.

Ms. Meryl appears, standing over me, grinning. "That is

so interesting. I've never actually gotten to try this feature before. Thanks for being idiot enough to deserve this punishment." She paces around my head, coming to stand next to my left hand. I follow her with my eyes. "So you heard the mayor explain why we have this system. Why you're here and not running amok in society." She kneels down, coming closer, and lowers her voice like she's telling me a secret. "That's why I became a security officer, you know. When I was younger I stayed out past curfew and saw the men doing maintenance. I went to the mayor the next morning. She decided I was fit for a job in enforcement, so she showed me the same presentation you saw today. I decided to take her up on her offer go into security. So I can protect us women and keep you men in your place."

She straightens up and cocks her head. Then she picks up her foot and slams it down on my hand, grinding her heel toward the floor.

I don't know if I can cry out. I don't know if I do. I can't hear over the noise inside my head, the screaming from shock and pain echoing around my mind as my hand breaks.

When the noise in my skull fades I'm gripped by the instinct to grab my hand, put pressure on it, hold it next to my body so it's safe. But I can't. I can't move to do any of those things, and that's the worst part.

My eyes are blurry and stinging. I realize Ms. Meryl is speaking again, like nothing just happened. "...the story about the Wars," she says. "I'm so curious. What did *Morgan* think of you after that?"

I shut my eyes again, trying not to listen, but the image of Morgan's expression flashes across my eyelids anyway. A pain deeper than the one in my hand burrows inside me.

"She was disgusted, wasn't she? Did she think you were her friend? Did you think she was your friend?" She snorts. "Whatever it was, you caused her pain. What you're feeling right now is retribution. A learning experience."

My hand throbs, sending jolts up my arm. But that's almost canceled out by the picture in my mind and the ache accompanying it. I try to force both away.

"But your hand will heal. You know what you need to have in order to learn? A reminder. Something that will be with you for a long time."

The buttons of my polo shirt are yanked open. I force myself to watch as she pulls out a knife, a small one with a slender blade. She studies my bare shoulder. "Let's see. How about an *M*? An *M* for Morgan. Will that serve as reminder enough?"

I understand what she's going to do a moment before the blade sinks into my skin. My teeth clench together, my mind starting to scream again, and Ms. Meryl traces an *M*, just like she said. I'm still wearing my class shirt, the blood staining the white fabric appears almost impossibly red.

My vision blurs again and I jerk my gaze away, gasping, wanting to run and knowing I can't. Ms. Meryl's cloudy form stands and towers over me again. I wait for her to gloat, to say something else, but she instead turns toward the door.

A new voice speaks from the doorway. "Lydia?" someone addresses Ms. Meryl. "You have a call."

"Stay here," Ms Meryl tells me sweetly, then her figure disappears and the gray color of the walls and ceiling overtakes my vision. Something runs down my cheek, splashing onto the floor.

The door closes, and I'm alone, blood spreading through my shirt and tears cutting rivers down my face.

I don't know how long it is until the door opens again. I am able to move now, though my limbs feel heavy, but I haven't stood up. I just let myself be yanked to my feet. The women who came for me pull me outside, practically dragging me when I stumble. The sky is dark and the streetlamps only illuminate some of the street.

I'm taken back to my dorm and dumped on my bed. I grit my teeth, refusing to make a sound when my now swollen hand falls against the edge of the mattress. The women quickly leave.

As soon as they close the door there's movement to my left. Han had been lying in his bed, he throws off his blankets and kneels beside me. For a moment he actually seems speechless. Then, "Neil."

"Han," I try to say, but only get so far as opening my mouth before I close it again. It's no use. This can't be the only punishment I'm going to get. Reassurances or complaints won't get me anywhere.

"Your shirt," Han whispers. "And your hand. What happened? No, never mind. I can guess what happened. Neil, what do I do?"

I shake my head slightly, trying to tell him I don't know. The bleeding from the cut stopped a while ago, the blood starting to dry on the wound. I have no idea about my hand. There is nothing I can say.

"We need Morgan," Han murmurs, and a different pain flashes through me. "She's studied this stuff, this medical stuff. She'd know what to do. She can help."

I finally speak, throat so constricted with the effort of not crying that I can barely force the two words out. "She won't."

"What?" I hear an unfamiliar emotion in his words. Fear. "Why wouldn't she?"

"She won't come back, Han." I turn my head away. "Morgan's never coming back."

CHAPTER 35
Morgan

How easy would it be?

My gaze locks on a rooftop in the distance. I've been standing here, on the edge of the rooftop garden, for I don't know how long. My breathing has slowed now. I feel calm. Detached. Indifferent enough to wonder how easy it would be to take just one step forward.

I probably wouldn't even feel the impact of the ground. It's likely my heart would stop first from shock. And then I'm sure the mayor would find some story to feed the City so no one would feel scared or confused. Because heaven forbid anyone know the truth.

And really, was not knowing the truth so horrible? I was stupid, but I was happy. Or, I thought I was happy. I felt more *real* during the weeks I snuck out to see Neil and Han. Life had a purpose, being with them, knowing them, and through the stress, having direction, looking for a change. I was happy with Neil. Thinking I was in love with him. No, I was. I loved him. Still love him. Who I believed he was, even if that's not who he is. Even if he's the same as all the men in history, I love who I thought I knew.

If I'd been asked this morning whether I'd prefer to know about men or not to know about men, I would have said the former.

But this evening I don't know what the truth is.

And now I'm here, on the roof, calmly thinking through the benefits of killing myself. Isn't that what Mayor Vee said happened in *Romeo and Juliet*? In the real love story? Romeo drives Juliet to kill herself. The truth is her undoing.

I tear my gaze from the distant rooftop, blinking hard. When I open my eyes I'm staring down at the street. Way down at the street. Vertigo overtakes me. My vision tilts, then spins, and it feels like my center of gravity is swooping, leaving me with no sense of up or down or anywhere. I might already be falling. I can't feel where my feet are on the edge. I can't feel anything at all. And for a moment, I'm relieved.

Then I do feel something. An impact. Something hits my side and wraps around my waist, yanking me backward. The roof flies toward me. With something tangible in my senses, panic rockets back into existence.

My body slams into a flowerbed. Stars burst in front of my eyes and the crushing feeling of having the wind knocked out of me fills my chest. I gag, rolling over, placing my hands in the dirt before I frantically draw in a breath. When the world stops spinning like a top I look to the side. "Mitchell." I choke out the words while taking in another sharp breath. He's sprawled next to me, gasping, watching me.

"Morgan." He reaches out, gripping my elbow. He moves his arm gingerly, but doesn't acknowledge the pain.

"Are you okay?" My voice sounds hoarse. "Your arm. Is it–"

"You were *falling*," he says, his eyes wide. But even as his eyelids open farther than normal, his eyes remain the same: flat and emotionless. Same as every Like. "I pulled you away from the edge, but I'm sorry I couldn't catch you better. Did you hit your head?"

"*I* should be asking *you* that." I scramble to my feet. Mulch clings to my shirt. I back away, but not toward the edge of the garden again, for the stairs this time, to run.

Mitchell pushes himself to his feet as well, ducking around plants to reach me. His hands catch my shoulders just as I pull open the door to the stairwell.

"Why were you *here*? I looked all *over* for you. Then I saw you on the edge of the building and ran up as fast as I could. I was so scared." He draws me in to a hug.

I put out my arms to stop him, before his perfect self can get any closer. "No you weren't," I say, barely moving my lips. "You didn't feel scared. You're a Like. You didn't feel anything."

"What are you saying? Of *course* I was scared." His gaze drops to meet mine, and I see the nothingness again, a wall, stopping me. It's so different from how Neil looks at me, when I feel like I can just lose myself in the vastness of his gaze. *No.*

The flatness in his eyes reminds me of the emptiness stretching beyond the edge of the roof. It reminds me that nothing about Mitchell is original. It reminds me that Likes are just reconstructed fakes. Perfect, beautiful, and fake, the ruins of what were once boys.

Flawless ruins.

"Morgan," Mitchell is whispering. "Don't be rash, please! I don't know why you were on the edge of the garden, but whatever it is, I can help you. I can make it better."

I jerk my shoulders from his hands. "You cannot help."

"I can!" He follows, reaching again. "Please listen to me. I love you, Morgan."

"*You don't love me,*" I scream, stepping back. "You're not even *real!*"

My foot hits air and drops to the second step of the stairs. I teeter for a moment, then grab the railing. But Mitchell's already lunged to catch me.

I don't think, just shake off his hand instinctively. His lack of balance does the rest. I gasp as his body hurtles past me and crashes to the steps. And keeps going. He tumbles down the flight of stairs, out of my sigh. I fly down after him as fast as I can, not giving myself time to think. Four flights below I find him.

My first, disjointed thought is I'm lucky I have the stomach for this. My second thought is more focused, more controlled, and it's that I need to do something *now*, and get help immediately.

I drop to my knees by Mitchell. He's on his back on the flat of the landing, mouth open, making gulping noises. His chest is lopsided, as if one side caved in, crushing his ribs. Blood spreads from his body onto the floor.

He coughs weakly, dark liquid trickling from his mouth.

Oh, no. His lungs were punctured. I hold my Pow to my mouth. "Mom?" My voice shakes when she answers my call. I tell her where I am. "Come. Now. With help. Please." Then I drop the Pow.

Mitchell's gaze moves slowly, drifting past mine. In this second I see emotion. Fear. Real fear. And then his eyes are empty again.

I do what first aid I can until doctors arrive, even though I know it's no use. The doctors swarm around, carting equipment and shouting orders. I fall back, and someone takes my hand. It's my mom. She's off-duty, not wearing her uniform.

I pull my hand away and drop to sit on the stairs. The other half of the steps is spattered with blood. I tuck my knees to my chest, watching, hoping for a miracle even though I know it's pointless. But after what seems like forever the emergency doctors finally slow down, glance at each other, and quietly gather equipment. Mom's gaze finds mine. One shared glance between us tells her what I know: Mitchell's dead. He can't be saved.

Mom takes me home. We get as far as the living room before Ross appears, blabbering about how concerned he is and what happened and how Mom still looks so beautiful even when she's stressed until Mom says, "Ross. Leave."

Her tone is sharp enough to quiet him, and he retreats. Mom leads me up the stairs and to her room, where she closes the door behind us. I don't realize I'm on the verge of crying until I sink down onto her green bedspread and find I can't see my own hands in front of my face because the tears are welling up and causing colors to swim nauseatingly.

Mom sits next to me and I lean into her, pressing my eyes against her shoulder. "He fell down the stairs," I say, my voice thick. "Because I pulled away from him and he lost his balance. And that was after he stopped me from falling off the building."

Mom doesn't freak out or demand to know what I was

doing in a position to fall off the building. I have a feeling she'll do that later, but for now she just rests her cheek against my hair and says, "Will you tell me now?"

I nod, and then explain, starting with Laney's Amora. By the time I'm done I can't help it; the tears roll down my cheeks. They soak into Mom's shirt, and I scrub at my eyes with the back of my hand.

Mom is quiet for a while. Then she says, "I couldn't talk to you about it before, with the threat hanging over my head, but now they've told you. I saw the same presentation. That's the test women go through in order to become doctors or biologists, or any profession requiring one to know men exist. And every time I think back to it, I know it's a lie."

I look up, opening my mouth, but she goes on, answering my question. "Yes, it was the truth, too. Those things happened. But they were presented with a lie. It was propaganda, to make the women hate the men and continue with the oppression."

"You think so?" I want to believe it and at the same time I don't want to believe anything.

Mom nods. "Consider this; what the women did and are still doing to the men, it's just as horrible as anything a man could have done in the past. And truthfully, how do we know all men did those terrible things, anyway? These boys, the ones in the Number Cities, they're just as ignorant as the women. They don't know anything about that history and they're raised without a chance to prove they're not heartless murderers."

It's like she's been thinking about this, waiting to say it, maybe for years. "Mom," I say, as the fabric of her shirt presses against my cheek, "if you believe that, why are you in birthing?"

"I didn't believe it at first," Mom says quietly. "After the presentation I thought it was justified, this system. But then I had my first job after training, and when I assisted in my first delivery, I was struck by the innocence of the babies. And then I realized I knew where the boy was going, when he was

271

taken away. I started to think."

"But you never did anything about it." It's more of a question than a statement.

Her hand, resting on my knee, trembles. "By that point I was pregnant. I made a plan because I didn't want to give up my son. I sent Ross away when I knew I was going into labor." Her eyes glaze over. "I hid the boy when Ross came home, and told him the dead baby had been taken away already."

I slowly look up. "My twin."

There are tears in her eyes too, wobbling, on the brink of falling. "It didn't work. They found him. I argued. And so the mayor at the time–Mayor Sarah–told me I had two choices. I could get over my *mood swing*, as she called it, and move on with my job and raising my daughter, or I could continue to make trouble. She said if I did that, then she would see to it my son was killed."

Cold shivers race up my spine. I know what Mom chose.

"She didn't understand what the big deal was either way," Mom continues. "But of course I quieted down. Played nice. I'm still playing nice."

"Mom," I say, trying not to think too hard, "if all those women have to know, I mean, they can't all be like Mayor Vee, right? There have to be some like you, who would protest. How are the lies still working, then?"

Mom stares at the opposite wall. "Not *all* doctors know. Only those in birthing. Same with other professions. And if anyone is...a problem, the mayor just threatens her or convinces her a job in one of the number cities is right for her. It's effective. Either way the skepticism is removed from Color Cities."

"But it seems crazy, now. How does no one *wonder*? About anything? About where the Likes come from?"

Now Mom meets my gaze. "Did *you* wonder, before all this?"

I hesitate. And shake my head.

"Our society's been this way for generations. It's how

272

we're *raised*. Not to question, to just accept and be happy. No one knows they should, or even could, do any different." Her hand squeezes mine. "I'm so sorry. You shouldn't have to deal with this. I should have kept it from you better, or made you tell me sooner. This is my fault. It's been my fault since they took my son." Her voice breaks.

I pull my hand out of hers and set it in my lap, focusing on it until my vision swims again. That's what they were, Mom's moods, the depression she never explained: her guilt, her hopelessness about her son. *My twin.*

Oh, no. What did I do? What did I let *happen?* Neil being dragged out of the office flashes through my mind. My eyes squeeze shut, but it doesn't help. He must hate me. He must truly hate me.

Stop, I tell myself. I can't keep doing this, can't keep losing it. I have to focus. I have to do something.

And I know what the first thing I have to do is in order to understand. I have to see Neil.

CHAPTER 36
Morgan

I walk back to the office building where Mitchell died. There's about an hour until curfew, and the streetlamps illuminate yellowy spots on the street. I stand across from the door to the building, just staring, replaying the conversation I heard Ross having with Mom before I left.

Ross: I heard from the mayor. She wants to talk to you.

Mom: What did she say about Morgan?

Ross: She said Morgan's not going to be held responsible for this. She understands it was an accident. Of course, what else would it be? She would like to talk to you both, though, tomorrow.

Mom: Only if Morgan's up to it.

Ross: Honey, it's the mayor.

Mom: And Morgan is my daughter, and I'm a doctor. The mayor can talk to Morgan only if she feels okay. And that decision is no one's but hers.

About that time, I'd left.

I start to walk now, toward the building, and my foot scuffs against something. I look down in time to see it roll into the edge of a circle of light. The whistle. The one Neil made for my birthday.

I pick it up. A crack runs up one side, opposite the holes. I gently press on it, smoothing it down, fitting the whistle back together as best I can. Then I pull my shoestring from my pocket and tie the whistle back around my neck.

I face the office building again. In my mind I see flashes of this afternoon, of Mitchell plunging down the stairs, of his sunken ribs with blood streaming out, of the fear flashing in his eyes just before they went blank again. The doctors tried to save him; but even the best doctor can't bring back someone who's died twice.

Because Mitchell did die twice. This was just his physical death. Mitchell, whoever he was before, had already died when he became a Like. He disappeared. And when Mitchell's body failed, there was nothing and nobody to supply the will to live. He just...died.

Those thoughts surge through my mind until I have to walk, trying to leave them behind. I have to concentrate. Have to figure out where I'm going tonight. Have to get ready.

It feels like any Saturday night when I sneak out in my polo and hat. Except it's a Tuesday and this time I head two districts over to wait, until the maintenance boys board the subway back to City 4. Then I slip in and act like I belong, which means I act like I don't belong by shuffling and keeping my head down, my shoulders hunched forward. Just like every boy.

The walk to the dorms in the darkness is familiar, too, as is the climb through the crowded staircase to dorm 302. The door isn't locked. Neil once told me only women's doors are locked. That the men don't get anything of value, nothing special to hold as their own, so why would they need locks?

I push it open. It's dark inside, the only light being a yellow strip on the floor cast by the small window. I assume both Han and Neil are asleep. Neither of them have maintenance tonight.

My feet make a slight shuffling noise as I step toward Neil's bed, debating whether I should wake him yet, or maybe I can just wait, and gather my thoughts. I can't see him, but I hear the soft sound of his breathing. It sounds almost peaceful, the opposite of the chaos in my mind.

Then I remember what I told Neil about assuming. And the next moment someone grabs my arms from behind. Before I can call out, a hand presses over my mouth.

"Shh," someone says while pulling me away from Neil's bed. I twist out of the grip and turn around.

The light cutting across the room catches half of Han's

face. One of his gray eyes stares at me, the glasses below it sliding down his nose. An eyebrow is cocked, but instead of asking me what the hell I'm doing like I expect, he just raises a finger to his lips.

"Try not to wake him," he whispers. "He finally fell asleep a few hours ago."

"Why…"

Han interrupts me with his own question. "What are you doing here?"

I bite my lip. "I had to see Neil. I mean, both of you. Did Neil tell you…?"

"He didn't exactly talk coherently," Han mutters. "But I got the gist of it. How could you let it happen? Didn't you try to do anything?" Now his eye narrows.

"Let *what* happen?" I panic, and spin to look at where Neil's asleep, even though I know I can't see. "Is he–?"

Han catches my arm and I turn back to him. He looks confused for a moment, then his expression softens into thoughtfulness. "Are you here to help, then?"

Am I? Am I still trying to help them? What do I believe?

It's easier to say I don't know when I'm not looking at Han, and feeling that the familiarity, the friendship, didn't disappear in one day. It's easier to be unsure when Neil's not asleep only feet away, sounding peaceful, sounding *innocent*, and when Han's not asking me if I'm still with them.

I am.

"Yes," I whisper. "What do I need to do?"

As soon as I say *yes,* Han pushes me toward the desk and the head of Neil's bed. I see him fumble for something, then the lamp turns on, casting a dim glow. Out of the corner of my eye I see Neil stir in his sleep, and turn toward him.

"Do something," Han says, his voice low. "Please."

Or, at least, I think he said please. The buzzing in my ears has come rushing back and I can't be sure.

I slowly lower myself to my knees, bringing myself closer, finding it impossible to swallow. A shiver runs through me, one of the horrible kinds. There's as much blood in his shirt as there was in Mitchell's, but I didn't react this way to that sight. Then I was collected, focused, slightly panicked, but nothing I couldn't handle. And now I feel like something's digging at my heart, just like something surely dug at Neil's skin to get the blood to flow.

I find myself looking up, searching Han's face for an explanation. He presses his mouth together, lips making a thin line.

"Punishment," he says quietly.

"They didn't get him medical attention?" My voice trembles.

Han shakes his head, rubbing his burn.

Neil's face is drawn even in sleep, a crease visible in the center of his forehead. So much less peaceful in the light. He's positioned awkwardly, too, with his left arm resting away from his body. I stare at it, at his hand, which is swollen and covered with dark bruises.

"Okay," I murmur, trying to force myself into the calm doctor mindset. "Bring me your pillowcase, Han."

Han obeys, uncharacteristically silent. But I don't dwell on his behavior as I wrap the pillowcase around my hand. "First thing is the shirt. Give me one of those blades Neil says he uses to whittle."

Once I have the blade I gently ease it under the collar of Neil's shirt, touching as little blood as possible. I know in some cases it's unavoidable, like when I did first aid on Mitchell, but now taking the safety measure helps me focus. I send Han to soak one of his towels in water. I slice away Neil's white polo, working it gently away from the skin in the areas where blood dried.

Now it's obvious where the blood originated. Dark clumps of it congeal on his shoulder, all around what appears to be four consecutive cuts. I use the towel to wipe the blood from the slightly swollen, lacerated shoulder. My hand shakes as I touch him, doctor mindset unable to control the reaction.

Han hears me gasp when I finally see the actual cut. He comes to peer over my shoulder, and his eyebrows fly

277

upward.

"*M*," he says, then looks at me.

I shake my head. No. That's not my initial carved into Neil's shoulder. It's just a letter. Nothing but a letter. Part of the alphabet. Needs to be bandaged.

I'm not sure how fast time is passing. My mind has slipped into a zone of concentration, and I'm grateful. After I'm done bandaging the cut and splinting his hand with Han's pillow and sheets, and after I've checked for other cuts or broken bones, I fall back on my heels, breathing deeply.

"I'm so sorry."

Han doesn't reply. He's silent for a minute before saying, "When he didn't show up for class, I thought I'd never get to tell him what I found out. But, of course, by then it wouldn't have mattered."

"What did you need to tell him?" I don't take my gaze off Neil.

In the corner of my vision I see Han take some of his lock-picking tools out of his pocket and put them in the desk drawer. "I wasn't doing invoices on Sunday. I was searching for Neil's record. It's a long story, but we never found it, and I decided to look in the Control Offices. I've never been in them before. The locks took me a while, which makes sense, as that's where a bunch of high-tech gadgetry is, and they probably want to keep it secure. But anyway, I managed to unlock the doors."

"And?" My lips barely move.

Han's bedsprings creak. "I only chanced a quick look, because it took me a while to find Neil's record. It was there, with a few other records from over the years, but I only read Neil's. The first page was the same as all the others we've found, basics. His birthday is in February, his eyes are brown. It had a second page, though."

The way his voice changes, how it becomes slightly more deliberate, makes me stare even harder at Neil, not wanting to see Han's face as he continues.

"Apparently," Han says, and I have to focus hard on

what he's saying so my mind won't block the words, "Neil's twin was dead at birth. He's listed as an extra on his file, meaning even though a few boys have been taken from Year 17 to become Likes, Neil's still expendable. And from what I could gather, if there isn't a shortage of men–meaning no accidental deaths in his year–by the time he passes Year 18, he's supposed to be terminated."

"Terminated."

"Terminated.   Killed.   Obliterated.   Abolished. Annihilated. Destroyed."

"Stop."

My voice trembles. I close my eyes, searching for something to hold on to, to stop the shaking. My hand curls around the whistle hanging from my neck. The crack presses against my skin.

Another minute passes. Then I hear Han stand and walk across the small room, stopping by the door. "Ah, I need to make use of the bathroom. I'll be back in a few minutes."

He leaves. Silence stretches in his absence. *Terminated.* Just the word sends a shock through me. One way or another, Neil is going to be taken. Taken from *me.* I don't care what men of the past did or didn't do. Right now I just want to put my arms around Neil and hold on tight until I'm sure he's safe and he'll be here forever.

I open my eyes and look at him. I want to study his face, as if I can see past his scars and eyes and mouth and into his brain to understand the world from his point of view, from a man's, to be sure once and for all I believe the right thing.

I can't seem to get through his face, however. But I'm content to study that.

I'm not content with the silence, though. I move closer, cautiously propping my arms on the mattress and resting my chin on them, inches from Neil's ear.

"Hey," I breathe, unsure what else to say. The obvious follow up is, "I'm sorry." But it's not enough. "I hope I helped. I hope it's less painful now. I hope you forgive me someday. I hope there's a someday for you to forgive me. I mean, I hope I see you again. I'll do whatever I can to make that happen, but…okay, never mind. No buts. I *will* see you again, and then you can choose whether to forgive me or not."

He doesn't reply. Not that I expected him to. I mean, he's unconscious. But still, I'm at a loss for words.

Kind of like when he was unsure what to do when I couldn't breathe after the fight. Maybe I should do what he did. He distracted me, and that allowed me to relax and focus on breathing, and feeling better.

I tug the whistle out from where it's pressed between my chest and the mattress. Then, cautiously, I blow into the mouthpiece.

The sound is quiet and breathy, the crack adding a second awkward whistle to. I experiment pressing down the little holes for a minute, then tuck the whistle away again, whispering, "I give up. But I tried."

I imagine him smiling, laughing, like when we were at the swimming pond. And how he smiled the day he gave me the whistle. The memory makes a smile of my own tug at the corners of my mouth. If I could go anywhere, I'd go back in time to that moment.

I reach toward him, gently brushing the backs of my knuckles against his hair. It tickles. I catch a lock between two fingers. It's soft, and it's real, and my hand is starting to shake so I withdraw it.

"Neil, I…" I let my barely audible voice trail into nothing. I don't know how to finish. Don't know what to do? Want you safe? Need you with me?

Love you?

I can taste the words on my tongue, wanting to be said. Wanting him to know. But when I try to comply, to say them, my heart wells and blocks my throat. I'm left with an empty sentence and nails digging into my palms as tears blur my vision from the truth of it.

I mouth the words instead. *Love you.* Then I slide my arms off the mattress and lean back until I can stand. I still can't swallow.

I meet Han on the way out of the room. "Leaving?" he whispers, but not in a surprised tone.

I nod. "Take care of him." I say the words with more authority than I have a right to.

He doesn't joke like last time. "I will." His gaze slides past me for a moment. Then he refocuses. "Will you come back?"

I meet his gaze. "I will. You…both of you need me." And I need you.

Han just nods.

Before I can say goodbye, an obnoxious noise rings through the hallway. The alarm. I jump, and Han scowls. On the bed, Neil stirs.

I give a last hurried nod to Han and slip out of the room. The walk back to the subway station is routine, and I hide and wait for the next departure, fighting the burning building against my eyelids. In the end, I win.

CHAPTER 37
Neil

Immeasurable time passes before the dream starts.

At first it's faint, her voice. Gradually it becomes louder, echoing and distant, as if I'm listening from underwater. Words fade in and out, sometimes clear, sometimes muffled.

I'm sorry. I hope... forgive me...someday for you...I mean...never...

Forgive her? I want to open my eyes, find her, tell her I wish she would come back. I don't want her to think I'm one of those monsters like the mayor said. I can't seem to find my eyes, though, or my legs or any other part of me. I'm just drifting, listening.

The next sound I hear can only be one thing: Morgan playing a whistle. Nothing else sounds quite as painful, or hilarious at the same time. Detached images of her laughing, and of me carving that whistle float through the emptiness.

The playing stops. *Tried*, her voice says, and I want to grin and joke and say *yeah, you tried, maybe if I showed you how to* actually *play it you could do more than try next time.*

What she says next is short, but clearer, like her voice moved right next to me. *Neil, I...*

She's so close. I struggle to turn in my nothingness, to face her voice, waiting for what seems like hours, but it could have been only seconds. Then the dream ends.

The next time I'm aware of anything, I can find my body. Once I do I also find the pain, deep aches emanating from my hand and my neck. It's not the same stinging pain, though, as it was before I finally fell asleep.

I wonder if this is also part of my dream. When I try to move my fingers to see them, I find they're held immobile, bound to something soft but firm. More senses flow into my consciousness. Sound, a ringing sound, the alarm. How am I going to go to work? Somehow I doubt I'll get a day off. Unless there's more planned for me.

The ringing fades. I can hear quieter noises now, voices. Han's talking to someone. Ms. Elliott? I'm not conscious enough for that to make sense.

Minutes pass as I debate whether or not to open my eyes. Dread keeps them shut as I hear Han speak again, and a soft voice answers before the door shuts. The floor by my pillow creaks. Someone's standing over me. My eyes squeeze tighter.

"Neil," Han says softly. "Are you awake?"

I let one more second pass, stretching out my time in the safety of the darkness. Then I open my eyes. I think I'm dreaming again, as the first thing I see are gray eyes, above me. "Morgan?"

A hand presses over my mouth to keep me from saying anything else. I refocus, and disappointment floods me as I see the blond hair and glasses framing the eyes. I'm not used to the disappointed feeling. My hopes are never high enough to fall. But in that one wild moment between being asleep and waking up, I wasn't myself.

Han's gaze flicks to the doorway, as if making sure we're alone. "How does it feel?" he demands.

"Better," I say, or try to say. No sound results. I try again. "Better."

"Oh, good." Han's expression visibly relaxes. "Good."

"How did I get to sleep?" I close my eyes again. All I can remember from last night is resisting the urge to toss and turn, and therefore my mind churned instead. Han was awake with me for hours. And then, somehow, I woke up with my hand set and my shoulder bandaged.

"I forced you to drink some alcohol. You were beyond resisting, and it obviously worked." Han sounds comfortable in his usual tone of nonchalant superiority.

I'm far beyond protesting. "What happened to me?"

"Morgan stopped by."

My eyes fly open. "Morgan?" Muscles in my torso clench as I struggle to sit up. "Does she hate me? I mean...us? Is she–"

Once again Han's hand cuts me off. He shoves me back against the mattress, shoulders suddenly stiff. I fight him for only a second before I see the new figure in the doorway. Figures, actually. Two women. And one is Ms. Meryl.

"Good morning," she says, surveying us. She walks the short distance to the edge of my bed. "What in the world happened here?"

I clench my teeth to keep from saying, *You know what happened. You made it happen.*

But that's not what she's talking about. She points at my hand, at the makeshift splint. "Is that a pillow? This is considered improper use of housing items." She fixes Han with a disdainful expression. "Untie it."

Han doesn't move as Ms. Meryl jabs a long finger at the sheets winding around the pillow, the material keeping my hand safe. I turn to catch his eye, wincing at the pain in my shoulder. Once Han looks at me I nod, telling him to do it, to avoid having this happen to him.

Han shakes his head. I glare, but he turns away. "No," he tells Ms. Meryl.

She seems pleased, pulling out her remote. Han puts on a good show, falling backward when she presses the button, face screwing up in what only I know is fake pain.

"I guess I will then." She yanks on the knot. I press the back of my other hand against my mouth, crushing my lower lip, to keep myself from screaming as the sheet unravels and the pillow falls away.

"You can't–" Han begins to protest, his voice shaking as he scrambles to his feet. Ms. Meryl quickly interrupts him.

"*You* should be preparing for work. Go. Now."

Han stares at her, his mouth hanging open. His image wavers as my eyes grow watery from the pain.

"*Now.*" Ms. Meryl punches at the remote again. I nod as well, silently begging him to leave. Han hesitates, then acts out the shock and retreats from the room. Ms. Meryl's silent companion watches him go, then both women face me.

"Consider yourself lucky," says Ms. Meryl. "You've been given a reprieve. A second chance."

She motions for me to stand up. As I struggle to push myself off the mattress, I brace myself for her to say, *So get going and get to work.* Instead they just make me put on a clean shirt, a process nearly impossible for me to do without crying, and lead me outside into the early morning darkness.

For the third time in less than twenty-four hours I find myself at the subway station. My feet stop by the main door, almost against my will, but a single shock from one of the remotes has me stumbling inside and down the stairs. When I come to a stop by the tracks I can feel my legs trembling. I cradle my broken hand against my stomach.

"Don't act so ungrateful," Ms. Meryl snaps. She walks over and glances at my shaking knees. "Most boys would be happy to be going to live in the Blue City."

And now my blood really does run cold. I don't say anything, just stumble back, edging closer to the subway tracks. I can only see the pit out of the corner of my eye, yet it seems to fill my entire vision. I take another step. I'd rather be there, under the wheels of a speeding subway, than where I know I'm going.

Hands grab me and hold me still. For a wild moment I fight them, desperate and, for a second, feeling empowered. I'm stronger than I thought. I throw off the woman and lunge backward. But she grabs my hand, the broken one, and that's all it takes. It's worse than the remotes. She twists my wrist around and I drop to the ground, in too much agony to resist.

I go into a state of detachment. I'm not aware of anything until I'm being shaken back into reality. Sterile white walls surround me. I vaguely remember getting off the subway in Blue City and walking through empty hallways to get here, but my mind doesn't supply any more information.

It's a new woman looking at me now, dressed in a spotless white lab coat. A doctor of some sort. And I can guess what sort.

"There you are. You were a bit dazed for a minute." She laughs, but it's not a real laugh, like when Morgan laughs. Morgan's eyes always close and crinkle up. This doctor surveys me as she chuckles, pulling a cart of medical equipment toward her. I'm sitting on the edge of a bed rimmed with metal and set up for medical practice, and yet I can feel the mattress is more comfortable than my own bed.

The doctor tilts her head. "Lie down," she instructs, still smiling.

"No." The word tumbles from my lips before I even consider stopping it. But like all of my attempts at resistance, it fails. The doctor just shrugs and taps her remote.

The feeling is the same as when Ms. Meryl immobilized me yesterday. I fall backward, striking my head on the metal framing. The doctor drags me by my shoulders to the top of the bed and positions my head on a pillow.

"There." She consults something on her wall before unhooking a piece of equipment from her rolling cart. I can only watch as the mask is placed over my nose and mouth. Something that smells too sweet fills my lungs. I try to hold my breath, but I'm already too dizzy.

"Just relax," the doctor says as the room spins. It rotates faster and faster until it no longer moves, it's just a blur of color, which slowly dissolves into darkness.

When the darkness melts away the mask is gone, and I'm alone. The first thing I notice is I can move again. As I sit up, my head spins. I clutch my skull with my hands to steady it.

Then I realize what I just did and pull my left hand in front of me. It's no longer swollen, or even bruised. I wiggle my fingers. Pricks of pain spike along them, but they move nonetheless. Quickly I check my shoulder, where the cut is, or *was*. It seems to have healed days, even weeks, early and is now just a scar, an 'M' etched into my skin.

Instead of relief, fear shoots through me. I swing my legs off the bed and stand up, looking around. The door to the room is closed. There's a keyhole on this side, but it probably locks from the outside too. They're certainly not going to leave it open. The medical equipment sits secured in a corner. And there's a full-length mirror beside the bed.

I know it was put there just for this, for me to look into. Therefore, I shouldn't do it. But I can't help myself. I step closer, then blink, wondering for one ignorant second who is blinking back at me, wearing a white shirt and black pants.

When I realize the obvious I feel only blank shock. My eyes stare at my reflection, trying to see past the illusion and to myself, the real me. Because this reflection has to be wrong. It's me, but it's not.

My skin is clear, completely clear. No sunburn, no blemishes, no scars. I check my arms and my torso and find the same condition. And the second most obvious thing is my hair. It's light now, so light it's blond at the tips. Everything's perfect, artistic, flawless. The only feature completely unchanged is my eyes. They're still dark, and they're still cast in shadow when I look down.

So I stare at my eyes, the one familiar thing about myself, for as long as I can bear to be by the mirror. Then I retreat, knowing by now it's useless to try the door or search for another way out. My mind concocts wild ideas of escape, but I can't focus on them. I just sink back on the edge of the bed and press my smooth hands against my eyelids so I don't have to see anything.

CHAPTER 38
Morgan

At around two o'clock in the afternoon, two things happen in rapid succession. The first is my mom trying to force-feed me to a bowl of rice because I haven't had an appetite all day, which she claims is not healthy. The second is Laney barreling into my bedroom.

My mom leaves and Laney tackles me–she is a football player, after all–knocking me into a sitting position on my bed while wrapping her arms around my neck. Her hair, now a deep gold color, obscures my vision.

"I'm so sorry," she gasps, leaning away to meet my gaze. I drop my gaze, but she pulls my chin back around so she can give me an intense stare. "I just heard. I was out practicing for a few hours and took my Pow off, so I didn't know until now and I can't believe this happened. I have to be here for you."

"I guess you are," I mumble, glancing around her for her omnipresent shadow. "Where's Lloyd?"

She looks confused for a moment. "He's not here. I...actually didn't tell him I came here; I just heard and ran right over to see you. Forget about our argument the other day, okay? I mean, I still don't believe you, but that doesn't matter right now. Eat your rice." She points at the bowl sitting untouched on my desk.

I shake my head, nearly gagging at the thought. I've been on the verge of nausea and consumed with listlessness the whole day, trying and failing to get some rest so I can be awake to go back to City 4 tonight. But I don't care. I'll sleepwalk there if I have to.

"Okay. I'll get you to eat later. Right now you need to talk. Or let me talk. Or you just cry on my shoulder. I'm so, so sorry about what happened. It's such a terrible accident."

I force back a lump in my throat, not letting myself

dwell on the word 'accident.' Laney sits with me in silence for a long time. I keep expecting to feel like she's a stranger, as if there's a wall between us. Everything she thinks is derived from the lies we've been told all our lives. And everything in my mind has to do with the last few months, all I've learned about reality; or, rather, the lack thereof.

But somehow Laney doesn't feel like just another part of the fabrication. Right now, as she's rubbing my shoulder and forcing herself to be quiet even though I know she has a million words on the tip of her tongue, she's real. Our years of friendship are real. And having something real, however inconsequential right now, lets me breathe a bit deeper.

An hour passes, or maybe two, while I try to find peace. Laney plays videos on her Pow and messages Lloyd to let him know she's fine and she'll see him this evening. Around three-thirty Laney finally does speak. "Okay, eat. Now."

I sigh, but reach for the rice. By this time it's crusty on top from sitting out so long. I tell Laney I'll find something else in the kitchen.

On my way down the steps I hear my mom at the front door, talking to someone. I stop to listen, and as I do I see Mia backing out to the street, saying "...check as fast as I can." She's holding a canvas bag. Something black pokes out. Somehow I doubt it's her ballet leotard. And speaking of ballet, shouldn't she be there right now?

Mia's out the door before I reach the bottom step. Mom's walking away, to the den. I follow her, stumbling once on the smooth floor as dizziness passes over me.

"Mom?" I lean heavily against the wall. I *really* need to nap soon.

Mom glances up, then turns back to the den closet, the one where she keeps her medical supplies. She's frantically searching through her supplies and key rings, seeming to grow more frustrated as she rejects items.

"Mom," I say again. "Why was Mia?"

Mom looks at me again, then at the time floating on the walls. "I have to go," she says, slamming the closet shut, two doctor coats draped over her arm. She still seems frustrated, though, as if she didn't find what she was looking for. "I don't have time to explain, but I will. Later."

"No," I say, lack of carbohydrates warring with sudden panic in my mind. "What happened?"

"Nothing," she says. "Yet." I don't believe her. As she passes I grab her hand, but she pulls away. "Morgan, I need you to do something for me right now. I need you to act normal."

I gape. Before I can reply she strides out the front door and into the afternoon.

I climb back up the stairs. Laney protests because I didn't bring anything up, and she *knew* I lied, and she'll be right back because she doesn't care how much I resist, she's going to make me eat. She returns with yogurt. We argue back and forth a while about me eating it, but it's bantering, something we used to do a lot. It comes naturally, and so it's easy for me to act *normal*.

Why?

It isn't until the light from my window is dimming to late afternoon that she says, "You need your strength to keep face," and we start to actually talk about something.

"To keep face? For you? Can't you deal with my anti-social face?" I mean to accompany the comment with an eye roll, but I just stifle a yawn instead.

Laney slowly shakes her head. "Um...not what I meant," she says. "You need to get ready."

I raise one eyebrow.

"I knew it," Laney exclaims. "I knew you'd be in denial. When I found out it would be tonight, I just knew it was too soon. You're not ready. But, I mean, it'll help, right? To move on and forget about Mitchell."

"What?"

"You probably don't think so *now*." Laney tries using a comforting tone. "Everyone was surprised when they first got the message about it, but my mom said it'll be good for you."

Without consciously doing it, I feel myself standing up

and taking a step away. "Laney. What are you talking about?"

The question is barely out of my mouth when I hear raised voices emanating from the hallway. My door swings open and Mom bursts in, followed by Ross.

"Honey, be reasonable," he's saying, reaching for Mom's hand. Mom moves her arm out of reach.

"Leave me alone, Ross." Mom's voice shakes with anger. "This is insane, and here you are just going along with it."

"The mayor made this decision." Ross's voice is calm and unfazed, like always. "She must have Morgan's best interests in mind."

"The hell she does." Mom turns to me. "I have to talk to you," she says urgently. "In private. But first, let me get a hold of Mayor Vee. I'll–"

"I can relay a message to her, if you'd like." A new voice joins the conversation as someone tall and blond strides through the doorway: Vaughn, the mayor's Like.

Mom recovers from her surprise quickly. "I'd like to speak to her in person, actually."

"Well," Vaughn says, "she's busy right now. You'll see her tonight, though. In the meanwhile, I can tell you're not ready. That's okay, you still have a little time. But Victoria instructed me to escort you."

"That won't be nec–" Mom starts to say, but I interrupt.

"Escort us where?" My voice should be more urgent, reflecting the panic twisting at my intestines, but it seems like the outside of me is unaffected. Almost like a shell. Almost like Neil's usual expression. Stony.

Vaughn regards me in an equally smooth manner. "To your Amora," he says simply.

CHAPTER 39
Neil

They leave me alone for a long time. Too long. I can't stand this. I try not looking at the mirror, but it's still there, taunting me, showing me a picture of white walls and a person I don't know every time I catch sight of it.

Finally, I snap. What do they think, I'll just sit here, staring at what they've done to me? I'll just *let* them, because they're women? What else can they do to me, except finish the Conversion, which will happen anyway?

These thoughts raging through my mind, I jump off the gurney. My feet hit the floor in a manner I'm not used to, not heavily, not unevenly, but almost gracefully. As if my center of balance has been perfected, too. Which, of course, it probably has.

I stride to the mirror and take in the image one more time. This is not me. And I'll prove it. Still staring at my eyes–those *are* my eyes–I grab the edges of the mirror and pull.

I have more power than I anticipated. I spin around, sending the mirror toppling past me. It crashes to the floor, landing on its side, base rolling to a secure position on the smooth surface a moment later. The mirror stays there, awkwardly propped up, as cracks form spider webs across the glass.

I kick it. I drive the heel of my shoe into the center, glass shattering and raining down from the frame to scatter across the floor. The pieces around me glint upwards, only reflecting slivers of my appearance, nothing recognizable.

I take a few deep breaths, then back away, settling against the gurney again. There are thousands of mirrors shipped to the Color cities every year. This one's easily replaceable. But right here, right now, there's nothing else in the room to burn images of the me that's not me into my eyes.

Then I hear noise.

I watch as the doorknob shakes, scraping noises echoing around the room. They've come back. Finally. Nausea swoops through my stomach, but I force it away. This is happening either way, and I'm going to spend my last few moments in my own head *calmly*.

But the door doesn't slide open right away. More scratching emits from the knob, as if something is poking around inside it.

My eyes widen. No. It's not...it's a trick. They've messed with my mind already, making me see things. And hear things. I scoot back further on the gurney, twisting the thin sheets between my fingers.

The scratching and clicking stops. I force myself to breathe. Nothing happens. Then the door opens and someone slips through.

They *definitely* messed with my mind.

Han catches my eye and puts a finger to his lips, using his other hand to push the door shut. It doesn't latch. And I wasn't planning on saying anything, anyway. They can make me see things, but they can't make me talk to my hallucinations.

I wonder if Morgan's going to walk in next.

Hallucination Han presses against the wall by the door, wearing his work shirt and clutching lock picks in the hand that's warning me to be quiet. As he looks at me, as he registers my appearance, horror seeps into his expression. I keep my own face stony.

"You–" he mouths, one arm twitching forward, as if to reach across the room to me.

I can't help it. I glare at him, face twisting into a scowl, and shake my head.

Hallucination Han closes his eyes and dramatically wipes his hand across his forehead in relief, but I can see he's shaking. Actually shaking. "You're not. Thank goodness. You're still you. I'd know that expression anywhere."

The words are out of my mouth before I can stop them. "Are you real?"

He nods once, then again, eyes wide. "Yes." Then he freezes, head cocked, and motions toward the door. He's listening.

I can hear words as well. They're faint, but audible.

"Hello," one woman says, tone formal but confused.

"Hi," another woman replies, more cheerfully. "I'm Dr. Rachel Waters."

Rachel Waters? The name triggers something in my memory. Waters. Morgan's last name. This is her mom?

"Oh. Mia," Morgan's mom says, "would you please hold the tray?"

There's another pause. Mia? As in Morgan's friend Mia? Mia and Morgan's mom are outside the door talking to someone, and Han is in my room?

I am crazy. Or dead. Or about to be both.

And if Mia, Han, and Morgan's mom are here, where's Morgan?

Does she still hate me?

Morgan's mom speaks again. "Thanks. Mia is my intern for today. She's here to observe."

Mia's not an intern; Mia's a ballerina. And Morgan mentioned Mia hates the sight of blood. How could she be an intern to Morgan's mom, the doctor?

My hands rub at my temples, my eyes squeezed shut. They're lying. Why?

"I'm Dr. Kayla Cazi," the other woman says. "From Yellow City. Are you scheduled to be down here?"

"Of course." Morgan's mom's voice is smooth. "Oh, were you here to perform a part-two Conversion?"

The other doctor answers. "Yes, in this room. It's the only one active today."

"Oh," Morgan's mom says again. "That can't be right. I got a notice about a change of staff. I'm to do the Conversion today. Mia's from another City, and no Conversions are scheduled there until Thursday, so we received special transport to see this one. Didn't...didn't anyone tell you?" Now the confusion has transformed into concern.

"Dr. Langston, who did the part-one Conversion, just told me to proceed at four o'clock," the other doctor says.

"There must have been a miscommunication. I'll have to ask later. But you're free to take a break, if you want. I'm sure you're invited to the Amora tonight."

"That poor girl's second Amora."

What second Amora? Who has a second Amora? How long until these questions make my head explode?

"How awful," the other doctor continues. "But exciting for her also. The mayor invited me to come, yes."

"I'll see you there, then," Morgan's mom says sweetly.

There's a slight pause. Then the other doctor says, "Are you *sure* you're supposed to be here? Do you have the key?"

"I do." The doorknob twists for a moment, then the door creaks open slightly. My gaze flies to Han, but he hasn't moved.

"All right," the other doctor says. "Thanks. Good luck."

"See you later," Morgan's mom replies. There's another few seconds of waiting, just waiting, and then the door opens fully and a figure in a white lab coat darts in. I clench my teeth. Behind her is another figure in a coat, holding a tray. She uses her foot to slam the door behind her. The lock clicks.

The girl holding the tray is Mia. She sees Han first, then slowly follows Han's gaze. When she catches sight of me the tray in her hand lurches, as if she came close to dropping it.

"Neil?" Her eyes stretch wide. "Neil, do you–?"

"I know who you are," I say, either too crazy to care about talking or starting to believe, maybe, they're actually here. As I speak, the sound of my voice shocks me. Last time I'd spoken above a whisper it sounded rough, like always. Now it's smoother, and stronger, even as it shakes.

"Oh, thank God." Mia's lips form the words as she kneels to set the tray down. Her expression borders on nausea. I don't blame her. The metal instruments on the tray are making my blood run cold from across the room. The other doctor carried it. For me. For the second part of the Conversion.

My knees shake as I push myself off the gurney. I take in the three people standing in front of me as I test my legs.

"Han, what's going on?"

"I think they're here to help, Neil."

I listen to Han, but I'm watching the woman, Morgan's mom, pacing around the edge of the room, looking lost in thought. "How did you...all of you...find..."

Han points at Mia. "I ran into her, and she told me about this."

"You *ran into* her?"

"In your city," Mia says. "I left early from ballet today when I heard Morgan was having another Amora tonight."

Morgan. It's Morgan who's having a second Amora.

And they're handing me to her on a silver platter.

"I stopped in the mayor's office," Mia continues, "because I had a feeling you might be...involved. And I saw on the wall that you were schedule for a part-two Conversion at four, so I went to Morgan's house. But her friend Laney was there, which meant I couldn't get to Morgan in time. So Rachel"–she nods toward Morgan's mom, who's pondering the broken mirror–"gave me Morgan's jeans and polo and hat. I remembered Morgan talking about how to get to your dorm. I was so freaked out, but I found it."

I feel two distinct, irrational emotions at realizing I'm going to be Morgan's Like. One is relief. At least it's Morgan. And the other is horror. I don't want her to see me like that. Likes disgust her. *I'd* disgust her.

Or, rather, my shell would.

"I came across Mia outside our room," Han tells me. "I ran back from work to check on you, and you weren't there, which was very upsetting by the way. I was going to be incredibly mad at you if you were already dead."

"We came back here on the subway," Mia says. "And we met Rachel in the Amora building, and she showed us this room, where Morgan saw Seffa's Like and freaked out. And you're under it, in a long hallway, full of creepy medical stuff. Neil, I'm so glad you're not...I mean, that you're okay."

"Rachel hadn't been able to find a key, so I picked all the locks," Han adds, trying for theatrical importance. Then his gaze flicks over me again and his bravado disappears. "Neil, your hand."

I glance at my left hand. Last time Han saw it, it was twice this size and purple. "I know."

"They fixed it?"

"Yes. No. It hurts to move it. But it's functional."

"And your shoulder?"

In reply I pull the collar of my shirt down. "The scar is there. They left it."

"Neil..." Han sounds like he wants to say a million other things to make me feel better or something. But I don't care. He doesn't have to say anything. I'm too busy trying to come to grips with the fact that he's actually here to listen anyway.

I'd almost forgotten about Morgan's mom. "Neil," she says, and I jump, facing her. She's definitely the woman from the picture Morgan showed me on the office wall. Except now she looks anxious instead of happy. "I'm–"

"Morgan's mom."

She nods. "Yes."

"How is she? I mean, how is Morgan?" I stumble over the question, rocking back and forth on my feet.

"She's not great. But we need to talk about you. You're scheduled to be presented at her Amora tonight." Morgan's mom starts to pace, fiddling with her lab coat.

Han steps in front of her. "Can we get him out of here?"

Morgan's mom slowly shakes her head. "There's no way to successfully run away in the given circumstances."

My right hand massages my left. Pain prickles in my bones. "Well, I'd rather die than undergo a Conversion."

"You can't *die*." Mia's eyes widen. "Do you know what that would do to Morgan?"

My expression remains stony, but something twists in

my ribcage. *What* would it do to Morgan? Has Mia talked to her? Maybe this means Morgan doesn't hate me? "Then what are we going to do?"

Morgan's mom stops pacing. "We're going to do the only thing we can for now, to keep everyone safe," she says, more to herself than any of us. "We're going to turn you into a Like."

An hour later, my mind feels like it's about to explode. Morgan's mom drilled the procedure into my head and made me practice, trying to prepare me for what I have to do. She finally stops, though, and claims she has to find a supply closet because I need a jacket and shoes, and then she has to run home to talk to Morgan. Han reopens the lock to let her out and she leaves with a few last-minute instructions.

Han seems to have had enough. He watches Morgan's mom leave the room, then slips out the door himself. I glance at Mia, and she frowns. Then she follows him.

Well, I'm not sitting here by myself. I hurry after them, the smooth floor cool beneath my feet, making sure not to latch the door behind me.

The hallways are empty. I only vaguely remember being dragged past these sterile white walls this morning. "What are you doing," I ask when Han and Mia stop in front of a door at the end of the hall. It has large red lettering across it reading *Do Not Enter.*

"I'm going to figure out what's in here," Han says. "We passed it on the way to your room. The door's cold and, I mean, 'Do Not Enter'—well, that's juicy."

"What if you're caught?" Mia peers over Han's shoulder as he starts to fiddle with the lock.

He shrugs. "Where would we be if Neil and I obeyed every 'Do Not Enter' sign when investigating where Kellan went? We'd be in Ignorantland, of course. Damn it, the pins reset." He retracts his tools and switches out one for a more slender pick. "If my vaguely possible prediction about the contents of this room is correct, then things might get a lot more interesting."

I consider what he said. "Things are interesting enough." I want him to hurry up. I feel exposed in the hallway, even though, according to Han, only a few people have a key to even get down here (and even fewer have the lock-picking skills, he added). Still, it's those few I'm worried about.

Mia touches the door and nods. "It's definitely cold. What do you think is in there?"

"I'll tell you when I get it open," Han replies. "If I'm wrong, then I will save myself the embarrassment of having jumped to conclusions. Also, once we see what's in there, I might be able to fabricate some tale about how I knew it all along. Ah! Here we go."

Han pockets his lock picks and pushes on the door. It swings open slowly. The space beyond is dark, but a few little green and red lights blink at us from the blackness.

This only seems to make Han more sure of himself. He beckons us in, feeling along the wall. As his hand slides over the surface the wall lights up, casting a dim glow over the contents of the room.

"Shut the door," Han tells Mia. She silently pushes the heavy door closed behind us. As we stand there, the cold permeates my thin clothing.

"Was your prediction right?" I say after a few seconds.

"I knew it all along."

The room is small, with a table in the corner. Han runs his fingertips over two boxes propped on the table. The sleek silver boxes sport green and red lights blinking from little buttons. Between the silver boxes is a black one, wider and flatter. Cords run from it to the boxes, and from the boxes to the wall. The whole thing just sits there.

"What is it?" Mia asks. I already have an idea, but I let Han explain.

"It's a computer. A very powerful computer. I've worked with these for inventory many times. And often I was able to explore them without the women noticing."

"Computer," Mia muses. "What's it do?"

Han presses a button on the flat middle section. The surface lights up, further illuminating the room.

"Computers are the ultimate control centers. They hold more power and information than any device, ever. I'm positive that behind all your fabulous walls and all-purpose devices, Mia, there's a computer. And considering the placement of *this* computer, I bet I know what it's behind."

"What?" Mia and I ask.

"The artificial intelligence for the Likes." Han pulls a drawer out from the table. In it is a slab of black material with letters and numbers on it and an oval attached to a cord. Keyboard and mouse. "This is great," he says, tapping on the keyboard. The screen changes as he does.

"So how does this help?" Mia peers closer.

Han examines the two boxes. "Maybe one's a backup," he says to himself.

"What if you broke them?" I suggest.

Han taps one of the boxes. "It's coated with some thick metal." Then he tries to shove it off the table. "And welded down, apparently. Perhaps so somebody can't break it? Just a thought."

"Then how does this help?" Mia repeats.

"There's more than one way to break a computer." Han adjusts his glasses. "I might be able to manipulate it from the inside."

"And what will manipulating it do?"

Han glances at Mia, then to me, then back to the computer. "I don't know yet."

I sit in the room. And sit. It's dim and the chair is hard, but I just sit still. I'm supposed to.

The door opens. Pulsing lights from the room outside flash against the wall in here. A woman walks in, the mayor's voice trailing her.

"…to convey how proud I am." The voice echoes around the small room.

I raise my head to look at the unfamiliar woman. Just

look, nothing more. I don't blink. I don't stand.

"Mason?" The woman studies me. I nod, expression calm. "It's almost time."

"I wanted to do something special for you," I hear the mayor say.

The woman indicates I should stand. I do so.

"To show you I'm on your side," the mayor finishes.

"Ready?" The woman points toward the door, toward the crowd.

I smile pleasantly. "Of course."

CHAPTER 40
Morgan

The only time Vaughn strays from sight is to let me put on Mom's black dress, and he insists Mom and Ross wait outside with him while Laney helps me change. Because, since I am so struck by tragedy, I am now two years old and can't dress myself.

To be somewhat fair, I did go into a state of mental nothingness once Vaughn told me I'd be having a second Amora. Well, I might have tried to run out the door first, but Ross caught me and held me back, saying something about how he knows I feel bad now, but once I have my new Like I'll feel much, much better about the whole thing. I only calmed down, though, when Mom grabbed my hand and said, "Morgan. It's okay. It's *okay*. Trust me."

Somehow she sounded like she knew what I was worried about. Neil. But she didn't–couldn't–tell me more in the present company. Her tone was the only thing that let me start breathing again. It was the same tone she'd used when I got sick at age two, and the same one she used when I freaked out about finals in class 14, the calm voice I heard when I had a bad day, even if she was in one of her own moods. It was real.

The Amora building is once again black and white. Laney steers me around the building to the table where my former classmates are sitting. Ross leads my mom away, to the designated parents' side of the main seating area.

The girls start to exclaim over me, saying how pretty I look and how sorry they are and how awful I must feel and how lucky I am to have *two* Amoras and what did I do with my hair, because it's absolutely gor-ge-ous tonight.

I feel myself shrinking away from their chatter, wanting no part of it. Laney puts a hand on my elbow and waves everyone to silence. I expect her to say something about my hair and the clip she put in, but instead she says, "Guys, really. This is hard enough without you all crowding her. Be quiet for once."

Gratitude sparks somewhere in my emotionless mind frame. I would've expected that gesture from Mia. Speaking of Mia... I turn, searching the room, and catch sight of her dashing through the main doors. She's wearing a white dress with one strap. I blink. How did she get my dress?

Mom carried her bag with her here, and a hanger poked out the top. She met Mia here and gave her the dress, and Mia must have changed in the monorail bathrooms across the street. Why? If Mia wanted the dress, why didn't she stay at my house when she stopped by earlier?

Mia comes right over to me, eyeing Laney, who still has her hand resting protectively on my arm.

"Morgan," Mia says slowly.

I twist to face her. "What?"

Mia's still looking at Laney. "Come find me when it starts."

"What?"

"Look," Mia murmurs, "don't freak out. I'll explain more later, but just don't freak out, okay?"

Which is almost exactly what Mom said. "Freak out about what?" I begin to stand, but Mia just glances at all the girls craning their necks to listen in and walks to the empty seat across the table.

The commencement ceremony starts seconds later. Mayor Vee takes the stage and addresses the room. "Welcome, all. I'd like to say a few special words here."

The building grows quiet. Mayor Vee wears a floor-length white gown, light lip-gloss, and heavy eyeliner, making her eyes bulge in an innocent and angelic manner.

"As you all know, a tragic event happened yesterday. Morgan Waters lost her Like, Mitchell, in an accident."

Some murmurs run through the crowd, and sympathetic looks flash my way, ignorant, sympathetic looks.

"So tonight," Mayor Vee continues, "we're going to make it all better. Morgan, could you come up here please?"

A pang of something passes through me. Adrenaline or panic? Now? I have to go up there now? It always happens at nine. Always.

Mia makes eye contact, and my feelings are mirrored in her expression. She won't get a chance to tell me anything. I wonder if Mayor Vee is doing this on purpose.

"Go," Laney whispers encouragingly. I stand slowly, my legs leaden as I walk toward the stage. I imagine my metallic joints grinding together as I climb the stairs and come to a stop before Mayor Vee.

Everyone else gets the cue, standing and gathering around the stage, as if they were just dancing, like it's nine o'clock and this is just another Presentation ceremony.

"Morgan." Mayor Vee places a hand on my shoulder. "I know you've been through a lot of tough events recently." Her gaze bore into mine, telling me she does know. More so than the crowd, who thinks she's just talking about Mitchell's death. "I am impressed at how you've handled these events. You're a strong young woman, and I want to convey to you just how proud I am."

She pauses, and the silence stretches on. I still stare into her eyes, looking but not seeing. A rush of images overtakes my vision, some relevant, some not. Almost all are of Neil. I feel my hand reach up and touch the cord around my neck, still attached to the whistle, which is covered by the neck of my dress. It anchors me, allowing me to listen to Mayor Vee as she goes on, voice echoing around the smooth, monochromatic walls. "So I wanted to do something special for you, to show you that I'm on your side."

She turns now, facing the dance floor. As usual, the people part to make a walkway. My mind cringes from the déjà vu, and suddenly I can't stand it. I shut my eyes tight, turning away, trying to drown out the *ooh*s of the crowd with the roar of my own muddled thoughts.

"Morgan, open your eyes." I shake my head, squeezing

them tighter, taking a wobbly step away from where I know the steps are.

The mayor grips my shoulders, spinning me around. "Open. Your. Eyes."

I have to sooner or later. I know. I can't be a wimp forever. So I open them now.

For a blissful moment the building is out of focus, just a blur of black and white. Then it snaps into coherence, and I'm staring right at him.

"Neil," I gasp.

He looks evenly back at me. His hair is too light, his skin too smooth, his smile too perfect. Only his eyes are completely unchanged, so I watch them as my stomach plummets miles beneath the stage.

"Hi," he says, in a voice that's too steady.

"No." I stumble backward. "No. Neil. *Neil.*" My voice is rising, nearing hysteria already. I catch glimpses of people in the crowd, looking at each other, whispering. Laney's face flashes across my vision, her expression confused, contrasting with Lloyd's blank one beside her.

Neil's voice reaches me again, sounding surprised. "What? My name is Mason. Wow, you're prettier than they told me."

"Don't *say* that." My voice trembles beyond any hope of controlling it. Terror races through me, practically pumping through my veins, like an acid in my bloodstream. He starts to walk toward me. I back away even further. My heel slips over the edge of the stage and I sway, trying to regain my balance.

"No, no, no," I whisper, or maybe scream, I don't know. I just don't want him any closer. It's not him. What did Mia say? *Don't freak out.* Too late, Mia.

He's only a step away. I whirl around, finding air. I teeter as I hit the ground, my center of gravity swinging wildly, and I see shoes land next to me. Shoes attached to feet that belong to Neil. Belong*ed* to Neil.

His arm wraps around my waist, steadying me, just like

when I got off the wall in City 4. But instead of tingles, I feel shivers of horror as a patronizing tone says, "Morgan, calm down."

"Don't," I say, gasping for air. "*Don't.*" I rip away, but my head spins too much. My knees slam against the floor. In my whirling vision I glimpse Mia's face, pushing through the crowd, and Laney's dress, making its way over, but they're not getting here fast enough.

Neil speaks above me, and his tone is urgent. "Morgan, *calm down.*"

I can't. I can't calm down. I put my hands to my face and they come away wet with tears. My breathing is short and frantic as panic overcomes me. The whistle swings free now, bumping my arms. I turn and press my face against Neil's leg, fighting sobs.

His leg moves and he crouches, putting his hands on my face and forcing me to meet his gaze. Unlike when I looked at Mayor Vee, I *see* as well. His eyes. They're not blank, like every other Like. It's as if I'm hallucinating he's there, somewhere, behind them.

I squeeze my eyes shut, but I can still feel him there, so close. "I'm sorry," I cry, wanting him to know how much I wish I had done something when I could. How much I wish he was still here. Wanting him to hear me, and knowing he can't.

My airway tightens further and my heart races in my throat until I can't breathe. When I open my eyes there are black clouds swirling at the edge of my vision. Last time this happened, I met Neil. Now it's because he's gone.

Except this time his hand moves off my face and tugs at the shoelace around my neck. He pulls it over my head and raises the whistle to his lips. When he starts to play, the sound fills my ears, blocking out the calls and the movement of the women, distracting me enough that the pressure on my lungs lessens and my head can stop spinning.

It's only seconds before I force my eyes back open and draw air into my lungs. Faces flash by my vision. Mia:

concerned, but not panicking. Mom: calculating, looking at something past me. Laney: freaked out.

Lloyd's face appears beside Laney's, and his arms wrap around hers. "No," he says. "Stay back."

"She's my friend," Laney screams back at him. "Let me go!"

Lloyd shakes his head. The next moment Laney's fist collides with the side of his nose. Lloyd falls back, pressing his hands to his face, red dripping onto his fingers. Then he's engulfed by the crowd.

I watch Laney cradle her hand and drop so her head is level with mine. "Breathe," she commands.

I nod, telling her I already am. As I do, the whistle stops playing. I turn my head, my gaze stopping within inches of his. Of whose? If it's not really Neil, then how did the Like know to play the whistle? Because only Neil, the real Neil, has ever done that for me. Would a Like know how to play? I doubt it. But if it is really Neil, then why is he so...flawless?

The chattering grows quiet and two tall, white heels plant themselves just inches from my knees. I slowly look up, and find myself locked in the glare of Mayor Vee.

"I thought you could take this in stride," she said. "I'm trying to show you I'm on your side. Isn't this what you wanted?"

"I wanted Neil," I whisper, so quietly I can barely hear myself. But Mayor Vee seems to understand.

"You got him," she says, voice low enough only Laney and I, and whoever is in Neil's head, can hear. "He's right there. He's just *better*. He looks better. He acts better. He's fit to be in *our* society now."

"You destroyed him."

"I *fixed* him."

I push myself up, gathering my feet beneath me. I'm a bit unsteady, but at least I'm now face to face with the mayor.

"You made an illusion." My words echo around the walls. "You and the other Mayors, you make everything an illusion. Every *Like* is a fake, a created personality." I turn to

307

Laney. "Lloyd isn't real. He's just another copy of a *perfect* partner. You're all so oblivious," I say to the room at large. My mouth opens, more words poised on my tongue, but Mayor Vee grabs my shoulders, leaning in close, stopping me.

"This behavior is unacceptable," she hisses. Behind her, people in the crowd gape, appearing blurry past the mayor's hair. A few faces seem out of place, too calm. "I'll have you live in a Number City, if you like *men* so much. You'll never have a daughter. You'll live with your Like, Mason, and you'll be content. Do you understand me?"

"Yes, *Mayor*," I say through clenched teeth. "I understand your intentions. But I can promise you that making me disappear, like women did with men, won't help anything. Your problems will stay here. This approach never solved anything."

"Be quiet." Her voice shakes with fury. "Obviously it was a mistake to trust you. You won't even work in a Number City at this point." Her eyes narrow into slits. "I think it's time this party came to an end."

Laney protests from behind me, reminding me there are other people here, watching, not understanding. The calm faces catch my attention again. One looks familiar, but Mayor Vee moves, bringing my attention back to her.

Mayor Vee beckons with her hands, and the next moment someone has my arm in a firm grasp. It's Ross, looking blankly down at me.

"Ross, let me go," I say, my voice surprisingly steady.

Ross shakes his head. Behind him I see Mom watching, body tense, like she's ready to lunge forward.

"I can't let you go, Morgan," Ross says calmly. "This is for your own good."

"You don't care about my own good," I tell him. "You only do what's in the mayor's best interests."

"Of course I do." Ross holds tighter as I try to rip away. Like-Neil grabs my other arm. "The mayor's interests are all of ours. And I do care about you."

I glare at him, hating the empty words.

Mayor Vee smiles. "Please escort Morgan to–"

Then it happens. Ross's hands tighten. His eyes switch from blank to unfocused, and suddenly his face goes slack.

They collapse. Every Like drops to the floor or slumps in his chair as if dead. The mayor cries out and falls to her knees by Vaughn.

That's all I see before Ross topples into me, his eyes rolling into his head. I fall to the ground beneath him, too surprised to hold his weight.

CHAPTER 41
Morgan

Women are screaming. Chaos rises from the crowd. I can't see from my position on the ground, trapped under Ross's limp form.

Then he's being lifted away, off of me, and I'm staring into the lights and not understanding what I see. It's the Like-Neil, dragging Ross off of my chest, and now Like-Neil crouches, taking my hand, pulling me to my feet.

Every other Like has dropped. But Like-Neil just watches me, fear etched into his too-perfect face as he clutches my hands and searches my gaze with his. It's real fear, and they're real eyes, the endless ones, and once again I feel the sensation of climbing into them and getting lost in the darkness.

Except Neil's holding my hand, so I'm not really lost.

I stand there for a moment, just staring, and then I say, in a tone way too normal for the question, "So you're not Mason, then?"

"I never was." Neil leans closer to be heard. "They found me just in time."

Now the relief hits. "Oh." I reach out with one hand to steady myself and my fingers twist around the material of his jacket. "What's happening?" I almost have to yell to make myself heard over the shrieks now echoing through the room.

"I don't know, this wasn't part of the plan."

Mom runs up and puts a hand on the back of my head. "Are you okay? Are you hurt?"

"Mom, *look around*," I shout, thinking everyone else can use more attention than me at this moment.

"I see it," she tells me. "I don't know what's going on, but are you–"

The rising panic drowns out her voice. I see women

shaking their Likes, crying, calling out, trying to understand. Laney crouches by Lloyd's form, her hands over her mouth, not crying, but terrified.

I focus on my mom. If anyone can fix it, she can. "*Do something.*"

Her brow furrows. Before she can move, however, someone runs up to us. Someone with blond hair and glasses.

"It worked?" he shouts, looking around, seeming surprised but not shocked.

"Han?" Mia appears next to us as I speak.

"You *did* it?" she calls to Han.

"That would appear to be the case," Han replies.

"What did you *do*?" Neil and I demand at the same time.

"I'd like to know as well," a cold voice adds.

Mayor Vee reappears. She shoves my mom out of the way and stands in front of Han, her expression wild. "Who the hell are you? How did you get here?"

"The subway. It's pretty convenient, though not as luxurious as the monorail, I must say."

The mayor's make-up laden eyes widen. "You're Nathan 17. I got an alert on you crossing the subway boundaries, but the security in your city couldn't find you. You should have been incapacitated."

"Yeah, about that…" Han grins, and I feel a strange urge to grin, too. Mayor Vee's face shows confusion, frustration, then deepens to hatred.

"Why did you come *here*?" Her gaze flicks toward me, then back to Han, making some connection. "There were others. More boys. How many did you talk to, Morgan? How many am I going to have to punish?"

I don't say anything, just let the screaming of the other women flow between us. Mayor Vee glares at me for another moment, then turns back to Han. "Tell me," she demands again, and pulls something from a pocket concealed on the waist of her dress. Her remote.

Han blinks at it, then takes a step toward her. Mayor Vee looks startled. "Don't come any closer. I *will* use this if you don't tell me right now."

"Well gee, I sure wouldn't want you to go to all that trouble," Han says seriously. "But on the other hand, I really don't care to tell you anything."

Mayor Vee flicks a knob on the remote. The instant she presses the button Han leaps forward and tears it from her hand. She gasps, shaking her head.

"I really should thank you." Han slides out of her reach before adding, "For not having them treat my burn properly. You have no idea how helpful that's been."

Mayor Vee can only gape. Han studies the remote curiously. Then the mayor finds her voice. "*Give it back*," she screams, lunging for Han.

Han skips out of the way, twisting the remote in his hands. The mayor reaches out again, but by now I've gathered myself and I slam into her, grabbing her arms. She claws at me, and Mia pins herself to the mayor's other side, restraining her.

"Neil." Han flicks the remote at Neil's feet. He glances down, then at his left hand, and finally at the mayor. Without another moment's hesitation he picks up his foot and slams it down on the remote.

The mayor shrieks in fury, but her scream is lost in the chaos. I glance at Mia. "What do we do?"

She shrugs. "Supply closet?"

"Good idea," someone says behind me.

I twist around. It's the librarian, Ms. Elliott, who disappeared the day I read *Romeo and Juliet*. How many more people can just appear at this Amora?

"Hi, Morgan," she says, her gaze flicking around.

"I don't remember putting you on the guest list," I say faintly as the mayor shrieks again.

"We crashed." Before I can ask who *we* are, she beckons behind her. Two more women appear, both wearing expressions of concentration. One looks like she's my mom's age and one might even be my grandma's age. They take Mayor Vee from Mia and I and pull her away toward the back of the room and the supply closet where I met Neil.

Neil and Han stare at Ms. Elliott, who nods at them, frowning when her gaze passes over Neil.

"Excuse me," Mom says, reaching out to touch Ms. Elliott's shoulder. "You were the librarian, so how–?"

Ms. Elliott holds up a finger to stop her, acting much more confident than the meek librarian I'd known. "First, please help us." She gestures around. I turn to face the crowd. Among the hysterical women and girls there are calm faces, the faces I saw over Mayor Vee's shoulder. The ones that don't fit. They're wearing pants and polos, not dresses, and they are trying to pacify the others, rearranging fallen Likes, slowly quelling the chaos. There must be a dozen of them.

Mom and Mia take this as a cue, both hurrying off to do the same. Laney clings to me now, saying, "I don't understand, I don't understand, Morgan," and I hear myself repeating, "Later, I'll tell you later," as a woman climbs up on the stage.

She's wearing a polo shirt like the other women with Ms. Elliott. She taps the microphone and calls for everyone's attention. Slowly the building quiets. The hysterical women are only too happy to give her their attention, to have someone explain.

The woman takes a deep breath and starts to talk, trying to explain the situation, what happened, the truth about Likes. About how she and other women work in Number Cities, and what Number Cities are, and how she and the others here disagree with the system. How they came to the Amora because Ms. Elliott thought there might be a situation, and how they are finally taking action. How they'll help everyone understand. There's more, but the words start to run together in my mind.

The women watch, confused, but at least they're listening, which is more than I can say for myself. I feel like I should climb up there and do something, but I also feel like I want to just let someone else handle things for the moment. Choosing the latter, I let Neil lead me to the side of the room while Han ascends to the stage to help the woman there explain.

Arms wrap gently around me, his cheek pressing against my ear. "Morgan, I–"

I spin around, pulling away, stopping when I can see his face. "I'm sorry," I whisper. I came so close to not being able to say this. Now I have to. I have to say it while I can. "I'm sorry," I repeat. "I should have done something when they took you away and I shouldn't have believed what she said."

I feel the lump rising in my throat again, everything inside of me raw with emotion, so I say the next part quickly. "I thought you were gone, but you're not, and even though you don't look like you, you're still there, so I have to tell you, right now. I love you. I love you I love you I love you. I'm so glad you're not one of them and not perfect because if you were perfect you wouldn't be Neil, and I love you, Neil."

I want to go on, but so many words are clogging my throat and mind that I can only close my eyes and breathe, just breathe.

Neil doesn't say anything, as if he understands I can't reply. He just pulls me in, hugs me again, and that's all I need. Sobs and words choke me, and tears stream down my face and into his shirt. But for the first time, I'm crying because I'm happy.

CHAPTER 42
Neil

Ms. Elliott finds me after the woman on the stage finishes talking. I vaguely recognized the woman as one of my teachers a few years ago, but further details escape me.

"Are you okay?" are the first words out of Ms. Elliott's mouth. I'm by the back of the room, where I can see women guarding the supply closet holding the mayor. Morgan went to help her mom decide care for the collapsed Likes while I was in the process of making my way toward Han, who is conversing with one of the Number City women and using emphatic hand gestures.

"Neil," Ms. Elliott says, and I blink, focusing on her.

"I'm..." I start to say, "okay," but it doesn't seem appropriate, so I just shrug helplessly. "I don't know." Then I add, quickly, "Thank you. I don't know how you–"

She shakes her head. "Don't thank us. We were almost too late. *This* never should have happened." She waves her hand at me, the *new* me.

I repress a shudder. Instead I nod at the Number City women. "Who are they? Why are they helping?"

Ms. Elliott purses her lips. "Not all women in the Number Cities are like Ms. Meryl. Shortly after I arrived in City 4 a group of women approached me, deciding I'd be a likely recruit for their...cause, I guess, is a good word for it. These are those women, the ones who think our society is cruel and unfair."

"The ones who see it as it is," I say immediately, clenching my hands. Pain shoots through my left fist.

She nods. "You've probably seen some of us talking during class."

I nod. "That's why you had me help? So you could talk?"

"Partly." She fiddles with the bottom of her polo. Now

that the imminent danger of the mayor has passed, she seems more like the timid teacher from City 4. "You also worked very well with the kids."

I shake my head. That hardly seems like the topic to be straying to right now. "What happens now?"

As I say it I look at her, and I'm struck by the unnaturalness of the gesture, of looking at a woman for guidance and answers.

She blinks. "I'm not sure. Once things here are somewhat settled, I'll talk to the other women and see what they think. We didn't plan ahead for this, we just got an alert that your friend Nathan crossed through the subway, and some women heard about Morgan Waters' second Amora tonight, and the fact that you were so severely punished…it was all so out of order. We came to observe only, but things changed."

"They did," I agree quietly. My gaze finds Morgan across the room. She has her back turned, kneeling over the prone form of a blond Like while her friend acts ready to pass out next to her. But just a glimpse of Morgan is enough to remind me of what she said, less than an hour ago, and to buffet me with entirely different emotions.

"We—the group, I mean—were talking about trying to gain access to the control center for the Likes' intelligence," Ms. Elliott is saying. "We just weren't sure what it was, or how it worked. Your friend Nathan seems to have done a brilliant job."

"You should tell him. I'm sure he'd be pleased."

She nods in agreement. "I guess for now, then, we should help. I just wanted to make sure you're all right."

"I'm better than the alternative."

She purses her lips again, but says nothing. I follow her across the room to where Morgan's mom is organizing a mass transportation of medical supplies to the Amora building. Shell-shocked women in dresses gather around her as she tells them what to do, what to bring, how to bring it, the women just nodding, like they need commands in order to function. I'm sure the truth will hit them hard later, when they stop to think.

It won't be easy. It won't be easy at all, not for a while. But maybe, somehow, it will be better.

It takes only a week to gain access to each of the other Color Cities' Like Computers and shut them down as well. Ms. Elliott and the group of Number City women organize each trip and the distribution of medical supplies, personnel, and knowledge. They also elicit the help of Han and other boys who've experimented with electronics to take down the computers backing the remotes and chips.

Those days are the busiest of my life, busier than working hours and hours, but I prefer this busy to the old busy. I spend a lot of time trying to explain to America what happened. Han and Morgan set up a live video of them telling the whole story. They encourage me to share as well, and I do, but I find I don't like being in front of the camera.

They broadcast the video to every wall and Pow in the nation. The group of women from City 4 find allies in other Number City women, while Han travels to the Number Cities to talk to the boys and encourage cooperation. They listen to him. He has charisma.

Meanwhile, the hospitals are full. Makeshift medical wards are set up in apartment buildings and vacant Academies. Morgan's mom explained how the Conversions take place, how every Like is first physically altered and then "programmed" through the chips already in their heads. The programming suppresses free will and directs the knowledge already in the men's brain into actions worthy of a Like. Then the Likes become dependent on the programming to function, which is directly connected to the computers.

When that connection is severed, every Like is affected. Half of them die immediately, and of the other half some go into comas. Others "awaken" soon after in a confused state, unable to remember anything since their Conversion. Rachel's Like, Ross, and Morgan's friend's Like, Lloyd, are in comas.

Ms. Elliott sets up a "Mayors' Residence" in a Blue City

hotel, where other boys and women willing to help keep the ex-Mayors of the Color Cities under close watch until we can decide how to proceed. Some other women are also in the hotel, such as Ms. Meryl. (Morgan voted we throw Ms. Meryl over the levies for the sharks, but her mother vetoed the idea.)

Right now we are trying to find out as much as possible about our situation while we manage it as best we can. Han and I stay with Morgan and her mom, assisting in daily research tasks. Morgan tries to spread the word that we're open to ideas on how to travel to another continent, like Europe. We talked about it, and we figure in order to fix a problem of this caliber we need an accurate, outside description of our history and pre-Wars government. But no one comes forth with any useful information.

A few days after we shut down the last computer, we finally search the physical articles in the mayor's office. We went through the files on her wall and all-purpose device, her Pow, the day after Morgan's second Amora and found documentation of Conversion schedules and disciplines, but didn't find any political or familial records.

It only takes Han five minutes to find the cabinet tucked away in a closet. We pull out the heavy piece of furniture. It's like a silver dresser, except with square drawers. There's a keyhole on every one, but it doesn't take Han long to grant us access with his lock picks.

We discover real papers stored in cream-colored folders, just like the ones in the offices in City 4. Han silently hands me the first one, and images of opening his to see just the one sheet, the *ULTIMATUM* written there, flash through my mind.

As with the ones in City 4, there are two pieces of paper. The one in my hand is the record of a boy I don't know, probably never did, as he was born ten years before me.

NAME/ DEVON
BY/2211
BD/0113
STAT/NONE
EYE/ BR, HAI/BLK, RAC/CAU.

But there's more on this one. It also has *ASGNCITY/4,*
MLIKE/JACOB, and *MOTHER/GOLDFYNE, JAEL.* The second
page has *CY/2228* and *CD/0809, CITY/YEL, LNAME/STEFAN*
and *WOMAN/NAJJYR, SOPHIA.*

I just gape, staring at the meticulous planning of some
boy's future nearly a decade ago. Wordlessly, I hand it to
Han, who passes it along. He digs through the rest of the files,
pulling out random ones.

"Parental, birth, and Like information about every boy
born in Blue City," he determines. "These date back decades.
But I don't understand what order the mayor has them in, it
doesn't seem to be alphabetical or chronological."

Morgan's mom gasps and drops down by the crate,
pushing Han aside to start pulling out stacks of files.

"Look for mine," she orders, pushing piles of folders at
each of us. "Find my son."

We go through hundreds, and there are thousands more,
cabinets upon cabinets still in the closet. I come across a few
names I recognize, but for nearly an hour I don't find mine,
Han's, or even Kellan's.

Then, finally, I open a folder containing just one page,
and a familiar name leaps out at me.

NAME/ NATHAN
BY/2221
BD/0630
STAT/ULTIMATUM
EYE/ GR, HAI/BLN, RAC/CAU.

"Han…" I start to say, but the words below catch my
attention before I finish. My gaze flicks over *ASGNCITY/4,* and
MLIKE/ROSS.

They stop on *MOTHER/WATERS, RACHEL.*
Waters, Rachel.

Morgan makes her way over to me, crawling around
stacks of roughly sorted files. "Neil, what's up?"

I shake my head and glance over at Morgan's mom.
Morgan's mom, Rachel. She sees me looking, and her eyes
widen as I hand over the file.

It takes her a moment to read it, gaze flicking to Han as soon as she sees the name at the top. But once she reads down to the bottom, she cries out, yanking the paper closer, reading it again. I see her hands tremble. In fact, all of her trembles as her gaze once again falls on Han.

Han pauses in his sorting of files, noticing everyone staring at him. "What? Do I have something in my teeth? I knew I shouldn't have eaten a poppy seed bun, but you just have so many *choices* here."

The file slips from her fingers. The next moment she's kneeling next to Han, crushing him in a tight embrace. "You're him," she says, voice cracking.

"I–why yes, I do happen to be a him. I thought we'd established that."

Rachel pulls away. Her cheeks have streaks on them. Tears. "Oh," she whispers, as if it's all she can think of to say.

"Rachel?" Han glances at the file on the floor and then back to her face. "What is it?"

"Call me Mom," she tells him.

Next to me, Morgan gasps. Mia, who joined us an hour ago, does as well. Han just gapes for a moment, then twists to face Morgan.

"I *knew* there was something I liked about you."

It takes a minute for the shock to wear off. Then I watch as Morgan grins. "I found you," she says.

And that happy feeling returns for everyone in the room.

CHAPTER 43
Morgan

The shock still hasn't worn off. I have a feeling it won't for an incredibly long time. Han–*Han*–is my twin. The entire time I stressed about finding my twin and learning who he is, it was Han. Mom keeps saying she should have known, we both have Ross's eyes, the same gray, and how could she not have noticed we even have the same chin? I just keep grinning, grinning at my mom, at Han, at Mia, at Neil.

As we're leaving the mayor's office I see something tucked beneath the desk. A book. I stop, letting everyone else go ahead, and pull the book out.

Romeo and Juliet. I stand there, holding it, seeing the faint crescent shape Mayor Vee's nail made ages ago. When I was the same as every other girl, sitting in here thinking about my Amora and not seeing through the mayor's lies.

I never did finish the story.

I sit down right here, back against the desk, and start reading. It takes a while for me to get into the dialogue, but then it's like time isn't even passing as I read to the last lines.

For never was a story of more woe
Than this of Juliet and her Romeo.

I close my eyes, taking deep breaths. Mayor Vee was right. Juliet killed herself over Romeo. But the mayor was also wrong; as in, she left out the part where Romeo, stricken with grief, killed himself first. And how Juliet didn't die because Romeo betrayed her or did any of the awful things Mayor Vee claimed were the fault of men, but because she couldn't live without him.

So that kind of love existed in Shakespeare's time. It existed until the Wars. It was beautiful, tragic, insane, *real*.

"Morgan?"

I look up. Neil hovers in the doorway, as if unsure

whether to disturb me. His new features still cause me to bite my lip, but every time I see his eyes the same tingles return.

"I'm coming." I pull myself to my feet. "I was just reading a book."

And I smile, because I know that kind of love exists now, too.

Three weeks after the Amora is a rainy Tuesday. Just like every morning of the previous near-month, the first thing I do is ask my mom what we're doing today.

"Well, more sorting through files," she says, preparing water for coffee. She's wearing her doctor's coat and a smile. Yes, a smile. She's happy. She and Han spend at least an hour each day sitting in the living room while she drills him about everything. I wouldn't be surprised if she's memorized his shoe size by now. And the whole thing makes me happy, too.

"Checking on the hospitals," Mom goes on, as if from a mental checklist. "Overseeing medical processes, talking to the women who are overseeing things in the other cities, and a lot of et cetera."

I nod along, leaning against the doorframe. Footsteps sound behind me, and Neil appears by my shoulder.

"Morning," he murmurs, then voices my same question. "What's on the agenda today?"

Mom starts to repeat herself, then stops. "You know what? For you guys, nothing. Not until this afternoon. Go take a break."

"A what?" Neil acts like he didn't hear correctly.

"A break," I explain, half-joking. "It's where you do nothing for a while. You don't work. You relax."

He looks confused. "I know. But why?"

I shoot my mom a smile. "Come on. I'll show you."

We head outside and start walking, the raindrops splashing against our skin. It's summery rain, and not unpleasant.

"Where are we going?"

"Shh."

He doesn't question me as we board the subway to City 4. It still runs back and forth on the three-hour schedule, and it still feels weird to just walk into the station and into a car without hiding.

As we ride, Neil glances at me, an amused smile playing around his lips. I have to stop myself from kissing him right here, because if I did I would forget to ask what's so funny.

"What?"

"We're on the subway," he says, "and look what you're wearing."

I look myself over. Jeans—my own jeans—and a green tank top. Now I feel the urge to laugh too. "I didn't even realize. I just waltzed onto the subway wearing my own clothes and didn't get in trouble."

"And I'm sitting with you. Not getting in trouble."

I lean my head on his shoulder. It *was* weird at first, seeing each other in the daytime, in Blue City, surrounded by women. It was also bizarre wearing my clothes and no hat and not worrying about being caught. Of course, we had a lot to do those first few days, so we didn't take time to dwell on the strangeness.

Once in City 4 Neil follows me through the drizzle again. We walk the streets without looking around corners, me trying to slouch and hide my face. There are a few boys outside and they glance at us, but that's all. It's exhilarating.

I lead him to where they took me on my third visit, the edge of the city. When Neil sees the wall his eyebrows, his too-perfect eyebrows, arch, and his eyes widen, as if the idea scares him.

"Come on," I insist, and pull him to the edge. He gives me a hand up, and once I'm on the top he finds a foothold. I grab his hand when he reaches up to me and he's able to grip the edge.

He hesitates a moment, as if he doesn't know if he can really do it. He spent his whole life knowing *can't*; it's hard for him to get in the habit of *can*.

"Come on," I say, not insisting this time, but asking.

He hoists himself up, flinching as he sits down, but then his face relaxes and transforms into an expression of surprise.

"You didn't trust me, I told you it would be fine."

Neil meets my gaze. His tone is nothing but serious. "Morgan, I trust you. More than anyone."

Shivers of the good kind run their course up my spine. "Okay," I say, trying not to get too lost in his gaze. "If that's the case, then turn around. You'll love it...trust me."

He does. I watch his face at first, as the shock melts into awe, and the beauty of the endless grass is reflected in his eyes. Then I, too, look out at the view, away from the chaos and into something different, where droplets cling to the plants undisturbed and flowers shimmer under the clouds.

We say nothing for a while.

Then Neil reaches for my hand. As he curls his fingers around mine I see him wince.

"What?" I stare at our fingers, then at his face.

"It still hurts." He shakes his head. "My hand. They 'fixed' it, but it still hurts to move it."

A spark of anger breaks the peace surrounding us. "Why didn't you tell someone? My mom would fix it."

"There was too much going on."

"That's ridiculous." I tug my hand away and cross my arms.

Neil rolls his eyes and sighs. "Maybe. But to me it's a luxury, okay? Being able to decide what I can and can't do about myself. I have to adjust to the idea of comfort. It'll take time."

I slowly shake my head.

"The system was put in place to keep peace. Keep women happy. To create a different world than in that story, *Romeo and Juliet*." I tilt my face up, meeting his gaze again. "But this world, it takes away the possibility of real. Real anything. Even happiness. There's contentment, but without anything to work for, there's no real accomplishment. Right now, now that things are changing, I feel happy. It's a different kind of happy than I've felt before. But it's more powerful."

"I didn't know happiness, period." Neil's right hand reaches up and trails down the side of my face. "Not until you forced your way into my life."

I close my eyes, heart feeling too big to be possible. His lips are softer, fuller against mine than they used to be, but I remind myself it's Neil, it's really Neil behind them, drawing me closer and making me feel like I'm a million miles in the sky. It's Neil, no matter what he looks like.

When he finally pulls away, he's breathing hard. So am I, but it has nothing to do with my breathing problems. We lean our foreheads together, so close I can't see his eyes clearly, but they are still dark and animated and Neil.

Then he says, "I never said it back to you, at your Amora. But I do, Morgan. Love you, I mean."

I should want him to say that. But somehow it sounds wrong, too much, to actually hear it. I shake my head, our bangs scratching between us. "You don't have to say it. In fact, please don't. No sappy talk, not yet. Can't you just kiss me again?"

"Okay." He sounds surprised, and not unhappy. But before he can do so, someone clears their throat.

I jump, and we break apart, spinning on the bricks to peer down to the lot with the dirt and the weeds.

A woman stands below us, hands on her hips, head tilted into the drizzle to face where we sit. She's tall, with light hair and a tan bag slung over her shoulder. I don't recognize her.

She regards us with a slightly interested expression before she speaks. "Morgan Waters?"

"Yes?" I sit up straight, resisting the urge to run or shield my face, reminding myself I don't have to hide this. Not anymore.

"I hear you want to go to Europe."

"Maybe," I say carefully.

"Well," she says, like she knows the answer is yes, "when you decide, let me know. I can get you there."

Kieryn Nicolas resides in central Pennsylvania with her parents, younger sister, and yellow lab. The three activities that she would like to take up most of her time are writing, Taekwondo, and being with her friends. The three things that actually take up most of her time are school, homework, and the REM cycle.